EPIPHANY

BOOK #1 OF FLATLINE FREQUENCY

K.D. BUSTER

Flume
Creek
Press

CHAPTER ONE

"Tell me your plan for the Peaksville Projects," the female caller said in a sinister voice.

The pilot lowered the boom mic from his lips, reduced his throttle, rolled his wings level, and yelled into his cellphone to drown out the propeller noise. "Everything's still a go!"

"Peaksville stakeholders have received fifty percent of National CABESA Initiative funding since 2013. Yet somehow, Peaksville has produced ninety percent of our complications."

"That was the past!" The pilot maneuvered to remain clear of clouds and mountainous terrain. "I handled it, Ma'am!"

"My Class of 2020 Peaksville Projects graduate in five weeks. Ten Projects have been accepted into ten different universities in ten different states."

"Understood!"

"Tell me your plan."

The man abruptly jerked the elevator controls back after inadvertently descending 200 feet in his small, single-engine airplane. "Nothing stops in Peaksville! Six Projects remain! Younger siblings! Nothing stops!"

"The *first* Peaksville Projects are my concern. The Class of 2020 will figure everything out during the first week in college when the pain stops."

"Understood, Ma'am!"

"Two choices: Calibrate my 2020 Projects; or terminate my 2020 Projects."

"We're trying."

"Try harder." The woman ended the phone call.

CHAPTER TWO

M y name is Marcus Flynn. I'm a high school Senior in Peaksville, a small town in North Idaho sandwiched between Washington, Montana, and Canada.

H ow did the Flynn family end up in Peaksville?

M arch 11, 2011. My Friday afternoon third grade experience.

Boy walks home from Japanese school to Army base housing. Boy knocked down by 9.0 earthquake in front of Sushi-Go-Round. Boy instinctively hugs cement telephone pole. Cement telephone pole beats boy like rented mule for sixty seconds. Motion stops. Boy releases white-knuckle death-grip. Boy hears thunderous footsteps coming from destroyed nuclear power plant. Godzilla destroys Tokyo. Boy evacuates to Idaho. Mom convinces Dad to retire from Army Rangers.

I made the Godzilla part up. The rest is true.

Y ou're thinking: Big deal, Marcus.

> *Boy survives Fukushima.*
> *Boy evacuates to wolf, bear and*
> *mountain lion country for safety.*
> *Great plan.*

T here's more to the story, I swear.
    Sometimes things are hidden in plain sight.

CHAPTER THREE

"Antoine! Are you going to swing or just stand there daydreaming about how hot I look?" Amy yelled from the west side of Peaksville Creek.

"You okay, Antoine?" Brianna whispered as Antoine zoned out.

"I'm good, Bree." Antoine clenched the rope tightly. "Here I come." Antoine sailed across Peaksville Creek towards Grace and me, leaving school grounds towards The Meadow.

I helped Antoine with his landing then quickly flung the rope swing back to Max. "Still got that headache, AJ?"

"Failed my AP Physics quiz today. I couldn't think."

Antoine's eyes looked tired and bloodshot. Antoine wasn't alone.

"Don't worry. We'll feel better after we swim." I didn't know what else to tell him.

"You're next, Bree," Max said, handing her the rope swing.

"Here goes nothing!" Brianna smiled at Antoine on the west side, grabbed the rope and swung with a funny scream to cheer him up.

Grace caught Brianna and laughed. "Gotcha, Bree!"

Antoine mustered a smile while rubbing his temples.

I caught the rope and flung it back to Max.

"Emma, you ready?" Max asked.

Emma nodded affirmatively and grabbed the rope swing. "I'm so tired."

"No rush, babe." Max rubbed her shoulder.

"Emma's hurting," Grace whispered to me.

I yelled from the west side. "Hold on tight, Emma!"

"Amy, your body double threw up again in school." Grace whispered. "Every day this month."

Amy Kernan whispered as her identical twin prepared to cross Peaksville Creek. "Maybe there's a bright side. April showers brings May flowers, right Grace?"

Amy always had something funny to say. Rain or shine.

"Alright, I'm ready!" Emma kicked her long muscular legs high into the air and gracefully sailed into the three o'clock sun.

Grace caught her then felt her forehead. "You're burning up, Emma."

"That breeze felt so good." Emma immediately sat next to Antoine on the downed cedar tree to rest. "I'm so tired, Antoine."

"Me too, Emma." Antoine and Emma leaned into each other.

"Last but not least!" I slung the long rope swing to Max. "Don't mess up! Here comes your dad at 9 o'clock over the tree line!"

Max yelled over the increasingly thunderous helicopter noise from his father's Bell 407. "Got it, Marcus!"

Max Burns looked to his left and swung from Peaksville School grounds towards The Meadow. Rotor wash rocked the majestic cedar trees and nearly blew us over.

I helped Max land and grabbed the rope. As a courtesy, I swung back towards Peaksville High School and looped our 100-foot rope over a large cedar tree branch for the others. I descended into the ravine and forded Peaksville Creek, jumping rock to rock.

Grace remained on the west bank with an extended hand after I climbed up the ravine. She greeted me with a beautiful smile and kiss on my right cheek.

"How's your headache, Marcus?"

I didn't answer. I playfully turned my head and pointed.

Grace kissed my other cheek. "How about now?"

I smiled. "Much better."

"Ah!" Grace screamed in fear and jumped.

"Everyone! Marcus is a weirdo! Run! Marcus pinched Grace's butt!" Amy took off running.

Grace pointed at Amy. "Guilty! I felt long fingernails!"

We initiated pursuit towards Amy into The Meadow laughing and holding hands.

I yelled in my best *Children of the Corn* voice. "Outlander!"

Amy sprinted towards The Boxcar giggling.

Nobody can catch Amy or Emma Kernan. Except my little brother Derrick.

"Get back here, Outlander!" Grace and I slowed to a jog through The Meadow. "Repent, Outlander!"

Amy ridiculously guarded her rear with both hands while running. "Marcus is a butt pincher!"

We slowed to a walk. "Outlander!"

Amy and Emma were also in Japan during the 2011 Japan earthquake. Mr. Kernan was flying COD's stationed at Naval Air Facility Atsugi. Amy and Emma were competing in a base track meet. The massive earthquake toppled over hurdles mid-race. Their third-grade competitors ran to the bleachers screaming. Except for two. The Kernan twins completed the race and received Gold and Silver medals.

They moved to Naval Air Station North Island San Diego in 2012. They became Junior Olympic track and field champions in 2013. Life was good on Coronado. When they moved to Peaksville in 2015, their migraines and heart problems began, ending their Junior Olympic careers before the end of freshman year.

"You'd think running through the fresh air would cure my headache!" Antoine yelled to Brianna running through The Meadow over the helicopter noise.

Brianna returned a compassionate smile.

Brianna had a secret: She loved Antoine.

Three people knew: Grace knew. I knew. Brianna knew. Antoine was the next in line to be number four.

Max jogged with Emma through the waist-high fountain grass while his father initiated a slow hover over The Meadow at thirty knots and two hundred feet. "Almost there, Emma!"

Emma stopped to vomit.

Amy looked back into The Meadow. "Hey Max! I figured it out! When you speak, my sister throws up!"

Grace Becker and I arrived to the The Boxcar hand-in-hand, one minute behind Amy. Ruby Kyle and Luke Bartholomew were inside tutoring twelve-year-old Jack Kernan and Gigi Becker.

Luke put down Jack's text book and confronted me in The Boxcar. "Hey, Marcus, Amy said you're some kind of Phantom Butt Pincher, mmm-kay? Butt pinching is against the rules in Peaksville, mmm-kay? Anyhow, my butt and Ruby's butt are officially declared off-limits, mmm-kay? They are like the Demilitarized Zone, mmm-kay? Instead of DMZ, think DMB, mmm-kay? Now apologize to young Jack and Gigi for setting a bad example, mmm-kay?"

Luke's dad was the local preacher. Mr. Bartholomew was probably home preparing for the Sunday service and reading Deuteronomy. Mr. Bartholomew's teenage son was in a broken-down old boxcar doing a *South Park* school counselor impersonation.

"Grace, tell 'Mr. Mackey' who pinched you."

"I don't want to say it was Amy." Grace paused. "But it was Amy."

Amy shrugged and smiled. "Maybe Grace imagined it."

A kiss from Grace, Amy's tomfoolery, and Luke's sermon made me momentarily forget about my headache.

Grace greeted her little sister Gigi Becker and Jack Kernan with a hug.

Brianna and Antoine arrived next, followed by Emma and Max.

I wasn't sure who looked worse, Emma or Antoine.

Max Burns hand-saluted goodbye to his father.

Mr. Burns, Vice-President of the Peaksville TSC, lowered his nose, added power, exited his low hover and departed to the east in his Bell 407.

"Hey little brother, getting ready for finals?" Emma Kernan quietly asked.

Jack smiled and nodded affirmatively.

Jack Kernan stopped speaking in 2016 at age eight, one year after moving from California with the twins. Luke and Ruby have been tutoring Jack daily for years.

"He's getting there, Emma." Ruby said. "And Gracie, you'd be proud of your little sister. Gigi and Jack are becoming math wizards."

Emma, in her weakened state, kissed young Jack on the top of the head as he completed a worksheet in The Boxcar.

"Max, what's Mr. Burns doing up there today?" Luke asked. "That was low."

"The Safety Corps is investigating another attempted child abduction in Peaksville. Dean Michaels announced it earlier. I guess that's why he's so low," Max said.

"Who is the child?" Antoine asked.

Amy interrupted. "It's me. People always try to steal me. Everyone wants me in their dungeon."

Max disagreed. "Amy, if I had a dungeon, I would abduct your twin, Emma. You joke around too much. Dungeons are serious places."

Emma gave Max a kiss. "Thanks, Max. You're so sweet."

Luke made an attractive offer. "Emma, please reconsider. My dungeon would have high speed internet, Amazon Alexa and stocked fridge."

Emma smiled. "Netflix?"

Luke maintained a serious face. "Streaming."

"Starbuck's Coffee?"

"On tap. As you wish, Buttercup."

"I'm sorry, honey." Emma hugged Max. "Too many choices."

I was still curious about the apparent abduction attempt. "Seriously, everyone. Nobody here can even afford to maintain a dungeon. Max, which child did they try to take?"

"No clue. Pop can't tell me. TSC child privacy laws."

The Boxcar went silent for about ten seconds as we digested the news about the attempted abduction. We could still hear the buzzing sound of the helicopter rotor blades less than one mile to the east.

Brianna addressed Jack and Gigi. "Do the middle school bookworms want to swim?"

"Yes!" Gigi exclaimed.

Jack nodded and smiled.

Ruby's dog, Kiche, heard Gigi's voice and leapt into The Boxcar.

Gigi smiled and scratched Kiche's belly. "Ruby, can we bring Wolfie?"

"One last math worksheet, Gigi." Smiles left Gigi and Jack's faces. "After that, yes. Kiche can join us." Smiles on the twelve-year-olds reappeared.

Jack and Gigi knelt down and aggressively gave Ruby's 150-pound Canadian Wolf and Anatolian Shepherd mix a hug. Kiche leaned into the 12-year-olds with her signature low-pitched, steady growl and rapidly licked their faces.

"Lover's Lagoon?" Luke asked.

"You betcha!" Grace said. "And thanks for tutoring Gigi."

"Yeah, ditto, Luke and Ruby!" Emma rubbed her forehead. "See you there, Jack."

Amy, Emma, Max, Antoine, Brianna, Grace and I jumped down from The Boxcar wearing swimsuits under our clothes.

"Marcus!" Luke stuck his head out the sliding wooden door. "The TSC said Lover's Cave is off limits, mmm-kay?"

I laughed. "Thanks, Luke."

Grace waved. "See you soon, Ruby!"

We faintly heard Gigi's voice as we trekked west. "Wolfie, let's get our homework done! We're going swimming!"

The seven of us walked from The Boxcar just north of Liberty Lake. My younger brothers Ryan and Derrick were enjoying Liberty Lake with Madison Goodwell and Gloria Becker. Gloria was the middle child between Grace and Gigi.

Derrick was perched on top of the twenty-foot high Deadman's Cliff wearing only his signature cutoff jeans. Ryan, Madison, and Gloria were treading water below in the small quarry-turned-lake.

Amy unnecessarily cupped her hands in front of her mouth to shout. "Attention, all losers! Winners are heading up Coldwater Creek to Lover's Lagoon. Join us only if you want to be like us!"

Madison laughed. "Sounds fun!"

"Count us in!" Gloria said.

"Ten minutes!" Ryan added.

Derrick jumped off Deadman's Cliff and yelled before his thunderous cannonball water entry. "Thirty minutes!"

"Oh yeah. The cedar trees," I told the other seniors as they continued walking around Liberty Lake.

"Cedar trees?" Emma asked.

Grace covered my mouth. "Derrick Flynn single-handedly saves five cedar trees per day from parasitic ivy, and thousands of cedar trees in the last few years. While we wander carefree through Peaksville Forest, Derrick zigzags from tree to tree, climbs them, and pulls down seventy-foot strands of parasitic ivy. He uses Mr. Flynn's Army Ranger knife, right, Marcus?"

I wasn't a fan of my brother Derrick's *Cedar Tree Parasite Prevention Program*. Grace released her hand so I could speak. "Right, Grace."

From Liberty Lake, we climbed up to the Elephant Rocks. This was a naturally carved formation of round, smooth boulders dividing an intricate series of smaller streams, waterslides, and small whirlpools on the east end of Coldwater Creek. These smaller streams rejoined to feed the Deadman's Cliff twenty-foot waterfall falling into Liberty Lake.

After five minutes of hiking up Coldwater Creek, Max stopped to comment. "Waste of time, Marcus."

"What's a waste of time?"

"Derrick's tree thing. There must be one hundred thousand trees in Peaksville Forest. Why save just one percent? Parasitic ivy serves a purpose. Weak trees die. Strong trees live. Parasites ensure survival of the fittest. Why kill parasites?"

I kept walking. I didn't agree with Max's sentiment. I also didn't particularly like conflict. "My problem is that Derrick climbs tall trees, not killing parasites."

Amy watched Derrick perform another cannonball in the distance while jumping from boulder to boulder in the Elephant Rocks. "Maybe he's *The One*."

I laughed. "This isn't *The Matrix*. This is Peaksville."

Amy gave me a serious look.

Grace gave me a similar look.

Antoine agreed. "Maybe Derrick is *Dauntless*?"

Mr. Burns buzzed overhead in his TSC Bell 407 at 200 feet in a slow hover.

I shook my head and let the helicopter noise drown out my next comment. "More like *Divergent*."

We continued walking up Coldwater Creek.

Antoine nudged Brianna. "Speaking of parasites."

Amy chimed in. "Look what the cat dragged in!"

Grace kindly exclaimed. "Hi Ben! Hi Tony!"

Ben's father, Mr. Light, the Peaksville TSC President, passed overhead in his Cessna 182 at only 500 feet and seventy knots.

Ben arrogantly smiled. "Y'all hear? Lover's Cave is now off-limits."

Brianna joked. "Says who?"

Tony Murdstone answered. "Says The Safety Corps."

Ben and Tony were not particularly likeable among the graduating Class of 2020.

I tried to be kind. "Thanks Ben. We already heard."

Ben shrugged. "Just saying."

We didn't respond. We silently stood at the Coldwater Creek bank waiting for the TSC Cadets to leave.

I broke the uncomfortable, two-minute-long silent standoff. "Good talk, Ben."

Ben and Tony turned and departed towards Peaksville.

Amy yelled in a ridiculous country accent as Mr. Light circled back in his Cessna 182. "I'm going to marry you, someday Ben Light!" Amy had outdone herself. Despite her migraine.

We laughed all the way up Coldwater Creek to Lover's Lagoon.

Amy joked. "That was my Alabama accent."

Emma sighed. "Can you tell that my twin has never been to Alabama?"

CHAPTER FOUR

D errick smiled at Ryan, Gloria and Madison in Liberty Lake treading water after his fifth cannonball. "Treehouse?"

"No," Ryan replied. "Lover's Lagoon."

"Treehouse. I'll be quick."

Madison climbed on Derrick's back. "How quick?"

"Twenty minutes, tops."

Gloria smiled and corrected Derrick. "Ten."

Derrick treaded water with his familiar passenger. "Fifteen."

Madison kissed Derrick on the cheek. "Deal!"

Derrick swam to the shore of Liberty Lake, towing Madison. "Come on slow pokes! Waiting on you!" Derrick joked as Mr. Burns performed another low, slow hover over Liberty Lake in his TSC helicopter.

Derrick tossed Madison her towel as she exited the cold, spring-fed lake.

Ryan handed Gloria her towel. "Derrick, headache gone?"

"It's everyday bro'." Derrick shook his head negatively and winked. "Liberty Lake helped though."

The four North Idaho adventurers dried off and walked north into Peaksville Forest, home of Derrick's spectacular, multi-level treehouse project.

F our additional Class of 2020 Peaksville Seniors trekked upstream, on the north bank of Coldwater Creek. Aaron, D'Andre, and Thomas walked alongside the Epley cowgirls riding horseback. Charlotte rode Jefferson, as her twelve-year-old sister Chloe rode Buckshot in trail.

Aaron Webster looked at his Casio G-Shock watch. "Amy said swimming starts at four o'clock at Lover's Lagoon."

D'Andre Jordan smiled and carefully marched up Coldwater Creek's bank. "Swimming sounds perfect."

Charlotte Epley looked back at Aaron from atop Jefferson and whispered. "Actually, Amy wants to go caving."

"Bulletin," Thomas said. "Lover's Cave is now off limits per the TSC."

"Bulletin," Aaron said. "Amy doesn't care."

Thomas became agitated. "So, we're rule-breakers?"

"Let me check, Tommy Boy." Aaron looked around. "That about sums it up."

Jefferson and Buckshot expertly negotiated the small, round river rocks.

"Big step up, DJ." Thomas Stallworth guided D'Andre.

Aaron held D'Andre's left arm.

Charlotte comforted D'Andre from Jefferson, her trusty steed. "How you feeling, DJ?"

D'Andre mustered a smile. "I've seen better days."

D'Andre and Antoine Jordan also experienced the 2011 Tokyo earthquake. Their father was the Senior Medical Officer on the USS George Washington aircraft carrier. The twins visited their father's carrier Friday afternoon after school, moored at Naval Station Yokosuka. The twin boys walked on the flight deck catwalk as the 9.0 earthquake struck. The seismic waves literally bounced the aircraft carrier up and down 12 inches on a vertical axis unlike the oblong, 36-inch horizontal motion on land.

Antoine tumbled from the catwalk. D'Andre instinctively grabbed Antoine's arm. Antoine hung sixty feet over the Yokosuka Harbor as the aircraft carrier violently bounced up and down for one minute. Starboard side mooring lines screamed under high tension. The Officer and Enlisted Brows (pedestrian ramp to ship) twisted like pretzels. The youngest sailor on the ship, eighteen-years-old and fresh out of Navy Base Great Lakes, saw Antoine dangling from the catwalk. He sprinted to the catwalk and helped D'Andre complete the rescue of his nine-year-old twin as the earthquake subsided.

The USS George Washington Captain awarded young D'Andre a Navy Commendation Medal for saving his twin.

They evacuated to Peaksville in 2014 and began getting headaches immediately. D'Andre was declared legally blind in during his Freshman year.

"I've been so tired lately," D'Andre said. "Being blind doesn't help."

"Hey DJ!" Chloe cheerfully rode Buckshot nearby.

"Yeah Chloe, what's up?"

"Want to ride Buckshot the rest of the way up Coldwater Creek?"

"If it's okay with Buckshot."

"Buckshot, can DJ have a horsey ride?" whispered twelve-year-old Chloe Epley. "Buckshot says absolutely!" Chloe jumped down.

Charlotte halted Jefferson and smiled.

Aaron and Thomas helped D'Andre. Chloe fed Buckshot a carrot and held his reins as D'Andre mounted.

Chloe walked alongside Buckshot as D'Andre smiled from ear to ear.

"Pretty fun, huh DJ?" Charlotte asked over the sound of Mr. Burns' TSC helicopter passing overhead performing monotonous search patterns.

"I wish my dad could see me up here, Charlie," D'Andre replied. "Almost makes me forget about my headaches."

"I miss your father, also," Charlotte sadly whispered atop Jefferson.

Charlotte turned her head and rode forward, hiding her tears. Dr. Jordan was the best pediatrician Peaksville before his fatal heart attack in 2016.

U pon reaching Lover's Lagoon, Emma Kernan embarrassingly face-palmed as Amy danced for laughs in the waterfall. "That's Amy, everyone! I'm Emma!"

Amy revisited her fake country accent as we stripped down to our swimsuits. "Any of you Peaksville Boys man enough to take little old me into Lover's Cave?" Amy innocently swirled her fingers through her drenched, long blonde hair in her swimsuit.

"I'll take you, Miss Amy!" Aaron joked in a country accent walking into Lover's Lagoon. "But I reckon it's off limits. Last thing I need is a TSC posse after me."

Amy rapidly cycled through ridiculous poses in the waterfall. "This hot body is not declared off-limits, though."

Laughter from the swimmers.

Grace dipped into the cold spring water of Lover's Lagoon. "Amy's going to make me pee."

Emma face-palmed again. "She's going to make me puke."

Charlotte joked as young Chloe secured Jefferson and Buckshot to a nearby cedar tree. "Let my horses get a drink first before you girls poison the water hole."

"You all seriously want to go caving?" Antoine yelled.

"Antoine." Brianna whispered and subtly pointed into the trees.

Grace helped Brianna try to cover. "Hey Ben! Hey Tony!"

Ben and Tony walked out from behind a large cedar. "Hey Grace. What's all this about caving?"

"Waving!" Max said as everyone waved at Ben and Tony.

"Actually, AJ said we are going shaving!" Amy drew some chuckles and strange looks.

Ben looked up as his father approached in his Cessna 182. "You understand Lover's Cave is off limits, right?"

"Ben, you understand my hot body is off-limits, right?" Amy rubbed her hands on her legs and stomach and performed a cannonball to celebrate her joke.

Everyone laughed treading water in the lagoon. Ben and Tony walked downstream towards Peaksville.

"They're gone," Aaron whispered after the Cessna 182 departed.

I swam into the group. "Alright, who's caving?"

"Shaving or caving?" Amy asked.

I laughed. "Caving."

Amy declared. "I'm in."

Antoine smiled. "Sounds fun."

Brianna swam closer to Antoine. "I'm in."

Aaron yelled from the shore. "I'm in!"

I pointed to the shore. "Okay, that's four. Aaron, grab two flashlights from my backpack."

"Got 'em, Marcus!"

"Thirty minutes in there, tops!" Grace said.

We last explored Lover's Cave in the Summer of 2019. But today was special. Dean Michaels reported that the TSC placed Lover's Cave off-limits, so Amy placed Lover's Cave on her to-do list.

Amy, Aaron, Antoine, and Brianna subtly walked behind the waterfall that beautifully cascaded over the cave entrance. One last TSC overflight by Mr. Light's Cessna 182. One last scan of the forest for the TSC Cadets, Ben and Tony.

Treading water in Lover's Lagoon, I nodded my head affirmatively and whispered loudly. "All clear."

"Be safe!" Grace added.

Aaron gave me a 'thumbs up' from under the waterfall as they entered the first large cavern. "See you in thirty."

"Antoine, you want to lead?" Aaron asked, handing him a flashlight.

"Sure, but I have three very simple rules in the cave."

"Three rules?" Brianna asked.

Amy smiled. "What are those?"

Antoine illuminated his own face with his flashlight for comedic effect. "Don't touch my butt. Don't touch my butt. And don't touch my butt."

Amy and Brianna looked each other, looked back at Antoine, and violently lunged at Antoine's rear with four open hands, causing him to scream and jump.

Aaron laughed. "Dang, Antoine, you scream like a five-year-old girl."

Antoine feigned weeping and victimhood. "Hold on, Aaron, I have to cry for a few minutes before we continue."

Brianna joked. "You said don't touch. You didn't mention grabbing."

The four Seniors carefully walked deeper into the darkness of Lover's Cave laughing.

Amy pinched Antoine one more time. "Any other rules, Antoine?"

"Um, no," Antoine said in a deep voice.

CHAPTER FIVE

"Derrick, that was five trees, brother!" Ryan said. "Off to Lover's Lagoon."

"Yeah, Derrick, what are you doing now?" Madison asked as Derrick climbed above The Treehouse."

"Five more minutes, Maddie! I promise!" Derrick yelled down to Madison from a weakened cedar tree covered in parasitic ivy.

"Does Mr. Flynn know Derrick does this, Ryan?" Gloria whispered as the TSC airplane passed over the tree line.

"Kind of," Ryan whispered. "Marcus wants Derrick to stop."

"Derrick says that all trees should be free to live a long life and die in their sleep at an old age." Madison whispered.

Ryan Flynn quietly stood and watched his younger brother slay the parasitic ivy wielding their father's Army knife high in a cedar tree.

Gloria noticed Ryan. "I see the gears turning, Ryan."

"My dad teaches us to be sheepdogs. He teaches us to protect the weak."

"What's wrong with that?"

"It's a lesson for later in life. Not for high school. Not for cedar trees."

Ryan, Gloria and Madison continued watching parasitic ivy fall from the cedars.

"Maybe Derrick has a gift," Madison said.

Ryan's eyes welled up with tears and immediately turned away from Gloria and Madison. Ryan yelled upwards. "Derrick, let's go!"

. . .

Antoine and Brianna led the Peaksville seniors deep into Lover's Cave.

"Ready to graduate, Amy?" Aaron asked.

Amy was slow to answer. "Five more weeks. Can't believe it."

"You ready Antoine?" Brianna asked.

"I try not to think about it, Bree. Too sad."

The four came to a fork in the cave with two options.

Brianna got closer to Antoine, slyly holding his hand under the guise of being afraid of the dark.

Antoine alternated the beam of his flashlight back and forth. "Amy, right or left?"

"Try left."

"Why left?"

"Why not?"

Antoine continued forward for two minutes before pointing his flashlight at a large jelly jar on the cave floor. "Amy, what's this?"

"There's something inside!" Brianna exclaimed. "It's a note!"

"What does it say, Bree?" Amy excitedly asked.

Antoine and Aaron anxiously illuminated the paper with the flashlight.

Brianna removed the lid, unfolded the note, and read aloud. "The cure to your symptoms is simply mine!"

THE CURE TO YOUR SYMPTOMS IS SIMPLY MINE.

"Symptoms?" Aaron asked.

"Symptoms," Amy replied. "Headaches, stomach aches, fatigue, nausea."

"Many Peaksville kids get them, Aaron," Antoine Jordan said. "You're pretty fortunate."

"You get 'em, AJ?"

"Every day. Especially when I wake up."

"Bree?"

"Same."

Aaron sighed. "Damn. Sorry."

Antoine chuckled. "It's not your fault, don't be sorry."

Amy examined the note. "There's a cure?"

Brianna gently set the empty jar on the cave floor, stuffed the cryptic note in her pocket, and doubled back. "Let's head back to Lover's Lagoon and show the others!"

. . .

G igi Becker whispered to Kiche while walking upstream with Jack. "Hey Wolfie! You like to swim. Don't you?"

Kiche playfully and gently responded to her twelve-year-old admirer with a nudge and a lick.

"Hey, Kiddos! Did you finish your homework down in The Boxcar?" Grace yelled from the middle of Lover's Lagoon.

Gigi and Jack raised a 'thumbs up' skipping along Coldwater Creek's north bank.

"They're all done!" Ruby walked closely with Luke.

Minutes later, Derrick, Ryan, Madison and Gloria arrived from The Treehouse.

Derrick quickly joined the swimmers with a spectacular cannonball.

"Marcus, anyone caving?" Luke asked over the helicopter noise.

I held up four fingers and nodded yes.

"They went in thirty minutes ago." Emma lounged with Max on a warm boulder in Lover's Lagoon.

Jack threw a North Idaho tamarack branch into the water.

Kiche instinctively followed the branch with a violent splash.

Jack and Gigi stopped to pet Buckshot and Jefferson.

Gigi joked while sinisterly looking at Charlotte in the lagoon. "Poor horsey. Did mean old Charlie tie you to a tree?"

Charlotte laughed. "Technically, mean young Chloe tied them up."

Luke and Ruby waded into the cold spring water.

Suddenly, out of nowhere, Thomas let loose a terrifying scream and was violently pulled down underwater. In North Idaho, we have bears, cougars, moose, coyotes, and wolves. Luckily for Thomas, we have no piranhas, hippos, or alligators. His scream was therefore likely indicative of a primitive, land-based mammal attack.

Two cave-dwelling, land-based mammals emerged from underwater. Aaron and Antoine, paddled away in a fit of laughter.

Thomas surfaced in a fit of anger.

Size 32 jean shorts were flung ashore by Aaron.

Thomas tried unsuccessfully to catch and dunk the pranksters.

"Did you losers miss us?" Amy, alongside Brianna, yelled from the waterfall before diving into Lover's Lagoon.

Brianna surfaced. "Marcus! Grace! We have something that might be important."

"Size 32 shorts?" Thomas joked while treading water in his underwear.

"No, even better," Amy replied with a smile. "Much, much hotter!"

"We found a note in Lover's Cave!" Brianna exclaimed. "The cure to your symptoms is simply mine."

"Makes no sense." Ryan watched the Cessna 182 pass overhead at 300 feet.

Thomas laughed. "Sounds like nonsense."

Amy treaded water. "Hey Tommy Boy, read *The Emperor has no Clothes* and write me a book report."

Charlotte threw Thomas his jean shorts and smiled. "Poor guy."

Grace looked at Brianna. "Interesting! What else, Bree?"

"That's all," Brianna said.

We peacefully swam for another ten minutes in the setting sun.

I whispered. "What do you think, Grace?"

Grace swam close and kissed my cheek. "I think someone cares."

The Bell 407 performed a loud, low pass.

"Someone cares? About us?"

"Maybe."

"Why?"

Grace kissed me again. "Why not?"

Emma and Max launched the old raft, riddled with makeshift patches.

Max smiled. "Who wants to ride down Coldwater Creek?"

Emma teased as the raft began to exit Lover's Lagoon. "Better hurry!"

The twelve-year-olds smiled and swam frantically towards Max and Emma on the raft. Gigi and Jack climbed onboard, followed by Chloe.

Chloe turned back to Lover's Lagoon once onboard. "Hey DJ! Please ride Buckshot to The Boxcar!"

D'Andre Jordan smiled. "Okay!"

Charlotte asked D'Andre. "DJ, do you *really* want to ride Buckshot again?" She already knew his answer.

D'Andre smiled. "Absolutely, Charlie!"

Brianna and Antoine helped D'Andre mount the horse.

Grace yelled downstream to the five floaters as Mr. Light performed a low pass in his TSC airplane. "Emma, you got the kiddos!"

"Got 'em!"

CHAPTER SIX

M ax skillfully navigated the old raft on the calm, clear waters of Coldwater Creek towards Peaksville as Emma rested her head on his shoulder. The three tired sixth-graders started to doze off on the ten-minute float trip until Chloe found her second wind.

"Jack, Gigi, the Rocks!" Chloe laughingly leapt off and swam to the waterslides of the Elephant Rocks in the setting sun.

Gigi woke up. "Chloe, wait for me!"

Jack politely helped Max and Emma stow the raft onto the rocky shore of Coldwater Creek.

"You're a gentleman and a scholar," Max said.

Jack smiled and jumped back into the cold, clear mountain stream to play with Chloe and Gigi in the maze of waterslides among large, smooth boulders.

"Any words yet?" Max whispered to Emma.

"It's been four years."

Emma lazily swam towards the playing children as The Safety Corps search plane returned.

"Damn. Four years of not talking. It'll come. How are your headaches?"

"Terrible. Nearly constant."

Max joined Emma on their favorite sun-heated rock outcropping as Jack, Gigi, and Chloe played on the natural waterslides nearby. "Have you told Nurse Light about the headaches?"

"No. Those shots. Every Monday we get those TSC shots. And for what?"

Max was not required to receive the shots. The Burns family was fairly insulated from any chemical or biological threats since Mr. Burns was Vice President of the local TSC. Max reportedly had one of the lowest threat levels in school.

"Do the shots hurt?"

Emma nodded and rested her head on Max's shoulder. "I just hate them."

We returned along Coldwater Creek far behind Max, Emma and the three middle schoolers. Charlotte rode Jefferson, D'Andre rode Buckshot, and the rest of us walked.

With the evening sun on our backs, Grace spotted Emma resting in the distance. Grace whispered to Amy. "Your twin is a real trooper."

Amy smiled.

Brianna sighed. "Hope we find the cure."

Ruby agreed as Kiche faithfully walked alongside. "Emma's body could use a break."

Antoine was skipping rocks. "The note seems real."

"Incomplete," I said. "Too cryptic."

Antoine agreed. "We need more clues."

Thomas was our resident skeptic. "There is no cure."

I skipped a rock across Coldwater Creek and challenged Thomas. "Alright Tommy Boy, explain the note."

Brianna recited the note. "The cure to your symptoms is simply mine."

"It's a big nothing-burger," Thomas explained as the TSC Bell 407 helicopter thundered overhead in a slow, ten-knot hover at one-hundred feet. "All kids have headaches. The note is nonsense."

I did not necessarily disagree with Thomas. But the note provided *hope*, and Thomas had no right to extinguish *hope*. "Dismissing the note as nonsense is foolish."

Grace smiled and squeezed my hand.

Thomas was preparing another dismissive statement.

Gigi interrupted while sliding down the dozens of small natural waterslides when she noticed Kiche leading us down Coldwater Creek. "Wolfie! Come here, girl!"

Kiche raised her ears and exploded into gallop downstream to the Elephant Rocks.

Ruby laughed. "Gracie, Kiche just adores Gigi."

The large she-wolf leapt and splashed near Gigi, Chloe, and Jack.

Chloe yelled in our direction over the TSC helicopter noise. "DJ, looking good on Buckshot!"

D'Andre smiled.

Charlotte agreed. "You should've been a cowboy!"

"Losers, pay attention! I'm only going to say this once!" Derrick yelled from atop Deadman's Cliff where Coldwater Creek poured noisily into Liberty Lake downstream of the Elephant Rocks. "Cliff jump and swim race to The Boxcar!"

"Luke, you in, buddy?" Ruby asked.

"Maybe Weakman's Cliff," Luke whispered.

I truly wanted Luke to get over his fears. "Doesn't count, Luke."

"Come on, Luke!" Aaron said.

Luke climbed down to the lower, 10-foot rocky shelf as others gathered around Derrick. "I'm good."

Derrick climbed 100-foot cedar trees with *No Apparent Fear Of Death*, or *NAFOD* as they say in the military. But Luke wouldn't jump feet first into Liberty Lake from a 20 feet ledge. I considered myself somewhere in that 80-foot gap between Derrick and Luke. Much closer to Luke's danger threshold.

We assembled on the rocky perch. Gigi, Jack and Chloe ran to join us with big smiles. I had as much chance of beating Amy or Derrick as the middle schoolers. Grace and I held hands on the edge of Deadman's Cliff.

Amy developed a devious look. "Okay losers. Here are the rules. Back away for a second while I explain."

Luke stood alone on Weakman's Cliff as we gathered around Amy.

Amy prematurely jumped into Liberty Lake and yelled in midair. "Ready, set, go!"

We laughed and jumped. Kiche excitedly ran back and forth on the rocks and watched the splashing children paddle ahead at full speed.

Luke jumped and swam frantically towards The Boxcar. He elevated his head to shout at Amy. "Here I come, cheater!"

Amy maintained her lead. "Weakman's Cliff Jumper say what?"

Amy and Luke hilariously bickered between breaths.

My little brother Derrick slowly passed them.

Charlotte led D'Andre on horseback around Liberty Lake to The Boxcar near Kiche.

"Go Derrick!" Madison proudly yelled ahead.

Derrick reached the shore first, turned, and extended his hand. "Here Amy, let me help you ashore. You look badly beaten."

"Sorry. Nobody told you, Derrick?" Amy attempted to pull Derrick back in the Liberty Lake. "This was a *seniors-only* race."

I winked at Derrick.

Derrick humbly smiled at Amy.

Amy obnoxiously celebrated. "I won, slow-pokes!"

Aaron scoffed. "You cheated."

Grace joked as 150-pound Kiche playfully licked her face. "What is it Lassie? Amy cheated? Derrick won?"

"Nice swimming, sixth-graders," Charlotte said to Chloe, Gigi, and Jack from atop Jefferson.

They smiled as the Bell 407 passed overhead.

Brianna asked. "What about the note?"

Thomas sarcastically smiled, jumped up into The Boxcar and shook his head negatively.

Ruby reached into her bookbag and gave Kiche a treat. "Marcus, what does it mean?"

Ruby asked *me*. Like I was supposed to know the solution to the riddle. I made eye contact with Emma. She was holding her stomach. Thomas didn't have the right to destroy hope. "It means we should look for more notes."

Grace smiled at me.

"Let's look tomorrow," Charlotte said.

Ruby agreed as she grabbed her backpack from The Boxcar. "Deal!"

"Race back to Peaksville through The Meadow?" Antoine asked.

Luke shrugged. "Count me out. Amy cheats."

Max's dad made a final low helicopter pass directly overhead. Everyone braced to avoid being knocked over by the rotor wash.

"One-two-three-go!" Luke yelled while entering a sprint.

Aaron instinctively restrained Amy as Luke gained separation.

Amy yelled. "Let me go, abusive man!"

We laughed.

Amy continued. "Ouch! Your man-hands are hurting my soft, womanly body. I'm actually Emma, not Amy!"

Aaron did his best to restrain Amy as Luke ran home.

Amy squirmed. "Grace, you're my witness! Mr. Man is man-handling me with his man-hands."

Grace was too busy laughing to respond.

Aaron warned Luke already running in the high grass. "Hurry, Luke!"

Amy bolted loose from Aaron's grip.

"Ha! Ha!" Amy joked while sprinting away. "See you tomorrow at school, losers!" Amy taunted over her shoulder before overtaking Luke in The Meadow with a ceremonious, loud slap on his rear.

CHAPTER SEVEN

"$\mathbf{G}$ ood afternoon, Peaksville students. Today is Tuesday, thirty-two days until graduation," Dean Michaels broadcasted over the school PA system just prior to 3 o'clock. "There's an eight-week summer internship opportunity at Peaksville Defense and Space Corporation. Kid-friendly PDS protects our innocent citizens in the Homeland through advanced military technology. Accepting applications immediately. Reminder, all Peaksville caves remain off limits. TSC Air Patrol continues to search for the attempted child abduction suspect. School's out. Be safe out there."

Charlotte slammed her locker. "Emma, how are you feeling?"

Ruby hurled her backpack over her shoulder. "Yeah, I heard you passed out this morning."

"I'm still dizzy." Emma sighed. "I just need to swim."

Charlotte helped Emma with her backpack. "Hope you feel better."

"Ruby!" Amy slammed her locker. "Are you up for caving?"

"After Luke and I finish tutoring the twelve-year-olds. Can you wait?"

"Yes, if you bring my she-wolf," Amy said. "She loves me the most, you know."

"Deal." Ruby smiled. "But that pup's all mine, Amy,"

Grace slammed her locker. "Ruby, my parents want to personally thank you and Luke with dinner sometime. Gigi's grades have been improving."

Ruby smiled. "That's so sweet."

I caught up with Grace. "Hey babe, how you feeling?"

Grace never complained.

Mr. Burns circled over the schoolyard in his Bell 407.

Grace snuck me a kiss as we exited Peaksville School. "Like a ray of sunshine, Marcus." Eloquently stated. Grace truly was *my* ray of sunshine.

" Charlie!" Chloe yelled running with Jack and Gigi from Peaksville Middle School. "Jack and Gigi want to ride horses to The Boxcar!"

Charlotte waited for the eager sixth-graders. "Let's hurry, kiddos!"

Ruby yelled to Chloe, Gigi and Jack. "Meet Luke and me at The Boxcar in thirty minutes! Bring your math workbooks!"

Charlotte flashed Ruby a 'thumbs up.'

Kiche greeted Ruby and Luke in the schoolyard with wolf-licks like clockwork.

Derrick approached the rope swing. "Anybody else feel warm today? Must have been ninety degrees in school."

I agreed.

D'Andre waited to comment until Mr. Light passed overhead in the TSC Cessna 182. "Little bit."

Aaron Webster hurled the rope back to Thomas Stallworth.

Thomas clumsily swung over the creek. "Maybe you were simply dehydrated, Derrick."

Brianna caught the rope from Thomas. "Tommy Boy! I saw you sweating in History class."

Antoine laughed and pointed. "Exposed!"

"What? I always sweat during quizzes and tests."

Luke joked. "You should. I've seen your grades."

Amy saw an opportunity. "I always look *hot* in school. Capital H. Capital O. Capital T. Every. Single. Day."

Aaron countered. "Dean Michaels agrees. Ben Light agrees. Nobody else agrees. But thanks for your opinion."

Amy retaliated by flicking Aaron's earlobe.

"Ow! What was that for?"

"For disrespecting my hotness."

Aaron joked back. "Agree to disagree."

Someone had to interrupt. One thing was on my mind. "Maybe we can find a cure."

Amy wasn't finished. "Marcus, there is no cure for my hotness. And maybe Bree is going to hurry and swing before sunset."

Brianna swung across. "Maybe Amy isn't as hot as she thinks!"

Amy yelled back. "Nonsense!"

Grace whispered to Emma. "Feeling better?"

Emma sighed. "I just need to swim, Gracie."

Max put his hand on her shoulder. "Possible reaction to yesterday's weekly shot?"

"Not sure."

Antoine watched Max's dad perform a low pass in his Bell 407 helicopter barely over the treeline. "Can't believe your dad flew earlier in the rain, Max. We heard him over the school roof all day long. Every ten minutes. Have they found the child abductor yet?"

Grace got a running start with the rope swing tight in her hands. "Doesn't seem like the TSC ever finds anyone!"

Max yelled as Grace glided over Peaksville Creek. "Maybe so, Grace! Maybe so!"

I caught Grace. Amy slung the long rope back to Emma and Max.

Max caught the rope and whispered. "You're next, Emma. Hold on tight."

Grace caught Emma after sailing over. "Love that smile."

Emma smiled 24/7 during her Freshman year. Then less and less. By her Senior year, Emma smiled only on rope swings and cliff jumps. Emma was ready to graduate.

O nce assembled on the west side of Peaksville Creek, we jogged through The Meadow as fast as Emma's tired body would let us.

Gloria Becker was already lounging next to Ryan, my not-so-little brother, in The Boxcar. Kiche jumped inside and rested her massive head on Ryan's lap.

Grace greeted Gloria. "Hey sis'!"

Ryan punched me on the shoulder to greet me. That hurt. No words were exchanged. I responded similarly. Now my hand hurt, also. Ryan acted like it didn't hurt him. Because it didn't. I resisted saying *ouch*. Grace rubbed my shoulder. To further humiliate me, Ryan's girlfriend Gloria rubbed my shoulder also.

Ruby and Luke climbed into The Boxcar and began to set up their tutorial papers for the middle schoolers who were due soon on horseback.

Emma arrived. "Ruby and Luke, you're doing God's work tutoring Jack."

Derrick Flynn whispered. "I can't believe it's been four years since Jack spoke."

Ruby Kyle nodded. "Give him time."

"What are the doctors saying?" Madison Goodwell asked.

Brianna Lopez answered for tired Emma. "I don't think Emma and Amy trust their family doctor."

I agreed. "There's a lot of that going around."

Amy rapidly slid the Boxcar door open and yelled inside. "Hey Losers!"

"Hey slowpoke," Derrick said.

"Kiche!" Amy playfully pointed to her cheek. "Give the awesome one a kiss."

Kiche wagged her tail, ran to Amy and excitedly licked her face.

"Any questions about loyalty, Ruby the Dog Owner?"

Ruby didn't back down. "She enjoys your dirty, sweaty face. She's trying to clean your pores."

Amy ignored the dissent and rubbed Kiche.

"Madison and I want to go caving with you, Amy," Derrick said.

Thomas spoke up. "It's still off-limits, right?"

We looked at Thomas with blank faces.

Amy broke the silence and looked around The Boxcar. "Maddie is invited. You can join me also, Derrick."

"Perfect." Derrick high-fived Madison.

Charlotte Epley and Jack Kernan arrived riding Jefferson. Chloe Epley and Gigi Becker arrived on Buckshot. Mr. Burns arrived overhead simultaneously in his Cessna 182 conducting his search pattern.

"Yee haw!" yelled Gigi while dismounting Buckshot. "Let's go caving!"

"Not so fast, Cowgirl," Luke said. "Ruby has one math worksheet for you guys."

The familiar sound of the TSC propeller and reciprocating six-cylinder Lycoming engine didn't help my headache. "Okay, then. Lover's Lagoon at four o'clock."

Charlotte grabbed her towel and stowed her schoolbag in The Boxcar. "Chloe, get Jefferson and Buckshot upstream safely, okay?"

Chloe gave a 'thumbs up' and smiled in unison with Jack and Gigi.

"We'll be quick, Charlie." Ruby organized her lesson plan on the floor of The Boxcar. "Alright, sixth-graders. School is in session."

Derrick's eyes lit up. "We have extra time, Maddie!" Derrick hustled north towards The Treehouse pulling Madison by her hand.

Gloria looked at Ryan as they followed. "The trees?"

Ryan nodded. "How'd you guess?"

I walked downhill towards Liberty Lake holding Grace's hand. "Careful Derrick! Don't climb too high!"

Chloe, Gigi and Jack flopped onto The Boxcar floor to study with Luke and Ruby.

"Wolfie," Gigi whispered to Kiche. "Sit by me, and I'll scratch your belly."

CHAPTER EIGHT

"Okay, boys, here's the protocol." Amy entered Liberty Lake and adjusted her swimsuit. "I swim. You watch. Questions?"

Charlotte, momentarily tending to Jefferson and Buckshot, subtly gesturing to Grace and me. "Speaking of watchers."

Grace lowered her feet into the clear, cold water of Liberty Lake. "Hi, Ben. Hi, Tony."

Ben didn't respond but creepily ogled Amy.

"Hi, Grace," Tony Murdstone mumbled.

"Amy, rumor is you entered Lover's Cave yesterday," Ben Light said as his TSC father droned northbound at five hundred feet and seventy knots in the Cessna 182.

Aaron laughed. "Ben, rumor is that you —"

"Whoa, easy, Aaron!" I knew where Aaron was heading and quickly interrupted.

Aaron and I made eye contact and smiled.

Ben and Tony quietly turned and walked back towards The Meadow.

Max Burns swam up to Emma. "How are you feeling?"

"Just tired."

"Headache?"

Emma nodded affirmatively.

"Getting better?"

"Cold water helps. But only a little."

I checked to ensure the TSC cadets were over the horizon. "Amy, can you find another note today?"

"I can try."

"Yesterday's note could be eighty years old," Thomas grumbled. "The cure to your symptoms is simply mine. It could be referring to the cure for Hoof and Mouth disease."

Amy replied. "You could only be so lucky, Tommy Boy."

D'Andre Jordan smiled. "Tommy Boy, be positive."

"I'm *positive* that there's no cure for my morning headaches," Thomas said. "How's that for positive?"

Antoine was treading water and saw his sightless brother's smile leave his face. "Not good enough, Thomas. We gotta have hope."

Thomas ran his mouth. "We can hope in one hand, and crap in the other. Then see which one gets filled first."

D'Andre shed a tear. "Enough, Tommy Boy! I *will* get my vision back!"

Charlotte and Brianna swam to D'Andre to comfort him.

My public self was angry with Thomas.

My private self was in agreement with him.

G loria looked up into the North Idaho cedars from the lower level of The Treehouse. "Ryan, explain again why your brother built a lookout platform seventy-five feet-high?"

Ryan yelled over the TSC helicopter noise. "I stopped trying to understand Derrick years ago!"

In 2017, Derrick single-handedly constructed The Treehouse platform five feet above the forest floor. The main level was a fully enclosed two-hundred square foot lounge complete with a ladder sloped metal roof, plywood walls, and clear, plastic windows. Above the main level was a makeshift ladder consisting of scrap two-by-four boards nailed into the trunk. This ladder provided access to a small wooden platform sixty-feet high, barely large enough for him to lounge on.

By 2020, The Treehouse had elevated another fifteen feet due to natural growth. The lower level was now twenty feet above the forest floor. The upper, semi-enclosed structure towered at seventy-five feet.

Derrick didn't actually lounge up top. He used it to scout for new growth of parasitic ivy in Peaksville Forest using Dad's Army Ranger binoculars.

Madison looked up. "That's odd. Derrick stopped cutting ivy."

Ryan waited for the TSC airplane noise to subside then yelled upwards. "Hey brother! You good up there?"

"Just resting!"

Ryan looked at the girls. "Yeah, he's too high."

"I'm done!" Derrick said moments later. "Let's go caving!"

Derrick began his descent.

Madison bit her fingernails. "Careful, Derrick!"

"Okay, Maddie!"

Derrick continued downward slowly, procedurally utilizing three points of constant contact.

Ryan initiated small talk with Gloria Becker while waiting for Derrick. "Can you believe Gracie is graduating?"

"Part of me is sad. Part of me says 'no more middle child treatment' between Grace and Gigi."

Ryan Flynn, also a middle child, silently understood.

Madison scoffed. "Get real, Gloria. Mrs. Becker loves you the most."

"I wish."

Derrick lost his footing, creating a loud cracking noise thirty feet above the lower terrace.

"Derrick!" Ryan yelled over the helicopter noise. "You good?"

"Got really dizzy! I'm good!" Derrick whispered to himself. "Damn."

Ryan covered his mouth. "Horrible time to get dizzy."

Derrick climbed down the ladder boards to The Treehouse lounge without any more slips.

"You're slower than usual, today," Ryan said.

"Your leg." Madison pulled Derrick's sock down to examine a wound. "It's bleeding."

Derrick covered the wound by pulling up his sock. "Just a flesh wound. Let's go caving."

Madison smiled. "For real? You're done? We can swim?"

"Only two more trees. I saw some hurting cedars from the lookout. Don't worry. They're on the way up Coldwater Creek."

Ryan complained. "Two insignificant trees?"

"Yeah, two cedar trees. Covered with parasitic ivy. Would you care if I named the two insignificant trees Ryan and Derrick?"

Gloria laughed. "Derrick you're amazing. Five trees per day."

Madison smiled.

Ryan kept his mouth shut. Almost. "Make it quick. And don't climb so high."

Ryan, Gloria, and Madison slowly tracked west toward Lover's Lagoon, just north of Coldwater Creek. Just slow enough for Derrick to slay parasites along the way.

. . .

Aaron Webster rested on the Elephant Rocks overlooking Liberty Lake watching the Bell 407 pass overhead. "Max, has Mr. Burns taught you how to fly helicopters?"

"I know just enough to be dangerous. I can get airborne. I can stay airborne. And I can land. Barely."

Mr. Burns pulled into a slow, thirty-knot hover at three hundred feet.

"Was Mr. Burns in the Army?" Antoine asked while cooling off in Coldwater Creek.

"Yeah, until 2013," Max said. "TSC pays more. Lot's more. Like triple. And he doesn't need to go to the sandbox to kill tangos."

I was sitting under a small natural waterslide listening with Grace. "Wonder if our dads served together."

"Maybe. Dad flew Army Rangers all the time."

Wasn't Dr. Jordan Army?" Charlotte asked.

Antoine answered without making eye contact. "Navy."

Charlotte immediately realized she just reminded the Jordan boys of their traumatic 2016 loss. "Navy. That's right."

Antoine replied. "Retired from the Navy, perfectly healthy."

D'Andre got a sad look on his face. "Died in his sleep on Thanksgiving."

The Jordan twins each silently wept.

I wanted to make it better as the Bell 407 thundered overhead. "I wish Dr. Jordan were still alive."

Grace, Brianna, and Charlotte gently placed their arms around Antoine and D'Andre.

Charlotte's eyes welled up with tears and sighed. "I'm sorry to make you sad."

Antoine wiped his eyes. "It's not your fault, Charlie."

Grace comforted the twins. "We loved Dr. Jordan."

Brianna rested her head on D'Andre. "So much."

Emma began to cry.

"Yeah," Amy said. "Doctors in Peaksville are all freaks and quacks now. Dr. Jordan was awesome."

Emma wiped her tears and rubbed her forehead. "Let's head upstream, my headache is returning. This is too sad."

Charlotte placed her arm around the Jordan twins. "Come on, guys."

Max and Aaron pulled the raft upstream toward Lover's Lagoon as we walked up Coldwater Creek.

Grace pointed towards distant tree noises. "Look! The Tree People!"

I yelled into Peaksville Forest. "Ryan! Tell Derrick he's done landscaping! Let's go!"

No response.

"I'll get them." Amy Kernan threw her arms around Aaron, Antoine, and D'Andre. "Madison! Gloria! Come upstream with us! I'll share all my boyfriends with you!"

Madison grabbed Gloria's hand and immediately ran towards us.

Gloria laughingly followed.

Amy rubbed it in. "Any questions on how to summon the Tree People, Marcus?"

I had a bad headache. I also had questions. But not about Amy punking me. I was still thinking about yesterday's note. I held Grace's hand and continued upstream. "Let's hurry."

"Amy, one! Marcus, zero!" Amy was about twenty feet behind me celebrating. "Whammy!"

Grace saw me crack and smile and squeezed my hand.

CHAPTER NINE

"Ruby! Luke! How did you beat us to Lover's Lagoon with the middle-schoolers?" Charlotte yelled.

Jefferson and Buckshot were properly tied to a large cedar near the shoreline.

"Chloe took us up the southern trail," Ruby Kyle replied.

"Chloe taught Jack and Gigi how to tie the horses up," Luke Bartholomew said.

"Jefferson is my buddy! Thanks Charlie!" Gigi yelled from underneath the waterfall in her swimsuit.

Mr. Light buzzed overhead in his Cessna 182 as we kicked our shoes off and prepared to swim.

"Luke, did Chloe get her homework done?" Charlotte asked.

"Perfectly! They're ready for tomorrow's math quiz."

Jack repeatedly hurled a large cedar branch into Lover's Lagoon for Kiche to fetch.

Ruby scanned the area for Ben and Tony. "We're still caving, right?"

"As soon as Derrick gets done saving the ten-thousand trees of Peaksville Forest," Marcus said.

"I heard you, Marcus!" Derrick yelled, approaching with a smile and finishing with a cannonball.

Splash!

"You guys aren't still preoccupied with yesterday's note, are you?" Thomas said.

"Sounds like you are, Tommy Boy," Antoine said.

"Maybe we'll find a unicorn in the cave, today!" Thomas yelled as the TSC helicopter thundered overhead at only twenty knots.

Grace whispered in my ear. "Ignore him."

"You all ready to cave?" Ruby asked wading in Lover's Lagoon.

"Waitin' on you!" Derrick joked while treading water.

The Peaksville cavers assembled close to the expansive cavern under the waterfall.

Gigi knelt down and whispered into Kiche's ear. "Wolfie. Stay by me in Lover's Cave. Okay?"

Kiche responded with a giant, full-faced lick.

Jack grabbed Madison's hand.

Ryan flipped on his flashlight. "Amy, you lead with Ruby, Gigi, and Kiche. Derrick and Maddie, you keep Chloe and Jack in the middle. Gloria and I will trail."

Chloe grabbed Derrick's right hand tightly. "It's chilly in here!"

Madison, holding Derrick's left hand, leaned around Derrick. "Stay close, Chloe."

Gloria grabbed Ryan's hand. "Alright Amy. Lead the way."

"Gigi, hold Kiche's collar," Ruby said. "Don't let go."

"You hear that, Wolfie?" Gigi whispered.

The nine cavers exited the initial cavern into the small, winding passageway leading deeper into the mountain.

Amy hunched forward, straightened out her right leg, illuminated her face, and looked backwards. "Walk this way."

Amy slumped down and dragged her stiff right leg on the rocky cave floor with every step.

Ruby laughed. "Are you for real?"

The sixth-graders laughed, hunched themselves over, and dragged their right legs like Amy.

Derrick addressed Chloe, Gigi, and Jack. "Don't encourage her, Kiddos."

Madison joked. "Derrick, what did we get ourselves into?"

Amy righted herself after about ten seconds and carefully navigated through the cave, always choosing the tallest passageways, always choosing left turns.

"Amy, it's been fifteen minutes. Ready to double back?" Ruby said.

Amy continued forward. "Hang on, almost there."

Gigi maintained a tight grip on Kiche's collar.

Moments later, Ruby saw a jelly jar on the cave floor and yelled. "There! Over there!"

Madison squeezed Derrick's hand. "Oh God. Please don't yell. You scared me, Ruby!"

Gigi exclaimed. "A note's inside! Can I open it?"

Amy illuminated the jar. "Of course."

Gigi released her grip on Kiche's collar and anxiously opened the jar.

G race and I lounged on a boulder in the middle of Lover's Lagoon. "It's getting dark soon, Grace. Think they're okay?"

Grace snuck me a kiss on the cheek. "They're fine, Marcus."

I made eye contact with Luke.

Luke subtly tapped his left wrist.

I replied with an affirmative nod.

Aaron and I made eye contact. Aaron pointed to an approaching evening thunderstorm. "Soon, we need to search for them."

I scanned the area for Ben and Tony, the TSC Cadets. Then, I made eye contact with Thomas who was near the waterfall and cave entrance. "Tommy Boy, can you holler inside?"

"I'm on it."

Thomas climbed up from Lover's Lagoon into the waterfall, cupped his hands together, and yelled into the mouth of Lover's Cave. "Ryan! Derrick! You in there?"

Thomas turned to us, shrugged his shoulders, and listened for a reply. Thomas waited in the cascading mountain waterfall and declared, "I don't believe —"

The confident declaration by Thomas was violently interrupted.

Ryan, Derrick, and young Jack executed a surprise attack on Thomas. All four boys splashed loudly into the lagoon.

Splash!

"Savage!" Aaron said to Brianna.

"Thomas, you were saying?" Antoine jokingly taunted. "I don't believe what?"

Amy celebrated before performing a cannonball. "Two days! Two notes! Are you not entertained?"

Splash!

Ruby, Gloria, Madison, Chloe, and Gigi jumped into the water. Kiche wagged her tail, emitted a strange howl, and jumped in after the girls.

Splash! *Splash*!

I pointed at the dark cloud rolling in. "Storms coming. Chloe, help your sister with Jefferson and Buckshot. Max and Emma, prepare the raft. Let's roll."

. . .

Inclement weather approached quickly, so we expedited our departure from Lover's Lagoon to navigate down Coldwater Creek.

D'Andre was the last to board the raft. "Alright, Amy. We float. You talk. Any questions?"

"Questions? Yes. I thought you'd never ask, D'Andre. First, let's all agree that I'm awesome. I'm beautiful. I'm smart —"

I interrupted. "Amy. The note."

Antoine paddled hard down Coldwater Creek to beat the storm. "Yeah, let's have it."

"I got this." Brianna snatched the note from Amy. "Carefully cross the stream to clean the stream."

CAREFULLY CROSS THE STREAM TO CLEAN THE STREAM.

Thomas scooped a handful of spring water from Coldwater Creek and drank it. "Too late. Stream's clean."

Gulp!

Amy watched Thomas, pointed upstream and gasped. "I wouldn't do that, I just —"

Grace kindly placed her hand on his shoulder. "It's a riddle, Tommy Boy."

Emma rubbed her temples and repeated the clues in a tired voice. "The cure to your symptoms is simply mine. Carefully cross the stream to clean the stream."

Luke and Antoine paddled as we all looked at each other with blank stares.

Riddles were not my forte. "Everyone sleep on it."

Charlotte and Jack rode past the raft on Jefferson, followed by Chloe and Gigi on Buckshot.

The Cessna 182 made a final low overflight as the cumulonimbus cloud matured.

Grace yelled to the riders. "Charlie, can you get Jack and Gigi to school tomorrow?"

Charlotte gave a 'thumbs up' as the we paddled downstream.

"Thanks, Charlie!"

Chloe, Gigi and Jack galloped to the Epley farm sleepover with big smiles.

Crack!

Lightning struck nearby. We quickly stowed the raft onto the Elephant Rocks, grabbed our backpacks from The Boxcar, and ran to Peaksville through The Meadow to beat the Tuesday evening storm.

CHAPTER TEN

"Good morning, Max." Nurse Light cheerfully greeted Max walking out of the vacant school medical office. "May I help you? Are you feeling ill, or something?"

"No thanks, Ma'am. Just looking for someone. But I guess the non-TSC children all get their shots on Mondays, right?"

"Right, Max. No shots on Wednesdays. I can give you a shot if you want," Nurse Light joked. "But Mr. Burns is the local TSC Vice-President. You have one of the lowest threat levels in Peaksville High School. You don't need shots, Max."

"Yes, Ma'am, I understand. Have a nice day, Ma'am." Max walked towards homeroom.

Max turned the corner, stopped, looked around, raised his sleeve and rubbed his upper left arm. Max subtly opened a bandage, taped it, and lowered his sleeve.

Emma yelled from down the hallway. "Hey Hot Stuff! Walk me to class or lose me forever!"

Max regained his composure and displayed his contagious smile. "Deal!"

Emma smiled despite her headache. "Where have you been?"

"I'll tell you later."

Before dismissal, I noticed Max opening his locker uncharacteristically slowly. "You alright?"

"Just tired. Is the flu going around?"

We caught Ben Light and Tony Murdstone creepily eavesdropping.

I whispered to Max. "Depends who you ask."

"Good afternoon, Peaksville students. Today is Wednesday, thirty-one days until graduation," Dean Michaels broadcasted on the school PA system. "Some extremely hazardous materials were found in the vicinity of the Peaksville Water Reservoir. The TSC Air Patrol is investigating and conducting 24/7 search patterns. All caves remain off limits. The search continues for the attempted child abduction suspect. School's out. Be safe out there."

Amy loudly joked to Ruby and Grace. "And now, for the bad news —"

Max rubbed his temples.

I helped him gather his books.

The dismissal exodus was overflown by Mr. Light executing an extremely low pass over the school roof, continuing his search pattern.

"Hey, Big Sis'!" Gigi yelled to Grace from the playground over the propeller noise. "Can Jack and I go with Chloe to the Epley farm? We want to ride again."

"Okay! You three stay with Charlie!"

Ruby was loyally met by Kiche in the schoolyard. "Math in thirty minutes, Gigi!"

Gigi departed with a playful frown, quickly followed by a 'thumbs up.'

A t the Peaksville Creek rope swing, Max subtly raised his left sleeve and whispered to Emma Kernan. "Emma, check it out."

"A bandage?" Emma asked. "What for?"

"One second." Max waited on Antoine to swing into The Meadow.

Emma looked at Max with an inquisitive look. "What happened?"

"I self-administered a sympathetic TSC shot today."

"Max, you have a super low threat level. Why?"

"For you."

"Why, Max?"

"To prove TSC shots aren't that bad."

"Go ahead, guys." Max yielded his turn at the rope swing. "We'll see you at The Boxcar."

Emma raised his sleeve to look again. "Max, you didn't."

"I did."

"What did Nurse Light say?"

"She almost caught me."

Emma sighed and hugged him. "Max."

Mr. Light intercepted Peaksville Creek then lazily rolled his TSC Cessna 182 into a left turn westward towards The Meadow.

Emma waited for the loud prop noise to subside. "How do you feel?"

"Good for two hours. Puked twice after lunch. My head is killing me, now."

"The weekly TSC shots must be bad, Max. You are proof!"

"Could be a bad reaction. Could be the HAZMAT the TSC found. Could be the flu."

Emma planted a kiss on his cheek. "Don't ever do that again."

Max handed Emma the rope. "Don't tell a soul."

Emma winked and swung across Peaksville Creek. "See you on the other side."

K iche entertained as we lounged around The Boxcar. The she-wolf was especially frisky and went person-to-person attempting to knock us over by sleighing into our ankles. Her wide smile revealed her long jaws with massive teeth.

Grace laughed. "She's like a bull in a china shop."

"I have a solution." I picked up a large stick and threw it into Liberty Lake. I realized my blunder when she returned soaking wet, just as frisky.

Luke and Ruby prepared a lesson inside for the middle schoolers as the sound of horses grew louder.

Luke peeked his head out of the sliding door. "Here comes the cavalry!"

"Howdy, partners!" Antoine tipped his imaginary cowboy hat. Charlotte and Jack rode in on Jefferson. Chloe and Gigi rode in on Buckshot.

"Wolfie, you're all wet!" Gigi exclaimed.

I looked upwards at Charlotte and petted Jefferson. "Charlotte, four o'clock at The Elephant Rocks for you and the twelve-year-olds."

"What for?"

Grace helped Gigi and Chloe dismount Buckshot. "Amy wants diversions as she enters Lover's Cave today."

"Diversions?"

I pointed upwards at the TSC helicopter in a slow, low hover overhead. "Diversions. Then we don't get seen entering the cave."

"Okay." Charlotte helped Jack dismount. "Sounds fun."

"After one quick worksheet," Ruby said.

"Aw!" Chloe and Gigi sang in unison while Kiche tackled Gigi.

I helped Gigi get free of Kiche's playful grip. "We should have warned you, Gigi. Kiche is in rare form."

Ruby helped me to corral Kiche. "Kiche thinks it's playtime."

Gigi smiled as I helped her stand up. "It's okay, Wolfie. We can play later." Gigi went back to securing the horses.

"Hey, Emma. Hey, Max," Aaron said over the Cessna 182 propeller noise.

"Liberty Lake for the three of us. Prepare for extreme tomfoolery. Max, are you feeling okay? You look rough."

Max looked at Emma during his answer. "Swimming will help. Just got overheated."

I looked at Amy. "Liberty Lake. What else?"

Amy looked around. "Luke and Antoine: On point at Lover's Lagoon. Tree People: Report to The Treehouse. Team Marcus: Coldwater Creek. Ruby and Brianna: Lover's Cave with the beautiful one, the one you love and respect the most. Me. Does everyone know their role?"

"Aye, aye! Captain!" Chloe yelled with an exaggerated, open-handed military salute before putting her arms around the shoulders of Jack and Gigi.

Amy looked at Chloe. "Outstanding, Lieutenant Epley! Carry On!"

Chloe returned a second salute and quickly led her little friends away from The Boxcar towards the water. "Let's roll!"

Luke laughed. "Woah! Nice try, Private Chloe! Get back here."

Ruby climbed into The Boxcar with Luke. "We'll be ready at four. Come on, kiddos."

Chloe, Jack and Gigi donned ridiculously sad faces, watched us disperse, and remained at The Boxcar for tutoring.

Luke addressed the sixth-graders. "Smile and we'll keep this under ten minutes."

Frowns morphed into ridiculous wide smiles.

CHAPTER ELEVEN

A aron swam with Emma and Max in Liberty Lake. "Looking better, Max."
Emma agreed while treading water. "Yeah, you looked rough earlier."

Max Burns looked at his watch as the TSC Bell 407 approached over the trees. "Coming up on four o'clock, Aaron. Describe this tomfoolery you speak of."

"Amy, Ruby, and Bree wanted multiple diversions since the cave has been declared off-limits by TSC."

Mr. Burns, flying solo in the small TSC search and rescue helicopter, was now clearly visible through his cockpit windscreen and starboard window.

Emma looked at Aaron and Max while treading water. "Shark."

"Shark?" Max asked in the rotor wash's piercing spray.

Emma splashed frantically in the abandoned, freshwater-filled, North Idaho quarry. "Shark!"

Max watched her flail. "Huh? Oh, I got it! Dad, help! Shark!"

Aaron laughed and splashed under the slow, thunderous helicopter. "Mr. Burns! There's a God-damned shark in Liberty Lake!"

Max continued. "It just bit off my legs, Dad! It's going to bite off my arms now!"

Mr. Burns rolled into a steep right turn at forty-five degrees angle of bank and added power.

Emma continued to splash. "Your dad's circling back."

Aaron yelled again as Mr. Burns approached just one-hundred feet overhead Liberty Lake. "I can't feel my legs!"

Max yelled. "I don't *have* any legs, Dad!"

Emma yelled under the helicopter's second and final pass. "We're going to need a bigger boat!"

"Don't leave us to die, Dad! I don't want to be shark chum! The boom! Lower your boom!" Max yelled in vain signaling with a right fist to his left chest as if he had a D-Ring. "Save me first!"

Aaron yelled as the helicopter departed to the north. "Don't go into the light, Emma!"

"He's gone," Emma calmly said.

Aaron relaxed and calmly treaded water. "I guess we're done."

Max smiled and treaded water. "That was a hell of a thing."

M adison heard the rotor blade noise approaching. She turned to Derrick, Ryan and Madison under The Treehouse. "Tree People, mobilize. Mr. Burns is inbound."

"Cavemen, your sticks," Gloria handed out sticks to Ryan and Derrick as helicopter noise grew louder. "Ready for the diversion."

Madison looked around. "Where's my stick?"

The other three smiled at her and raised their clubs in the air as the helicopter noise increased.

Madison backed up slowly. "Oh crap!"

"Get cavegirl!" Ryan grunted in his best caveman voice. "Get cavegirl!"

Madison ran around the cedars screaming.

Derrick ran with his club in his hand. "Thor want cavegirl!"

"Cavegirl one club cavegirl two!" Gloria yelled with her club in the air.

The TSC helicopter slowly passed over the treeline in a thirty-knot hover.

"He's gone, he's gone," Madison stopped and put her hands in the air, requesting a truce.

The Safety Corps helicopter quickly circled back overhead.

"Pterodactyl return!" Gloria grunted in a cavegirl voice.

Derrick raised his club. "Food!"

"Cavegirl run more!" Ryan instructed.

Madison ran, laughed and screamed. "Why me?"

Derrick grunted and chased her through the trees. "Cavegirl make good wife for Thor!"

Visually, Ryan was sadly the most convincing caveman. "Cavegirl make sandwich!"

Gloria played along as the cedars waved in the rotor wash. "Cavegirl jealous! Cavegirl eliminate second cavegirl to have prehistoric Flynn caveman babies all by herself!"

The helicopter passed overhead once more and departed to the west.

"He's gone!" Madison yelled, laughed, ran, and hoped for a truce. "He's gone!"

Gloria, Derrick, and Ryan lowered their clubs.

Ryan looked up. "Pterodactyl fly into sun. Caveman sad."

Gloria stopped running. "Cavegirl done with diversion."

Derrick hugged Madison and sat with her on a large North Idaho boulder among the tall, dense cedars. "Caveman tired. Caveman want sandwich."

"Hi, Charlie! Hi, Chloe, Jack and Gigi! Secure the horses. Just in time!" Grace stood on the lone sandy shore of Coldwater Creek, one thousand feet upstream of the Elephant Rocks. The four dismounted Jefferson and Buckshot and quickly tended to them.

Ruby and Luke continued upstream to Lover's Lagoon on foot.

"What's the plan, Grace?" Charlotte asked.

Grace and I continued to gather stones. "Setting up our diversion for Amy, Ruby and Brianna."

"It's a six-foot diameter circle of rocks on the sand," Charlotte raised her eyebrows.

The TSC aircraft noise grew louder.

"Gigi, quick! Lie in the fire pit on your back and don't move," Grace said. "Ever been sacrificed?"

"Not yet!" Gigi laughed on the sand. "Sacrifice me!"

I nodded. "You heard it, natives. Gigi said sacrifice her."

Mr. Burns entered a left-hand orbit at two hundred feet. Grace, Charlotte, D'Andre, Chloe, Jack and I initiated tribal chanting and dancing clock-wise around Gigi in the sacrificial rock pit. Thomas rubbed two sticks together over Gigi as if to start a fire.

Thomas looked up. "Don't stop, here comes Mr. Light."

The small, noisy Cessna 182 entered a tight, left-hand orbit just 300 feet above the Bell 407.

"God of Peaksville!" D'Andre chanted ridiculously. "We are sacrificing this abnormally-thin, willing sixth-grader on Wednesday so we humble seniors can have a small, meager lunch on Thursday!"

I danced and circled Gigi Becker with the others. "God of Coldwater Creek! Please keep the Class of 2020 headache-free in return for our paltry, skinny offering!"

"They're flying west!" Charlotte watched both TSC aircraft roll wings level and depart in tandem up Coldwater Creek towards Lover's Lagoon.

"Great acting, everyone," Grace said.

Charlotte laughed and helped Gigi stand up. "Especially you."

Thomas frantically continued trying to start a fire with two sticks.

Chloe laughed. "Any sparks, Tommy Boy?"

Thomas immediately threw the cold driftwood into the creek. "Ouch, it's hot!"

"Yeah, right." I laughed. "Nice try, Tommy Boy!"

"Oh, God. What are Antoine and Luke doing on those rocks?" Brianna asked Amy and Ruby. The three seniors peeked outside at Antoine and Luke from Lover's Cave through the cascading waterfall.

"My eyes are burning. Kiche, come with us. You gentle, innocent she-wolf." Amy knelt on one knee holding a flashlight.

Ruby gawked. "Is Luke dancing?"

Brianna joked. "Amy Kernan. Asked for distractions. Got distractions."

Amy watched Luke. "More like got *convulsions*."

"Come on, ladies. Let's go caving," Ruby said.

Two TSC aircraft approached Lover's Lagoon from the east under 500 feet.

"Not yet. I can't keep my eyes off Luke's overbite." Brianna peeked out at Antoine and Luke dancing on separate large boulders in Lover's Lagoon.

Ruby looked up. "Don't get seen."

Amy joked. "Bree, don't look anymore. You'll catch something."

"This is our diversion? Luke looks like he is having a physiological episode," Ruby said.

The three girls hid as the helicopter and airplane entered left orbits over the two dancers.

"There's nothing like good dancing," Amy joked over the sound of the waterfall and aircraft noise. "And this is *nothing* like good dancing."

"Is this legal in Idaho?" Ruby asked. "Has to be a law against this."

"Check out Luke's dancing. Why are his thumbs up in the air?" Brianna asked.

"Hitchhiking?" Amy asked.

"Not sure because Luke gets two thumbs down from me," Ruby joked.

Amy, Ruby and Brianna remained hidden from the approaching TSC aircraft, both flying barely over the treeline.

"Is this some kind of a dance-off?" Brianna asked.

"The dance-off worked. They dance." Amy said. "And *off* we go."

The three seniors turned on their flashlights and walked deeper into Lover's Cave. Ruby addressed her she-wolf. "Come on, Kiche. Sorry you had to see that."

Amy agreed. "Animal cruelty."

CHAPTER TWELVE

R uby walked deeper inside Lover's Cave for fifteen minutes. "I don't think I can find a third note. My eyes are still burning,"

"Yeah, wonder if Antoine and Luke are still dancing," Amy said.

"Probably got tired," Brianna said.

Amy pointed with a flashlight beam. "Here's our left turn, ladies. And here's our jelly jar. Empty?"

Ruby sighed. "Amy, that's not where Gigi left it yesterday."

"You're right."

Brianna shook a paper bag. "Want to go farther? I brought popcorn."

Ruby sighed. "I'm not hungry. Thanks, though."

"I think Bree means for our trail and eventual return."

Ruby cleared her throat. "Oh! I know. Ahem. Just kidding. Let's go farther. Amy and Bree lead and drop popcorn. Kiche and I will follow."

"R yan?"

"Yeah?"

"Maddie and I were talking." Gloria Becker lounged on the lower level of The Treehouse as Derrick Flynn hacked down parasitic ivy from cedars.

"About what?"

Madison paused. "We don't want to hurt your feelings."

"What is it?"

Madison hesitated, glanced at Gloria, then sternly faced Ryan. "We think you had an advantage during our caveman diversion."

"What are you saying?"

Gloria smirked. "What she is saying is —"

Madison solemnly placed her hand on Ryan's shoulder. "It's just that —"

Gloria smiled. "Some people are closer to cavemen than other people."

Ryan sat up. "What do you mean?"

"We don't think you had to act like a caveman," Gloria said.

"What's that supposed to mean?"

Gloria looked at her watch. "Whoops! Time to go to Lover's Lagoon."

"Caveman understand insult," Ryan said. "Caveman sad."

"Derrick! That was five trees! Let's go!" Madison yelled.

"Waiting on you." Derrick calmly stood on the forest floor twenty feet under The Treehouse.

Gloria laughed. "How did you get down there?"

Ryan, Madison, and Gloria stood up and prepared to climb down.

"Caveman finish early chopping down parasitic ivy?" Madison joked walking backwards to the treehouse ladder.

Ryan reached for Madison. "Madison, no!" Ryan was too late.

Madison extended her arms and clenched her hands, grabbing only air. Madison quickly disappeared from Ryan and Gloria's view. She fell backwards off the twenty-foot platform and screamed in fear.

Gloria lunged forward, also too late. "Maddie!"

Ryan and Gloria panicked as Madison plummeted backwards to the forest floor.

Silence.

Ryan and Gloria rushed to the ledge and looked down. "Maddie?"

"Cavegirl fall for caveman!" Derrick held Madison safely in his strong arms after her fall.

"Derrick Flynn!" Madison yelled. "I love you!" Madison threw her trembling arms around his shoulders and cried.

Brianna Lopez led the two cavers deeper into Lover's Cave while dropping popcorn. "Daylight!"

Amy turned off her flashlight. "Lover's Lagoon?"

Ruby studied the light. "There's no waterfall."

"It's beautiful," Brianna said.

"The sunset is amazing!" Amy said.

Ruby exited the cave with Kiche. "We're on the west side of Lover's Mountain! We found The Forbidden Zone!"

Brianna looked around. "The TFZ? It's like another world. Forests. Mountains. Mesas. Rock formations. Rivers. Waterfalls. Birds chirping,"

Amy studied the sky. "No airplanes or airplane noise. The Safety Corps says this is off-limits."

"How could the TFZ be forbidden?" Ruby asked. "It's like heaven."

"Bree and Ruby! Look! Kiche found something!" Amy leaned over. "A jelly jar!"

Brianna smiled. "A note? What does it say?"

Amy opened the jar and read the note. "The source of your symptoms is drawn to the cure."

THE SOURCE OF YOUR SYMPTOMS
IS DRAWN TO THE CURE.

"Huh?" Brianna replied.

"The cure to your symptoms is simply mine, carefully cross the stream to clean the stream, and now this?" Ruby sighed. "You guys believe this stuff?"

"I have to believe," Amy stuffed the note in her pocket. "My twin sister, Emma, throws up daily. My little brother, Jack, hasn't spoken in four years. Our Olympic track and field dreams are shattered. I have to believe."

"Someone's trying to help us?" Brianna asked.

Ruby looked around. "Who?"

Amy reentered the cave. "Let's backtrack to the lagoon. My fan club awaits. They get so worried about me."

"Your fan club?" Ruby laughed. "You mean your dancers, Luke and Antoine?"

"I don't manage my mailing lists. If people want to join, they can join."

"It's getting deep." Brianna smiled and turned on her flashlight again. "Follow the popcorn. I dropped lots."

Amy advanced into the cave for five minutes. "Bree?"

"Yeah?" Brianna responded.

"Not seeing popcorn."

"What do you mean?"

"No popcorn," Amy said.

The three swept their flashlights back and forth and continued forward.

"Umm, Ruby?" Amy shined her flashlight on Kiche's large she-wolf face. "Does Kiche, I don't know, like popcorn?"

The three seniors simultaneously shined flashlights at Kiche.

Kiche licked her lips.

"Kiche?" Brianna leaned into Kiche's face and smelled her breath.

"Guilty?" Amy asked.

"Guilty!" Ruby stated.

"Dirty. Little. Rat." Brianna received a lick on her face.

Ruby corrected Brianna. "Big rat."

"Kiche, this time you lead." Amy scratched Kiche behind the ears. "Take us home, girl."

"Mr. Burns circled back over us twice at Liberty Lake!" Aaron swam in Lover's Lagoon. "Our shark attack was realistic and believable. Well-planned. Superb acting. Great execution. Our diversion rocked!"

Gloria laughed. "You all should have seen the look on Madison's face when she realized that she was the only caveman with no club!"

Grace joked. "Thomas, you were rubbing those sticks together pretty vigorously next to Gigi. There was no fire, but I thought you were going to pull a muscle."

"Mr. Light and Mr. Burns circled our Gigi-sacrifice three times on Coldwater Creek," Charlotte said. "Antoine and Luke, what was your diversion here in the lagoon?"

"We just stood on the boulders," Luke said as an evening thunderstorm approached.

"You just stood there?" Emma joked while swimming in the lagoon.

I was suspicious. "That's all, Luke?"

"Yeah, we just stood there."

Max was curious. "Did my Dad circle back to watch you?"

Luke shook his head affirmatively. "Yeah, he pretty much did a slow hover overhead for five minutes."

Aaron joined in. "The TSC helicopter hovered. Over you two. Standing on rocks. Five minutes?"

Luke and Antoine looked guilty of concealing something.

"I call bullcrap," Aaron said.

"I guess we have no great story," Antoine said.

CHAPTER THIRTEEN

"**P**eaksville Class of 2020!" Amy suddenly yelled the darkness of Lover's Cave. "Prepare to be entertained!" Amy, Ruby and Brianna ran out of Lover's Cave and performed synchronized cannonballs into the lagoon.

Splash!

Ruby surfaced and yelled. "What's wrong, Luke and Antoine!"

Brianna treaded water and smiled. "Did you get tired?"

Thomas interrogated the cavers. "They didn't just stand there?"

Amy laughed. "Stand there? Ha!"

Raindrops began to fall on Lover's Lagoon.

"That's their story and they're sticking to it!" Brianna looked at the approaching storm west of Lover's Lagoon. "Saved by the rain."

Charlotte prepared Jefferson and Buckshot. "Hope you girls got pictures."

Amy winked. "It broke our camera."

Lightning cracked nearby.

I helped Grace exit the lagoon. "Here comes the rain, party people!"

"Yeah." Antoine nodded suspiciously. "It's starting to rain, better go!"

Amy joked. "It was *Raining Men* earlier! Wasn't it Antoine?"

"Too much information." I laughed. "Let's roll."

Ruby boarded the raft. "Marcus! The Forbidden Zone! We found it!" "You found the TFZ? How? Where?"

Amy kicked a leg up from Lover's Lagoon to enter the raft. "Superior navigation skills."

"Can you guys find it again?" Emma paddled with Max into Coldwater Creek.

"It depends."

Amy, Brianna, and Ruby simultaneously looked at Kiche.

Kiche crouched low and licked her lips.

"Probably." Brianna nodded. "Even without my popcorn trail."

"See you at The Boxcar!" Charlotte and Jack rode Jefferson down Coldwater Creek.

"Bye, Wolfie!" Gigi sat behind Chloe on Buckshot.

"Check this out. A third note." Amy unfolded the wet note. "The source of your symptoms is drawn to the cure."

Ruby found a seat on the raft. "It was in a jar at the *west* mouth of Lover's Cave. Overlooking the TFZ!"

Ryan paddled down Coldwater Creek. "Fascinating."

"What does it mean?" D'Andre asked as rainfall intensified.

"It means someone is messing with us." Thomas smirked. "Spreading false hope and more nonsense."

"Tommy Boy!" Grace scolded.

Crack!

Lightning struck one mile from us in Peaksville Forest.

"That's our cue." I helped everyone exit the raft in heavy rain at The Elephant Rocks. "No more swimming. Let's get home."

W e circled the north end of Liberty Lake and sprinted for The Boxcar in the storm.

Gloria arrived soaking wet and jumped inside. "Whew! That was easy!"

We laughed and climbed inside.

"Get up here, girl!" Grace said.

Kiche effortlessly jumped inside The Boxcar.

Brianna towel-dried her hair and laughed. "Hey Antoine, time for you and 'Son of a Preacher Man' to share your talents with those who missed the dance-off at Lover's Lagoon."

Madison placed her hand over Chloe's eyes. "Can the twelve-year-olds watch?"

Amy covered Jack and Gigi's eyes. "It's PG-13."

Charlotte walked to the Boxcar door. "Where *is* Luke?"

Crack!

More lightning.

I sensed something was wrong and yelled outside. "Luke!"

"Oh, God! Luke's on Deadman's Cliff!" Grace exclaimed frantically.

Thomas replied. "No way!"

Luke, despite his fear of heights, despite the violent thunderstorm, stood twenty feet over Liberty Lake with his arms extended vertically in the pouring rain.

"Luke!" I yelled. "Come here, man!"

No response.

Derrick jumped down. "He's going to be struck by lightning."

"Kiche!" Ruby knelt on one knee. "Go get him girl! Go get Luke!" Ruby slapped Kiche on her hind quarters.

The Canadian Wolf and Anatolian mix leapt down from The Boxcar in full gallop around the north, rocky shore of Liberty Lake.

Charlotte jumped down and mounted Jefferson. "Stay there, Luke!"

Emma gasped. "He's not answering."

Grace agreed. "He's crying."

Charlotte expertly rode Jefferson towards Luke.

Kiche won the race to Deadman's Cliff and tackled Luke.

"Kiche, easy girl!" Charlotte yelled ahead as Kiche rapidly licked away Luke's tears. Charlotte dismounted and ran to hug Luke. "It's okay, Luke. Everything's okay. Let's go home."

Luke cried.

Charlotte returned to The Boxcar with her right hand on Jefferson's halter and her left arm around Luke.

"Y ou okay, buddy?" I asked as Luke climbed inside. The girls all greeted Luke with hugs for several minutes.

We waited for the hugs to end.

Ryan joked. "Looks okay to me."

"Ryan!" Gloria scolded with her head on Luke's shoulder.

Antoine defended Ryan. "Luke's got five girls mugging and hugging him on the couch."

"You good, Luke?" Aaron said.

"What's wrong, Luke," Ruby quietly whispered next to Luke.

"When I was thirteen," Luke cried. "I was struck by lightning."

"So, you realize lightning is bad," I said.

"Marcus!" Grace slapped my knee. "Let him talk."

"We remember," Ruby said.

Charlotte held Luke's hand. "You were sad about that?"

"No, not sad," Luke said. "I wanted to be struck again today."

Everyone gasped.

"Why, Luke?" Brianna asked.

Luke cried. "Because for a week, my headaches were gone."

"Then the headaches returned?" Charlotte asked quietly.

"Yes. Every morning for the last five years," Luke wept. "I go to bed. No headache. I wake up. Headache."

I quizzed Luke. "The lightning strike cured your headache?"

Thomas shook his head negatively. "Yeah, but that's probably just —"

"Tommy Boy!" Grace scolded.

Kiche nudged Ruby and Charlotte aside to lick away Luke's tears.

"Everything's going to be okay, Luke." Gigi scratched Kiche and whispered. "Good Wolfie!"

"Luke, we're going to find you that cure," I said.

Luke looked me in the eyes.

"I promise."

G race rubbed Luke's knee. "It's okay."
      Brianna rubbed his other knee.

Amy obnoxiously rubbed Luke's face and hair to upset the boys.

Derrick stood up. "Is this actually happening?"

Aaron stood up. "Luke's fine."

"I'm done." Ryan stood up. "Dude is being loved on by multiple Peaksville girls."

"Dude can't even dance," Antoine said. "Where is the justice?"

"Alright, Luke," D'Andre said. "We know your game."

"Luke, you know they're kidding, right?" I asked.

Luke raised one thumb up from the couch with a covert smirk after reaching his arms around several girls.

Ryan looked outside. "Charlie, your horses are officially soaked."

"Chloe, Gigi, and Jack." Charlotte comforted Luke with the other Class of 2020 senior girls. "Prepare Buckshot and Jefferson."

Gloria gave Luke a kiss on the cheek, followed by all of the other girls, deliberately slow, one by one.

Aaron exited The Boxcar. "Can't watch anymore."

Antoine jumped into the heavy rain. "See you, Luke."

Derrick followed Antoine. "Let's go, fellas."

Max grabbed his backpack. "Jack, sorry you had to watch that, little man."

"Life isn't like that." Antoine explained to the middle-schooler. "You gotta earn it. Luke didn't earn it through his dancing, today."

Ryan jumped down. "There are more ethical ways to get girls, Jack. When you are old enough."

Chloe yelled inside. "Charlie! Jefferson and Buckshot are ready!"

Soaking wet, we all ran home through The Meadow. We swung across Peaksville Creek, ran through the schoolyard, and scattered into our neighborhood homes in the pouring rain.

Charlotte, Chloe, Jack and Gigi returned the horses to the Epley farm.

"Hey Jack and Gigi!" Mrs. Epley greeted the riders from her farmhouse porch. "What a storm!"

Jack dismounted Jefferson and smiled.

"Hello, Mrs. Epley!" Gigi replied.

"Charlotte and Chloe, dry towels for wiping down Bucky and Jeff are already in the barn. Mr. Epley and I were worried about you. Hot chocolate in ten minutes."

"Where you been, Max? Weather grounded Mr. Light and me two hours ago." Mr. Burns, wearing his TSC flight suit in their kitchen, stood with his arms crossed.

"Just hanging with friends, Dad."

Mr. Burns pointed at Max's arm. "What's that?"

"What's what?" Max said.

"Your left arm. That's a TSC shot bandage."

Max realized he forgot to remove it. "It's nothing."

"Don't lie to me."

"What's the big deal?" Max asked.

"'Fess up." Mr. Burns became angrier. "Now."

"I took a sympathetic TSC shot for Emma. To show her TSC shots aren't that bad."

Mr. Burns looked around for something to break. He left the kitchen to cool off. He returned. "What's the big deal, you ask? Tell me how you feel?"

"Guilty?"

"Your health. How do you feel?"

"I think I caught the flu today or something. I'm better now. Except for my headache."

Mr. Burns angrily left the room again.

Max heard Mr. Burns take out his frustration on living room furniture. He returned with something shiny in his hand.

"Chill, Dad."

Mr. Burns showed Max a large metallic disc.

"What is it?"

"A strong magnet. Keep it away from computers. Keep it away from metal or you'll lose a finger."

Max received the silver, three-pound, hockey puck-shaped magnet in his hand.

"What should I do with it?"

"Slide it into a volleyball kneepad. Wear this on your calf overnight."

"Are you kidding?"

"Do I sound like I'm kidding?

"Why?"

"Fixes headaches."

Max was confused. "Can I share it?"

"It fixes *your* headache. Nobody else's headache."

"But Dad, my friends —"

"Absolutely not." Mr. Burns angrily pointed a finger in his son's face. "You want that SUV for graduation? You want me to pay for college? Promise you'll keep our secret. Promise to return it to my dresser before school."

Max quietly looked at the magnet.

"Promise me!" Mr. Burns instructed.

Max walked towards his bedroom with the magnet, turned around, and looked at Mr. Burns. "I promise."

CHAPTER FOURTEEN

At seven o'clock in the morning, Max was awakened by the thunderous noise of his father's TSC helicopter.

Mr. Burns hovered one hundred feet over his bedroom for one minute then raised his visor to make eye contact with Max in his bedroom window.

Max got up, approached the window and looked up.

Mr. Burns added power, lowered his nose, and departed to the west towards Peaksville High School.

Max reached down and felt the magnet on his calf. Max slid the magnet from the volleyball kneepad and looked at it. Max was headache-free, feeling great, just like he has felt his whole life. The magnet worked. But how?

Mrs. Burns walked into Max's bedroom. "What was that about, Max? Dad almost destroyed our roof."

Max quickly hid the magnet. "Not sure, Mom."

"By the way, Dad said to return something you borrowed. Sound familiar?"

"Got it, Mom. I'm on it." Max prepared for school. Conflicting thoughts raced through his head. Max felt no ethical obligation to return something that could help Emma. But Max did make a promise. Max considered the withholding of his graduation SUV an empty threat. Max considered using forgetfulness as his excuse. Max figured that breaking one promise for one day is better than keeping a valuable secret from Emma forever. Max loved Emma.

Max made up his mind and slid the magnet into his backpack and departed for school. "Bye, Mom!"

. . .

"Good afternoon, Peaksville students. Today is Thursday, thirty days until graduation." Dean Michaels transmitted his PA system pre-dismissal announcements. "The TSC Air Patrol is searching day and night for the weekend's attempted child abduction suspect. Suspects who deposited HAZMAT near the reservoir yesterday remain at large. A reminder that Peaksville Defense and Space Corporation is taking applications for summer STEM internships. All caves are considered dangerous and remain off limits. School's out. Be safe out there."

"The only thing dangerous in Lover's Cave is my hot body," Amy whispered near her locker preparing to leave school.

Ruby laughed. "Luke, you up for caving today?"

"Sounds great, Ruby."

Antoine checked his six for TSC cadets and whispered. "Can I go?"

"Ruby, you're caving with the dance troupe?" Aaron whispered.

Ben creepily eavesdropped.

Amy slammed her locker. "More like just a troupe with no dance. By the way. Ben, take a picture. It'll last longer."

Ben ignored Amy and walked away.

Everyone exited school and saw the middle-schoolers waiting.

Ruby yelled over the sound of the schoolyard airplane propeller noise. "Jack, Gigi, Chloe! See you in twenty minutes at The Boxcar! Science prep today!"

Max caught up with Emma in the schoolyard.

Emma smiled. "Hey Max, how's your flu?"

"I feel better. How about you?"

"Only puked once. Better than most days."

Max snuck a kiss on Emma's cheek under the roar of his father's Bell 407 rotor blades. "See you out west in about twenty minutes. I have something for you. Later."

"Gigi and Jack! Welcome back sweethearts." Mrs. Epley cheerfully smiled. "We have a surprise for you today. Charlotte and Chloe, do you want to go introduce them to Daisy?"

"Sure, Mom," Charlotte said.

"My dad has been too busy with the cattle, hogs, chickens and crops." Charlotte walked Gigi and Jack into the barn. "Daisy doesn't get ridden enough anymore."

"You have a girl horse?" Gigi excitedly asked.

Charlotte nodded and arrived to the stables. "Gigi and Jack, meet Daisy!"

Jack smiled.

"She's beautiful." Gigi petted her nose. "Is she friendly?"

"Friendly?" Mr. Epley entered the barn after shutting down his John Deere tractor. "Friendliest horse in North Idaho. Very gentle. Can you ride Daisy for me?"

"What do you think, Gigi and Jack?" Charlotte asked.

Gigi and Jack had wide smiles while stroking Daisy's nose and mane. "Can Jack and I ride you today?"

Daisy happily soaked up the attention and hugged Gigi with her head.

Gigi laughed while pinned to Daisy's chest. "Is she hugging me?"

Charlotte nodded.

"She likes you both. I can tell." Mr. Epley reached into a feedbag. "Here, feed Daisy these carrots as Charlotte gets her saddled up."

G race jogged through The Meadow towards The Boxcar. "Maddie, watch out for those cavemen today."

"Especially Flynn cavemen." Madison pointed at Derrick and Ryan. "The most primitive."

Derrick immediately grabbed Madison and lifted her over his shoulder while jogging.

Gloria laughed. "Madison find strong caveman."

Mr. Burns initiated a thirty-knot hover over the runners at one hundred feet.

"Wonder if they caught that shark in Liberty Lake," Aaron joked.

D'Andre ran with Brianna's help. "Poor Gigi. Sacrificed at age twelve."

Brianna laughed. "Poor Gigi? You apparently weren't in Lover's Lagoon for the dance off."

"Yeah, Gigi wasn't the only thing sacrificed yesterday." Amy jogged through The Meadow. "My innocence was sacrificed."

"Innocence!" Aaron laughed. "Ha!"

Amy bumped Aaron.

Derrick suddenly stopped jogging with Madison still riding over his shoulder. He slouched, rolled his eyes upwards, and collapsed.

Madison fell with him in the high grass. "Derrick!"

"Derrick! You okay, brother?" Ryan said nervously over the sound of the rotor blades.

I ran towards the commotion and found my youngest brother passed out. "What happened?"

"Derrick just fainted." Madison gently placed her hands on his cheeks.

"What the heck?" Derrick opened his eyes. "How did you guys get here?"

"Derrick, it's okay, sweety." Grace softly said. "You passed out."

I looked at Ryan. "Let's get him to The Boxcar."

Ryan agreed.

We picked up Derrick and slow walked him to The Boxcar.

Mr. Burns departed from his hover overhead and departed back to Peaksville.

M ax jumped in The Boxcar with Derrick resting on the couch. "What happened?"

Emma greeted Max. "Derrick passed out."

Charlotte Epley arrived on horseback. "How is he?"

Chloe rode up on Buckshot, followed by Jack and Gigi on Daisy.

I looked at Charlotte and whispered. "He looks pale."

Charlotte turned to the middle-schoolers. "Stay on your horses."

Gloria and Grace Becker looked at each other. "Mom can help!"

Grace looked at Charlotte. "Charlie, can you ride Derrick and Madison to our home? Our mom can take a look at him. She was an Army medic."

I walked closer to Charlotte. "Charlie, don't ride Derrick to Peaksville Hospital. Last year we took Derrick to the ER twice. It was a disaster. Derrick passed out both times. They said he faked it."

"Understood, Marcus!" Charlotte said with a wink.

" M adison, climb up on Buckshot with Chloe," Charlotte instructed. "Jack and Gigi, ride alongside us. Daisy will follow just fine."

Antoine, Luke and I helped Derrick safely mount Jefferson behind Charlotte.

"How we doing, buddy?" Charlotte calmly whispered.

Derrick opened his eyes. "Dizzy."

"Alright, Derrick. Wrap your arms around me. Hold on tight."

Derrick held on.

"Ready?"

"Born ready," Derrick softly mumbled.

Grace approached Buckshot. "Chloe and Madison, ride next to Jack and Gigi. Keep 'em safe."

Chloe gave her a 'thumbs up.'

I nervously watched Charlotte ride my brother to Mrs. Becker's home. Best athlete in Peaksville High School history. Derrick Flynn should *not* be fainting.

CHAPTER FIFTEEN

W e solemnly sat in The Boxcar with the horses halfway to Peaksville.
Ryan was the first to speak. "Damn."

"What are we going to do?" D'Andre Jordan asked.

"The cure," I said. "We're going to find the cure."

"It's not that simple." Thomas Stallworth immediately received cold looks.

"Who's caving?" Amy Kernan looked around. "I'm three for three for those keeping score. Tired of winning. Who's turn today?"

Ruby Kyle petted Kiche as the TSC airplane circled three hundred feet over The Boxcar in a tight left turn. "I'm taking the dance troupe."

"Let's cool off first," Antoine Jordan said.

"Concur," Luke said. "I thought I was going to pass out in The Meadow. Derrick beat me to it."

"Yes, Marcus." Grace whispered. "We need to find a cure."

I nodded. "Liberty Lake first. Then Lover's Cave."

G race looked around, stood up and jumped down from The Boxcar. "Everyone ready?"

Max Burns gestured for Emma Kernan to stay behind and yelled outside. "We'll catch up!"

Most of us quickly dipped into Liberty Lake.

Emma eagerly listened to Max in The Boxcar.

"Emma, can you keep a secret?" Max asked over the propeller noise.

The TSC Cessna 182 continued orbiting.

"Of course, Max."

"How's your headache, Emma?"

"Always the same. You're stalling. What's up?"

Max looked around and removed the three-pound disc-shaped magnet from his pocket. "Here's what's up."

"What is it?"

Ben Light and Tony Murdstone walked into sight momentarily.

"Hold on." Max stowed the magnet and directed Emma's attention towards the nosy TSC Cadets who were ogling into The Boxcar. Max and Emma found a more private area and continued speaking.

"A magnet."

"A magnet?"

"A very, very strong magnet. Wear this on your calf tonight in a volleyball kneepad. Keep it away from metal, it'll crush your fingers. Keep it far from computers or electronics. Bring it to school tomorrow. Tell nobody."

Laughter and splashing could be heard from Liberty Lake.

"Why, Max?" Emma asked.

"Tell nobody. Not even family. Promise?"

"I promise."

"Hide it here. Don't swim with it. Take it home. Wear it all night. I need it tomorrow morning. Understand?"

Emma nodded.

Max hid the magnet in Emma's backpack and kissed Emma on the cheek. "Let's go swim."

C hloe sat between Gigi and Jack in the family room. "Thanks for the grilled cheeses!"

Mrs. Becker smiled. "My pleasure, Cowgirl."

Gigi peeked into Gloria's room. "Is Derrick okay, Mom?"

"Madison and Charlotte are in there with him, now. He's sleeping like a baby. Here Jack, bring the girls these sandwiches."

Jack stood up and delivered the food.

Chloe rubbed her forehead and smiled. "Mrs. Becker, we are hoping to find a cure."

"I heard about the notes from the cave."

"For now, here are some apple quarters for those beautiful horses mowing my front lawn." Mrs. Becker walked to the kitchen then returned. "An apple a day keeps the doctor away."

. . .

T he cavers prepared to enter Lover's Cave.
        Downstream Coldwater Creek at The Elephant Rocks, Amy Kernan was tanning between Grace and Emma in bikinis. "Grace, do you think this diversion is dangerous?"

"Oh, God. Here we go." Grace Becker laughed. "Why is this dangerous?"

"Because if a TSC pilot flies over and sees my hot body. He could have a physiological episode then crash and burn."

Emma Kernan looked at her twin. "What you're saying is we're overshooting. Our distraction for Ruby and the dance troupe duo could result in loss of life or destruction of property."

"Not we. Just me." Amy leaned back on the giant boulders. "A tragic consequence to fixating on my legs, my arms, my hair, my stomach —"

"We get the picture!" Grace interrupted. "Anyhow, here comes the TSC helicopter over the trees from Peaksville."

"Quickly!" Amy squirted suntan oil into their hands. "Distribute, Distract, Destroy!" The three seniors rubbed the suntan oil all over their bodies.

Mr. Burns overflew them at forty knots at one hundred feet.

Amy confidently quipped and relaxed on the rock. "He'll be back. For me."

The Bell 407 continued to the west up Coldwater Creek over the horizon toward the cavers in Lover's Lagoon.

Silence. The helicopter noise dissipated.

Grace sat up. "Amy, I don't think he's coming back."

Emma sat up. "Not even an obligatory wing dip."

Grace joked. "The only thing destroyed was Amy's ego."

"Crash and burn." Emma joked. "Amy, did that cold spray from the rotor wash feel good? Because you got roasted."

"Laugh it up, losers." Amy sat up. "There's only so much I could do with two liabilities next to me. Even perfect beauty has its limits. A Blue Angel formation flight requires skilled wingmen to impress."

I treaded water in Lover's Lagoon. "I hope Derrick's okay."
        Aaron splashed me in the face. "Derrick's a tough kid."
I laughed and splashed back.
Aaron was already underwater.
D'Andre treaded water. "Gloria, Mrs. Becker was a US Army medic?"
"Twenty years, DJ. She was a combat medic."
D'Andre smiled. "Derrick will be fine."

I looked at Aaron and whispered. "He's fainting more and more."

Aaron smiled and whispered back. "Stop worrying. He's fine."

Splash!

Aaron splashed me in the face again to cheer me up.

It wasn't working.

"R uby, fast! Get the dance troupe inside." Brianna treaded water in Lover's Lagoon. "Mr. Burns is inbound!"

Ruby led Antoine and Luke into Lover's Cave from beneath the waterfall as Kiche followed.

Antoine Jordan walked into the initial large cavern. "Ruby. Question. How can Luke and I be a dance troupe? I'm the only dancer. Doesn't that make only *me* the dance troupe?"

Ruby entered the first narrow cave to the left. "Two people are required to make a troupe, correct?"

Antoine looked at Luke. "I'm asking for an exception to the rule."

Kiche led the three deeper into the darkness.

Ruby shrugged. "Luke is in your dance troupe. Deal with it. You don't always get to choose who's in your dance troupe."

Antoine marched deeper into the dark cave and complained to Ruby. "A citizen has the Constitutional right to select their own troupe members. It's in the Bill of Rights. Freedom of Assembly."

Ruby laughed. "Elections have consequences. Write your Congressman."

Luke aimed the flashlight at his own face. "You and me, Antoine. Peaksville High Dance Troupe. Trust me on this. We'll make t-shirts. We'll be famous."

B rianna laughed as Grace and the Kernan twins walked up Coldwater Creek. "You three look like a fire hazard,"

I couldn't believe what I was seeing. "What's up with the suntan oil?"

"Is that 10W-30?" Ryan joked.

Aaron laughed. "Pennzoil or Quaker State?"

Amy submerged into Lover's Lagoon with Grace and Emma. "Laugh, laugh, laugh, losers. None of you get to check under the hood."

Grace joined Amy in the cold water. "We failed."

Emma sat on a large boulder and dipped her feet in the water. "Max, your dad overflew us. No wing dip. No orbit. If he had a horn, he wouldn't have honked."

Amy shouted over the sound of Mr. Light's TSC airplane passing overhead. "You two failed. Not me."

"Hey Amy?" D'Andre said.

"You want to tell me you love me, DJ. Get it over with."

"Well, I just wanted to say that —"

Amy swam in a suntan oil slick. "Cough it up, Buttercup."

D'Andre hesitated. "Well I'm blind and all, but —"

"You wish you could see me, right? I get it."

"Not exactly." D'Andre continued. "I just wanted to say that your twin sister Emma sounds much hotter than you."

Aaron yelled. "Savage!"

I've only seen Amy blush a few times. This was one of them. "Amy, you got roasted."

Amy went underwater in Lover's Lagoon and attempted to change the subject.

Ryan waited for her to surface. "Amy, swim under the cold waterfall to soothe that burn!"

Thomas joined in. "Amy needs to submit her official *Hurt Feelings Report* to the TSC tomorrow."

Emma pointed into Peaksville Forest. "There's an Aloe plant over that hill, Amy."

Amy went on the offensive. "Betrayer! Emma, my own twin sister. Even my own flesh and blood joins in my persecution. You should be ashamed of yourself for spreading lies and associating with these sinners."

CHAPTER SIXTEEN

Antoine walked forward in Lover's Cave in search of a fourth note. "Ruby, you know the way to the TFZ, right?"

"I'm following Kiche. Look at her go!"

"Kiche, are you a she-wolf or a hound dog?" Luke asked.

Ruby looked forward. "Hey check it out. Daylight."

The 2020 seniors trekked another fifty feet to the west side of the mountain.

Luke looked around. "Ruby, the sunset. It's incredible!"

Antoine smiled at their wondrous discovery. "This is forbidden?"

Luke overlooked the natural beauty of The Forbidden Zone. "It's like a dream!"

Ruby vigorously scratched Kiche and slipped her a treat. "Good girl!"

Antoine pointed nearby. "Ruby, is that the jelly jar?"

"Another note!" Luke said.

Ruby opened the jar while Antoine anxiously inquired. "What does it say, Ruby?"

"Travel right into the light, before the night, above the white, under the rainbow."

TRAVEL RIGHT INTO THE LIGHT, BEFORE THE NIGHT,
ABOVE THE WHITE, UNDER THE RAINBOW.

L uke scratched his head. "What?"

Antoine paused. "Directions?"

Luke shrugged. "Partial directions at best."

"Not sure." Ruby looked at her watch. "Let's double back to Peaksville."

"I want to explore The Forbidden Zone." Antoine looked to the west. "Someday."

I lounged next to Grace on a large boulder in Lover's Lagoon. "What do you all think about The Forbidden Zone?"

Brianna lounged nearby. "It's beautiful."

"Why is the TFZ forbidden?" Gloria asked.

"I'm sure the TSC has a good reason." Thomas explained. "They're the smart ones."

"Tommy Boy is right." Aaron Webster looked at me and winked. "I'm agree the TSC has a good reason. We shall explore the TFZ to find out that reason."

"You can't." Thomas continued. "That's illegal."

Aaron became angry. "So, don't go, Tommy Boy! It's as simple as that."

I lay on my back and watched the underbelly of the TSC Cessna 182 pass directly over Lover's Lagoon as we waited for the cavers. "That's ten Lover's Lagoon overflights in sixty minutes."

Thomas shrugged. "I hope Mr. Light finds the bad guys."

Aaron and I made eye contact.

Grace pinched me and whispered. "You can't change Tommy Boy. Don't say any more."

Emma rubbed her temples and rested with Max.

Grace rested her head on my shoulder and whispered. "Marcus, let's find out why the TFZ is forbidden."

R yan subtly motioned to the east side of Lover's Lagoon that feeds into Coldwater Creek. "Here comes Ben."

"Hello, boys!" Grace kindly said to Ben and Tony standing on the bank.

"Hi Grace," Tony Murdstone said.

Mr. Burns buzzed overhead in the TSC helicopter.

Ben looked around. "Nobody is entering Lover's Cave? Correct?"

We remained silent and ignored the question for ten seconds.

Amy broke the silence. "Sorry Ben. Kind of busy. Biology finals approaching. Studying parasites, germs, bacteria. Different ways for hosts to eliminate parasites. Stuff like that."

Ben looked at me. "Hey Marcus, where's your little brother Derrick? Around this time isn't Derrick usually saving Peaksville forest?"

"Hey Ben," Ryan said. "Around this time aren't you and the neighbor's cat —"

"Ryan!" Gloria slapped his knee.

Aaron and Amy chuckled.

"Beautiful day, isn't it Ben and Tony?" Grace asked.

"Yeah, I guess so."

The TSC helicopter departed from its noisy, slow orbit.

Ben and Tony turned and walked down Coldwater Creek towards Peaksville.

Aaron smiled and treaded water. "Gloria, never interrupt Ryan when he has something very important to share. That was *going* to be epic."

E mma looked at her watch. "How long have those three been in there?"

Max lounged on the raft in the middle of the lagoon. "Sixty-five minutes!"

D'Andre Jordan treaded water. "Luke and Antoine probably stopped to dance to about three or four songs."

Grace sighed. "Poor Ruby."

"More like poor Kiche," Amy said.

Brianna swam and checked her Lady G-Shock. "Luke's probably a great dancer in a very dark cave."

Amy whispered to D'Andre in a peculiar, sinister tone. "D'Andre! Let's play a trick on Antoine and Luke when they return."

"Okay. Count me in —" D'Andre was violently interrupted. "Arrrgh!"

Antoine and Luke secretly swam underwater from under the waterfall, pantsed D'Andre, and threw his jean shorts onto the raft with Aaron.

"Real cool. Pants the blind dude. Duly noted." D'Andre smilingly said amid laughter.

"D'Andre!" Aaron threw D'Andre his shorts. "Always wear proper protective pants in the pond, please."

D'Andre pulled up his shorts while treading water. "My Spidey-Sense tells me Amy was an accomplice."

Amy tried not to laugh. "I'm the victim here, D'Andre. You hurt my feelings earlier. You said Emma sounds hotter than me. I'm still hurt."

"I see shorts flying around! You all need a little more time alone?" Charlotte rode up the north shore of Coldwater Creek on Jefferson.

Chloe slowly rode Buckshot one hundred feet behind her sister.

Gigi and Jack followed on Daisy.

Aaron yelled downstream. "D'Andre didn't realize Idaho trouser trout was out of season!"

Amy smirked. "And endangered."

"Charlie, they stole my shorts!"

"Whatever you say, D'Andre." Charlotte joked. "Keep your pants on. Here come the sixth-graders."

Chloe approached behind her big sister on horseback. "Why is Coldwater Creek so oily today?"

Gigi looked around. "Did a supertanker crash?"

Aaron nodded and looked at Amy. "More or less."

Brianna smiled at Grace, Amy, and Emma. "Don't ask!"

I looked at Charlotte. "How's our tree whisperer?"

"Derrick is resting with Maddie. He's fine. Grace, your mom said pizza at the Becker home in one hour."

"Perfect!" Emma was piggy-backing on Max near the waterfall.

Antoine prepared the raft. "Awesome!"

"Wolfie! Did you miss me?" Gigi yelled.

Kiche's eyes and ears perked up on the lagoon shore. Kiche was nestled strategically between Ryan and Gloria on a large boulder, lounging in the warm setting sun.

Aaron boarded the raft. "Who wants to float down Coldwater Creek?"

"Are pants required at the pizza party?" Amy climbed into the raft and looked at D'Andre. "Asking for a friend."

Charlotte turned Jefferson downstream towards Peaksville. "Probably. We'll put the horses to bed then meet you at Gracie's. Let's go, kiddos."

I waited until a few minutes of silent paddling down Coldwater Creek before asking. "Ruby, did you and the dance troupe discover a fourth note?"

Ruby lounged next to Luke. "We did. Travel right into the light, before the night, above the white, under the rainbow."

We drifted downstream under the low pass of a Cessna 182 and digested the clue.

"Directions to the cure," I said.

Grace looked at me and silently nodded affirmatively. Ruby, Amy, Emma, Brianna, and Gloria all made eye contact with Grace. No words required.

Thomas shrugged. "Someone's messing with us."

Ryan saw that I wasn't interested in debating Thomas. "Not necessarily, Tommy Boy."

Grace exited the raft at The Elephant Rocks, walked with me around Liberty Lake and whispered. "The cure, Marcus. It exists. Maybe in the TFZ."

. . .

W e gathered our backpacks from The Boxcar and headed to the Becker home for pizza.

Mr. Burns buzzed overhead at over one hundred knots in The Meadow at full power.

Vroom!

Aaron fell after being caught by surprise. "Holy crap, that was low!"

Max watched his father depart towards Peaksville Municipal Airport and pulled Emma aside.

"Emma," Max Burns whispered with a secretive look. "Volleyball kneepad on your calf. Magnet inside all night. Tell nobody. Bring it tomorrow."

"Tomorrow tell me why."

"Tomorrow, you'll *know* why."

Emma gave Max a kiss on the cheek. "Okay."

"My dad's flying angry." Max pointed at the eastbound Bell 407 fifty feet over the trees. "Enjoy the pizza. Gotta get home. Bye, Emma."

One more kiss. "Bye, Max."

CHAPTER SEVENTEEN

M adison sidestepped through the Friday lunch line. "How you feeling today, Derrick?"

"Headache's kicking my butt. Hopefully I won't pass out before the annual track and field event."

Emma joined Max in the lunch line, slipped the magnet into his pocket, and whispered. "Four years of morning headaches. How —"

Max nervously interrupted. "Quiet."

Emma loaded her tray more than usual. "How did it work, Max?"

"You promised. Not here. My dad is pissed."

Max found an empty lunch table.

Emma sat and softly whispered. "Can Amy and Jack —"

"Stop." Max interrupted. "You don't understand. My dad smashed my PS4. He kicked a hole in my door. I thought he was going to kick a hole in *me* last night."

"Maybe *you* don't understand, Max. Amy threw up this morning. Jack hasn't spoken in four years. They're family. Why can't —"

"Drop it." Max interrupted again and concluded their lunch conversation. "You made a promise. Keep your promise."

Emma dumped her food in the trash. "See you at track and field."

T he 2020 Peaksville High School Track and Field games started at two o'clock on Friday.

Derrick won another event.

Ryan and I congratulated our brother over the schoolyard TSC airplane noise.

"Derrick, you just broke three school records," Ryan said.

I smiled. "You looked amazing out there."

Derrick vomited then humbly answered. "I wish I felt as good as I looked."

Aaron patted him on the back. "Derrick, you puked during a five-minute mile. Ben was so pissed."

Luke smiled. "You actually broke four records, Derrick. Ben lost to you by two full steps in the eight hundred. The TSC scorekeeper obviously cheated. Everyone saw you win by a mile."

Thomas shrugged. "The TSC scorekeepers don't lie. It was close but probably just an illusion. Setting three records is still great, Derrick!"

Aaron quickly stopped me from correcting Thomas.

Antoine smiled. "Here comes Emma."

Grace hugged Emma. "Two school records!"

Charlotte laughed. "Nice job, girl!"

Amy looked at her twin curiously. "Yeah, you smoked me. You ran like we both used to run back in California Junior Olympics. How?"

Emma made eye contact with Max and shrugged. "Just a good day, I guess."

"Good afternoon, Peaksville students. Today is Friday. Four more weeks of school," Dean Michaels broadcasted on the loudspeakers outside before dismissal. "Congratulations to Ben Light for breaking the all-time record in the eight hundred during Peaksville School's TSC Invitational. Great job, Ben! Lots of students have reported headaches and stomach aches. Peaksville State University Medical School released a study concluding that young people can reduce illnesses twenty percent by drinking eight glasses of water per day. Due to recent suspicious activity at the reservoir and elsewhere, The Meadow and all areas west of The Meadow have been declared off limits by the TSC for your safety. TSC has partnered with KidCare Counseling Services to solve problematic anti-authority behavior. It's okay to refer a friend for counseling if they question authority. As usual, please report all violations to the TSC. Have a great weekend. School's out. Be safe out there."

Ryan angrily asked. "What the hell was that all about?"

Madison asked. "Ben Light broke a record? Derrick beat Ben by two steps."

I agreed. "They cheated for Ben."

Aaron slung his backpack over his shoulder. "What's this turn in a friend crap? Who would do that?"

"Not a friend," Brianna said.

Ruby sighed. "We can't swim anymore? Liberty Lake, Coldwater Creek, and Lover's Lagoon are all off limits now?"

"Let's go to my farm," Charlotte said. "It's Friday, let's build a campfire."

"Thanks Charlie. Sounds perfect," Grace said.

Antoine pulled Emma aside. "Emma. We're friends, right?"

"Yes, Antoine, of course. Why?"

"I saw you run like the wind today, Emma. I also heard you and Max talking at lunch about —"

"Woah!" Emma interrupted. "Max is in trouble about that. And that was a private conversation."

Tears welled in Antoine's eyes. "D'Andre has been blind for four years. If you knew something, Emma, would you share it with us?"

"You don't understand, Antoine."

"Would you share it?"

"Life isn't that simple."

Antoine tearfully waited for Emma to change her mind.

"Sorry, Antoine. I can't help you."

G igi yelled to Kiche at the Epley farm. "Wolfie! Come her girl!"

Kiche ran at Gigi wagging her giant, furry tail.

Gigi whispered in her ear while petting her belly. "Wolfie, I like Daisy. But you'll always be my favorite."

Luke, Aaron and I built a giant campfire using an old, dried-out pile of scrap cedar, birch and tamarack courtesy of Mr. Epley.

Grace, Ruby, Charlotte and Emma prepared hamburgers, corn, and potatoes for the barbeque.

Ryan, Gloria, Derrick and Madison threw a Frisbee.

The TSC Bell 407 helicopter and Cessna 182 airplane conducted search patterns for the child abductors at three hundred feet over the children at two-minute intervals.

Emma worked in the kitchen and whispered to Grace once the two were alone. "Got a minute?"

Grace smiled and stopped shucking corn. "Always for you, Emma. What's up?"

"I feel perfect. No headache. No stomachache. Perfect."

"I heard. That's great."

Emma and Grace continued shucking corn.

Grace playfully bumped shoulders with Emma. "Something's up. What is it?"

"I have a dilemma."

"Want to share?"

"I know which path is the right path."

Grace laughed. "That was easy. Need any other advice?"

Emma looked around to ensure privacy. "The right path has consequences. I would have to lie. I would have to break a promise. And I would lose Max."

Grace stopped shucking corn. "That's quite a dilemma. What if you choose the wrong path?"

"I wouldn't lie. I wouldn't break a promise. I would keep Max."

"Sounds better."

"But everyone else suffers."

"Sounds worse."

"What do you personally gain by choosing the right path?"

"I would gain nothing. But family and friends gain things."

"What kind of things would family and friends gain?"

Emma began to cry. "Health. Hope. Freedom. Life."

Grace calmly hugged Emma. "Pretty heavy stuff."

"Grace, what should I do?"

"Follow your heart. The right path is always the hardest path."

I was the last of a dozen to board Charlotte's hay-filled trailer. "Good to go, Charlie!"

Charlotte smoothly let out the John Deere tractor clutch while simultaneously advancing the throttle.

Gigi smiled at Chloe and Jack. "Wee!"

Madison held Derrick's hand. "This is great."

Antoine yelled over the tractor and TSC airplane propeller noise. "Only four weeks until graduation!"

Brianna leaned into him. "Don't say that, Antoine. Unless you want me to cry."

Charlotte circled her pond, barn, and chicken coop in high gear.

I couldn't get the clues off my mind. "What do you all think about those four cave notes?"

Luke looked at me. "I think someone wants to help us."

"Why doesn't this *mysterious helper* just tell us the answer to his riddles?" Thomas asked.

Amy laughed. "Tommy Boy obviously doesn't understand the purpose of a riddle."

Aaron agreed. "Amy's got a point. The best teachers don't give answers. The best teachers ask questions."

"Maybe the mysterious helper is a teacher," Madison Goodwell said.

I looked at Aaron. "Maybe the mysterious helper is in danger."

Aaron nodded and pointed at me. "Bingo."

I saw Derrick began to slump and fall from the back of the trailer. "Ryan!"

Ryan instinctively grabbed the Derrick's shirt with his strong grip and pulled him back in.

Aaron quickly helped as Madison screamed. "Derrick!"

Derrick was pale. "Hey brother, you good?"

No answer.

"Charlie!" I yelled forward over the diesel engine noise. "Hold up for a minute!"

"How did this farm get here?" Derrick rubbed his eyes and slowly regained his situational awareness.

Charlotte stopped the tractor.

Madison was visibly shaken. "You okay, Derrick?"

"Yeah, my headache got the best of me."

I made solemn eye contact with our middle brother, Ryan.

Aaron Webster looked ahead at Charlotte on the John Deere. "Charlie, can we get our track and field champion back to the farmhouse?"

"Sure thing. Everyone hold on tight!" Charlotte initiated an accelerating left turn towards her farmhouse.

R uby lounged near the campfire. "Emma, check it out. That was a short hayride."

Charlotte parked the tractor and secured the engine.

Mr. Burns passed overhead the Epley farmhouse in the TSC search helicopter at three hundred feet as Derrick was led to the campfire.

Ryan gently lowered Derrick into a lounge chair. "Emma's fellow gold medalist tried to take an unannounced nap."

Aaron nodded. "A dirt nap."

"Everything okay, Derrick?" Emma asked.

Brianna handed Derrick a cold water as he relaxed. "Derrick got a little dizzy."

Grace watched Emma's pensive posture and quietly whispered to me. "There is a cure, Marcus."

I whispered back to Grace. "How do you know?"

"Can't say."

I sank into deep thought with a thousand-yard stare. Suddenly, out of the corner of my eye, I saw D'Andre collapse at the red, wooden barn. "DJ!"

Aaron, Luke, Antoine, and I bolted immediately into a full sprint. As we arrived, Kiche was licking D'Andre's face as he lay motionless.

I pulled the massive, gentle she-wolf back. "Jack and Gigi, grab Kiche for us!"

Antoine shook D'Andre. "Wake up, brother!"

"He's out cold!" Luke yelled to Charlotte.

Aaron gently placed a sweatshirt under D'Andre's head.

Grace looked at Gloria. "Call Mom. Tell her D'Andre fainted."

Charlotte ran to prepare Jefferson. "Chloe, get Buckshot!"

Chloe sprinted.

Charlotte returned on horseback. "AJ, climb up with Chloe. I'll take D'Andre when he's ready to be lifted."

"Someone said that name?" D'Andre mumbled. "Who there was said that my —"

Brianna whispered calmly. "Charlie did. Just relax, DJ. You passed out."

Antoine mounted Buckshot behind Chloe.

Gloria returned. "Charlie, my mom said bring him over."

Charlotte steadied Jefferson as Ryan and I lifted D'Andre. "He better ride in front of me. I can hold him better."

D'Andre mumbled once atop Jefferson. "Pizza."

We laughed.

Charlotte gave a 'thumbs up' carefully rode to the Becker home with Chloe and Antoine in trail.

CHAPTER EIGHTEEN

W e settled into lounge chairs at the campfire.

Amy cracked open a Diet Coke. "DJ actually said 'pizza' climbing onto Jefferson. Didn't he?"

Brianna laughed. "I heard it, too."

Thomas explained. "He was probably delirious."

Aaron smiled. "Negative, Tommy Boy. He's probably already eating pizza in the Becker home. He's not delirious."

Brianna waited for the TSC helicopter noise to dissipate. "Hope DJ's okay."

I observed Mr. Burns alone in the right seat. "Emma, where's Max this evening?"

"Grounded," Emma said.

Grace studied Emma's comments and mannerisms.

"Grounded?" Luke asked. "Max is eighteen."

"What did he do?" Thomas asked.

Grace gently nudged me.

"Not sure," Emma said, cryptically looking at Grace.

"Marcus and I might be going away for a few days," Grace said.

I looked at her with surprise. "We are?"

"The cure. It's out there. I really believe that."

Ryan looked at me. "Where? The TFZ?"

I looked at Grace, who was publicly volunteering me for something.

"Travel right into the light, before the night, above the white, under the rainbow," Brianna recited from memory.

"Carefully cross the stream to clean the stream," Luke said.

"The source of your symptoms is drawn to the cure," Madison said.

"The cure to the symptoms is simply mine," Ruby said.

"It's not real," Thomas said.

"You're not real, Tommy Boy," Aaron joked.

I took a stand. "It's not practical. Or reasonable. Those clues might lead to nowhere."

Derrick removed the water bottle from his forehead to speak. "Marcus, above the white. The White River."

Ryan nodded. "And 'right into the light, before the night' means travel west, before sunset."

"Above the white." Luke stood up and faced the sunset and used his hands to orient himself. "Stay north of the White River as you travel west."

Derrick reached into his pocket and tossed me something. "Take Dad's Army Ranger compass."

I sighed. "Then what? Under the rainbow? I've seen ten rainbows in my whole life. Tops. How is a rare meteorological phenomenon going to happen as we trek?" I made a solid point and nodded at our campfire with confidence.

Thomas was the only one who nodded back.

Fail.

Grace practically made me fall out of my chair. "Marcus and I will leave tomorrow at noon for The Forbidden Zone."

"Excuse me?"

Gloria looked her older sister. "When will you return? You graduate in four weeks."

I agreed with Gloria. "Yeah, listen to your sister."

Grace grabbed me by the hand. "After we find the cure."

I sighed.

Derrick returned the cold bottle to his forehead.

Grace was right.

"Paging Ruby Kyle to the chicken coop!" Mrs. Epley yelled towards the campfire in the moonlight. "Ruby Kyle to the chicken coop, please!"

We all looked at Ruby.

Ruby scanned the area. "Kiche?"

Grace smiled. "No."

Gigi looked around. "Wolfie?"

We all got up in unison and ran toward the chicken coop.

"Kiche!" Ryan exclaimed.

"Right this way, Ruby Kyle," Mrs. Epley said.

Mrs. Epley blocked the door to the chicken coop. "First, let's talk. What kind of dog is Kiche?"

"Half Canadian wolf. Half Anatolian Shepherd. Why?" Ruby nervously approached the chicken coop.

"How much does Kiche weigh? About one hundred and thirty?"

"One hundred fifty." Ruby was trembling.

"Ladies and gentlemen." Mrs. Epley opened the door to the chicken coop. "Behold, Kiche. The ferocious she-wolf."

Ruby first witnessed Kiche in the coop. "No way."

Amy tried to see. "Feathers?"

I peeked inside. "Huh?"

Brianna gasped. "You've got to be kidding me."

Grace picked up one of the hens. "I don't believe it."

Kiche lay prone in the middle of the chicken coop. Five hens slept on her back. Ten more hens were nestled under her sides for warmth. Dozens of hens were circling Kiche as if for protection.

Ruby looked around for feathers. "Kiche? How many did you eat?"

Kiche saw Ruby, lay still and kept her muzzle flat on the ground in the chicken coop between her massive paws. Kiche was not guilty of eating the Epley's chickens. Kiche was guilty of letting her *maternal instincts* overpower her *wolf instincts*.

Mrs. Epley laughed. "I found her and had to show you. Kiche is a perfect LGD!"

Ruby smiled. "I'm speechless."

I looked at Mrs. Epley. "What's an LGD?"

Mrs. Epley explained. "Livestock Guardian Dog. Twenty years ago, outsiders introduced 200 pound Canadian wolves into North Idaho. Now, the giant wolves are a problem. People own LGD's to protect their livestock from depredations. Kiche is perfect."

Ruby explained to Mrs. Epley. "My dad trained Kiche to be an LGD for some goats we owned before he was killed."

Gigi smiled and petted Kiche. "I guess the training stuck. Right, Wolfie?"

Mrs. Epley scratched Ruby's back. "Mr. Kyle's legacy lives on in more ways than one, Sweetheart."

"What a beautiful creature," Brianna said as the chickens appeared to enjoy Kiche's furry coat.

Mrs. Epley took a picture of Kiche.

Thomas was confused. "But Kiche is half wolf."

Mrs. Epley laughed. "That's why I took a picture, Tommy Boy!"

Kiche looked up and licked Gigi on the face.

Amy joked. "You are supposed to *eat* the chickens."

Aaron laughed. "Maybe Kiche has an identity crisis. A wolf in sheepdog's clothing."

I scratched Kiche's ears. "Good girl."

Grace placed another hen on Kiche's back. "That's some dog, Ruby Kyle."

G race, Ruby and I walked to the Becker home with Kiche. When we arrived, Charlotte and Chloe were in the front yard preparing Jefferson and Buckshot for the ride home in the dissipating civil twilight.

"Hi Charlotte!"

"Howdy, Marcus!" Charlotte said.

"How's DJ?" Grace asked.

"Better." Charlotte said. "Inside eating pizza with Antoine."

Ruby smiled. "Figures."

"Grace, your mom laughed when I told her 'pizza' was his first word after waking up."

Grace looked at Charlotte. "Charlie, tomorrow Marcus and I leave for the TFZ to look for the cure."

"I'm going with you," Antoine mumbled from the doorstep with pizza in his mouth.

I approached the porch. "Antoine, you stay here. Look after D'Andre."

Chloe secured Buckshot and walked to pet Kiche.

"What about school?" Charlotte asked.

Ruby winked. "Dean Michaels said the flu is going around. You both are officially home with the flu."

I nodded. "Good cover."

"Charlie, better get those horses to bed," Grace said in the civil twilight.

"See you tomorrow at The Boxcar at noon," I said.

"But that's off limits now," Charlotte replied.

I shrugged. "Everything's off-limits."

"And when everything's off-limits," Ruby Kyle said, "nothing's off-limits."

I smiled at Ruby. "Bingo!"

CHAPTER NINETEEN

Antoine swam in Liberty Lake as the Cessna and Bell passed overhead every few minutes. "TSC flies on Saturday mornings? Are we in trouble?"

"Strength in numbers," Brianna said lounging on the rocks.

Aaron nodded. "Bree is right. We must resist. Or this area will be off-limits forever. I know how they operate. My dad is TSC."

I feebly attempted to make an analogy. "Kind of like the ants disobeying the grasshoppers in *A Bug's Life*."

"Huh?" Antoine said.

Derrick emerged from Peaksville Forest and yelled. "More like passive non-compliance!"

"What's that?" D'Andre asked.

"A form of resistance against oppression," Ryan answered for Derrick. "POW's use it as a survival tactic."

My brothers' historical analogies dwarfed my cartoon-based analogy.

Madison stood atop Deadman's Cliff before jumping. "Derrick, where have you been, Sweetie?"

"Derrick arrived at eleven," Luke said. "The Parasite Slayer went straight into the forest."

Derrick tapped his dad's US Army Ranger knife on his belt. "Ten trees saved."

Luke surfaced after jumping from Weakman's Cliff. "Emma, where's Max? Still grounded?"

Emma nodded. "Still grounded."

Charlotte arrived on Jefferson with the three twelve-year-olds riding Buckshot and Daisy in trail.

Amy yelled from the middle of Liberty Lake with her ridiculous country accent. "Howdy, Charlie!"

Charlotte performed an exaggerated tip of her cowboy hat. "Howdy, Amy!"

Ruby greeted Charlotte. "Does Mrs. Epley need to hire my LGD, today?"

"Ha! My mom showed me the pictures. Adorable."

Grace and I stood ready with bags packed.

Thomas joked. "Hey Marcus Polo and Sacajawea! Ready for Manifest Destiny Part Two?"

"We do require a jack ass to haul our provisions. Are you for-hire?" I felt like my response overshot.

Grace slapped my rear.

Overshot confirmed.

Derrick, pre-cannonball, yelled from Deadman's Cliff in his jean shorts. "You all want company walking up Coldwater Creek?"

"Sure!"

Derrick jumped and yelled on the way down. "Be right there!"

Splash!

We all walked together from The Boxcar towards Lover's Cave.

Amy asked me a legitimate question passing The Elephant Rocks. "Marcus, what do you expect to find in the TFZ?"

I laughed. "Do you want my honest answer? I think —"

Grace interrupted me with an elbow.

"I'll answer that. We're going to find the cure."

Thomas walked with us up the north shore of Coldwater Creek. "Possible wild goose chase. Or possible trap."

Amy disagreed. "No way, Tommy Boy. The notes are real."

"I agree," Ruby said.

"Grace is right to follow her instincts," Brianna said as Mr. Light's airplane passed overhead.

Luke whispered. "My instinct tells us we are being watched. Look to the south. In the trees."

Everyone faced across Coldwater Creek. Ben Light and Tony Murdstone vacated their hiding spots behind cedar trees.

Aaron preemptively yelled. "Ben, you guys realize this is off-limits, right?"

Ryan backed up Aaron. "Yeah, Dean Michaels told us to report all violators."

"This is a citizen's arrest," Luke said.

"Put your hands on the tree," Antoine said.

"I'm going to personally file a report to the TSC President!" Amy said looking up at the Cessna. "Oh wait, that's Mr. Light. And he's flying in off-limits areas. Like father, like son."

Ben and Tony turned east and walked towards Peaksville.

"Got everything you need?" Luke and the boys crowded around me at Lover's Lagoon.

"Probably not," I joked.

"Toothbrush?" Ryan joked.

"I have everything dad taught us to pack," I whispered to Ryan. "Ryan, you take care of Derrick."

Ryan solemnly whispered. "No worries, brother."

"Grace, hurry back, okay," Amy said as Mr. Burns buzzed over Lover's Lagoon in the TSC helicopter.

Brianna wept. "I'll miss you, Gracie."

"Don't cry Bree. It will only be a few days."

"Be careful, Grace," Gloria said. "See you soon."

"Love you guys." Grace hugged her sisters and friends.

Derrick stood near the waterfall with Ruby. "Marcus and Grace. Kiche is ready to lead us through Lover's Cave to the TFZ."

Ryan hugged me. "Marcus, be careful."

Antoine approached me and whispered with tears in his eyes. "Marcus, you find that cure, buddy. For DJ."

I flipped on my flashlight once inside Lover's Cave. "Derrick, you're caving with us to the TFZ?"

"Ruby thought I should come see you off."

Ruby winked.

Kiche eagerly led the four adventurers. "Okay, Marcus and Grace. There are only three choices to make navigating through. Always choose the tallest passageway. They also happen to be left turns. Right turns upon return. You should never have to duck your head at any point."

Grace repeated the instructions. "Tallest passageways."

I helped. "Left turns outbound. Right turns inbound."

After fifteen minutes of caving to the west side of the mountain, Ruby reiterated. "You never need to crawl. That knowledge alone gets you back to Peaksville."

I broke the silence after a few more minutes thinking about what Thomas said. "What if these notes *are* a trap?"

"They aren't," Grace said.

"You have to *want* to be saved." Derrick walked forward in the darkness. "Or you *can't* be saved."

"Saved by whom. Saved from what?" I mumbled.

Ruby laughed. "That's for you to find out."

We continued for a few more minutes.

"Derrick."

"Yeah brother."

I pointed my flashlight on my own face. "Quit cutting down parasitic ivy. Quit trying to save the forest. Quit climbing tall trees. You can't save them all. Just quit."

"Marcus, stop!" Grace marched forward in Lover's Cave.

"But Derrick's wasting his time."

"Daylight!" Grace said.

"Wow! The TFZ!" Derrick smiled. "It's like heaven!"

"Just don't tell Mr. Light or Dean Michaels," Ruby said.

"It's beautiful." Grace silently stood, perched over The Forbidden Zone.

"What's that?" I pointed to the cave entrance floor.

"No way!" Ruby quickly unscrewed the jelly jar lid. "A fifth note."

"What does it say?" Derrick said.

Ruby cleared her throat then read the note. "He will guide you along the best pathway and watch over you."

HE WILL GUIDE YOU
ALONG THE BEST PATHWAY
AND WATCH OVER YOU.

This fifth note didn't inspire me in the least bit. "I would rather have a good magnetic heading."

Ruby nodded. "Interesting. But who is *he*?"

Derrick shrugged. "The person who wrote the note?"

"It seems biblical," Ruby said.

Grace smiled. "All is well."

Derrick shook my hand as the girls hugged goodbye. "Take care of yourself, Marcus."

"See you in a few days, little brother. Hopefully with the cure."

"Definitely with the cure!" Grace exclaimed before we walked down the steep mountain path into the TFZ.

Ruby waved. "Love you guys!"

We walked downhill for about one minute. I stopped and looked back up at Lover's Cave west entrance. "Hold on, Gracie."

Derrick remained in the mouth of the cave with Kiche at his side. I initiated a military salute with my right hand. Derrick solemnly returned the salute.

Ruby noticed tears running down Derrick's cheeks. "They'll be fine." She thoughtfully draped her arms over Derrick from behind and rested her head on his strong shoulders.

Grace and I continued westward into The Forbidden Zone.

CHAPTER TWENTY

Charlotte swam in Lover's Lagoon. "Maybe Marcus and Grace will find the fountain of youth in the TFZ."

Luke treaded water. "Maybe the cure is located in a neighboring town."

"Maybe the cure is a strange plant only found in the TFZ," Antoine said.

Amy smiled. "By strange plant, do you mean some type of weed?"

Ryan laughed. "Would our symptoms go up in smoke?"

Thomas pointed. "Wishful thinking. Here come Ruby and Derrick."

Aaron yelled. "All good?"

"Yes." Ruby nodded. "All good!"

Derrick stood with Kiche near the waterfall and pensively stared into the forest.

"Come on, Derrick!" Madison read his sadness. "Let's go home."

Charlotte climbed out of the water onto a boulder. "Marcus and Grace will be fine."

Gloria said. "Pizza at my house?"

D'Andre smiled. "Pizza? Count me in."

Amy giggled.

Madison softly spoke with her open hand extended. "Derrick?"

"Something isn't right." Derrick shrugged. "I don't have a good feeling about this."

Madison hugged Derrick. "Let's walk to the Becker home and relax."

. . .

I walked down the mountain with Grace deeper into the TFZ. "Travel right into the light, before the night."

"We head west. After we intercept the White River," Grace said. "Then a rainbow."

I tapped my device. "My dad's Army Ranger compass is spinning,"

"Is it broken?"

I shrugged. "This region is famous for rare earth metals. The TFZ must be worse than Peaksville for magnetic interference."

Grace marched forward. "Let's follow the sun. All is well."

"Hold on. Do you notice anything?"

Grace stopped and looked around. "Notice what?"

"Listen."

"I don't hear anything."

"Exactly. No TSC airplane noise. For forty-five minutes."

Grace smiled. "Only birds chirping."

We walked another ten minutes in the silence. "I feel guilty. Are we are being disloyal to the TSC? They keep us safe. We should obey."

Grace smiled, held my hand, and continued walking. She waited another ten minutes before responding. "You know what they call this?"

I shrugged. "What?"

"Freedom."

Aaron lazily paddled the raft down Coldwater Creek abeam the horses. "Got some tired rafters over here, Charlie!"

Chloe expertly rode Buckshot.

Gigi and Jack proudly trailed on Daisy with wide smiles.

Charlotte, horseback on Jefferson, replied to Aaron. "Too much excitement. Everyone is tired."

Madison slept soundly in the noon sun leaning back on Derrick.

Ruby and Luke were sound asleep.

Amy slept on Aaron's shoulder as he calmly paddled.

Brianna peacefully slept in Antoine's arms.

Aaron attempted to turn the ten-minute trip downstream into a fifteen-minute trip by back-paddling to steer. Aaron and Ryan gently arrested the forward movement of the raft at The Elephant Rocks.

Aaron whispered. "Rise and shine, rafters."

The approaching TSC Bell 407 helicopter woke any remaining sleepers.

Brianna held her forehead. "Oh, my headache. It's horrible."

Amy agreed. "Me too, Bree. I went to sleep without a headache."

Luke woke up rubbing his temples. "How can a headache develop during a ten-minute nap?"

Thomas covered his eyes. "Same here. Must be the sunlight."

Emma, headache-free for thirty-six hours, watched and listened.

Most continued to Liberty Lake to swim, some were too fatigued.

Madison Goodwell woke up last. Derrick helped her exit the raft onto The Elephant Rocks. "Derrick, walk with me."

"What's up?"

Madison whispered. "I had a dream. My dad was slaying parasitic ivy in Peaksville Forest with you. He had a shaggy beard and was dressed like a mountain man. Derrick, my dad was a nanotech engineer kidnapped during a business trip to Dubai in the United Arab Emirates. He *wasn't* a mountain man."

Derrick listened over the Cessna 182 propeller noise. "Interesting dream, Maddie."

"There's more. My dad smiled at me. Then, he pointed upstream. What does it mean?"

"He pointed west?"

"Into the sunset." The two sophomores continued walking to The Boxcar. "I think so."

"Possibly the TFZ?"

Madison nodded then hugged Derrick. "I miss my dad."

We walked west through the TFZ, picking huckleberries along the way, a North Idaho wild delicacy. "Grace, do you hear something?"

Grace stopped to listen. "Rushing water?"

I approached the top of a rocky ridge. "Rapids!"

Grace smiled at me. "The White River!"

I extended my right arm towards the sunset, holding Grace's hand with my left. "So now, we trek west on the north bank of the White River."

"Then we look for a rainbow."

"A rainbow in the clear blue sky? Just past the unicorn?"

"Oh, Marcus." Grace marched forward. "That's ridiculous. Everyone knows that only leprechauns hang out near rainbows."

Marcus sighed.

"He will guide us along the best pathway."

"The leprechaun?"

Grace pinched me.

· · ·

D'Andre, Luke, Ruby and Brianna floated in the middle of Liberty Lake. Kiche played fetch with Gigi, Chloe, and Jack near The Boxcar.

Ryan, Antoine and Aaron waited impatiently behind Thomas on Deadman's Cliff.

Aaron snapped. "Your turn, Tommy Boy. Going to jump?"

"Do you think we're in trouble for being in a restricted area?" Ryan asked.

Aaron shrugged. "What are they going to do? Send us to North Idaho and make us live in Peaksville?"

Ryan laughed.

"Thomas, they invented this new thing they like to call *jumping*!" Antoine said.

Mr. Light's TSC Cessna 182 conducted another 360-degree, left-hand eighty-knot orbit only three hundred feet above the children.

"Jump, Tommy Boy. Before Marcus and Grace return with the cure," Antoine said.

Ruby looked up to the twenty-foot cliff from Liberty Lake. "Tommy Boy? You okay up there?"

No response.

Luke looked up at Thomas. "Ryan! Tommy Boy's wobbling!"

Thomas, standing on the ledge, fell down to his knees and quickly slumped forward.

Ryan lunged forward to grab him by the feet.

Too late.

Thomas collapsed, fell head first, slipped from Ryan's grip, and plunged awkwardly into Liberty Lake.

Splash!

Ruby and Luke raced to Thomas. Ruby arrived first. Ruby grabbed his right arm with her right hand, spun him, turned his limp body away from her, pulled him close, reached her left arm around his neck, and grabbed his right armpit to swim Thomas to safety.

Thomas began to regain situational awareness with his chin elevated inside Ruby's left elbow. "I'm good. I got it. I'm okay."

Ruby ignored Thomas and kept swimming. Ruby was trained to always complete her rescue. Ruby squeezed her left arm tighter around his neck, holding his right armpit as she performed the side stroke with Thomas safely on his back.

"Ruby?"

Thomas was trapped and along for the ride.

Aaron yelled from Deadman's Cliff after Ruby reached the east shore of Liberty Lake near The Boxcar. "Is he okay?"

"Tommy Boy, you good?" Antoine yelled.

Mr. Light rolled wings level in his Cessna 182 and departed his low orbit.

Thomas gave a 'thumbs up.' "I'm good. Just dehydrated, I guess."

Ruby lay on her back exhausted and out of breath next to Thomas on the rocky shore.

"Ruby, are *you* good?" Charlotte asked.

Ruby exhaustedly nodded and relaxed on her back.

Kiche remedied the situation with dozens of giant licks to Ruby's face.

The TSC Bell 407 helicopter performed a thunderous low pass over Liberty Lake at nearly 100 knots.

"Charlie, can you ride our totally radical *X-Games* cliff jumper to Mrs. Becker?" Luke asked.

Ryan giggled. "Cliff jumper."

Aaron laughed. "More like cliff *faller*."

G race and I paralleled the White River into the TFZ sunset.

"Hey Marcus."

"What's up?"

"Whoever finds the rainbow first gets the pot of gold."

"Deal!"

Grace laughed. "Pay up, Bub!"

Grace stopped and pointed ahead at a majestic, hundred-foot tall natural red rock formation shaped like a rainbow.

"What is that? And did you just call me Bub?"

Grace celebrated. "Grace discovered rock formation. Grace names rock formation. Grace shall call it Rainbow Bridge. And Grace shall receive pot of gold per verbal contract."

I sighed and marched forward.

C harlotte and Thomas dismounted Jefferson at Mrs. Becker's home under the roar of the TSC helicopter. "Special delivery for Mrs. Becker. I have one cliff jumper. Dizzy, wet and hungry."

Mrs. Becker smiled. "Thanks, Charlie. Hello, Mr. Stallworth. Here early for some pizza?"

Thomas slowly mumbled. "Yes ma'am. Felt a little dizzy at Liberty Lake. I'm okay now. Just dehydrated."

"That's okay, Thomas. Come inside and pop in a movie. I'll get some dinner started."

Charlotte escorted Thomas inside. "Tommy Boy performed a Peter Pan off

Deadman's Cliff. Eyes closed. Big splash. Thankfully, the cold water woke him up."

"Sounds exciting. Glad you're okay, Thomas. Make yourself at home."

"Thank you, ma'am."

Charlotte whispered. "Mrs. Becker, Derrick and Ruby walked Grace and Marcus into the TFZ through the mountain. Grace asked me to pass that she will be fine."

Mrs. Becker smiled. "Miss Epley, you read my mind."

Charlotte mounted Jefferson. "I have to run home to help Chloe, Gigi, and Jack put the horses to bed."

Mrs. Becker smiled. "All Gigi talks about anymore is Daisy."

"Your daughter Gigi's a natural cowgirl."

"Pizza and movie night, Charlie! See you later?"

Charlotte rode off on Jefferson. "Sure thing, Mrs. Becker! Thanks!"

I stoked our small campfire in my makeshift fire pit under Rainbow Bridge with a long branch. "No clues. No cure. No pot of gold."

Grace hugged me as we rested next to our campfire. "All is well."

I stood up and continued assembly of our small tent. "What if we don't find anything tomorrow?"

Grace attempted to lightly toast her marshmallow under the stars. "Tomorrow will be a good day."

"What if tomorrow's a bad day? We may go home empty-handed."

"Marcus, think positively. We found a gallon of huckleberries."

"But not the cure."

"Not yet."

"Grace, we searched for two hours before sunset."

"Relax, Marcus." Grace smiled. "He will guide us along the best pathway and watch over us."

I pointed at our fire. "Watch over your marshmallow. It's burning."

Mrs. Becker delivered another tray of pizza and soda into the television room. "Feeling better, Tommy Boy?"

"Much better, Ma'am. I was just dehydrated. Still have my headache but that's normal."

The TSC Air Patrol continued their noisy search patterns over the Peaksville community well into Saturday evening.

"Enough!" Ryan turned up the television volume and looked up. "Sounds like Mr. Burns is trying to land his helicopter on the Becker roof."

Luke threw a pillow at the ceiling. "Mr. Burns! Trying to watch a movie down here!"

"Hope Marcus and Grace are doing okay in the TFZ," Charlotte said.

"Hope they found the landmarks," Gloria said.

"Hope they have enough food," Brianna said.

Antoine pointed at Kiche. "Speaking of food."

Gigi scratched behind Kiche's ears and whispered. "Wolfie, your mouth is watering."

Kiche sat patiently awaiting any accidental or benevolent pizza scraps.

Brianna laughed. "Hungry like the wolf."

Amy sighed. "Bree, ever seen a wolf that wasn't hungry?"

Luke held up a piece of pizza. "Ruby, I have a stomach ache. Can I give Kiche my piece?"

"Sure, just guard your fingers. Kiche, no bite!"

Luke nervously placed the pizza on his hand with closed fingers, as if to feed a horse. "Easy, girl."

Kiche tilted her head sideways and gently removed the pizza from Luke's possession, devoured the sausage and pepperoni pizza slice with one impressive chomp, and quickly returned to her original begging posture.

Brianna laughed. "It's gone?"

Antoine gasped. "Wow."

Luke was relieved to retain his fingers. "She didn't even chew."

Thomas guarded his own slice of pizza by pulling it closer. "Mine."

Amy laughed at Thomas. "Mine?"

Ryan rubbed Kiche's shoulders. "Scary girl."

D'Andre entered the television room. "Did someone feed a piece of Mrs. Becker's delicious pizza to a dog?"

Charlotte laughed. "Not just any dog."

Gigi hugged Kiche. "Wolfie!"

CHAPTER TWENTY-ONE

The sunrise illuminated our small tent under Rainbow Bridge in The Forbidden Zone. Birds sang their morning rituals. Trees rustled in the cool morning breeze.

I whispered. "Grace?"

Grace remained asleep in the warm sleeping bag.

I exited the tent and quietly secured the tent zipper. I immediately continued yesterday's search, carefully scouring the red rocks for any sign of a clue.

The sounds of nature gave me an uneasy feeling. I hadn't seen The Safety Corps aircraft in nearly twenty-four hours. For the first time in many years, I wasn't woken up by a TSC aircraft. The absence of the TSC airplane's reciprocating engine and propeller was deafening. The lack of vibration from the TSC helicopter's rotor blades was unnerving.

Gloria whispered in her family room among the slumbering Sunday morning guests. "Good morning, Charlie. Go help yourself to some breakfast."

D'Andre woke on the couch to the startling sensation of Kiche licking his eyes. "Hey girl." D'Andre smiled and covered his face. "Why are you doing that?"

Ruby whispered. "Welcome to my world, D'Andre. She's my daily alarm clock."

Brianna sighed. "The airplane and helicopter noise kept waking me up for the past two hours. Every. Five. Minutes."

Gigi whispered. "Wolfie, want to go outside?"

Kiche wagged violently until Gigi opened the back door.

D'Andre whispered to Ruby and Brianna. "You guys want to hear about my dream?"

Brianna nudged closer as others slept. "We'd love to!"

D'Andre whispered. "My father, Doctor Jordan, was in my dream. Antoine and I were nine years old. It was sunny. We were on the Yokosuka Navy base in Japan. I could still see. The three of us were playing catch. Dad was in his Navy whites with black shoulder boards. Mom was watching us. Sitting. Smiling. Drinking lemonade. I could see everything. The birds. The trees. The clouds. My family. I could see the threads of the baseball spinning in the air. Dad was still alive. Everything was wonderful. Almost too wonderful."

Ruby whispered. "That was beautiful, DJ."

Brianna cried. "We loved Dr. Jordan. Thanks for sharing that with us."

D'Andre tearfully whispered. "Then my dad said something to me in the dream."

Brianna whispered. "What was it, D'Andre?"

"He said. My dad said. Something like. Things have to get worse before they get better."

Ruby and Brianna listened. "Wow."

"I'm blind." D'Andre cried. "How much worse do things have to get?"

G race peeked her head out of the tent. "Good morning, Sunshine."

I grilled bacon in the morning sun under Rainbow Bridge and smiled.

"How long have you been up, Marcus?"

"Two hours."

Grace rubbed the sleep from her eyes and took a deep breath. "Smells really good. And I have no morning headache or chest pain."

"Same here."

"Find anything?"

"Nothing. Want to help me take a look around after we eat?"

Grace smiled. "After breakfast. I'm starving."

M rs. Becker prepared breakfast with Gloria's help. "Good morning, Thomas. All better?"

"Yes ma'am. Except for my morning headache. Which is normal, anyway."

Luke walked into the kitchen rubbing his temples. "Breakfast smells great."

Mrs. Becker smiled. "Grab a plate and enjoy."

Luke and Thomas sat down near Antoine and Brianna.

Antoine poured syrup his pancakes. "Tommy Boy, we have a legitimate, ongoing debate. I scored your dive a 5.5, Bree is giving you a 6.5."

Brianna maintained a straight face. "It seemed so effortless."

Antoine disagreed. "He was unconscious."

"So."

Luke sided with Antoine. "Bree, how can you score Tommy Boy a 6.5 without a full rotation?"

Thomas scraped eggs onto his plate and tried to ignore them. "Yuck it up."

"6.5," Brianna said.

"5.5." Antoine disagreed. "And my score is generous. Water entry was atrocious."

Thomas quietly ate breakfast for another thirty seconds.

Luke broke the silence. "Random arm and leg flailing. One point deducted."

Brianna smiled. "Stoic and entertaining facial expression until impact. One point added."

Thomas slowly looked at Antoine and Luke. "Hardy. Har. Har."

Mr. Light flew his TSC airplane directly over the Becker home at three hundred feet.

Gigi snuck Kiche a piece of bacon and whispered from across the breakfast table. "Tommy Boy, ignore the dance troupe. Wolfie and I loved your dive."

Thomas looked up and smiled. "High-five, Gigi."

The bright-eyed twelve-year-old enthusiastically slapped his raised palm.

"Smart child, Mrs. Becker."

I searched under the hot sun in the TFZ. "It's been two hours. All we found was an old arrowhead, deer antlers, a toad and a rusty pick axe."

Grace rubbed my back. "Something must be here. I know it."

"How do you know it?" Marcus asked.

We sat down on a large red rock near overlooking our campsite under the shade of Rainbow Bridge. "Faith, Marcus."

"Huh?"

"There's a reason why we're here."

I looked at Grace. "What's the reason?"

"The cure."

"The cure to what?"

"See, Marcus." Grace nudged me with her shoulder. "There you go again."

I sighed. "You're not making any sense."

Grace kissed me. "You'll figure it out."

. . .

B rianna Lopez splashed into Liberty Lake from the rope swing, surfaced, and looked at Thomas. "New rules! No stupid human tricks today!"

"Whew!" Gloria Becker slowly submerged in her jean shorts and bikini top. "Cold water!"

Amy yelled before jumping from Deadman's Cliff. "Don't worry, Gloria! My hot body will warm it up!"

Max Burns arrived as his father performed a low pass in his TSC helicopter.

Emma yelled towards The Boxcar. "Max! You made it!"

Charlotte yelled from the rope swing. "Swim, Max!"

Max saw Luke near the edge of Deadman's Cliff. "Only if Luke jumps!"

D'Andre floated on an inner tube. "Luke! Try closing your eyes. It works for me."

Aaron laughed. "And for Tommy Boy!"

Amy treaded water. "Jump, you chicken! I'll let you touch my butt!"

Luke sprinted down to Weakman's Cliff, jumped feet first into Liberty Lake and began frantically swimming towards Amy. "Didn't say from where!"

Amy nervously back-paddled. "Oh, crap!"

Luke determinedly swam with all of his might and rapidly approached.

Amy laughed too hard to swim well. "Help!"

Madison warned nearby. "Better swim, Amy."

Aaron smiled. "I never saw Luke swim so quickly."

Derrick sighed. "I never saw Amy swim so *slowly*."

Amy yelled laughingly as Luke approached. "This butt is reserved for the brave!" She kept back paddling. "For the courageous! And the strong!"

After one final stroke, Luke reached and squeezed her rear end.

Amy screamed. "Yipe!"

Ruby sighed. "Oh, please! Amy suddenly forgets how to swim."

Brianna and Charlotte nodded. "Sudden Non-swimmer Syndrome."

Emma sprang from Liberty lake in her one-piece bathing suit and approached Max near The Boxcar. "Hey. I've been waiting for you."

"Want me to touch your butt?" Max joked.

The TSC helicopter slowly passed overhead in a twenty-knot hover into the ten-knot headwind.

"No. I mean yes. I mean not right now." Emma whispered as everyone swam. "My headache returned. That thing that I borrowed. Can I borrow it again?"

Max didn't answer.

"Max?"

Max pointed at the slow-moving helicopter. "He'll kill me."

"He can't kill you when he's airborne."

"You don't know my dad well enough."

Emma whispered in his ear. "I'll let you touch my butt."

Emma yelped in a high-pitched voice similar to her twin's yelp.

Max displayed a guilty smile. "I'll be back."

Max ran towards Peaksville through The Meadow.

G race and I walked under Rainbow Bridge looking for a clue, a cure, or anything. "How does the fifth note read again? He'll guide you on the worst possible pathway and ignore you?"

Grace replied with her comforting smile. "Marcus! He will guide you along the *best* pathway and watch over you."

"Forgot. The leprechaun, right?"

"Marcus! That's it! I know where we need to go!"

"Home?"

Grace pulled my hand and pointed it upwards. "Where is the best pathway to watch over us?"

I realized she was referring to Rainbow Bridge. "An airplane?"

"No."

"Rainbow Bridge?"

"Yes."

"No deal!"

"Yes deal!"

"That rock is one hundred feet high. Too dangerous."

Grace approached the nearest leg of the spectacular geological rock formation and looked up.

"Marcus, it's at least thirty feet wide up there. We can do this."

I shook my head negatively. "It'll collapse."

"It survives four-foot snow loads each winter."

I shrugged.

"Dinosaurs used to walk on that rock bridge."

I nodded. "That's why they went extinct. They fell."

Grace grabbed my hand and smiled.

I wasn't going to win this one.

M ax returned with his contagious smile to The Boxcar. "Chloe! Gigi! Jack! It's Sunday afternoon, go swim!"

Chloe held a pencil in her hand. "But we did swim."

Gigi explained. "Jack got a bad headache so we took a break."

Luke held up a math workbook. "Three weeks until finals."

"Just making sure they're ready," Ruby said.

Mr. Burns buzzed Liberty Lake in the TSC helicopter just over the treeline.

Luke peeked outside The Boxcar's sliding old wooden door. "There goes your dad again, Max."

"Max, did the TSC find the bad guys yet?" Gigi asked while scratching Kiche's belly.

"Still looking."

Chloe looked up from her homework. "Hope they find them."

Max nodded.

Twelve-year-old Jack rubbed his temples.

"Are we in trouble for breaking the new TSC restriction?" Luke asked.

Max shrugged his shoulders. "If you absolutely, positively have to break the rules, do it in a group."

Emma walked towards The Boxcar soaking wet in her swimsuit, towel-drying her long, blonde hair. "Hey, stranger!"

"Hey, Emma."

Max subtly nodded to initiate a private conversation behind The Boxcar.

Emma followed. "Sure."

Max carefully scanned the area. Four sophomores were deep in the woods at The Treehouse. Luke and Ruby were inside tutoring Chloe, Gigi and Jack. Amy was two-hundred feet away in Liberty Lake entertaining Charlotte, Brianna, Antoine, D'Andre, Aaron, and Thomas. Marcus and Grace were exploring the TFZ. Ben and Tony hadn't been seen all day. And no aircraft were currently passing overhead.

Assured of privacy, Max reached into his pocket and slid the three-pound magnet into Emma's backpack.

"Emma," Max said sternly. "Bring this to homeroom tomorrow. Last time ever. Only *you* can use it."

"Thanks, Max."

"Promise?"

Emma quietly responded with a kiss.

"If my dad kills me for this, I will be *very* mad at you," Max said, halfway joking.

Emma stowed her backpack, smiled and performed a running jump into Liberty Lake. "Bye, Max!"

Max ran home to Peaksville and attempted to elude his father's Bell 407.

Antoine intercepted Emma in the cold water. "How are your headaches?"

Emma assumed a guarded posture. "Why do you ask?"

Antoine treaded water next to Emma. "We're good friends, right?"

"Of course."

Antoine whispered. "I watched you and Max. Can you share that thing with me?"

Emma swam next to Antoine expressionless with no response.

"D'Andre and I can keep a secret. Please, Emma. I promise."

Emma Kernan slowly swam away from Antoine Jordan. Emma noticed tears in Antoine's eyes a few minutes later. Emma saw her twin sister Amy, holding her head. Emma saw her brother Jack, unable to speak. Emma saw Antoine's brother D'Andre, unable to see.

Emma slowly swam to Antoine. "Maybe."

CHAPTER TWENTY-TWO

Ryan Flynn yelled seventy-five feet up into a cedar tree. "Derrick! You're too high, brother!"

Derrick yelled over the sound of the TSC airplane propeller and slayed parasitic ivy with his father's US Army Ranger knife. "Oh, ye of little faith!"

Madison Goodwell lounged with Ryan and Gloria in the lower level of The Treehouse. "Peaksville Forest actually looks healthier each year."

Ryan responded. "Impossible. One person can't make a difference."

Gloria disagreed. "One person can stop the engine of the world."

"Huh?" Ryan replied.

"Read it in a book."

Ryan shrugged.

"Look at him go!" Gloria Becker looked up at Derrick Flynn. "My dad said Derrick reminds him of a recruit from his basic training. There was something distinctly different about this one guy. Everyone knew it. That Marine later earned the Congressional Medal of Honor in the sandbox. My dad says Derrick is saving trees right now, but someday Derrick will be saving fellow soldiers or sailors in battle."

Madison smiled proudly, looked up and admired her beau.

Ryan began to disagree but was interrupted by a large ivy strand falling on his head.

. . .

W e hiked up the southern slope of Rainbow Bridge. "Happy now, Grace? Ready to head home?"

"We haven't reached the summit."

I licked my finger and held it in the air as Grace pulled my other hand uphill. "Wind's picking up."

"You're right, Marcus. The breeze feels great!"

"You remind me of Derrick."

A bald eagle soared overhead and screeched loudly.

Grace watched the massive bird in flight. "Beautiful. Perfectly free."

"Well, at least the bird is free. Tell me when I'm *perfectly free* to return to Peaksville where I'm perfectly free."

Grace hiked faster towards the Rainbow Bridge summit and pulled my hand. "Bah! Humbug!"

I carefully examined our seventy-foot drop. "Slow down, Grace. We're getting pretty high."

Grace winked. "It's getting more level."

I sighed and followed.

D errick yelled down to Ryan, Gloria, and Madison who were still lounging in The Treehouse. "The trees look amazing from up here!"

Madison yelled. "Derrick, come down! Let's go swim!"

Mr. Light, the Peaksville TSC President and Chief Pilot, continued his three hundred-foot, eight-knot search pattern over Peaksville Forest.

Mr. Burns flew his TSC Bell 407 helicopter in loose cruise formation behind the Cessna 182.

"Derrick, finish!" Ryan exclaimed.

"Finishing!"

"Good! Finish!"

Derrick mumbled. "I have a headache anyway!"

"How many trees, Parasite Slayer?" Gloria yelled.

"Twenty-five!" Derrick yelled down proudly over the propeller noise.

Madison yelled. "Great!"

"Only ten thousand more to go," Ryan whispered to Gloria and Madison.

Gloria smiled. "Ryan, we know you're proud of your little brother."

Madison watched Derrick begin his descent from seventy-five feet and whispered. "He's amazing."

. . .

"**A**my!" D'Andre yelled down standing on Deadman's Cliff. "That touching of the butt deal with Luke? Is a poor blind kid from East Peaksville entitled to that special offer on Sundays?"

Amy explained treading water as the TSC airplane passed overhead. "If you catch it, you can touch it! I'm a fast swimmer, D'Andre. No handouts! No hard feelings! There's no such thing as a free butt touch!"

"Deal!" D'Andre yelled. Emma and D'Andre quickly held hands, jumped twenty-foot and plunged into Liberty Lake.

"Unassisted!" Amy cited more rules and back-paddled slowly with a smile.

D'Andre surfaced and broke into a sprint towards Amy.

"Holy crap!" Amy said. "He can swim!"

Charlotte laughed. "Better hurry, Amy!"

Brianna joked. "Defend the butt!"

Thomas coached. "Straight ahead D'Andre, slightly left."

Aaron coached from the inner tube. "Listen for her splashes."

"Little right," Emma said.

D'Andre methodically swam forward and listened attentively.

"Betrayer!" Amy joked paddling away. "My twin sister is a betrayer!"

Gigi laughed. "You're making too much noise, Amy! Stop talking!"

Amy instinctively went underwater.

Antoine coached. "Turn right. She's under. Perfect! Speed up!"

Chloe yelled from near the rope swing with Jack and Gigi. "Left, D'Andre!"

"To your left!" Ruby instructed to D'Andre as Amy tried to hide under the surface.

D'Andre dove underwater.

"Yowwwweee! I said touch my butt, not grab a handful and put it in your pocket!"

Antoine laughed. "That's how blind people see."

"It's true, Amy." Luke laughed. "It's like Braille."

D'Andre smiled.

"I think they call it imprinting." Aaron added.

"Imprinting." Amy rubbed her bottom. "That's for sure."

The TSC airplane and helicopter initiated low overhead orbits before circling back to The Treehouse.

Luke swam to D'Andre with a celebratory tone. "DJ, welcome to the club."

D'Andre smiled. "Let's go make t-shirts."

. . .

W e summited Rainbow Bridge.
Grace exclaimed. "Marcus! A jelly jar!"

I was fairly preoccupied with our precarious perch one hundred feet above the TFZ rocky floor. "Cool."

Grace retrieved a piece of paper from the jar. "Rise and shine, bright to your right, turn west at tower, and track to trestle."

RISE AND SHINE,
BRIGHT TO YOUR RIGHT,
TURN WEST AT TOWER,
AND TRACK TO TRESTLE.

I observed the setting sun. "Bright to your right? Let's trek south."
Grace disagreed. "Rise and shine means morning. We trek north. Then west at a tower."

I threw my backpack over my shoulder. "North it is. Let's roll."

Grace disagreed again. "It's getting dark soon."

"Tomorrow is Monday. What about school?"

"He will guide us and watch over us. Besides, we have the flu. Right?"

I sighed. "Oh, brother."

R yan yelled upwards from The Treehouse. "Careful descending, Derrick. It's getting dark!"

Gloria yelled. "One step at a time!"

The port red and starboard green wingtip navigation lights were now becoming clearly visible on Mr. Light's TSC Cessna 182 as he passed over Derrick again. The forest floor was becoming quite dark under the cedar tree canopy. At sixty feet, Derrick was still illuminated by the sun on the horizon. Derrick paused during his descent to look west at the sunset.

Derrick yelled down. "How do you think Marcus and Grace are doing in the TFZ?"

Madison sighed and cupped her hands. "Swimmingly! You just be careful and come down, Derrick!"

. . .

I looked at my watch atop Rainbow Bridge. "Getting late. Let's head down and build a campfire. Cold breeze is moving in."

Grace stowed the sixth note in her backpack and sat down. "Not so fast, cowboy. Have a seat and warm me up, Marcus."

"But the sun's going down."

Grace patted the smooth red rock and smiled. "I know."

R yan waited as Derrick slowly climbed down the giant cedar. "Gloria, is the Becker Pizzeria open on a Sunday night?"

"The Becker Pizzeria is always open." Gloria smiled. "Especially for you."

Ryan yelled over the helicopter noise "Derrick! Let's roll! Now!"

Gloria gave Ryan 'the look' and yelled up to Derrick. "Take your time!"

No response.

"You feel that cold breeze blowing in?" Madison asked Gloria and Ryan.

Ryan yelled. "Derrick!"

No response.

Madison gasped. "Derrick's hugging the tree trunk."

Ryan yelled louder. "Derrick, say something!"

Madison nervously looked up. "Derrick?"

No response.

Gloria instinctively started running towards Liberty Lake. "I'll get the others."

Ryan prepared to climb the cedar. "Something's wrong, Maddie."

" W e should set up our camp," I said deep in The Forbidden Zone atop the natural rock formation.

Grace leaned against me with her eyes closed and whispered. "Too comfy."

"I'm serious, Grace. I have a bad feeling up here. Let's get down."

Grace nestled in my arms in the cool evening breeze. "Hold me for a few more minutes and you have a deal."

C harlotte approached on horseback with Gloria riding tandem.

Madison frantically waved her arms. "Over here, Charlie!"

Charlotte skillfully rode Jefferson through the cedars. "Which tree?"

Madison pointed and wiped her tears. "Ryan's climbing."

Charlotte and Gloria came to a halt and quickly dismounted. Charlotte grabbed the rope from Jefferson's saddle, threw it over her shoulder and climbed the tree. "Ryan, how we doing up there?"

Ryan exhaustedly yelled. "Almost there, Charlie. Catching my breath."

"On my way!"

Ruby arrived on foot from Liberty Lake with Luke, the three twelve-year-olds, and Kiche. "What happened?"

Madison held Gloria's hand. "Derrick's still not answering. He's way up there. I'm scared."

Kiche sensed the danger and responded with a series of frustrated growls, pacing and circling. Gigi unsuccessfully tried to pet Kiche to calm her down. Kiche repeatedly nudged Madison who was now audibly crying.

"Ryan, can you reach him?" Aaron yelled over the propeller noise.

Ryan carefully ascended. "Almost!"

Ryan grabbed Derrick's belt and pulled it closer to the tree. "Derrick."

Derrick whispered. "Ryan?"

"Brother, I can't do this alone."

Derrick slowly regained consciousness and examined the situation. "Why are you tugging my belt? And why are you out of breath?"

"Very funny."

The cedar tree swayed in the breeze.

Derrick rubbed his eyes. "I passed out?"

"You passed out."

Charlotte waited on a large branch halfway up the cedar.

"You got him, Ryan?" Amy yelled upwards.

"We're coming down!" Ryan yelled down into the darkness.

The Flynn brothers reinitiated Derrick's descent.

CHAPTER TWENTY-THREE

I whispered on the red, thirty-foot wide, rocky plateau of Rainbow Bridge as Grace slumbered in my arms. "Grace?"

I spoke slightly louder. "Grace."

Grace quietly responded. "Yes?"

"You fell asleep."

"You woke me up."

"We need to get down. It's getting dark."

Grace whispered. "Will you keep me warm at our campsite?"

"I'll build a campfire," I extended my hand to pull Grace up. "And I'll keep you warm."

"Forever?"

"Forever. But first we have to start down."

We carefully began our descent on the southern slope with the sixth note. Grace squeezed my hand as we walked down the naturally arch-shaped rock formation in the amber twilight.

Grace paused. "That's weird. Wind shifted."

I agreed. "And it's getting colder."

Gigi Becker tended to Kiche and yelled up into the darkness. "Take your time, Derrick!"

Kiche quietly howled with each breath in Gigi's arms.

Ryan cautiously climbed down holding Derrick's belt. "Twenty-five today?"

The red and green wingtip navigation lights and red rotating beacon under the fuselage of the hovering TSC helicopter were now lighting up the trees as darkness loomed.

"Twenty-five what?"

"Trees, Derrick. You saved twenty-five trees."

"Oh."

Ryan was drenched with sweat from the rapid ascent. "You okay?"

Derrick stopped fifty feet above the forest floor. "My vision."

Charlotte, out of breath, waited ten feet below Ryan and Derrick with her rope. "Ryan, is he okay?"

Ryan shook his head negatively.

Derrick whispered to Ryan. "Worst. Headache. Ever."

"Let's rest, then."

Derrick opened his eyes and whispered. "Ryan, they're hurting me."

Ryan clinched Derrick's belt tighter. "What's hurting you?"

Derrick shook his head 'no' handed a strand of parasitic ivy to Ryan. "I said *they* are hurting me. But today, I think they're killing me."

Ryan looked down anxiously and yelled over the helicopter noise. "Charlie! Be ready down there!"

W e carefully continued down the south leg of Rainbow Bridge. "Hope nobody stole our campsite."

Grace smiled. "Marcus, we have the whole TFZ to ourselves."

"Just you and me?"

Grace jumped onto my back. "Just you and me."

I received a kiss on the cheek from my new piggy-back passenger. "Then nobody is guiding us and watching over us."

Grace patted her pocket. "Marcus, someone had to leave this sixth note for us."

"Then we *don't* have the whole TFZ to ourselves. Can't have it both ways, Gracie."

"Oh, ye of little faith."

D errick collapsed over Ryan's shoulders fifty feet above the forest floor. "Derrick's unconscious!"

"Oh God!" Madison whimpered.

"Take your time, Ryan," Brianna said.

The TSC helicopter slowly orbited overhead, with only navigation and strobe lights visible in the darkness.

"You got this, Ryan!" Aaron declared firmly.

"No hurry, Ryan," Ruby said.

Gigi calmed Kiche.

Ryan yelled down. "I can't do this!"

"You *can* do this!" Amy said.

Ryan, drenched in sweat, looked at his brother. "Okay, I can do this."

Derrick's two arms and two legs were limp and hanging freely.

Ryan held Derrick over his right shoulder using his right hand. He gripped branches with his left hand. Ryan's legs were exhausted from the rapid climb and shook with pain under the added weight.

"Derrick, wake up." Ryan whispered. "I can't do this alone."

Crack!

The load-bearing ability of the cedar branches quickly became an issue. Charlotte threw some rope up from ten feet below. "Ryan, secure Derrick if you can. Maybe to his belt. Take your time, buddy."

Ryan examined the precarious situation. The rope was within two feet. Ryan's left arm now hugged the tree trunk. Ryan utilized a Fireman's Carry holding Derrick's body over his right shoulder. Parasitic ivy had become tangled around his left foot. The branch under his right foot was weakening.

Ryan made a decision. First, clear the parasitic ivy from his foot. Second, secure the rope.

Ryan attempted to raise his left foot to free his leg from the ivy. This proved unsuccessful. Ryan then carefully crouched down to release the ivy by hand. Now in a crouching position, Ryan had almost released the ivy with his left hand. But he had lost his reference point and balance. His unconscious brother began to slide forward on his right shoulder a bit, causing a weight shift. Ryan slammed the tree trunk with his left hand to stop the forward motion.

Wham!

Luke gasped. "Ryan, you okay?"

"He's struggling." Aaron jumped onto a branch and sped upwards. "I'm going up!"

Suddenly Ryan and Derrick tumbled backwards from the tree branch. Charlotte was unsuccessful at arresting their rapid, uncontrolled descent. Ryan instinctively grabbed Derrick by the wrist while falling. Both came to a rest below Charlotte, about thirty-five feet above ground. Ryan was face down on a branch holding Derrick's left arm with his right hand.

Aaron climbed the cedar. "I'm almost there."

Derrick's left wrist began to slip out of Ryan's sweaty grip. "I'm losing him."

Madison cried and whispered softly. "Please don't."

The TSC helicopter passed overhead in a slow thirty-knot hover slightly below the Cessna 182 in a higher orbit.

Aaron was five feet below Derrick. "Hold on, Ryan!"

"He's slipping!"

Aaron precariously reached for Derrick's shirt.

Ryan whispered and cried. "I'm sorry, Derrick."

Derrick's wet wrist and hand slipped from Ryan's sweaty grip.

Aaron held the shirt as it ripped from Derrick's torso.

Slam! Bang! Crash!

Derrick violently crashed through four branches during his thirty-five-foot fall. Antoine, Luke, and Thomas caught Derrick's limp body before impacting the forest floor.

Kiche immediately broke free of Gigi's grip to lick Derrick's wounds before Ruby pulled her back.

The boys gently placed Derrick flat on the ground.

Madison leapt to his side in tears.

Charlotte descended from the cedar and ran to untie Jefferson.

Aaron helped Ryan climb down before Ryan could visually acquire the blood on Derrick in the dark.

Gloria found a puncture wound on his chest that bubbled out blood with each breath. "Charlie, can you ride Derrick to Peaksville Hospital?"

Charlotte nodded affirmatively and mounted Jefferson.

Gloria examined the rhythmic bubbling. "Sucking chest wound. Charlie, do you have duck-tape?"

Charlotte reached into her saddle bag and tossed a roll. "Here!"

"Aaron, rip me three pieces, each four inches long!"

Luke and Antoine helped.

Gloria Becker covered the sucking chest wound with her PHS student ID card. She secured three pieces of tape, allowing Derrick's lungs to exhale through the hole, but not inhale.

"Done!" Gloria yelled. "Onto the horse!"

Thomas, Antoine and Luke quickly lifted Derrick onto Jefferson.

Ryan hugged Derrick tightly and cried. "I got you now buddy. I got you now. It's okay."

Aaron had to release Ryan's grip to allow the boys to secure his brother.

Derrick, bleeding from his right ear and nostrils, opened his eyes and laboriously whispered to Ryan. "Tell Marcus I'm sorry."

Madison sobbed. "I love you, Derrick."

Derrick looked down at Madison and smiled.

Charlotte secured her grip and galloped away to Peaksville.

Ryan cried on his knees. "I'm sorry, brother! I wasn't strong enough."

N ightfall approached too quickly.
Grace reassembled our tent under Rainbow Bridge.
I built our Sunday night campfire. "Got cold. Didn't it?"

"That just means you have to work harder to keep me warm."

The cool breeze picked up from the east. The cedar trees near Rainbow Bridge swayed and sang in unison. Grace and I looked up and admired the natural beauty of The Forbidden Zone.

"Grace, what kind of trees are those again?"

"Cedars. You should know. Your little brother is single-handedly saving Peaksville Forest from invasive parasitic ivy.

"Cedars, huh? They seem to be talking to us."

"What do you think they are saying, Marcus?"

"I don't know. I never really listened to them."

R yan entered the ER lobby of Peaksville Hospital and yelled. "Derrick! Where's Derrick Flynn? Where's my brother?"

Charlotte quickly walked up to Ryan and hugged him. "I rode as fast as I could."

Ryan examined the pitiful expression of Charlotte. "No way, Charlie. Don't talk like that. Knock it off! I need to talk with Derrick. I have something to ask him. Let me talk to Derrick!"

The Peaksville children filled the lobby. Ryan watched distraught Charlotte shake her head 'no' at Madison.

Madison wailed helplessly.

Ryan cried. "No Charlie! Don't shake your head! Don't be doing that stuff. Where's Derrick?"

Nurse Light lovingly approached Ryan. "I'll take you to see your brother."

Ryan quickly hugging Mrs. Light. "Thank God you're here, Mrs. Light. Derrick's okay, right?"

Nurse Light led Ryan towards Derrick's ER room. "Your parents are on their way. Ryan sweetie, normally we wait to notify parents first."

"No." Ryan interrupted. "Stop talking like that. Just take me to my brother. I need to speak with Derrick, Nurse Light."

Nurse Light showed Ryan the Pediatric ER room with Derrick covered. "Derrick passed away upon arrival. His lungs were punctured and filled with blood. We couldn't save him. I'm so sorry, Ryan."

Ryan slowly walked towards his brother Derrick who was fully-draped in a white cloth in the small room.

The other children gathered in the doorway near Nurse Light as the Bell 407 could be heard orbiting overhead.

Ryan cried as he hugged the young, lifeless body of Derrick Flynn. "I'm sorry, little brother. It was my fault. You didn't do anything wrong."

Ruby, Charlotte, Brianna, Amy and Emma slowly approached Ryan and placed their hands upon his back as he wept miserably.

Gloria and Madison gently placed their hands upon Derrick's feet and sobbed loudly.

Luke, Aaron, Antoine, D'Andre, and Thomas remained near the doorway in deference to Ryan.

Nurse Light remained outside consoling young Jack, Gigi, and Chloe.

Ryan held Derrick's lifeless hand. "I'm so sorry."

Twelve-year-old Jack Kernan tearfully prepared for bed as the TSC Cessna 182 conducted its low, round-the-clock Sunday night search patterns over the Peaksville neighborhood homes.

Amy brushed her hair after showering. "I can't believe Derrick is gone."

Emma tucked Jack into his bed. "Derrick mentioned a terrible headache before he died."

"I heard that." Amy said.

"Do you both still have headaches?" Emma asked.

Amy nodded. "Every day. Waking up is the worst."

Jack nodded his head affirmatively as Emma scratched his back.

Emma reached into her backpack. "I don't have them."

Amy watched attentively. "Since when?"

"Wednesday."

Jack sat up in his bed.

Emma showed them the three-pound, hockey puck-shaped shiny magnet.

"Take turns wearing this on your leg tonight," Emma said.

Amy asked examined the strange metal object. "On our leg? Why? What is it?"

"It's a magnet. A dangerously strong magnet. Max Burns needs it in homeroom. Tell nobody. Do not thank Max. He thinks I borrowed it for myself only."

"Is this how you smoked the 400m and 1600m races on Friday?"

"I think so."

"How does it cure headaches?" Amy asked pressing it up to her calf.

"It just does." Emma shrugged. "At least it cured mine."

Amy looked at her little brother. "Jack, you first."

Emma slid the volleyball kneepad over Jack's calf and slid the magnet inside the kneepad.

The TSC airplane passed over their roof.

Emma kissed Jack goodnight and set an alarm. "Leave this on as you sleep, Jack. I'll set my alarm for two o'clock in the morning. Then it's Amy's turn until breakfast."

W e lay on our backs next to the campfire under Rainbow Bridge. "I've never seen so many stars."

Grace quietly rested in the moonlight. "Must be millions of them."

"Look!" I pointed. "A shooting star!"

Grace watched it shoot across the North Idaho big sky. "Beautiful. And just like that, now it's gone."

"Too fast for its own good."

"What do you mean?" Grace asked.

"The other stars get to shine forever. That shooting star should have maintained a low profile."

Grace disagreed. "Maybe the shooting star knew something the other stars didn't know. Maybe it spread magical stardust into the universe."

"Now it's extinguished."

Grace kissed me. "But its memory lives forever."

CHAPTER TWENTY-FOUR

M r. Kernan greeted Amy, Emma, and Jack at the breakfast table. "You three are up early."

Amy kissed her dad. "We feel great. No headaches!"

Mr. Kernan smiled. "Fantastic. How about you, Jack?"

Jack walked to his chair with a waffle, big smile, and 'thumbs up.'

Emma held the three-pound magnet. "Ask us why, Dad."

"Why?"

"Amy and Jack wore this magnet on our legs last night. No morning headache. First time in five years."

Mr. Kernan stopped eating. "Doesn't make sense. On your leg?"

Emma handed him the magnet. "Max Burns loaned it to me Wednesday. Five days, headache-free for me. Check it out. But don't break your fingers."

Mr. Kernan examined the strength of the magnet against his keychain. After dislodging his keys, he tossed the puck-shaped object in the air towards the refrigerator. The magnet accelerated and slammed against it creating a report like a gunshot.

Mr. Kernan laterally slid the magnet to remove it from the formerly dent-free refrigerator. "Does the TSC know about this?"

Emma stuffed the magnet in her backpack. "Max Burns already got in trouble. Don't tell anyone, Dad."

Amy lifted her backpack. "Off to school, Dad."

Emma smiled. "Four weeks until graduation."

Mr. Kernan received kisses from Emma and Amy and a high-five from young Jack before they walked out the door. "I love you!"

Mr. Burns slowly passed two hundred feet over the Kernan home in his TSC Bell 407 helicopter.

The retired Navy pilot wandered into the family room and reminisced about his twin daughters' Junior Olympic trophies accrued during their healthy years. He popped in a VCR home video cassette to listen to the sound of Jack's voice.

"Rise and shine!" Grace read note six aloud as we packed our tent under Rainbow Bridge. "Bright to your right, turn west at the tower, and track to the trestle."

I looked at my father's Army Ranger compass. "Still spinning."

Grace playfully spun me so I faced north, tapped my right shoulder, and pointed at the sunrise. "Who needs a compass when you have the sun?"

I stuffed our sleeping bags, secured our backpack zippers, and extinguished our campfire embers. "Before we go deeper into the TFZ, do you still have the other five notes?"

Grace smiled, sat down, patted the rocky surface next to her, and pulled the notes from her pocket. "Let's review them. Thanks for asking."

I sat in the cool morning breeze of the TFZ.

"Note one. The cure to the symptoms is simply mine."

Deer in the headlights. I wasn't good at riddles.

"Note two. Carefully cross the stream to clean the stream."

North Idaho mountain streams were naturally clean.

"Note three. The source of your symptoms is drawn to the cure."

Note to self. Don't enroll in Modern American Riddles 101 in college.

"Note four. Travel right into the light, before the night, above the white, under the rainbow."

For the record, the note was over the rainbow. Not under.

Grace stood up to recite the next one. "My favorite. He will guide you along the best pathway and watch over you."

"Never did see that leprechaun." I stood up and donned my backpack. "What's next, Sacajawea?"

"North to the tower."

"Hopefully it's a tower of chocolate-chip cookies."

Grace smiled.

. . .

Nurse Light hugged Ryan Flynn in her Peaksville High School office. "Oh, Ryan. I'm so sorry. Derrick was such a good, wonderful boy."

Ryan sat and prepared for his Monday morning TSC shot. "Thank you, Mrs. Light. Derrick always loved you like a second mother."

Nurse Light held a needle in her right hand. "You didn't need to attend school today."

Other students entered the nurse's office. "I wanted to be with friends. I couldn't stop crying at home. So, I came to school."

Nurse Light leaned over Ryan to administer the shot. "Well, this week's TSC shot won't hurt a bit."

Ryan sat still. "That was easy. Didn't even feel it."

Nurse Light hugged Ryan again then cycled through the Peaksville students one by one.

Amy watched and waited. She always went last, hoping Nurse Light would run out of shots. Something was different about Nurse Light's technique. Amy sat and carefully observed the shots administered to Emma, Luke, Charlotte, Gloria, Brianna and others. When it was her turn, Amy broke her routine. This time, Amy carefully watched Nurse Light's hands. Nurse Light attempted to shield Amy's view with her elbow.

"Um, ouch?" Amy joked.

Nurse Light smiled and winked at Amy. "Goodbye, funny girl."

Amy smiled and walked out.

Amy quickly caught Emma, Charlotte, and Brianna in the hallway. "They were fake."

"What was fake?" Emma replied.

Amy ripped off their bandages. "The shots. She didn't stick any of us. I watched. No blood."

Emma looked at her arm. "Mrs. Light faked our TSC shots this week?"

Brianna agreed. "I noticed she shielded more than usual. And no pain this time!"

Charlotte examined her arm. "Why?"

Amy shrugged. "I don't know."

Mr. Kernan dialed his phone from his living room.
"Hello?"

"Bud? It's me, Jack Kernan."

"Good morning, Jack."

"Are you still the local TSC President?"

"TSC Chief Pilot, also. You should fly with us, Jack. Great pay. Great benefits.

No aircraft carrier to land on during a South China Sea typhoon, but Rug and I try to keep it fun."

"No, thanks, Bud. I'm calling about the children. You're aware of the unexplained medical problems with Peaksville children since 2013?"

"We think we may have it narrowed down to bioterrorism and intentional contamination of the Peaksville reservoir. That investigation is ongoing. We poke holes in the sky daily looking for bad guys. What's up?"

Mr. Kernan explained. "Here's the deal. Amy, Emma, and Jack Jr. wore this large magnet on their legs overnight. This morning, no headache, stomach pain, fatigue or chest pain. Apparently, Emma borrowed it from Max Burns. They say 'if you see something, say something.' I just figured the TSC should know."

"Thanks for sharing, Jack. I'll take it from here. Oh, and please don't mention the magnet to anyone else. Citizens tend to get hysterical easily."

"Thanks, Bud."

Mr. Light hung up his phone and called Mr. Burns.

"Rug, it's Bud. We got problems."

W e hiked north for two hours in the Monday morning TFZ sun. Grace looked ahead. "That must be the tower."

"That's just a rock."

"A towering rock."

"I figured it would be man-made."

Grace examined the fifty-foot-diameter natural rock structure towering nearly one hundred feet above the rocky, shale surface. "It's amazing."

"So now we turn west."

Grace agreed. "Yes."

"My compass is still spinning," I said.

North Idaho was situated 49 degrees north, placing us slightly closer to the North Pole than the Equator. The noon sun, well south of us, was somewhat unreliable for navigation.

Grace evaluated the sun's position. "Then how do we find the trestle?"

I smiled and sat down. "Ask me at three o'clock. For now, what are you doing for lunch?"

Grace cheerfully replied. "No plans!"

"Join me for lunch at the Rock Tower?" I asked.

Grace sat on a boulder. "A lunch date?"

I reached into my bag, prepared two PBJ sandwiches with my folding tool and handed one to Grace.

"A hobo multi-utensil combo tool." Grace sighed. "How romantic."

. . .

Mr. Kernan entered Peaksville Bread Company restaurant at noon. "Thanks for coming, fellas."

Mr. Bartholomew kindly replied. "Our pleasure, Jack."

Mr. Flynn, Mr. Becker and Mr. Epley were already seated.

Mr. Kernan first addressed Mr. Flynn. "Frank, my dear friend. Peaksville is heartbroken over the loss of Derrick."

Mr. Becker solemnly contributed condolences. "Such an amazing young boy."

"Thanks everyone. Derrick always enjoyed the friendship of all of your children."

The waitress brought five iced teas to the table.

"What's on your mind, Jack?" Mr. Epley asked.

"It's about our families. It's about Peaksville's unexplained childhood illnesses. Emma borrowed a magnet from Max Burns. Our children wore it on their legs. It cured their headaches overnight."

Mr. Flynn whispered. "A magnet?"

Mr. Bartholomew lowered his drink. "On their legs?"

Mr. Becker clinched his fist. "Those damn TSC shots are supposed to alleviate the symptoms."

Mr. Epley shook his head. "What the hell is going on in Peaksville?"

Mr. Kernan scanned the restaurant and quietly pulled a letter from his folder. "I drafted a letter from Peaksville parents to Congresswoman Abby Walker. I'm requesting a Congressional Investigation."

Mr. Flynn pulled out a pen. "Where do I sign, Jack?"

Tony Murdstone's father suddenly approached their table. "Hey fellas!"

Mr. Kernan instinctively stowed the letter to Abby Walker. "Hey, how's the microwave business?"

"Heating up," Mr. Murdstone said expecting a laugh.

Zero laughter.

Mr. Murdstone stood at their table as five seconds of uncomfortable silence elapsed. "Hey, you all look busy. Take care."

Mr. Flynn whispered. "Never did like that guy."

Mr. Becker, a Marine Corps veteran, broadcasted as if he was speaking over gunfire and mortar rounds. "He sat alone in his car last week for three hours near the park where Jack, Chloe and Gigi play were playing."

Mr. Kernan looked around and whispered. "Definitely something strange about the Murdstone family."

. . .

D ean Michaels initiated the three o'clock announcements as the TSC helicopter passed over Peaksville High School's roof. "Good afternoon, Peaksville students. Today is Monday. Only nineteen school days remaining. There was another attempted child abduction on Saturday. Also, the search continues for the suspects targeting the Peaksville reservoir and water supply. All areas west of The Meadow remain off limits. Caves are off-limits. School's out. Be safe out there."

Emma noticed Ben Light and Tony Murdstone creeping around during dismissal. Still in possession of the magnet, Emma eluded interaction with Max. Emma quickly slammed her locker and defiantly shouted to Amy, Brianna, and Ruby. "Let's go swim!"

Kiche, like clockwork, playfully intercepted Ruby in the schoolyard as she walked to the Peaksville Creek rope swing. "How's my baby girl?"

Brianna joked as Kiche wagged and licked. "That's a big baby!"

Max intended to retrieve the magnet from Emma, but the girls quickly entered The Meadow. Max tried to follow Emma into the restricted area.

Mr. Burns pulled into a slow hover over the rule-breaking high school students.

Max looked up and returned to Peaksville. "Dang."

Charlotte and Chloe escorted Jack and Gigi to the Epley farm.

Antoine Jordan observed that Max stopped at Peaksville Creek under his father's Bell 407. Antoine presumed that Emma may have still had the mysterious object. Antoine crossed the rope swing, hiked west towards Liberty Lake, and planned to speak with Emma privately.

G race woke under the southern face of the Rock Tower leaning on her mountaineering backpack. "Marcus, wake up."

"How long did I sleep?"

Grace nervously signaled and whispered. "In the thicket. Something moved."

I slowly sat up. "What was it?"

"A four-legged animal. Bigger than a large dog. Wolf-sized. Behind those rocks."

I looked at the southwesterly sun for situational awareness. "We better go."

Grace held my hand and whispered. "Let's get to the trestle."

I quietly donned my backpack, helped Grace with her straps, and faced west. "Let's roll."

We cautiously evacuated and scanned the area for wildlife.

Grace finally spoke after a ten-minute westward hike. "Train tracks."

"Now we're cooking."

Grace silently walked westward another ten minutes. "It didn't move like a dog."

"Say again?"

"That animal at the Rock Tower. It moved like —"

"Like what?" I asked.

"Like a cat."

CHAPTER TWENTY-FIVE

Luke, Aaron, D'Andre and Thomas joined the girls for a Monday swim in Liberty Lake.

Antoine played fetch with Kiche on the shore and hoped to catch Emma alone.

Amy swam up to the boys. "Hey boys! How would you categorize me? A nine or a ten? Or maybe an eleven? Just be honest."

The TSC Cessna 182 buzzed overhead and initiated a three hundred-foot, thirty-degree angle of bank orbit.

"Do you require the answer in decimal or fraction format?" Aaron, the likely Class of 2020 Valedictorian, rubbed his chin. "I would need to take a good look at your hypotenuse to solve this equation accurately."

Amy treaded water towards Aaron. "Careful what you ask for, Einstein."

"Be right back." Emma quietly paddled to shore.

Brianna laughed. "Amy, you make me forget all about my headache."

Emma climbed out of Liberty Lake and walked to her backpack. Antoine nonchalantly joined Emma behind The Boxcar under a canopy of trees. Emma scanned the area.

Ben Light, hiding behind a nearby tree, eluded her sight.

"Antoine." Emma whispered and handed Antoine the magnet. "Wear this on your calf tonight in bed using a volleyball kneepad. Wake up at two in the morning and put it on D'Andre's leg. I *need* this in homeroom tomorrow. Promise me you'll tell nobody."

Antoine hid the magnet under The Boxcar. "I promise."

Antoine and Emma heard a stick break in the woods and paused to listen.

Emma looked around for five seconds. "Probably an animal."
Max rapidly approached The Boxcar from The Meadow and yelled. "Emma!"
Antoine instinctively departed for Liberty Lake to join the others.
Emma greeted Max, smiled and whispered. "Hey, I forgot it. Sorry. Is tomorrow okay?"
The TSC helicopter roared over the treeline at two hundred feet.
Max looked up. "Dammit, Emma. My dad's flying angry again."
Emma futilely donned her 'I'm sorry' face. "Tomorrow?"
Max sighed, angrily spun and briskly walked home to Peaksville.

W e trekked west on the old railroad tracks for ten minutes. "Is that a trestle?"
"That's a trestle," Grace replied.
I stepped onto the decommissioned train bridge and cautiously peered below into the ravine. "Is it safe?"
Grace, blessed with cat-like situational awareness, picked up a jelly jar. "Marcus! Another note!" Grace removed the note and set the jar down. "Carefully cross, track the track, right at the roar to the ropes."

CAREFULLY CROSS,
TRACK THE TRACK,
RIGHT AT THE ROAR
TO THE ROPES.

G race inspected the stability of the railway bridge. "Okay. Simple. Right at the roar."
We commenced the trestle passage, two hundred feet over the river.
"What roar? What ropes?" I asked.
No response.
I looked down the railroad tie gaps. We were so high, we couldn't hear the whitewater rapids below. "What if a train comes?"
No response.
"Grace?"
Grace smiled.
I carefully walked forward, step by step. "Does the idea of a train make you smile?"

"Don't be silly, Marcus. This broken-down, old bridge can't hold a train."
Not a comforting response.

L uke threw a football with Aaron, Thomas and Antoine in Liberty Lake. "I
miss Derrick."

"Me too." Aaron caught the football. "Life isn't fair."

Antoine treaded water. "I hope Marcus and Grace return soon."

"Poor Marcus." Luke nodded. "It's just too sad to think about."

Aaron errantly skipped the football up and out of Liberty Lake towards The
Boxcar. "Whoops, sorry Antoine!"

Antoine yelled over the thunderous sound of the TSC Bell 407 helicopter. "No
worries! I'll get it!" He ran up the slope from the water, retrieved the football, and
punted towards Thomas, Aaron and Luke in Liberty Lake.

Luke yelled and swam to the ball. "I got it!"

"I'll be right down!" Antoine wandered behind The Boxcar to verify his
magnet hiding place. "Emma?" Antoine signaled for Emma to swim ashore.

Emma paddled ashore on her inner tube and approached dripping wet.
"What's up?"

"You moved it?"

"You're joking."

"Why would I joke?"

"You lost it? Already? You swam with it?"

"You saw me hide it. Right here. Remember?"

"You swam with it! It's at the bottom of Liberty Lake! That was a rock quarry.
It's gone forever. You loser! Totally irresponsible! You idiot! Max is going to
kill me!"

"Emma." Antoine whispered. "I swear —"

"Don't *ever* talk to me again, loser! *Ever!*" She grabbed her backpack and
began walking home through The Meadow.

Antoine cried and whispered. "I hid it right here."

Emma angrily exclaimed over the helicopter rotor noise. "I said don't talk to
me, loser!"

W e continued westward in the Sunday evening sunlight deeper into The
Forbidden Zone. The rusty railroad tracks converged into a small river.

I stopped to throw some rocks into the rushing water on the right. "I'm hungry,
Grace."

"Yep, my stomach's growling, too."

I threw another rock into the whitewater rapids. "Tell me if your stomach roars."

Grace looked around. "What sound does a river make?"

My skipping rock didn't skip as intended. "Splash?"

"Does a river roar?"

"Right at the roar." I laughed and threw another rock in the river. "Good call, Sacajawea. Hidden in plain sight. Then where are the ropes?"

Grace looked around and secretly discovered the next checkpoint. "Feeling sporty?"

"Not particularly. Why?"

Grace led me to the river. "Surprise!"

I saw the old ropes. "Oh, hell no!"

We hiked down the loose, rocky shale bank towards the river. Three questionable ropes were suspended ten feet over the fast-moving mountain river.

Grace smiled. "Tell you what, next person who finds a jelly jar is awesome."

I looked around.

Grace stopped me. "No looking. First make the deal."

"Deal." I scanned around quickly.

Grace immediately pointed and yelled. "A jelly jar!"

I didn't share her enthusiasm. "First of all, you cheated. Second of all, the note is going to tell us to cross this rope bridge."

She smiled and read the note. "Carefully cross the stream to clean the stream. The cure to the symptoms is simply mine."

CAREFULLY CROSS THE STREAM TO CLEAN THE STREAM. THE CURE TO THE SYMPTOMS IS SIMPLY MINE.

"We've been down this road before."

"This is the stream, Marcus!"

I inspected the forty-foot ropes tied to cedar trees on either bank. One lower rope appeared to be designed to support a person's feet. Two upper ropes served as left and right handholds. The clear, cold, four feet deep water easily exceeded five miles per hour.

"Crossing the stream cleans the stream? I call bullcrap. This stream is already clean. It's mountain spring water and melted snow."

Grace carefully scanned the mountain rising above the opposing riverbank. "It's a riddle, silly."

"What are you looking at?"

Grace pointed upwards. "Up there! The cure to the symptoms is simply mine!"

"Explain."

Grace grabbed the two upper ropes and stepped onto on the lower rope. "Marcus, the word 'mine' is not a possessive pronoun. It's a noun, silly."

B en Light waited for his father to taxi into the Peaksville Municipal Airport fuel pits.

Mr. Light secured his engine, chocked his nose wheel, grounded the Cessna 182 to a grounding station using a metal cable, and slung the fuel hose over his shoulder. "Hello, Ben. How's my favorite TSC Cadet?"

"Your favorite TSC Cadet just recovered something dangerous."

"Dangerous?"

"Dangerous contraband."

Mr. Light commenced fueling with 100 Octane Low Lead gasoline. "How dangerous?"

"As dangerous as one hundred dollars."

Mr. Light lectured his son. "Ben. You already get a large TSC Cadet salary."

"No deal?"

Mr. Light retrieved one hundred dollars from his wallet. "Your older brother never acted like this."

Ben counted the cash twice, pocketed the cash in his jeans, and handed the three-pound magnet to his father. "Brian's gone. Remember, Dad?"

"Where did you get this?"

"Antoine Jordan lost it near Liberty Lake. I found it. Fair and square."

Mr. Light looked down and inspected the large magnet as 100LL began to spill. "Dad. You're killing the concrete."

Mr. Light rapidly secured the rusty nozzle. "Damn."

Ben exited the Peaksville Municipal Airport flightline one hundred dollars richer.

Mr. Light immediately called Mr. Burns. "Rug, meet me on the flight line."

"What's up?"

"Something's definitely going on in Peaksville."

"Where are you?"

"Fuel pits."

"See you in five mikes."

CHAPTER TWENTY-SIX

I crossed the Rope Bridge ten paces behind Grace. "Careful, sweetie."

Grace looked back at me from the halfway point. "Just a walk in the park."

I didn't share her flippant, easy-going enthusiasm. "Look straight ahead."

Grace reached the west bank of the swift river. "Piece of cake!"

I got within ten feet of the west bank. "Is the rope supposed to droop this close to the water?"

"Shouldn't have brought that rock collection in your backpack."

I tried to ignore the condition of the three ropes, the cold river rushing under my hiking boots, and Grace's inopportune rock collection joke.

"If I fall in," I looked downstream. "You have to rescue me."

"You're fine. Relax."

"Fine, she says." I nervously continued then leapt from the ropes onto the north bank into Grace's arms. "I made it." I expected Grace to celebrate with me!

Grace obliviously turned and calmly pointed uphill. "Look, an old sign. West Peaksville Neodymium Mine."

M r. Kernan heard crying after dinner after the TSC Bell 407 passed overhead. "You okay, Emma?"

Emma wept in the family room.

Amy explained. "Emma never returned the magnet to Max."

"Why?"

"Antoine lost it."

"Does Max know?"

Emma wiped her eyes. "No."

"Tomorrow, you should apologize."

Emma cried. "Here's the worst part. I yelled at Antoine today so horribly. I called him a loser and an irresponsible idiot."

"Then you should to apologize to Antoine, also."

"Okay, Dad."

Mr. Kernan sat down. "My chest has been bothering me for a few hours."

"You okay, Dad?" Amy asked.

"I'm fine." Mr. Kernan rested on the sofa. "Everyone still headache free?"

Jack responded with a bright-eyed 'thumbs up' as the TSC Cessna 182 flew down their street at three hundred feet.

I joked about the abandoned, partially boarded-up West Peaksville Neodymium Mine. "Why did it have to be a mine. Why couldn't a *mime*?"

Grace laughed. "For real?"

"Yeah, the mime could pantomime the cure."

"I'll take a mine over a mime any day."

I inspected the old, wooden-beamed frame surrounding the entrance. "Either way, we're in a box."

Grace ventured deeper inside.

I declined to follow. "Seems dangerous, Gracie."

Grace found a torch, matchbox, and can of petroleum strategically placed at the entrance.

I laughed. "A torch? Hasn't 'he who watches over us' ever heard of a flashlight?"

Grace smiled and held up another note. "Let's find out."

"Where'd you get that?"

Grace pointed at an empty jar and read the note. "The source of your symptoms is drawn to the cure. In forty-eight hours, you will be unattractive, invisible, and free."

THE SOURCE OF YOUR SYMPTOMS
IS DRAWN TO THE CURE.
IN FORTY-EIGHT HOURS, YOU WILL BE
UNATTRACTIVE, INVISIBLE, AND FREE.

"**U**nattractive? Is someone inside waiting to beat us with an ugly stick?"

Grace laughed. "Don't you want to be free, Marcus?"

"I'm already free. But invisible sounds fun."

Grace gave me a stern look. "What if we aren't really free? What if we only think we are free?"

I scoffed at her suggestion. "Trust me. I live in North Idaho. I'm free."

Grace shrugged.

I removed a flashlight from my backpack, flipped it on, and began to inspect the mine. Suddenly, the metal flashlight jumped from my hand, traveled sideways, and slammed onto the rocky wall of the cavern entrance.

Wham!

Grace touched the metal flashlight, now stuck to the cave wall.

"Woah."

Grace pulled the flashlight from the wall using all of her strength.

I looked at Grace. "What kind of mine is this again?"

Emma stuffed her completed homework into her backpack and prepared for bed.

Amy walked into her bedroom and whispered. "Emma, Max is knocking."

"Thanks." Emma apprehensively answered the front door. "Hi Max!"

"Where is it?"

Emma deflected with a fake yawn. "Max, it's nine o'clock on a Monday night. Can I bring it to school?"

"No, you can't bring it to school."

Emma froze.

"Do you know *why* you can't bring it to school?"

Emma nervously replied as the TSC helicopter orbited. "Why?"

"Because Antoine lost it, you broke your promise, and my dad showed it to me an hour ago. That's why."

"Mr. Burns has the magnet? I don't understand."

"You promised you wouldn't share it. There are consequences."

Max turned and walked away.

The Bell 407 green and red navigation lights and white strobe lights illuminated the dark street. Rotor wash fanned Emma's trees.

Max yelled. "Don't act like a victim, Emma!"

Emma cried and yelled over the engine noise. "I had to share it. That expectation wasn't fair!"

Max continued walking down the street. "Consequences!"

. . .

O ur campfire outside the West Peaksville Neodymium Mine slowly perished. I scanned the dark sky as the cold air from higher altitudes began to descend down the mountain. "No more shooting star."

Grace cheerfully lay on her back looking up. "It's lighting up the sky somewhere. Just as bright. Just as fast."

The cedar trees sang in the breeze. "Why does my brother believe he can save all the trees from the parasitic ivy?"

No answer.

"Do you believe this old mine holds the cure?"

No answer.

"Do you *really* believe it, Grace?"

Grace carefully crafting her answer in the cool evening breeze. "My father told me his Marine Corps unit won all of their battles because they *believed* they would win."

I looked to the sky. "Nobody is shooting at us in Peaksville."

Grace rested her head on my shoulder. "I can't explain. I just know that someone is attempting to save the children of Peaksville."

"Save us from what? We aren't in danger."

"You mentioned Mr. Flynn taught you the sheepdog lesson."

"Yes."

"Did he teach you about wolves and sheep, Marcus?"

"Yeah, why?"

"Gloria, Gigi and I heard that lesson many times also. My father's Marine Corps version is probably similar to Mr. Flynn's Army Ranger version."

Grace lay on her back and gazed at the stars.

"Explain yourself."

"Promise you'll listen?"

I sat up. "Yes."

"I don't want to hurt your feelings."

"I'm thick-skinned. Like *Teflon*."

Grace sat up. "Okay, here it is, Marcus. A good sheepdog doesn't simply bury his head in the sand. A good sheepdog acknowledges that wolves exist. A good sheepdog knows history. A good sheepdog can identify a wolf in *sheep's* clothing. A good sheepdog can also identify a wolf in *sheepdog's* clothing. A good sheepdog is alert 24/7. A good sheepdog protects the flock."

We lay back down and looked up at the stars.

I needed to be a better sheepdog.

CHAPTER TWENTY-SEVEN

First thing Tuesday morning, Dean Michaels invited Amy Kernan into his Peaksville High School office. "Is everything okay? Have you been feeling okay? No problems at home?"

Nurse Light quietly sat near Amy in his school office.

Amy, finally headache-free, nervously replied. "What's this about?"

Dean Michaels initiated small talk. "What's that book in your hand?"

"*Fahrenheit 451.*"

Dean Michaels looked at Nurse Light. "Didn't we ban that book?"

Nurse Light shrugged.

Dean Michaels studied the book cover and looked at Amy. "What's it about?"

"Book burners and tyranny disguised under the color of law."

Dean Michaels momentarily paused to evaluate Amy's response. "Anyhow, I just wanted to make sure that you and Emma are doing alright. Jack is being interviewed in Peaksville Middle School. Has the Kernan family been feeling okay lately? Are you getting enough sleep? Your father is a military veteran. Is he getting the help he needs? I assume that PTSD is a horrible, horrible thing to live with. Things must be very stressful for him especially."

"What are you saying?"

"We can't legally tell you due to HIPPA laws. Just realize that the VA runs many outreach programs for veterans."

Amy looked at Nurse Light. "Huh?"

"How about Emma and Max. Are they still dating?"

Amy looked at Nurse Light again, stood up and walked to the door. "Ma'am, I'm going back to class."

"That will be all, Amy. You're excused. Remember that The Safety Corps offers free counseling and support for all Peaksville citizens."

E mma Kernan looked around and whispered in the hallway. "D'Andre. Brianna. Thomas. Come here."

Mr. Burns hovered noisily over Peaksville High School.

"Can't believe you and Max broke up," D'Andre said.

Emma whispered. "Bree, have you spoken with Antoine?"

Brianna nodded. "Yeah. Antoine cried this morning. What did you say to him yesterday?"

"Oh, God. Horrible things. I was so mean. I need to apologize after school at Liberty Lake."

D'Andre whispered. "Antoine feels really badly. He said he lost something of yours but can't find it. He's very sorry."

"I'm such a jerk. Tonight, I'll fix it," Emma said.

Brianna whispered. "Speaking of feeling badly, you guys have terrible headaches today?"

D'Andre replied. "Worse than ever."

Thomas replied. "Like an icepick."

Emma didn't reply, then she was saved by the bell. "Gotta go. Let's swim later."

D ean Michaels initiated a midday PA system announcement. His message was partially obscured by the sound of the TSC Cessna 182. "Peaksville students, just a quick announcement. Stomach aches and headaches have been reported today. Keep washing your hands. That's all."

Click!

Madison placed her lunch tray on the table. "Gloria, you're looking a little rough."

Gloria's head dropped forward.

"Gloria?" Charlotte asked.

No response.

Madison pointed. "Ryan!"

Gloria collapsed to the left from her lunch seat. Ryan dove sideways and prevented her head from striking the tile cafeteria floor.

Crash!

Ruby scrambled to her aid. "Gloria, are you okay?"

Brianna felt her forehead. "She's burning up."

Emma stood and ran towards the cafeteria kitchen. "I'll get ice."

Gloria slowly regained consciousness. "What happened?"

Madison comforted her friend. "You passed out."

Mr. Light executed another noisy low pass over the school roof.

Ben Light walked by the lunch table and looked upward. "Sound of freedom!"

Ryan gently held Gloria's head in his hands and looked at Ben. "What did that dipshit just say?"

Luke Bartholomew looked at Ryan. "Don't worry about him."

Aaron Webster whispered to Ryan. "We'll get him later."

Dean Michaels broadcasted his daily pre-dismissal announcements. "Good afternoon, Peaksville students. Today is Tuesday. The Safety Corps of Peaksville is recruiting new TSC Junior Cadets for the 2020-2021 school year. We are looking for motivated children that value their freedom. The TSC keeps our innocent citizens safe. Aviation training is available and encouraged. Accepting applications immediately. The TSC Air Patrol is searching for suspects who stole dangerous HAZMAT from the local hardware store. School's out. Be safe out there."

Amy slammed her locker. "Anyone get called to the office today besides Emma and me?"

"What did you war criminals do now?" Luke asked.

"Nothing," Amy said.

"It was creepy," Emma said.

Brianna laughed. "How creepy?"

Amy grabbed her backpack. "Dean Michaels questioned *both* of us about Max."

Brianna looked at Emma. "Why?"

Emma sighed. "We broke up last night, Bree."

"Dean Michaels knew? Yuck!"

D'Andre walked with Emma into the schoolyard. "Very strange."

"Sometimes the truth is stranger than fiction," Ruby said.

Mr. Burns noisily hovered over the schoolyard in a slow, left-hand orbit.

Aaron chuckled. "Dean Michaels just earned a starring role in my 2020 Cringe Compilation Video."

"That creep even asked Emma and me about our father," Amy said.

"Dang," Luke said.

Thomas scoffed. "Maybe he's concerned about the welfare of his student body."

Amy hugged Thomas and whispered into his ear. "Maybe you should be concerned about the welfare of *this* student body, Tommy Boy?"

Thomas froze.

Amy pulled Thomas closer. "Would you like to call me into *your* office?"

Brianna sighed. "Now *that's* creepy!"

Ruby giggled. "Better release Tommy Boy go before something happens, Amy."

Aaron nodded. "Congratulations, Amy. You, too, just made my Cringe Compilation."

Gloria laughed and rubbed her temples. "My headache is killing me. Swim with me, Amy."

Amy release her grip from Thomas. "That's a big 10-4, good buddy."

Charlotte smiled. "I'll swing by Peaksville Middle School to get Gigi, Jack and Chloe. See you later at Liberty Lake on horseback."

CHAPTER TWENTY-EIGHT

Antoine, Thomas and Aaron jumped off Deadman's Cliff in the afternoon sun in tandem.

Splash!

Luke performed multiple solo cannonballs off Weakman's Cliff.

Brianna, D'Andre, Gloria, Ruby, and the Kernan twins relaxed on inner-tubes on Liberty Lake.

Charlotte and the three sixth-graders arrived on horseback.

Emma finally mustered up the courage to apologize to Antoine. "I'm going to go say sorry now."

Aaron and Thomas waited in line for Antoine to jump in the water as Emma swam close to Deadman's Cliff and waited below in her innertube.

Mr. Light circled overhead at seventy-five knots in his Cessna 182.

Aaron yelled. "Hey Luke! Why don't you join the *men* up here?"

Luke defended himself. "Sorry, losers! The girls like *my* cannonballs! Not yours!"

Mr. Burns passed overhead at thirty knots in his Bell 407.

Aaron laughed. "Not a bad comeback from down there in the kiddie pool area, Luke!"

Antoine dizzily teetered on the edge of Deadman's Cliff.

Emma yelled from below. "Antoine is falling!"

Aaron and Thomas attempted to grab Antoine and failed.

Antoine clumsily fell twenty feet into Liberty Lake, submerged immediately and didn't surface.

Splash!

Emma hurled her innertube in Antoine's direction and vigorously swam at full speed. She dove underwater to find him and pulled him to the surface.

Emma instinctively initiated a water rescue.

Luke yelled. "Charlie! Antoine's out cold!"

Charlotte untied Jefferson and galloped to the shore.

Emma expertly side-kicked with Antoine's chin and face safely elevated.

Gigi harnessed Kiche ashore. "Wolfie, stay back, girl."

Ruby and Charlotte pulled Antoine ashore as Emma collapsed on dry land.

Brianna cried. "He's not breathing!"

Gloria Becker immediately performed CPR on Antoine utilizing her mother's Army medic training.

Brianna checked. "He's breathing again! And he has a pulse!"

Antoine was unconscious.

C harlotte pointed. "Chloe, you and DJ ride on Buckshot to Peaksville Hospital with me."

Luke and Aaron lifted Antoine's limp body onto Jefferson.

Emma, still exhausted from the water rescue, sobbed helplessly. "Antoine?"

Brianna cried. "Antoine, wake up!"

Charlotte directed the twelve-year-olds. "Gigi and Jack, ride Daisy to Mrs. Jordan. Tell her Antoine's hurt. Then ride to your mom, Gigi. Have them both meet us at Peaksville Hospital. Okay?"

"Got it, Charlie." Gigi replied from atop Daisy with Jack.

The noisy TSC airplane departed its overhead orbit.

Charlotte rode away with Antoine.

Emma screamed. "I'm sorry, Antoine! I'm sorry!"

A t six o'clock in Peaksville Hospital, Antoine's vital signs were stabilized. But he remained unconscious. D'Andre Jordan, Mrs. Jordan, Brianna Lopez, and Mrs. Becker sat at his bedside as others waited in the lobby.

Mr. Kernan arrived into the ER lobby. "Amy, what happened?"

Amy cried. "Dad, AJ passed out and fell in Liberty Lake."

"Emma rescued Antoine," Gloria said.

"Gloria performed CPR," Charlotte said.

Nurse Light smiled. "Then Charlotte rode Antoine to the ER. Jack, these kids are heroes."

"How's Antoine?"

Nurse Light uneasily whispered. "Still unconscious."

"Mr. Kernan, what the hell is going on in Peaksville?" Ryan Flynn said.

"I don't know. Congresswoman Abby Walker needs to investigate these daily headaches and heart problems you've experienced since 2013. She still hasn't responded."

Mr. Kernan handed his daughter one hundred dollars. "Amy, buy dinner for Mrs. Jordan, Mrs. Becker, and Nurse Light. Then buy pizza and soda for the children with the leftover money."

Amy took the cash. "Where are you going, Dad?"

"I'm going to get to the bottom of this."

"Sorry I'm late." Mr. Kernan joined Mr. Bartholomew, Mr. Epley, Mr. Flynn and Mr. Becker at Peaksville Bread Company.

"Any word from Abby?" Mr. Epley asked.

"No response. Our busy representative is not responding."

Mr. Becker angrily grumbled in his Marine Corps loud-talker voice. "Tokyo Abby's too busy bragging about gifting our hard-earned tax money to Peaksville Defense and Space Corporation, Peaksville Institutes of Health and PsytoSCOPE Nanotech Corporation."

"Jack, do you think Antoine's injury is related to Derrick's death?" Mr. Flynn asked quietly.

Mr. Kernan nodded affirmatively.

"How?" Mr. Flynn asked.

Mr. Kernan shrugged.

Mr. Epley saw Mr. Murdstone enter Peaksville Bread Company and quietly quipped. "Speaking of headaches —"

Mr. Murdstone overtly avoided eye contact with the five fathers. Mr. Kernan instinctively hid the rough draft of their second letter to Representative Walker.

Mr. Becker adjusted his USMC hat and expressed his thoughts aloud. "Murdstone's not a headache. He's a pain in the ass."

"Something's rotten in Peaksville," Pastor Bartholomew said.

"Can the TSC investigate this?" Mr. Epley asked.

Mr. Kernan nodded. "Bud Light said he would investigate."

Mr. Becker shook his head. "Do you trust that guy?"

Mr. Kernan paused. "Yes."

Grace lay back outside the West Peaksville Neodymium Mine entrance. "Can you believe we're spending our second night in an abandoned mine?"

"Better than a mud hut," I joked.

Grace sighed under the stars. "I guess this isn't torture."

I stoked our campfire embers with a long cedar branch. "Grace, do you think courage is hereditary?"

Grace carefully reflected for five seconds. "No."

"Why is my little brother Derrick courageous like my dad?"

She shrugged. "It could be learned."

"Why didn't I learn courage from my dad?"

"Maybe Derrick learned courage from you."

I disagreed. "But I don't consider myself courageous."

Grace paused. "Does Derrick consider himself courageous?"

"Probably not."

"Does your dad consider himself courageous?"

"Certainly not."

"Interesting."

"What's interesting?"

Grace lay in my arms in the cool mountain breeze. "Your modesty is interesting, Marcus. Some courageous people *pretend* to be humble. The Flynn family is different. Your modesty and humility is genuine."

M r. Light phoned Mr. Burns. "Rug, got a minute?"
      "Sure, Bud."

"Just got a call from General Voigt."

"At ten o'clock on a Tuesday night?"

"Queen Bee wants all five problems solved."

Mr. Burns paused. "Solved?"

Mr. Light confirmed. "Solved."

No response.

"You still there, Rug?"

"Yeah. I'm still here. When?"

"Queen Bee said immediately."

Mr. Burns digested the information. "It's going to be a rough week. All five?"

"All five." Mr. Light paused. "According to General Voigt, Queen Bee is unhappy with me."

"Damn. I'll notify Web and Nuke."

CHAPTER TWENTY-NINE

Ryan joked on Wednesday morning in Peaksville High School's student lounge before the first bell. "Looking kind of rough, Luke,"

"Tired. Couldn't sleep. The annoying TSC search plane and search helicopter must have flown down my street one hundred times last night."

Thomas was concerned. "Must have been another attempted child abduction or attempted reservoir poinsoning."

Ryan sighed. "Tommy Boy."

"What?"

Charlotte leaned forward over the table and whispered. "Seems odd to search all night in a subdivision."

Aaron concurred. "I agree with Charlie. The Bell 407 has a FLIR pod. Either you see a guy, or you don't. Why drive back and forth one hundred times?"

Charlotte asked. "Anyone know if Antoine woke up?"

Ruby shook her head negatively.

Brianna ran into the lounge crying with D'Andre. "Oh, God. Did you hear?"

"Hear what, Bree?" Aaron said.

"Mr. Kernan had a heart attack," Brianna said.

D'Andre cried. "He died in his sleep."

"Heart attack?" Charlotte asked.

"Mr. Kernan was fit as a fiddle," Ryan said.

"He just bought us pizza last night," Luke said.

"He just wrote our Congresswoman. Fighting for us kids," Ryan said.

"Is Antoine okay?" Aaron asked.

Brianna cried. "It's bad. Peaksville Hospital said Antoine's in a coma."

Ruby cried and hugged D'Andre and Brianna. "This is too sad."

Aaron whispered. "Ryan, check out Ben Light over there with Tony Murdstone. Ben just smiled at us and rubbed his eyes like he's crying."

Madison confirmed it. "Disgraceful. Nurse Light is so wonderful. Unlike Ben."

Ruby wiped her eyes. "Ben is so evil."

"I saw Ben, too." Gloria cried. "Was that really directed at us?"

Brianna nodded.

"That dipshit just signed his own death warrant," Ryan said.

"Good afternoon, Peaksville students. Today is Wednesday," Dean Michaels cheerfully announced on the Peaksville High School public address system at three o'clock. "Our town reservoir has apparently been intentionally contaminated. A boil order is in effect. Peaksville TSC is investigating. The contamination can induce severe headaches, heart problems or in severe cases, death. Peaksville State University Medical School recently released a study about heart health. They studied one thousand military veterans between the ages of eighteen and fifty-five. PSU learned that ninety minutes of daily outdoor activity can reduce the likelihood of heart problems by thirty-five percent. TSC Air Patrol is searching the area. School's out. Be safe out there."

"I'm not buying anything Michaels says." Aaron stood at the drinking fountain. "I smell horsecrap."

Luke stuffed his backpack with homework. "Yeah, why isn't this water fountain secured?"

Ryan obnoxiously gargled the water. "Peaksville water. Tastes great. Less filling."

Thomas exclaimed from the hallway as lockers slammed. "I wouldn't drink that! Dean Michaels said it's contaminated."

Luke laughed. "You trust Dean Michaels?"

"Of course," Thomas replied.

"Maybe Dean Michaels is contaminated," Aaron said.

Ryan exited Peaksville High School with Thomas under the slow-moving TSC helicopter. "Don't trust Dean Michaels, Tommy Boy."

"Said two dozen abducted kids in the Dean Michaels Dungeon," Aaron joked.

Thomas sighed. "Dean Michaels does *not* have a dungeon."

Brianna entered Antoine's Peaksville Hospital ER room with D'Andre. "Emma, we heard about your dad."

Emma hugged Brianna. "Oh, Bree!"

"Emma! How long have you been here?" D'Andre asked.

"Since noon. I need Antoine to wake up. I need to say sorry."

"Emma, we loved Mr. Kernan," D'Andre said.

"Thanks. Jack Junior found him this morning. Poor little guy."

"Heart attack?" Brianna asked.

"That's what the paramedic told us. But —"

"But what, Emma?" D'Andre asked.

"A few things. I called 911. Peaksville Ambulance arrived in less than sixty seconds. The paramedic verbalized that my father had a heart attack on my doorstep."

"What's wrong with that?"

"The 911 telephone conversation. I said we need an ambulance. No details. No names. I panicked and hung up. But these paramedics knew details about Dad."

"Suspicious," D'Andre said.

"One more thing. We found red burn marks on Dad's chest."

Amy and Jack arrived to Antoine's hospital room.

"From paramedic equipment?" Brianna asked.

Jack shook his head negatively and looked at his twin sisters.

Emma replied. "Paramedics didn't attempt to revive Dad."

Amy agreed. "There were four dime-sized red burns. Two in front near his heart, two on his back. They were *burns*!"

"What's happening to Peaksville?" D'Andre cried.

I successfully completed one hour of *unsuccessful* fishing near the abandoned West Peaksville Neodymium Mine. "It's officially been forty-eight hours. Am I unattractive, invisible and free yet?"

Grace joked. "Unattractive to the fish. Obviously!"

Okay, Grace burned me. I changed the subject. "Do you feel free yet?"

"Free of headaches, stomach pain, and chest pain. Also, I'm not waking up feeling like I'm in a sauna," Grace said.

"Same here. Then again, it's sixty-five degrees inside the mine."

"Maybe we found the cure, Marcus."

I patiently waited for a fish to bite my hook. "Okay, I'll bite. What's the cure?"

Grace shrugged. "Possibly the magnetic cave."

"Magnets don't cure people, Grace. Doctors cure people. Pharmaceutical drugs cure people. Biotech research cures people. Peaksville Institutes of Health cures people."

Grace laughed. "You sound like an advertisement. Are they paying you to say that?"

I sighed and reeled in my fishing line.

"I used to believe that stuff, Marcus. I can think more clearly without my daily headache. My opinions changed this weekend. Don't you have a different perspective now? Don't you *feel* differently? Don't you *think* differently?"

I shrugged and cast my line into the river. "Fair enough."

Grace whistled and hummed.

"You're going to scare the fish."

She laughed, looked at her watch and hummed quieter.

I changed the subject to stop the humming. "You think we're in trouble?"

Grace smiled. "We're home in bed sick. Influenza, right?"

"Good point."

Grace resumed her humming.

"Besides, what could they possibly do to us?" My fishing line was quickly taken out by my first trout. "When we're catching fish in the TFZ!"

Grace Becker laughed as I wrestled the trout. "Mr. Flynn would be proud, Marcus!"

CHAPTER THIRTY

A aron ran into homeroom at eight o'clock on Thursday morning. "Ruby! Oh God, Ruby! Horrible news! Mr. Becker and Mr. Flynn. They both died in their sleep! Heart attacks!"

Ruby cried, stood up and ran to the door. "How can that be, Aaron?"

Aaron shrugged.

Ruby pulled his hand. "Let's go see Nurse Light!"

Aaron and Ruby intercepted Brianna, Madison, Thomas, Emma and Amy in the hallway and told them the bad news.

They all continued to see Nurse Light as Dean Michaels calmly broadcasted on the PA system. "Peaksville High School water fountains are secured until further notice due to suspected terrorist contamination at Peaksville reservoir. TSC is investigating."

Aaron angrily responded as the students approached the Nurse's Office. "Horsecrap!"

Ruby hysterically cried. "Mrs. Light! Is it true? Marcus and Grace's fathers both died last night?"

Nurse Light tearfully replied. "Oh, Ruby. It's so much worse! Luke and Charlotte's fathers died last night, too."

Aaron angrily asked. "Mr. Bartholomew and Mr. Epley? How? Five healthy fathers died in two nights? Five fatal heart attacks?"

Thomas raised his hand before speaking. "Dean Michaels just said the water supply was —"

Aaron interrupted him with an angry stare.

The TSC airplane performed a low, slow pass over Peaksville High School.

"Nurse Light, what do you know? Please tell us," Aaron said.

"Aaron, I love you kids so much. Go to your homeroom. Just leave me here to cry."

Ruby, Amy, Emma, Madison, and Brianna hugged Mrs. Light as the children exited her office.

Aaron kicked a locker in the hallway in tears. "Nurse Light knows something. She doesn't like it. But she knows something. I'll find out what's going on. My dad volunteers with The Safety Corps."

"Good afternoon, Peaksville students. Today is Thursday," Dean Michaels broadcasted before afternoon dismissal. "Entering restricted areas west of school including the TFZ remains grounds for expulsion and inability to graduate. Peaksville TSC has removed the boil order but the search continues for reservoir contamination suspects. It's cold and flu season. Peaksville State University released a study recently revealing that regularly washing your hands before meals reduces mild to severe health problems by sixty percent and improves heart health by twenty percent. Reminder that the Peaksville TSC Junior Cadet program continues to accept applications for summer internships and the 2020-2021 school year. School's out. Be safe out there."

Aaron slammed his locker in anger and slung his backpack over his shoulder.

Emma exited school under Mr. Light's orbiting Cessna 182. "Aaron, swim with us!"

"First let's get Ryan, Luke, Gloria, Gigi, Charlotte and Chloe."

"I'll go with you," Emma said.

Aaron and Emma led their sad, grieving friends on a walk to Liberty Lake.

Madison greeted her friends who paddled to the middle of Liberty Lake on inner tubes. "We are so, so sorry."

Ruby Kyle cried to Ryan as he sobbed. "Ryan, you lost Derrick and your dad in the same week. Give me a hug, buddy."

Gloria tearfully joined her friends and treaded water. "How are we going to tell Marcus and Grace?"

"What do we tell them?" Ryan said.

"We tell them the truth," Luke said.

"Our fathers were murdered," Amy said.

Thomas disagreed. "That's pure speculation."

"We're burying six loved ones tomorrow and Antoine's in a coma, Tommy Boy," Aaron said. "Wake up and smell the coffee."

Ryan became angry. "Aren't you paying attention?"

Thomas argued. "It would be on the evening news if they were killed. Besides, the water supply was contaminated by terrorists."

Aaron laughed at Thomas. "Tommy Boy, you fainted and fell Saturday. Oh, let me guess, the flu? Or was it the water supply?"

"I was dehydrated."

Luke threw his arms up. "You can't have it both ways, Tommy Boy. Not enough water? Too much contaminated water? Which one is it?"

The TSC Bell 407 helicopter initiated a twenty-knot hover at one hundred feet over Liberty Lake.

Emma, careful not to lose her temper, scolded Thomas Stallworth. "Tommy Boy, something evil is going on. Admit it. You don't need to understand. Just admit something is wrong."

"See!" Thomas pointed as the rotor wash sprayed the children. "The TSC is looking for the terrorists."

Aaron watched Mr. Burns fly solo in the right seat and whispered to Ryan. "Humpty Dumpty didn't fall from the cedar tree. Humpty Dumpty was pushed."

Ryan whispered back while treading water. "How?"

Aaron shrugged. "I'll find out."

*S*plash!
    The swimmers immediately turned their heads to Deadman's Cliff.

Grace surfaced with a smile.

I yelled cheerfully and impacted the water.

Splash!

Gloria and Gigi cried. "Oh, Grace!"

I was excited to debrief our five-day TFZ expedition. "Happy Thursday, everyone!"

Grace and I paddled towards our sobbing friends.

I whispered to Grace as we swam closer. "Something is wrong."

Luke and Aaron maintained their composure.

"Tears!" Grace fearfully evoked an emotionally defensive posture. "You guys *really* missed us."

Ruby softly replied. "Of course, Grace."

I suspiciously scanned the group as Madison wept. "Madison, where's Derrick? I've never seen you two apart."

Madison responded with a loud, pitiful cry. "Oh, Marcus —"

Something *was* wrong. "Ryan, where's Derrick?"

"I tried so hard! It was my fault! I wasn't strong enough —"

Aaron interrupted Ryan. "It wasn't Ryan's fault. Ryan climbed sixty feet to save Derrick."

My heart sank. "Where's Derrick?"

Luke cried. "Marcus —"

I swam to Luke. "Say it."

"Derrick died. Saving the cedars."

I reflected silently and treaded water in the middle of Liberty Lake as a breeze rustled through the cedar trees. I angrily erupted with a powerful roar towards Peaksville Forest. "Derrick!"

"Come on." Ruby wisely made a suggestion. "Let's all swim ashore."

We cried and slowly paddled ashore on inner tubes holding hands.

Kiche playfully greeted everyone with a wagging tail and plenty of licks.

Gigi sobbed and hugged Kiche. "Oh, Wolfie."

It was like a dream. A nightmare. It didn't feel real. Derrick was gone.

Luke helped us enter The Boxcar.

Emma wept and looked at us. "Sit with us."

Amy wept. "There's more."

Grace cried and attempted to smile. "Better news?"

Amy shook her head negatively.

"Other news?"

Emma nodded and wept.

Ruby looked around. "Worse news."

Charlotte broke down crying and hugged Grace. "Oh, Grace."

Luke carefully filtered the looming news. "After Derrick died. Antoine went into a coma."

Grace wept. "That's terrible. I'm sorry, D'Andre."

"There's more," D'Andre said.

"Our dad died in his sleep on Tuesday," Amy said.

Grace cried. "Mr. Kernan? Oh, God."

Charlotte held Chloe's hand. "Our dad also died in his sleep last night."

Grace began to shut down and stare into space.

I felt faint.

Luke cried. "My dad also died in his sleep last night."

"Three dads and Derrick?" I asked.

Aaron wept. "Marcus there's more."

I shook my head and tried to block out what I knew was next. "That's all. I don't want to hear any more."

Grace turned her head towards her sisters. "Gloria? Gigi? What's going on?"

Ryan, Gloria and Gigi wailed loudly and covered their faces.

I yelled. "Ryan? Look at me! Knock it the hell off, Ryan! Cut the crap! I don't want to hear any more of this!"

Ryan couldn't verbalize the horror. "I can't, Marcus!"

"Ryan! Where's Dad?"

Ryan wailed and collapsed.

"Where's my dad?"

"Your fathers," Ruby said.

"They both died in their sleep last night," Emma said.

"We're sorry," Aaron said angrily wiping tears from his face.

We wept miserably.

Kiche leaned heavily on our legs.

Mr. Light orbited his TSC Cessna 182 in a left turn at three hundred feet over The Boxcar during five minutes of weeping.

I looked at Aaron. "Five dads? Five heart attacks? And Derrick?"

Aaron nodded affirmatively with a determined expression.

"Where's Antoine?" Grace asked.

"Peaksville Hospital. Bree is with him," Ruby said.

I cried for several minutes then stood. "DJ, let's go see your brother."

Aaron, Amy and D'Andre solemnly walked us to Peaksville Hospital. The others went home to comfort our mothers and prepare for the Friday afternoon funeral.

"I missed you both." Nurse Light whispered to Grace and me in the hospital hallway. "I'm so sorry for your losses."

Grace hugged Nurse Light and cried.

"Glad you're safe. Bree's inside with Antoine. Go on in."

Brianna Lopez stood and hugged Grace. "Oh, Grace."

I quietly wept when I saw Antoine.

"Is Antoine okay?" Grace sadly asked.

"He's in a coma."

I was overcome with sadness and could barely speak. "Antoine. Wake up, buddy."

No response.

"Can Antoine hear me, Bree?"

Brianna nodded. "I think so."

I checked the doorway and whispered. "Antoine, we found a place in the TFZ. It cured our headaches."

"You have no headaches?" Brianna whispered.

Grace whispered to Brianna. "There's an abandoned neodymium magnet mine in the TFZ. Somehow it cured our symptoms."

Aaron Webster was curious. "D'Andre and Amy? You get headaches like Brianna, right?"

"Every day, bro'," D'Andre nodded.

Amy gasped. "A magnet mine?"

I nodded. "A very strong magnet mine."

Aaron stared at Amy. "You look like you saw a ghost."

Amy's gears were turning. "Emma, Jack and I wore a large magnet Sunday night on our legs. We've been headache free since Monday morning. First time since middle school."

"Magnets cure headaches?" Aaron asked. "Can't be."

Amy shrugged. "Seems odd, I know. It weighed three pounds. Max stole it from his dad. Emma snuck it to Antoine. Antoine lost it. Mr. Burns found it. Max and Emma fought and broke up over this magnet."

"How does it work?" Brianna asked.

I noticed a strange TSC doctor eavesdropping in the doorway and cleared my throat. "Hold on."

Amy posed theatrically. "This shirt makes my teenage boobs look bigger. Check 'em out everyone!"

The disheveled TSC doctor quickly left.

"Okay, that got rid of Doctor Creep-a-Sneak-Peek." Amy looked at Grace and me. "My dad told four other dads about the magnet. They wrote Congresswoman Abby Walker. She ignored them. Our five dads died in their sleep."

Grace whispered. "Marcus, our dads *were* murdered."

I made eye contact with Aaron. "Maybe Derrick, also?"

Aaron angrily nodded affirmatively.

I whispered. "Bree and DJ, want to be headache free?"

They were too sad to smile. "Yes!"

"Pack your bags. Tomorrow, after the funeral." I looked at my friend, Aaron. "We all travel to the TFZ for the weekend."

M r. Webster greeted Aaron. "Good evening, son. Can you join us tomorrow at three o'clock for a TSC meeting?"

Mrs. Webster smiled. "We're investigating the Peaksville water contamination. You can start your TSC Junior Cadet training."

"Three o'clock? Tomorrow's Friday. You aren't going to the funeral?"

Mr. Webster ignored Aaron's question. "Mr. Light's been asking about you this week. Ben Light and Tony Murdstone each make one thousand dollars weekly as TSC Cadets. Pretty good money for a teenager."

"Let me think." Aaron interrupted with a comedic pause. "Um, no."

Aaron defiantly walked down the hallway to his room. The spare bedroom was padlocked as usual. He annoyingly pounded his clenched fist on the secured door. "Mom, what's in this room?"

Mrs. Webster sipped her glass of water. "Some TSC equipment. Manuals. Logbooks. PDS Engineering stuff. Just things. Why?"

"Can I see it?"

Mr. Webster drank some water. "No."

"How's that Peaksville water taste? Tap water didn't kill our friends. I knew that was horsecrap."

Aaron looked at the padlocked room once more then slammed his bedroom door.

CHAPTER THIRTY-ONE

F riday morning, the TSC aircraft repeatedly executed multiple low, loud passes over Peaksville High School.

"Every five minutes?" Luke exclaimed after the Bell 407 rattled the windows again.

"Is Mr. Burns landing on the roof?" D'Andre asked.

"Anyone have earplugs?" Aaron joked.

"I wish." Ryan rubbed his forehead. "This noise gives me a headache."

I knew Ryan was hurting. "Hang in there, brother. By Sunday, you'll be headache free."

"I hope so."

Luke pointed at the wall clock. "Two more minutes until noon. We should have skipped. My whole body is aching."

Dean Michaels broadcasted his pre-dismissal announcements. "Good afternoon, Peaksville students. Today is Friday. Students interested in the TSC Junior Cadet program are all invited to attend the TSC water contamination investigation meeting at three o'clock. Or, stop by The Safety Corps kiosk for free stuff or to join our TSC family. Just a reminder, restricted areas are restricted for *your* safety. Have a spectacular day. School's out. Be safe out there."

"Join the TSC family?" Luke said.

Aaron slammed his locker and looked at me. "Have a spectacular day? Is Dean Michaels stupid? We have a funeral at three o'clock for six loved ones, and Dean Michaels invites the school to a TSC meeting? Horsecrap!"

Aaron didn't lose a father or brother. Aaron didn't get the Army Ranger dinner table sheepdog lecture for eighteen years on Sunday nights. Why was Aaron angry, and not me?

Grace was right.

I needed to be a better sheepdog.

The funeral came too soon for Grace and me at Peaksville Memorial Cemetery. We had only known about the mass-tragedy for twenty-four hours.

The small chapel could only accommodate one casket, so the six caskets were displayed on a hilltop outside in the grass near the American flag among the cedar trees. Kiche faithfully lay at the base of Derrick's casket. She sadly tucked her head between her front paws in the grass.

The local Marine Corps recruiting station provided a color guard, rifle team, and bugler for the funeral.

The Safety Corps provided low, loud Cessna 182 overflights during the ceremony. Didn't the TSC have a three o'clock meeting? Didn't Mr. Light know we had a funeral procession? Didn't Mr. Light notice the funeral procession from his airplane? After all, he droned back and forth at no more than three hundred feet directly overhead. Ten times!

It was my turn to deliver the eulogy that I prepared all morning. I stood up and walked to the podium.

I looked at Charlotte and Chloe Epley who both tearfully smiled. "Ladies and gentlemen, we remember a fourth-generation North Idaho farmer who sowed the nourishment of love and fellowship into Peaksville's hearts."

I looked at Luke Bartholomew as Ruby Kyle placed a loving hand on his shoulder. "We remember a preacher and retired Navy Chaplain who taught Peaksville about faith, hope, and redemption."

I looked at Grace, Gloria, and Gigi Becker who kept their composure remarkably well. "We remember a retired Marine who, through his heroism and bravery, taught Peaksville about sacrifice and patriotism."

I looked at Emma, Amy and Jack Kernan as they comforted their mother. "We remember a retired Navy pilot who proudly earned his Angel Wings this week." I waited ten seconds for the Cessna 182 to pass. "Mr. Kernan will eternally guard our freedoms from above, far above our national airspace."

I looked at my brother Ryan and my mother. "We remember a retired Army Ranger who didn't teach with words, but with actions. My father's patriotic life lessons about loyalty and dedication will stay with us forever."

"Lastly, we remember a Peaksville Sophomore. The perfect son, perfect brother, and perfect friend." I looked at Madison Goodwell as she wept. "At the young age of fifteen, Derrick somehow possessed the positive traits of all five of our fallen fathers. Derrick protected the weak, the oppressed, and those without a voice. Derrick was taken from us too soon."

I looked at Derrick's casket guarded by Kiche. "Derrick Flynn, you were the best of us."

I returned to my seat with dry eyes.

Bang!

The rifle volley was more than I could take.

Tears!

The bugler sounded Taps.

Tears!

Folded flags were militarily presented to our five families by the USMC recruiting officer.

Tears!

Ruby Kyle hugged me first after the ceremony concluded. "That was beautiful, Marcus."

I was too tired and despondent to politely and properly respond to Ruby's kind words. I wiped my eyes. "Did everyone get the word about tonight?"

"Eight o'clock. Everyone knows."

"Nice job up there. I don't think I could have done that." Aaron shook my hand. "I'll be there for sure, buddy."

Thomas whispered. "Marcus, do you really think it will help our headaches?"

I nodded. "Trust us, Thomas."

CHAPTER THIRTY-TWO

Aaron Webster angrily hustled home after the funeral. He quickly confirmed that his parents were still at the TSC water contamination meeting. Aaron hurried to the master bedroom and scanned all known parental hiding spots for keys.

Within two minutes, Aaron unlocked the padlock on the spare bedroom.

Aaron entered and found an eighteen-inch, cylinder-shaped, matte-black, electronic device curiously mounted on a large black camera tripod pointing at the draped window. The strange high-tech medical machine appeared to be currently energized with two amber LED lights illuminated. He observed multiple stacks of logbooks professionally embossed with the official seal of Peaksville Institutes of Health and individually labelled with names of Aaron's friends.

Emma's PIH logbook was open. Aaron paged through and found repetitive hand-written entries for the previous week.

Tuesday 3:33am Project Emma
RFID drop lock
Tuesday 3:57am Project Emma
RFID drop lock
Tuesday 4:02am Project Emma ALERT
Require new PsytoSCOPE Imaging Probes

A my and Jack's logbooks displayed similar recent *RFID drop lock* entries. Marcus and Grace's four-day absence from Peaksville was documented as *AWOL*. Aaron quickly grabbed Derrick's logbook to observe Sunday, the day Derrick died.

Sunday 4:10am Project Derrick
Brain Stem (39 min, 12 sec)
Sunday 5:22am Project Derrick
Heart (4 min, 48 sec)
Sunday 5:29am Project Derrick
Frontal Lobe (18 min, 5 sec)
Sunday 1:30pm Project Derrick
Brain Stem (22 min, 10 sec)
Sunday 6:02pm CABESA UPDATE
Project Derrick Terminated

A aron peeked outside the secretive window. The Webster home, perched on a hill, was uniquely situated overlooking Peaksville. Within two hundred feet of this window, Aaron could see the Flynn, Becker, Jordan and Kernan homes.

Aaron saw D'Andre, Gigi, and Grace walking home from the funeral on his street.

Mr. Webster's machine came to life. It pivoted left as electronic servo motors seemed to operate autonomously. The long black cylinder locked onto and slowly tracked Aaron's friends through the drapes. One larger green LED light illuminated twice, followed by a red LED light. The machine re-centered after D'Andre, Gigi, and Grace exited line-of-sight. The green and red LED lights were replaced by the two amber LED lights.

A digital report immediately displayed on a nearby computer screen.

Friday 4:47pm Project D'Andre
Right Eye insert (43 sec)
Friday 4:48pm Project Gigi
Frontal Lobe (38 sec)
Friday 4:49pm Unknown Project
RFID drop lock

In a fit of rage, Aaron grabbed a baseball bat and violently destroyed the machine. The high school senior shattered the strange, delicately constructed device into pieces.

The garage door below energized.

Aaron stuffed sixteen PIH logbooks and random, portable TSC devices into a backpack. He quickly located his pre-packed weekend backpack and ran outside.

Mr. Webster exited the garage and smiled. "How was the funeral, son?"

"Derrick was such a nice boy," Mrs. Webster said in a sickening-sweet voice.

Aaron held up Derrick's PIH logbook. "You mean Project Derrick?"

Beep! Beep!

Mr. Webster locked his $147,500 Mercedes Benz AMG G-Class SUV with his key fob. "Aaron, calm down."

"You've been hurting my friends since 2013."

Mr. Webster smiled. "Nobody has been hurting anyone."

"Aaron, those books contain sensitive medical information about minors," Mrs. Webster said.

Mr. Webster extended an open hand. "Hand me those logbooks. You're violating TSC, PIH, and HIPPA laws. Children have privacy rights, Aaron."

Aaron backed away on the front lawn and pointed to the window. "LASER Engineer, huh pop? Better engineer yourself a new weapon."

Mr. Webster struggled to maintain his composure. "Son, those are medical instruments."

Aaron gained separation, walking backwards off the front lawn.

Mrs. Webster whispered. "Why can't he be more like Ben?"

"I heard that, Mom!"

Mr. Webster yelled while standing near his G-Wagen. "You didn't achieve Valedictorian without our help! You think you have raw talent, Aaron?"

"This is horsecrap!" Aaron broke into a sprint.

Mrs. Webster yelled. "This is all for you, Aaron!"

Aaron angrily jogged away toting evidence of his parents' inhumanity. He passed the Flynn, Kernan and Becker homes but was too ashamed to knock.

Aaron slowed his pace to a walk.

"Murdstone," He mumbled to himself. Aaron walked to the doorstep, slowed his heart rate with deep breaths, and knocked.

Mr. Murdstone opened the door. "Hi Aaron. We missed you today at the TSC Cadet Summer Kickoff."

"Yes, Sir. Is Tony here?"

"Just a second." Mr. Murdstone turned upstairs. "Tony!"

Tony entered the foyer.

Mr. Murdstone walked away into the living room.

Aaron whispered and signaled for Tony to walk outside. "Got a minute?"

Tony shrugged and seemed shocked. "What's up?"

"We aren't the best of friends. I'm not a TSC Cadet like you and Ben."

"And?"

"But you and Ben are very different. Right?"

Tony shrugged. "I guess."

Aaron cautiously whispered. "Tony. My parents have hurt our classmates since 2013. Every day."

"How?"

Aaron Webster scanned the dozens of homes within line-of-sight. The Murdstone home was also uniquely central and elevated.

"Does Mr. Murdstone padlock rooms? Are any rooms off-limits to you?"

Tony looked up at a specific window. "How'd you know?"

"What's inside?"

"It's padlocked. My dad calls it his TSC room."

Aaron noticed Ben Light approaching from several homes away.

"Why?"

"I've probably said too much. See you, Murdstone."

Aaron walked into the sunset hauling two backpacks.

Tony studied the secretive window and neighborhood homes.

Ben dismounted his new mountain bike on Tony's lawn. "What was that about?"

"Just math homework."

Ben watched Aaron depart and whispered. "Don't trust him."

CHAPTER THIRTY-THREE

The Friday evening sun had set on Liberty Lake.

Grace and I arrived at the rendezvous point.

Jack, Gigi, and Chloe played fetch with Kiche in the civil twilight.

The sad, tired high schoolers assembled inside The Boxcar and listened to the galloping footsteps of Kiche outside and intermittent propeller noise.

I looked around The Boxcar. "Who's missing?"

"Thomas," Ruby said.

I looked at Grace. "Damn."

Brianna shrugged her shoulders. "Tommy Boy said he had a horrible headache."

D'Andre nodded. "He told us the TFZ wouldn't help his headache. I don't think he's coming."

Grace whispered. "Let's get him, Marcus."

It was eight thirty and quickly getting darker. Everyone was tired. We had a four-hour night hike to the West Peaksville Neodymium Mine. I flipped on my flashlight. "Let's roll."

Gigi retrieved her backpack from The Boxcar. "Wolfie, we're going on a trip."

I led us around Liberty Lake towards the Elephant Rocks.

Emma adjusted her backpack on the go. "Aaron's missing also."

"Aaron, too?"

Amy directed her flashlight beam onto Ryan's rear end for laughs. "That's odd. Aaron is a mischief hound."

Charlotte laughed. "Like you, Amy?"

The TSC Bell 407 helicopter passed overhead in an ominously slow hover with green and red navigation lights, white flashing strobes, and a high-intensity search light illuminating us. We disregarded the airborne TSC threat and silently intercepted the north bank of Coldwater Creek to trek west.

Walking south of Peaksville Forest where Derrick had fallen, Madison grabbed Gloria's hand and unsuccessfully used the darkness and rustling trees to conceal her tears.

I looked into Peaksville Forest and spontaneously joined Madison's sorrowful weeping. Grace participated and squeezed my hand harder.

Kiche stopped, raised her ears, and swept her nose high in the air, and sniffed the westerly breeze from Lover's Lagoon.

Gigi knelt down and whispered. "You smell something, Wolfie?"

Kiche emitted a low-pitched steady growl as the hair on her spine stood up.

Ruby scanned and whispered. "What is it, girl?"

We froze.

Kiche instinctively stood sideways between us and the threat.

Ruby watched. "That's the Anatolian in her."

Kiche growled one last time and charged toward the entrance to Lover's Cave with her ears tucked back.

Amy whispered. "And that's the wolf in her!"

Ruby screamed in the dark. "Kiche!"

I ran after Kiche into the night and attempted to illuminate her path. "Everyone stay here!"

Luke yelled. "Marcus, it's not safe!"

My remaining brother, Ryan, sprinted after me. "Marcus, wait!"

I ran with my flashlight towards the mouth of Lover's Cave hearing strange, muffled canine whimpers. "Kiche, where are you, girl?"

Ryan followed me in the darkness. "Marcus, no!"

I walked just inside Lover's Cave to find Kiche on an unidentified human pinned on the ground. "Kiche, no!"

I caught my breath and heard familiar laughter coming from under Kiche. "Aaron? What are you doing down there?"

"Ask the wolf. She knocked me down and licked my face about fifty times."

Ryan successfully pulled Kiche from Aaron after I failed. "Damn, you guys scared me."

I extended my hand to Aaron and pulled him up. "You going?"

"I'm going."

"It's safe!" I shouted across the lagoon. "Kiche found Aaron!"

The girls quickly entered Lover's Cave. "Aaron!"

Luke sighed. "I figured you were a wild animal."

Amy gave Aaron a ridiculously sensual hug. "You figured *right!*"

Ruby pointed her flashlight into the first passageway. "Kiche! Before I vomit. Lead us through to the TFZ."

After carefully navigating Lover's Cave, we arrived and secured our flashlights momentarily to observe the serene beauty of The Forbidden Zone. The quiet, western TFZ sky comforted our grief-stricken hikers.

The cedar trees calmly sang in the moonlight.

Gigi whispered. "Wolfie, it's like Heaven."

Chloe tapped me on the shoulder and yawned.

"Piggyback?"

Chloe nodded.

Grace smiled as I heaved the middle-schooler up on my back.

Ryan held Gloria's hand. "So many stars."

"It's so quiet." D'Andre used Emma's sleeve as a guide.

"I wish Antoine could be here," Brianna whispered.

Charlotte comforted her. "Nurse Light will take good care of him."

Jack slept while riding piggyback on Charlotte.

Gigi exhaustedly tapped Ryan on the shoulder and hitched a ride down the mountain path towards White River.

Ryan lifted her up with one arm.

Grace and I led our Peaksville friends westward just north of White River. With no helicopter or propeller noise, the three sixth-graders slept soundly during the first hour.

I looked up at the sky beneath the Rainbow Bridge and sadly whispered to Grace. "I guess shooting stars really do burn out."

We walked north for ten minutes towards the Rock Tower.

Cedar trees loudly sang in a sudden, cool night breeze.

Grace whispered. "Jet wash."

"What?"

"Jet wash. Navy and Marine Corps air support flew so low over my father's Marine infantry platoon, they could sometimes feel jet wash. These cedar trees are swaying from the shooting star's jet wash."

I was silently satisfied with Grace's analogy.

But I didn't admit it.

G race noticed Chloe's eyes in the moonlight. "Your precious cargo woke up, Marcus."

I marched forward, leading the weary flock. "Doing okay, Sport?"

Chloe whispered. "Bad dream."

Grace rubbed the twelve-year-old's back.

"Marcus, did someone murder my dad?"

I finally felt anger. The anger felt appropriate and natural. "Sometimes life isn't fair."

"Why, though? He was only a poor farmer. He wasn't military like the other dads. Why did *my* dad have to die?"

"Because Mr. Epley stood up to evil."

"Aren't we standing up to evil? Aren't bad people going to hurt us?"

"Are you asking Grace or me."

Grace silently squeezed my hand tightly. "You, Marcus."

"We have someone watching over us, Chloe."

Grace released her grip on my hand and smiled in the moonlight.

I hoisted the sad sixth-grader higher on my back.

Chloe closed her eyes and rested her head on my shoulder.

Gloria whispered as Chloe, Gigi, and Jack slept. "Hey big sis', is that the Rock Tower up ahead?"

Grace nodded affirmatively.

Kiche ran twenty feet ahead, menacingly faced the Rock Tower, and initiated a terrifying growl.

"Something's up." Ryan scanned the area. "Kiche smells danger."

"What is it, girl?" I whispered.

Ruby held back Kiche as she assumed her fighting posture.

Ryan accidently woke up Gigi. "What do you think Ruby? Should we send Kiche?"

"Too dark." Ruby looked around. "Too dangerous."

Amy lifted Gigi from Ryan's back. "Whatever's out there has home field advantage."

Brianna held D'Andre's arm. "I'm scared."

Gigi whispered from Amy's back. "Wolfie, will you protect us?"

"Stay together." Grace motioned with her hands. "Keep walking."

Emma grabbed Aaron's hand. "Grace is right."

Ruby looked at me and led my hand to Kiche's collar. "Hold her tightly, Marcus. Only release her if you see the threat charging us."

I maintained a white-knuckled, death-grip around Kiche's collar with Chloe onboard squeezing me.

"Want me to carry Chloe?" Aaron asked.

"No." I harnessed the aggravated she-wolf. "On second thought, yes. You'd better take her."

I didn't see the threat. Just like before. "Ruby, do you really think there's something there?"

Kiche growled into the darkness.

Ruby nodded. "I trust Kiche."

"I believe you." I walked Kiche towards the westbound group. "Let's roll."

Ruby and I quickly caught up and intercepted the tracks.

Grace sighed. "Remind me to never travel alone in the TFZ."

CHAPTER THIRTY-FOUR

Charlotte approached the ravine. "This must be the trestle."

"Looks dangerous," Luke said.

Grace stepped out to lead the way. "Easier to cross at night."

"Why?" Brianna asked.

"We can't see how high we are."

Amy laughed and commenced her crossing. "Good point."

D'Andre, led by Brianna, agreed. "Grace is right."

"Partially right." Aaron cryptically commented as he navigated the railroad ties. "Sometimes invisible things can hurt you. Or even kill you."

Ruby held Kiche's collar on the old, wooden trestle and curiously responded. "Example please, Aaron."

"Ultraviolet light." Aaron carried Chloe. "Can't see it. But it burns you."

"Ryan's armpits." Amy joked. "Can't see them. But they burn your nose."

Gloria laughed. "I've seen them."

Amy sighed dramatically. "TMI."

"No more joking." Luke nervously advanced, step-by-step. "Trying to cross a trestle, here."

I helped illuminate the trestle passage. "Concentrate, everyone. Watch your step."

Charlotte walked and yawned. "What a horrible week. Even my mom had a headache all week. She never gets headaches."

Brianna sighed. "Poor Antoine."

I agreed as we finished crossing. "Unconscious for four days. Not looking good."

Grace pinched me in the dark and performed damage control. "Antoine will wake up soon."

Luke marched forward. "Dean Michaels said rule-breakers won't graduate. Maybe Thomas is safer at home."

Aaron disagreed. "Not necessarily safer. Thomas lives between the Light and Murdstone homes."

Luke didn't understand. "Mr. Light is the local TSC President. Mr. Murdstone also works for The Safety Corps. That is the definition of *safety*. No crime on *that* street, for sure."

"Peaksville has crime. More than you think."

I didn't understand. "What kind of crime?"

"Invisible crime."

We hiked thirty minutes on the railroad tracks.

Grace led us downhill towards the rushing water. "Last thing!"

I looked around and gently tapped a few shoulders. "Better wake up the twelve-year-olds for the rope bridge. No piggy-backing."

"Rope bridge?" Luke turned visibly pale in the moonlight and crossed his arms. Even more than normal. "Negative! It's after midnight."

Grace pointed up the opposing mountain slope and comforted Luke. "Luke, we're almost there."

Ruby studied the speed of the cold river. "What about Kiche?"

Amy pointed her finger. "Ryan."

Ryan heard his name. "Ryan what?"

"Ryan carries the she-wolf."

"You're the strongest, Ryan," Marcus said.

"I'm not strong enough."

Gloria squeezed his hand. "Yes, you are, Ryan."

"I'll drop her."

"No, you won't, brother," I said.

"Kiche won't let me. She may bite me."

"Call her," Ruby said.

Ryan mumbled quietly. "Come here, girl."

Kiche ran to Ryan, snaked her long body around his legs, placed her large front paws on his shoulders, and licked his face repeatedly.

"Like I said," Amy joked. "Ryan carries the she-wolf."

Grace yelled from the middle of the rope bridge. "Come on guys! Piece of cake."

Luke helped Jack climb down from his back. "I'll go last."

Jack rubbed the sleep from his eyes, grabbed the two upper ropes, and methodically followed Grace.

"Very brave." Amy watched. "Maybe on the way home, Jack should carry Luke."

Ryan was next. "Alright, fur ball. Get up here."

"You can do this, Ryan," Ruby whispered.

Ryan picked Kiche up like a lamb and slowly negotiated the suspension bridge with his one hundred and fifty-pound passenger. "Ruby, didn't they have a miniature version of this breed?"

Ruby chuckled. "Kiche was the runt."

Gloria bit her fingernails. "Take your time, Ryan."

Ryan yelled nervously passing the halfway point. "I can't see my feet! How much clearance do I have?"

"Let me check." I shined my flashlight.

The lower rope precariously sagged within one foot of the dark, cold, rapids.

Grace quickly yelled from the west side. "Plenty of room!"

Ryan continued step-by-step.

I couldn't lose Ryan. "Almost there, brother."

Ryan exhaustedly whispered as Kiche excitedly leapt from his tired arms. "We did it, Kiche."

Grace slipped Kiche a treat. "Who's my chunky puppy?"

Others nervously crossed the Rope Bridge.

"Your turn, Luke." I encouraged my most fearful friend forward. "Easy stuff. I'll go last."

Luke grabbed the upper ropes and checked them for tension and stability. "Stay close."

"Sure thing."

Luke apprehensively stopped at the halfway point. "That mine will cure my morning headaches, right?"

"Don't stop." I was suspended over the cold, rushing water behind Luke. "I promise. Now pay attention. Let's get this over with."

Luke and I arrived on terra firma. "Nice job, Luke."

Grace smiled and pointed upwards to the mine entrance. "The cure to the symptoms is simply mine."

Charlotte commenced the steep climb. "I'm so tired."

. . .

A aron arrived at the old mine entrance. "West Peaksville Neodymium Mine? This place really helps your headaches?"

"Absolutely."

"How?"

I shrugged.

Aaron experimented and held his metal flashlight two feet from the mine entrance bulkhead.

"Aaron, keep metal away from the mine," I warned.

He continued. "Just testing it."

Slam! His flashlight hit the wall and stuck.

Ryan, wearing a large, metal-framed backpack, noisily slammed into the wall.

Amy sought out tired laughter. "Ryan is why we can't have nice things."

Luke was amazed. "Wow."

"I'm stuck." Ryan helplessly looked at Luke. "Little help?"

Luke yawned and checked his wristwatch. "I'll get you in the morning."

Gloria and Madison sympathetically pried Ryan free.

Charlotte knocked on the wall. "Neodymium, huh?"

Aaron felt the mineral's texture. "Neodymium. 'Nd.' Element number 60. It's the strongest rare earth magnet. It's sparingly used in lightweight headphones, electric motors, and oil filter traps to capture small metallic shavings from gasoline engines."

Amy winked. "Sorry, Aaron. There's is no room inside for your brain."

Ruby ventured inside with Kiche. "Amazing!"

Emma and Grace unrolled sleeping bags and readied Gigi, Chloe and Jack for bed.

I unfurled my sleeping bag deep inside the neodymium mine next to Grace. "Get some sleep, sports fans. And remember, the source of your symptoms is drawn to the cure. In forty-eight hours, you will be unattractive, invisible, and free."

Brianna helped D'Andre navigate the mine entrance. "Marcus, we've been *free* since 1783!"

D'Andre disagreed. "Speak for yourself. That's 1863 for some of us."

Amy tickled Ryan. "Ryan's been *unattractive* for sixteen years!"

Ryan light-heartedly retaliated. "How would you like to be *invisible* forever, Amy?"

Aaron slid into his sleeping bag. "Marcus, how long have you guys had headaches?"

"Every day since about 2013."

"Except of course the last five days for Marcus and me," Grace said.

Brianna agreed. "Since roughly middle school for me."

"Why do you ask?"

Aaron shrugged. "Just asking."

Ten minutes later, Emma noticed Aaron crying in his sleeping bag. "Why are you crying, Aaron?"

Aaron whispered. "Tough week."

Emma scooted closer and whispered. "Tough week is right."

Aaron continued to cry. "Emma?"

"Yes, Aaron?"

"Sorry about your headaches."

Emma softly ran her hand through his hair. "Nobody causes headaches."

Aaron sniffled. "Sorry Mr. Kernan died."

"Thanks."

"I wish my dad was like Mr. Kernan."

Emma leaned over in the dark mine, hugged Aaron and kissed him on his cheek. "Get some sleep, buddy."

CHAPTER THIRTY-FIVE

In the two-story Murdstone home in an otherwise quiet Peaksville neighborhood, Tony awoke to the repetitively annoying sound of a single-engine propeller airplane droning down his street at eighty knots. Mr. Light initiated his Saturday-morning, three-hundred-foot search pattern at five o'clock, monotonously flying down Tony's street every four minutes. Tony rolled out of bed after the tenth flyby, went downstairs to eat cereal, and found a note on the kitchen table.

Tony,
Attending all-day microwave distributor conference
in Shady Valley. Sorry for late notice. Food in fridge.
Love, Mom and Dad

Recovering from an uncharacteristically restless night's sleep, Tony studied the periodic passing of the TSC airplane and attempted to make sense of Aaron's cryptic conversation.

Fairly confident that the TSC airplane was not legitimately searching for child abduction suspects before sunrise, Tony wandered upstairs to investigate Mr. Murdstone's padlocked TSC room. Not particularly gifted with Aaron's cunning ingenuity, Tony finally found his father's key after an exhausting one-hour search.

Cautiously entering the room, the conflicted TSC cadet noticed a strange, cone-shaped high-tech device mounted on a tripod near pointing at the window blinds. On the digital screen, Tony read an ominous message.

CABESA Project Thomas
PsytoSCOPE Imaging Probe FREQ: 205.245 Mhz
Microwave intensity: 72%
Beam Width: 4 inches
Target: Frontal Lobe
Duration: 4:33am – 5:45am

A wall monitor displayed the thermal image of a boy asleep with color-coded and numerically displayed temperature readings for his entire body. The boy's forehead was hottest at 102.4 degrees Fahrenheit. His beating heart and its function was clearly depicted as if the boy was obtaining an MRI in a hospital room.

Tony gently peeked outside the blinds, confirming his suspicion. The strange machine was pointed directly at the bedroom of his neighbor, Thomas Stallworth.

"Microwave Distributor. That's for sure," Tony mumbled about his father's fictive employment title.

Tony found a logbook entitled *PIH Project Derrick*. He also found dozens of books such as *PIH Experimental Child Psychology, Peaksville Defense and Space Corporation MEDWEAP Operator Manual*, and *TSC MEDWEAP Field Manual*.

He picked up a logbook entitled *PIH Project Antoine* and paged to the most recent April 2020 daily entries. "Oh, God. My dad is keeping Antoine in a coma."

Tony closed the blinds, stuffed the *PIH Project Antoine* logbook in his backpack, padlocked the room, and returned Mr. Murdstone's key to its hiding place. He collected seven thousand dollars of TSC cadet cash payments, his passport, and some clothes. Three weeks before his 2020 Peaksville High School graduation, Tony Murdstone walked out his front door.

I woke up in the dark neodymium mine, quietly slid out of my sleeping bag, and carefully stepped around a dozen slumbering TFZ adventurers.

I adjusted my tired eyes under the noon sun.

Luke and Ruby were supervising as Jack, Chloe, and Gigi played with Kiche and panned for gold in a small, spring-fed mountain tributary.

Ryan greeted me. "Hey, Marcus."

I sat next to him on a warm boulder and curiously whispered. "How you feeling?"

Ryan had apparently been crying. "No fatigue. No headaches. No stomach aches. No rapid heartbeats. No chest pains."

"Great!"

"But I still feel miserable."

"Why?"

"I dropped Derrick. I had him. Then I dropped him."

"You tried." I suddenly realized Ryan had been carrying this burden all week. "You didn't do anything wrong."

"I didn't protect him. I'm sorry, Marcus. I hope someday God forgives me."

My brother cried in the mountain breeze.

Once, our father told us a story about a Gulf War firefight gone bad. My dad sobbed. I froze.

I couldn't comfort Dad then.

I couldn't comfort Ryan now.

I needed to be a better family member.

M r. Light phoned General Voigt, the Peaksville Defense and Space CEO and retired USAF pilot. "Bad news, Sir."

"It's Saturday afternoon. How bad can it be, Bud?"

"Bad. Web's kid found his project room. Stole sixteen PIH Project Logbooks. Destroyed a $900,000 tripod MEDWEAP. Stole a portable weapon."

General Voigt paused. "A TSC Cadet did all that?"

"The Webster boy isn't a TSC cadet. He's best friends with Marcus Flynn, our oldest project."

"Totally unforgiveable. Totally un-American."

"Thirteen of the fifteen remaining Projects are believed to be in the TFZ."

"Damn."

"General Voigt, should I inform Queen Bee?"

"You better not. She isn't going to be happy. I'll call her. Thank me."

"Thank you, Sir."

"What about air support in the TFZ?"

"Our attitude gyros and heading instruments spin in the TFZ due to the rare earth metal deposits. Too dangerous."

General Voigt didn't respond.

Mr. Light continued. "Besides, Sir. The PsytoSCOPE nanotechnology RFID imaging probes in their blood will be scrambled."

"Then reintroduce more."

"Monday morning at school, Sir."

"Damn."

Mr. Light waited ten seconds for General Voigt to speak.

"I'll call Queen Bee, Bud."

"Thank you, Sir."

"*You* are responsible for law enforcement in Peaksville. Start enforcing the law. Lots of wolves out there, Bud. Time for you to tend to your Peaksville flock and start acting like a sheepdog."

"Wilco, Sir."

W e huddled around our Saturday evening campfire telling stories about Derrick, Antoine and our fathers.

Ruby helped Jack, Chloe and Gigi construct their marshmallow, chocolate, and graham cracker S'Mores.

Brianna Lopez gently placed dried tamarack and cedar branches into the fire. "Maybe Antoine will wake up today."

D'Andre smiled. "Maybe Antoine is already home from Peaksville Hospital."

Grace warmed her hands over the campfire. "I like the way Bree and DJ think."

"I still feel responsible for Antoine fainting." Emma sighed. "I was just so mean to him. I'm sorry, everyone."

Aaron kept Emma warm in the cool, night TFZ breeze. "You aren't responsible, Emma. Trust me."

I leaned back on a boulder with my arm around Grace. "I still can't believe Derrick and my dad are gone. I thought Derrick would live forever. He had so much to contribute."

Luke Bartholomew, warmly situated between Charlotte and Ruby, agreed. "Derrick was like our dads. That generation knew about sacrifice."

Charlotte Epley cried. "My dad just began to sow our crops. The tractors are difficult to operate. My mother is terrified. We could foreclose on the farm."

Gloria Becker lounged back in Ryan's arms. "It's all like a bad dream."

"This week reminds me of my dad dying." Ruby Kyle wept. "I miss his voice. I want to hear it again."

Jack Kernan walked over, sat on Ruby's lap, and hugged her.

Ruby smiled. "Oh, Jack! We're going to get your voice back. I miss *your voice* the most!"

"I can't remember my dad's or Antoine's face," D'Andre said. "Every night, before I go to bed, I try to remember what you all look like."

Amy sighed. "Here's a refresher, DJ. Charlotte looks like a Cabbage Patch doll.

Ruby looks like a Strawberry Shortcake doll. And I look like a Barbie doll." She utilized a comedic pause. "Oh yeah. Ryan looks like Sasquatch."

D'Andre laughed. "Amy sounds like a Chatty Cathy doll."

"Ha! If you're man enough, D'Andre, pull my string," Amy said.

Chloe, Gigi and Jack giggled.

Amy was our grief therapist in the TFZ moonlight.

Grace laughed as Kiche slept at her feet. "You're too much, Amy!"

Emma snuggled closer to Aaron outside West Peaksville Neodymium Mine.

Aaron pensively sat between the Kernan twins. "How do you all suppose Derrick and your dads were murdered?"

I replied first. "The water contamination story seems like disinformation. Emporer Hirohito had Tokyo Rose. Adolf Hitler had Goebbels. Saddam Hussein had Baghdad Bob. Peaksville TSC has Dean Michaels."

Aaron smiled. "Concur on the Dean Michaels analysis. The TSC spreads more daily horsecrap than Jefferson and Buckshot."

Chloe, Gigi and Jack giggled again.

Aaron looked around. "Any other ideas?"

Grace shrugged. "Poison?"

"Too hard to target within a family." Aaron shook his head negatively. "Next question. *Who* murdered Derrick and your dads?"

"Organized crime?" I suggested.

Aaron pointed at me. "Bingo. But *who*?"

I shrugged my shoulders. "Hopefully the TSC is investigating."

Aaron leaned back and disengaged.

"Look!" Madison pointed into the sky. "A shooting star!"

Grace squeezed my hand tightly as we watched.

"Make a wish, everybody," Ruby said.

Madison cried. "I want Derrick back."

CHAPTER THIRTY-SIX

S unday arrived.
    I woke up in the West Peaksville Neodymium Mine and walked towards the light.

Grace smiled as everyone enjoyed their lunch. "Good afternoon, sleepy head."

Charlotte grabbed my hand and pulled me from the cavern entrance, precariously framed by old wooden beams. "Join us, Marcus!"

Chloe smiled. "No headache!"

Brianna agreed. "We feel great! It's like we're young again."

Aaron looked at Brianna. "We *are* young, Bree. Chronic pain is not normal for high school kids."

Brianna smiled. "You know what I mean."

"Amazing!" Luke cheerfully ate his sandwich on a warm boulder between Ruby and Charlotte. "This is how I felt immediately after the lightning strike years ago."

Amy looked around at the TFZ explorers. She immediately spotted D'Andre, who had a great looking lunch. D'Andre utilized a knife, fork, and a bib. "D'Andre?"

D'Andre paused. "Yes, Amy."

Silent laughter.

"Whatcha got there, buddy?"

"Chicken-fried steak, red potatoes, applesauce and green beans."

More silent laughter from the peanut gallery.

"Did Betty Crocker or Martha Stewart make that lunch for you?"

D'Andre stopped eating. "You guys are laughing at me? Whose side are you on? Amy's or mine?"

Brianna laughed and hugged him. "Your side, DJ."

I laughed.

Amy looked at me. "Marcus?"

I should have remained quiet. "Yes, Amy?"

"Seriously, dude. You cut off the crust and made four PBJ triangles?"

My dad warned me about the Army's law of Thermal Dynamics. Heat is automatically transferred from the hot object to the cold object. DJ was the hot object. I was the cold object.

I made a feeble attempt to deflect the heat. "My *mom* cut the triangles, not me."

Laughter.

D'Andre smiled, knowing the heat was off of him. "Triangles?"

I fed one of my crust-less PBJ triangles to Kiche and looked at my watch. "We have to pack and go to make it home before sunset."

Fifteen more school days.

Grace initiated our Sunday afternoon easterly trek home by crossing the Rope Bridge. "Who's next?"

Luke quietly slimed his way to last in line.

Jack effortlessly followed Grace and smiled.

Ryan's hiking boots momentarily dipped into the cold river carrying Kiche. The tensile strength of the lower rope apparently weakened.

Luke crossed second to last, exhibiting more fear in the daylight than in the moonlight.

I forded the river, performed a headcount, and climbed up the rocky bank to the railroad tracks. "Let's roll."

We precariously completed passage over the trestle and hiked towards the Rock Tower into a stiff, fifteen-knot headwind.

Approaching the Rock Tower, Kiche growled and rapidly swept her long muzzle left and right, high the air.

"Danger." Ruby stopped walking. "Same place."

I looked around. "False alarm? I don't see anything."

"Look at the hair on Kiche's back." Aaron pointed. "That's one thousand years of wolf instinct talking."

"Aaron's right." Ruby held Jack's hand. "Kiche's ancestors are warning her."

I trusted Aaron and Ruby and grabbed Grace's hand. "Let's walk."

We continued past the Rock Tower.

Wham!

Luke was violently struck by a mountain lion from above. Luke offered his right forearm as his only defense.

Ruby's loving, playful, harmless Livestock Guardian Dog AKA 'Wolfie' instantly transformed into a wild animal. She leapt onto the two-hundred-pound male cougar and sunk her powerful jaws into its nape.

The hungry cougar angrily released Luke's forearm and launched a high-pitched, terrifying attack onto Kiche.

Ryan dragged Luke clear of the battle.

Kiche tightened her deadly spinal neck grip as the cat attempted to tear her to shreds with five feline weapons. The cougar spun and sunk twenty long claws into Kiche's belly, causing Kiche to audibly whimper in pain.

Kee-yai!

Kiche retaliated and ferociously inflicted deep wounds into the bloody cougar.

More horrific whimpers from Kiche.

Ryan screamed and lunged forward. "I can't watch this anymore!"

I instinctively grabbed Ryan. "She's got this!"

The cougar dangerously sunk his teeth into the underside of Kiche's furry neck, throttled her breathing, and began to win.

Kee-yai! Kee-yai!

Ruby cried. "Ryan, she's dying!"

Gigi screamed at the top of her lungs. "Wolfie!"

Ryan made another attempt to save Kiche.

I held my only brother back with all my strength.

The whimpers stopped.

Ruby cried as Kiche began to expire on her back.

Jack Kernan bolted from Ruby's grip and exploded into the fight. The twelve-year-old repeatedly kicked the mountain lion in the gut and screamed at the top of his lungs.

"Aaaaaaaahhhhh!"

Emma screamed. "Jack, no!"

My brother broke free of my grip and ran to Jack's aid.

"Roar!"

The wounded mountain lion complained then swiftly retreated into the rocky North Idaho forest.

Ruby ran to Kiche in tears. "My puppy!"

Kiche's breathed slowly and laboriously through her bloody jowls as she lay dying.

Grace and Gloria attempted to shore up open neck wounds with their fingers.

Ruby lovingly stroked her bloody fur.

Gigi tearfully knelt down and whispered in her ear. "Wolfie, you can't die, too."

Kiche coughed, opened her eyes, and planted a long, bloody lick up Gigi's cheek.

Ruby sobbed and hugged Kiche. "Good girl, Kiche! Good girl!"

R yan carried Kiche in the Sunday afternoon TFZ sunlight clear of the Rock Tower until it was safe enough for Grace to treat and bandage Luke's injured forearm.

Kiche finally found the strength to drink water and accept snacks from sixteen thankful children.

Ryan picked her up again and carried her beyond Rainbow Bridge, White River, up Lover's Mountain, and through Lover's Cave. Ryan was a horse. He clearly inherited my father's strength.

Ryan was also secretly angry with me. He wanted to be the sheepdog. I stopped him. I made a mistake and learned something.

Never restrain a sheepdog.

W e arrived to The Boxcar on Sunday evening. My friends were all headache-free for the first time in years.

Thanks to an anonymous sheepdog who leaves notes in jelly jars.

W e rested at The Boxcar and noticed Tony Murdstone standing in the nearby forest.

Grace greeted him as usual. "Hi, Tony."

Tony waved. "Hi, Grace."

Ryan was less than cordial. "Where's Mother Goose?"

No response from Tony.

Aaron asked us to stay behind and wait. "I got this." He whispered with Tony for about one minute.

Tony reached into his backpack, and handed Aaron some items.

Aaron shook his hand and rejoined us at the The Boxcar.

Tony turned, walked west away from Peaksville, and disappeared into the sunset.

"What was that about?"

Aaron looked at me. "Tony's running away."

"Why?"

Aaron shrugged.

CHAPTER THIRTY-SEVEN

Amy arrived early for the Monday morning TSC shot ritual in Nurse Light's office.

"Want to go first, Amy?"

Amy sat in the corner and smiled. "You know me better than that."

Nurse Light snuck Amy a bag of M&M's. "Then sit back and enjoy the show."

Amy watched carefully as Nurse Light faked every shot for the second week in a row.

Gloria received her 'shot' as Amy joked. "How do you keep it from hurting so much?"

Nurse Light bandaged Gloria's arm and smiled. "Ancient Chinese secret, Amy."

Gloria, head-ache free, giggled and began to leave.

Nurse Light stopped her. "Gloria, hang out for a minute."

Amy's turn. She sat and ate M&M's. "Ouch?"

"You're done, Amy. Get out of here."

Gloria looked at her watch as the homeroom bell sounded. "Something wrong?"

Nurse Light nodded and whispered. "I'll make this quick, Gloria. You went to Peaksville Hospital six weeks ago and had a mammogram. Does it still hurt?"

"Yes."

"It's not a cist, Gloria. Take these pills for thirty days."

Gloria was shocked. "What?"

"Trust me. This is our secret. They wanted you to advance to stage four before telling you."

"Oh, God."

"Our secret, Gloria. Don't repeat this. It's not safe. Okay?"

Gloria stuffed the pills in her bag. "Okay."

Nurse Light kissed her forehead and wiped her tears. "Get to class, sweetie."

G eneral Voigt unenthusiastically answered his phone. "Bud, the hair on the back of my neck instinctively stands up when I see your name appear on my *iPhone*. I assigned the *Star Wars Imperial Death March* as your ringtone."

Bud didn't immediately speak.

"Just kidding, Bud. What's happening?"

"Bad news."

"Figured as much."

"Nuke's boy ran away. The TSC Cadet."

"You're breaking my balls, Bud."

"We're fixing it. Dean Michaels cleaned out his locker as if he never existed."

"That's a start. What if the Murdstone boy returns?"

"We have a contingency plan."

"I won't tell Queen Bee. She had a cow yesterday and is still recovering."

"Literally or figuratively?"

General Voigt didn't answer.

Mr. Light broke the silence. "Thank you, Sir."

"Any more Peaksville news?"

"No, Sir."

"I'm hanging up before things change."

Click!

I intercepted Aaron after the first period. "Aaron, the teacher didn't read Tony Murdstone's name during rollcall. Tony's desk was gone."

"I heard."

"Bad news." I whispered to Aaron. "Tommy Boy threw up and passed out during PE."

"Damn."

Ben Light walked by as his father overflew the school roof.

I waited for Ben to leave. "Tommy Boy said he needed to hydrate."

Aaron whispered. "He needs to go to the mine."

I shrugged. "I don't think he wants to go."

Aaron whispered. "I have an idea."

"Good afternoon, Peaksville students. Today is Monday. Less than three weeks of school remain," Dean Michaels broadcasted on the PA system.

Aaron slammed his locker and zipped his backpack. "Stand by for the daily dose of horsecrap."

"The TSC is investigating another attempted child abduction this past weekend in our community. TSC Air Patrol continues low search patterns for your safety. We are installing multiple SMIR stations for you to submit Suspected Mental Illness Reports. Classmates experiencing psychological problems can be referred confidentially with a SMIR to Dr. Hands at KidCare Counseling Services, a trusted TSC partner. Peaksville State University Optometry School released a new study. Accidentally staring at the sun each day for three seconds can lead to a thirty-one to ninety-four percent loss of vision. Please visit Dr. Schultz of Peaksville Optometry for more information. School's out. Be safe out there."

I tapped Luke on the shoulder. "Want to go stare at the sun with me?"

"Dude, that's crazy. I'm going to SMIR you!"

Aaron yelled down the hallway. "Hey Marcus, Operation TOMMY BOY begins in five mikes."

I laughed, not knowing what Aaron just signed me up for. "What's that?"

"You'll see."

Luke smiled. "Can I come?"

"Yes, I'll feel safer." Aaron joked. "Please come, Luke. Mountain lions tend to attack you first apparently."

Luke sighed.

Ruby nestled into Luke's non-injured arm, and smiled. "I'll protect you Luke."

"Where are we going?" Thomas asked.

Aaron walked Thomas through the subdivision. "Here's the deal. Thomas, how do you feel?"

"Headache. Heart hurts. Tired. Like crap."

The TSC Cessna 182 buzzed overhead at three hundred feet. "Want to go to the mine? Everyone who went is pain free."

Thomas shook his head negatively. "No."

Aaron questioned his resilience. "Why not?"

Thomas shrugged. "I respect authority and the TFZ is off limits."

Aaron stopped on a street corner. "Let's make a deal, Tommy Boy. If you fall down, you go to the mine tomorrow with Marcus."

"With *me*?" I had absolutely no idea what Aaron was planning.

"You'll just push me over. No deal."

Aaron disagreed. "We won't physically touch you."

Luke, Ruby and I smiled as if a magic trick was approaching.

Thomas looked ill.

"Deal, Tommy Boy? Nobody will touch you."

Thomas was clearly in pain. "Deal."

Aaron stood and checked his watch. "How do you feel now, Tommy Boy?"

"Dizzy."

Aaron looked at the Murdstone home and checked his watch.

I didn't understand. "Aaron, what are we waiting for?"

"For Tommy Boy to fall down."

"Why?"

"If he falls down, he'll go to the mine. That's the deal."

Thomas rubbed his temple and began to wobble. "Little dizzier."

"How do you know he's going to fall down?"

"Stand behind him." Aaron whispered to Luke and me. "Get ready to catch him."

Luke and I side-stepped into position.

More wobble.

Ruby got nervous. "Tommy Boy?"

Aaron whispered and spoke slowly. "Wait for it."

Thomas dropped his head forward, fainted, and collapsed as Luke and I grabbed his arms.

Ruby couldn't believe it. "How did you know?"

Aaron slowly looked at the Murdstone home. "Sometimes, things are hidden in plain sight."

Ruby looked suspiciously at the Murdstone home. "Let's carry Tommy Boy to Mrs. Becker."

I was still trying to figure out Aaron's magic trick.

CHAPTER THIRTY-EIGHT

I arrived at The Boxcar at five o'clock in the morning as planned.

Grace brought Thomas with the sunrise at her back. "Good morning, Marcus!"

"You both ready?"

"Sorry we're late. It took my mom a while to wake up Tommy Boy. Then we swung by his home. Mrs. Stallworth wanted to pack him some food and drinks."

"Understood. How we feeling Tommy Boy?"

"Like crap. Terrible headache. Nothing new."

"Are you sure that you want to go?"

Thomas shrugged. "I made a deal with Aaron, right."

I threw my backpack over my shoulder. "Fair enough. Let's roll."

"Are you sure that a boarded up mine will help with my headaches and stomach aches?"

Grace hugged Thomas and smiled. "Trust us."

R yan returned from the lunch line with seconds. "Without a headache, I actually feel hungry."

Amy mumbled. "Said the 400-pound Sasquatch."

Gloria sipped her orange juice as the Bell 407 buzzed the cafeteria roof. "I feel great."

Luke smiled. "I could actually read the SmartBoard in class."

Brianna opened her apple juice and whispered. "How does the mine work? I aced my quizzes. I don't feel pain. Why is the West Peaksville Neodymium Mine special?"

Emma shrugged. "I don't know, Bree. Something about neodymium magnets. Aaron, what do you think?"

Aaron was daydreaming, watching Ben Light's table as the Cessna 182 passed two hundred feet overhead.

"Aaron?"

"I can't believe it."

"Can't believe what?"

"When you hear the next TSC flyover, look at Ben's eyes."

Forty-five seconds later, Mr. Burns executed a slow hover over the cafeteria roof.

"Now." Aaron whispered over the rotor noise. "Look at Ben."

Ben established eye contact with the children, looked up at the roof, then reestablished eye contact.

"Seven overflights during our fifteen-minute lunch. Seven times Ben looked at us."

Ryan became angry. "Why should we even care about Ben?"

Aaron shrugged. "Because Ben cares about you."

I scanned our environment as we circumvented the Rock Tower. "This is where Luke fed his arm to a mountain lion."

Thomas cautiously advanced. "I saw Luke's bandage."

I pointed. "Kiche saved Luke's life right there."

Grace nodded. "Then Jack saved Kiche."

Thomas slowed down and looked at us. "Excuse me? Jack did what?"

I nodded. "The twelve-year-old Kernan boy kicked a fully-grown male mountain lion in the gut five times."

Grace agreed. "Jack screamed. Top of his lungs."

Thomas quietly hiked for another minute then whispered. "Kiche killed it?"

Grace pointed into the forest. "It was bloody and wounded. It whimpered away."

I carelessly threw a rock into the bushes. "Over there."

Grace punitively clenched my hand.

I looked at Thomas. "We think it's dead."

Grace corrected me. "We *hope* it's dead."

. . .

G loria found Ryan in the hallway at 2:55 p.m. "Do you think Grace and Marcus are in trouble for skipping again?"

Ryan nodded affirmatively. "Dean Michaels frowned at me after lunch."

"He always does."

"Worse than usual."

Gloria heard the PA system energize over the Cessna 182 propeller noise. "Speak of the devil."

"Good afternoon, Peaksville students. Today is Tuesday. Thirteen more days of school. The Safety Corps Air Patrol conducts low altitude search patterns 24 hours per day to find suspects responsible for poisoning the reservoir last week. Summer Internship opportunities exist at Peaksville Institutes of Health. The PIH and other local North Idaho military and health industry stakeholders receive a combined one trillion dollars annually towards the 2013 CABESA Initiative and 2013 National Nanotechnology Initiative. The Cooperative Adolescent Biotech Experimental Science Act is a multi-agency and multi-disciplinary kid-friendly initiative designed to eradicate cancer from our society. The PIH keeps our innocent citizens healthy and accepts internship applications for qualified students. All Class of 2020 Seniors intending to graduate require a solid attendance record. School's out. Be safe out there."

N urse Light removed her famous Huckleberry Pie from the oven. "Bud, it's nice to have you home for dinner."

Mr. Burns buzzed down the street in the TSC Bell 407 helicopter.

Ben nodded and reviewed his TSC Cadet PQS. "Yeah, Dad. You must have 120 hours of flight time already this month. I don't know how you do it."

Mr. Light focused as CNH News delivered a segment comparing Russian and American missile defense systems. "Oh, sorry. Talking to me?"

Nurse Light cheerfully repeated herself. "We said it's nice to have you home, honey."

No response.

CNH News went to a commercial break. "Honey, did the Projects get their PsytoSCOPE shots this week?"

"Projects?" Nurse Light sliced the steaming pie into eight triangles. "Oh, The children. Yes, why?"

Ben looked at Mr. Light and covertly shook his head negatively.

"Just asking. Billions invested into these children. I just want them to be safe. That's all."

"Huckleberry pie!" Nurse Light watched Ben and Mr. Light exchange secretive looks. "Hot and ready!"

Mr. Light reclined in his favorite chair and kicked his feet up. "By the way, we'll need you at the TSC meeting later tonight. And that pie smells delicious."

G race and Thomas roasted squirrels over the campfire just outside the West Peaksville Neodymium Mine entrance.

Thomas spun his skinned critter with pride and precision. "That's some good squirrel, Marcus."

"Glad you like them. My dad taught me Army Ranger survival skills. Tomorrow we'll eat snakes."

Thomas paused his manual rotisserie spinning motion. "Really?"

Grace laughed. "He's just kidding."

"Whew. Scared me." He began to spin the squirrel again." Anyways, thanks for taking me here."

Grace smiled. "No more headache, Tommy Boy?"

"First time since sixth grade. No headache."

CHAPTER THIRTY-NINE

"Oh, say does that star-spangled banner yet wave
O'er the land of the free
And the home of the brave."

General Voigt initiated the CABESA Initiative conference call hosted by Peaksville Defense and Space Corporation.

"I open these meetings with the Star-Spangled Banner and the CABESA Core Values: Faith, Family, and Freedom. You can't have one without the other. The Queen Bee apologized for her absence, she is attending an event at *Boys and Girls Club of America* fundraising for her next campaign. Swamp, you have the lead."

"My name is Colonel Marsh, Callsign *Swamp*, I'm from the Pentagon, and I'm here to help."

Laughter on the conference call.

General Voigt sighed.

"No really. Who am I? The USAF MEDWEAP Program Manager. Yes, there are five hundred USAF officers nationwide masquerading with this job title. I assure you, they're all imposters. I am *the* MEDWEAP Program Manager. I'm kind of a big deal."

More laughter.

"What do I do? I have ten bosses in the Pentagon. All one-star to four-star Generals. I produce ten PowerPoint briefs per week to help my bosses obtain funding for your CABESA Initiative programs. Unfortunately, my bosses are afraid of their bosses, so my PowerPoints rarely leave their MS Outlook inboxes.

"To actually obtain funding for your Peaksville programs in Washington DC, I rely on a Congressional college intern from Georgetown. She can get any appropriation written into the annual National Defense Authorization Act in exchange for one Double Chocolaty Chip Crème Frappuccino Grande from the K Street Starbuck's. If your funding request exceeds ten billion dollars, she requires a Spinach, Feta & Cage Free Egg White Breakfast Wrap. What's the matter with kids these days?"

General Voigt sighed. "Are you finished yet, Swamp?"

"Not yet, Sir." Colonel Marsh continued. "I recently visited Peaksville. Bud briefed me about dangerous North Idaho 'tree wells' *after* I fell in a North Idaho 'tree well' snow skiing with him at Schweitzer Mountain. My right leg continues to heal nicely, Bud.

"Hoping for a more comprehensive safety brief prior to my July water-ski trip to Lake Pend Oreille (*pronounced Ponderay*)."

General Voigt looked at his watch.

"Kudos to the sixteen Peaksville Projects that were volunteered, or '*volun-told*,' at young ages to replace the sandbox insurgents from Durka-durka-stan for PDS weapons testing. Land of the free, home of the brave, right? More time with my family in CONUS. My wife is happy. Thank you, children of Peaksville.

That's all for now from the Pentagon. In flight school, we learned to keep it either short or funny. I'm going to quickly hand it back to you General Voigt, since my presentation was neither short nor funny."

"We're down to *fifteen* Projects, Swamp," General Voigt said.

"Sorry to hear that. Not really. Anyhow, fifteen is a good round number."

"Isn't it bedtime for you on the east coast, Swamp?" General Voigt sighed. "Who's next?"

"I'll go next. I'm the *one and only* CABESA Command Center Project Manager at the PIH. My name is Dr. Hertz. Callsign Dr. Hertz."

Laughter.

"All kidding aside, at the PIH we are developing strategies to meet United Nations end of century mandated population goals with selective precision. Our two hundred and fifty local scientists coordinate with the TSC to resolve recent target acquisition problems. That's all I got."

"Your turn, PNC." General Voigt said.

"I'm Dr. Braun, CEO of PsytoSCOPE Nanotech Corporation. Swamp, I had a callsign in East Berlin but that was many years ago. PsytoSCOPE Lot-22 Imaging Probes have been reduced from 7 microns to 5 microns. Lot-21 RFID's inconveniently lodged in the liver instead of remaining in the bloodstream to properly pool in the heart and head for MEDWEAP targeting. That's all I have, General."

Mr. Light raised his hand. "Dr. Braun, can you guarantee 6-mile targeting with your Lot-22 probes using modern MEDWEAP's?"

"Bud, through medical advances, the airborne Peaksville Defense and Space weapons will be able to effectively interrogate and target tangos at 8 miles line-of-sight and 4 miles through drywall and composite roofing, even using our new Lot-22 Cytoflow 5-micron probes.

"Nice work, Doctor Braun," General Voigt declared. "Next."

"I'm Dr. Moriarty. Director of Experimental Child Psychology at Peaksville State University. Bud, I got to hand it to you. Your selectees appear to be teenage graduates from Navy SERE school. Next time Projects are selected, can we choose non-military children? These are tougher than the PIH Spider Monkeys we retired in 2013. Their pain thresholds are through the roof, so to speak. Half of their parents were war heroes. These kids seem like the cast of *The Great Escape*. It's been frustrating and expensive."

Mr. Light ignored the criticism.

"I'm Dr. Klein from INLINE Pharmaceuticals here in Peaksville. I'm going to piggy-back on what Dr. Moriarty said. We have prescribed zero psychotropic drugs to CABESA Projects. Zero pain medications after seven years of pain? Phenomenal. Who are these kids?"

"I'm Dr. Hands from KidCare Counseling Services. Zero of the sixteen Peaksville Projects volunteer for psychological counseling? Other cities are batting a thousand."

Mr. Light looked at Mr. Burns. "We're working on it. In my defense, zero PIH Spider Monkeys referred themselves for counseling or pain meds."

Colonel Marsh was heard on the conference call making monkey noises from the Pentagon.

"Ooh, ooh, ooh. Ah, ah, ah."

"Bud and Swamp, this is not amusing to the stakeholders," General Voigt said.

Dr. Klein nodded. "We are having trouble renewing our CABESA funding this year."

"Give us another two weeks," Dean Michaels said.

"The first ten projects graduate in two weeks!" Dr. Hands said.

"Bud, the screw-ups seem to all be TSC screw-ups," Dr. Moriarty said.

Mr. Burns defended Mr. Light. "We're all in this together. Copy all. We'll turn up the heat on the projects."

Colonel Marsh commented from the Pentagon. "Dr. Feelgood, email me if you need more INLINE pharmaceutical funding, for real. I also know this local guy in DC who can get opioids for cheap. For the projects, of course."

Dr. Klein laughed and signaled 'okay' to Colonel Marsh via teleconference.

General Voigt sighed. "Thanks Swamp. I think. Nurse Light, shot program on track?"

"Yes, Sir." Nurse Light nervously dropped her pen. "Every Monday."

Mr. Burns made eye contact with Mr. Light.

"Is PSU Psychology programming and messaging being delivered to the students?"

Dean Michaels nodded. "Every afternoon, General Voigt."

"Bud, did you receive the PsytoSCOPE package?"

"Yes, Sir."

"When's the drop?"

"This week, Sir."

"Make it quick. I understand the Projects are currently midnight. Time is money."

CHAPTER FORTY

B rianna helped D'Andre gather his homework at 2:50pm as the Cessna 182 rattled Peaksville High School at two hundred feet. "DJ, want to visit Antoine with me in the hospital after school?"

"I'll join you at six o'clock after swimming, Bree."

"Six o'clock? Deal!" Brianna replied cheerfully. "Nurse Light can sneak us free dinner."

Mr. Burns overflew the roof in the Bell 407 helicopter in a loud, twenty-knot hover.

Gloria smiled. "Ryan, this week is amazing. I can think. I can see. I'm getting A's on my quizzes and homework!"

Ryan didn't respond.

"Ryan?"

Ryan nudged Gloria and whispered. "Ben watched us as the helicopter passed overhead."

"Still doing it?" Gloria whispered. "He's a creep."

Aaron slammed his locker. "He's worse than you know."

D ean Michaels initiated the pre-dismissal announcements. "Good afternoon, Peaksville students. Today is Wednesday. The local TSC HAZMAT Team is investigating local reports of environmental and biological terrorism. Noxious and hazardous materials were found in vicinity of Peaksville High School. Several children have reported respiratory problems and headaches."

Luke nudged Ruby. "What's he talking about?"

"The HAZMAT Team has sealed off the area and begun the cleanup. TSC Air Patrol is actively performing search patterns for suspected terrorists. There was another report of a scary man in the woods with a LASER toy scaring children. Local mental health experts from KidCare Counseling Services look forward to receiving SMIR referrals to assist students with daily struggles. Please remain clear of restricted areas for your safety. School is dismissed. Be safe out there."

Emma walked outside as Mr. Light overflew the playground. "The LASER toy story is ridiculous."

"I agree." Aaron nodded. "My father is a LASER engineer for PDS."

Charlotte saw Luke. "Swim with us!"

Luke smiled. "Ruby and I are tutoring the kiddos first. How about four o'clock?"

Charlotte preferred a simple 'okay.' "See you then, Luke!"

Thomas and I checked our squirrel traps down by the river while Grace slept in the mine.

"I bet you miss Derrick and your dad." Thomas caught me off guard.

I began to reply but got choked up.

"Sorry."

I reset a trap and threw a squirrel into my bag. "I can't believe they're gone."

Thomas caught me off guard again. "You're lucky. I never had a brother or sister."

"I wish that I was a better big brother to Derrick. He'd probably still be alive."

"Don't say that, Marcus."

I lowered another squirrel from its elevated predicament. "Number seven."

Thomas looked at me. "Sorry I'm always so obtuse and stubborn. I consider you my brother. Thanks for taking me here, Marcus."

The sunbathers lounged on the Elephant Rocks after school.

The TSC Cessna 182 intermittently buzzed overhead.

Gloria leaned on Ryan. "What a beautiful day!"

Chloe, Gigi, and Jack giggled in the cold, smooth waterslides between the large boulders.

Emma, Amy, Ruby, Charlotte and Madison slept and sunned in their bathing suits on a large warm rock.

Aaron whispered to Luke. "Don't do it."

D'Andre blindly smiled in the sunlight. "Don't do what?"

Aaron smiled at Luke.

Aaron whispered. "Luke was going to splash Ryan."

D'Andre whispered. "I'll do it. Where's Ryan?"

Aaron and Luke positioned D'Andre for his cold, spring water assault. Ryan and Gloria watched from afar.

Luke coached D'Andre. "Straight ahead. Ryan's asleep. Just like this. Let it rip."

D'Andre manually flooded the adjacent boulder with cold water.

Emma, Amy, Ruby, Charlotte and Madison woke up and screamed. "DJ!"

D'Andre immediately distinguished the five high-pitched voices from Ryan's voice. "Luke and Aaron made me do it!"

Luke and Aaron shrugged their shoulders and pointed at D'Andre as the Cessna 182 buzzed overhead at only sixty knots.

S*plat!*
A strange, loud clapping sound was heard from the large boulder. The startled children looked around and found a thin, gel residue on the boulder near the Kernan twins.

Ruby approached the object. "What is it?"

Within three seconds, the thirteen children began to cough, choke, and gag.

"Get —" Ryan attempted to yell 'get out of here' but couldn't finish without coughing.

The halfway submerged sixth-graders coughed and gasped for air as Ryan instinctively carried all three of them towards the bank of Coldwater Creek.

Luke guided D'Andre clear of the mysterious, gaseous contaminant as everyone followed.

The sinus and lung pain caused the children to gasp for air for the next five minutes.

Emma coughed. "What was that?"

Luke coughed, pointed and mumbled. "Plane."

"Agree." Aaron coughed. "Mr. Light. Dropped. Something."

The children desperately splashed mountain spring water into their faces and mouths.

"Are we dying?" Ruby cried to Luke.

"It hurts," Amy cried.

Gloria pointed at herself and coughed. "My house."

. . .

Thomas and I climbed uphill towards the TFZ mine entrance.

Grace smiled and prepared a campfire by stacking multiple fallen tamarack and cedar branches. "Hi fellas."

I returned a smile. "Hope you're okay with squirrel, Gracie."

"Two nights in a row? But are the squirrels okay with it?"

Thomas nodded and displayed our catch. "They were just hanging around down by the river."

"I shaved some cedar kindling with my Gerber for you guys. I figured you manly-men wanted to honors on the evening's fire-lighting ritual."

"Step aside, Miss Becker." I proudly wielded my father's Zippo Lighter with the Army Ranger logo. "Men at work."

Multiple attempts.

Click! Click! Click!

My Zippo was empty.

Grace quietly extended her hand holding a full Bic Lighter. "Need a light?"

Thomas laughed.

The TSC Air Patrol noisily orbited the small, rural North Idaho community.

Mrs. Becker brought Chloe, Jack and Gigi iced teas as they whimpered on the living room couch. "Are your lungs starting to feel better?"

Jack held his chest and shook his head negatively.

"What was it, Mom?" Gloria asked in a scratchy voice.

Mr. Becker tended to D'Andre who was burning up.

"You all say it dropped from a Cessna?"

Ryan, Luke, Amy, Emma, Madison and Charlotte all shook their heads affirmatively in pain.

"The TSC Cessna? The Cessna flying over our home right now piloted by Mr. Light?"

Ruby nodded and whispered. "It splatted on the rock and left a gel residue."

Gloria held her sternum. "What is it, Mom?"

"I saw some things in the Army when I was a combat medic in the sandbox. But —"

Aaron winced in pain. "But what, Mrs. Becker?"

"I shouldn't speculate. I really don't know what happened. I'm just surprised Congress hasn't responded to our letters."

.   .   .

Thomas enjoyed the evening campfire in the fresh mountain breeze. "So many stars."

Grace yawned as the fire gradually extinguished. "Peaceful here, isn't it Tommy Boy?"

Thomas nodded. "I really appreciate you both missing school for me."

I handed Thomas my last can of Arizona Green Tea. "Our pleasure."

"Thanks, Marcus!"

Thomas took a drink. "Sorry I'm so stubborn."

"You're just confidently skeptical." Grace winked. "It's fine."

I looked at my watch. "I wonder what we are missing in Peaksville."

Thomas sighed. "Probably not much."

CHAPTER FORTY-ONE

Mrs. Becker monitored the thirteen Peaksville children during their Wednesday night sleepover.

Charlotte joined Luke, Ryan and Gloria at the breakfast table while Amy prepared pancakes.

Gloria whispered and grimaced. "Good morning."

Mrs. Becker scratched Charlotte's back. "Feeling better, Charlie?"

Charlotte shook her head. "The aircraft noise all night made my lungs hurt worse."

Aaron entered the kitchen holding his chest. "Say again, Charlie?"

Charlotte pointed up. "The propeller and rotor noise makes it worse."

"Remember you said that." Aaron walked to the window and observed the Cessna 182 performing a left-hand orbit over the Becker home. "Okay, Charlie?"

"Why?"

"I can't say yet."

Charlotte looked at her pancakes. "Are these? Are these pancakes in the shape of? Oh my God!"

Mrs. Becker blushed and pointed to the stove. "Amy is making them."

Amy joked in a scratchy voice. "Charlie, your pancake needs lots of hot, wet syrup."

Madison giggled and covered her face. "Rated-R pancakes?"

Amy handed Aaron his breakfast pancake. "Whoops! Aaron, yours doesn't quite fit on the plate."

Mrs. Becker face-palmed. "Amy Kernan!"

. . .

G race enjoyed her Thursday morning stroll down to the river while Thomas and I slept deep inside the West Peaksville Neodymium Mine.

After filling our three canvas and plastic canteens with cold mountain stream water, Grace hung them on the wood beams framing the mine opening, and proceeded inside. Before she walked into the darkness, she felt some dust and gravel sprinkle into her hair.

Suddenly, the rocky ceiling collapsed.

Crash!

The wood beams failed. Grace attempted to leap outside to safety but was knocked in the forehead by a falling beam.

Grace Becker lay in the collapsed passageway coated in dust, bleeding, and trapped under heavy rock.

B rianna intercepted Ruby, Emma and Luke before Thursday homeroom and whispered. "I was visiting Antoine in Peaksville Hospital when that *thing* happened. Are you guys okay?"

"Our lungs and sinuses, Bree." Ruby shook her head. "It's so bad."

Emma struggled to whisper. "It hurts."

Luke sat down and held his chest. "I feel so thirsty."

Ben Light wielded a creepy smile as the Bell 407 helicopter buzzed two-hundred feet over the school roof in a slow hover.

Ruby nudged Luke. "Ben's doing it again."

Dean Michaels initiated a quick announcement before the first bell. "The Safety Corps is performing a toxic HAZMAT cleanup behind the school. Water fountains and sinks have been secured for your safety. Many children reported respiratory problems from this HAZMAT. The TSC cares for adolescent health and safety and is conducting a search for your safety. Remember to drink lots of water and wash your hands to stay healthy. Dean Michaels, out."

G race's lower body was pinned by a several rocks, each weighing over one hundred pounds. "Marcus!"

No answer.

"Marcus! Tommy Boy!"

Grace was officially alone, quickly developing circulation problems and unable to budge the rocks crushing her legs.

She looked around.

Her backpack and Gerber knife were buried in the rubble.

There were three canteens, one was nearby. Grace reached for it, drank some water and cleaned her head wound.

Grace reattempted pushing the rocks from her legs.

Too heavy.

Grace spotted a dried, firm tamarack walking stick eight feet away. She removed the canteen strap and tried to lasso the stick.

Too far.

Grace tied a rock to the strap and lassoed the second canteen.

Grace connected two canteen straps and lassoed the third canteen.

Grace connected the third strap and lassoed the walking stick.

Got it!

Using the long, dried branch, Grace made several attempts to free her legs.

"Why doesn't this work?"

Grace remembered her Physics homework and placed a small rock under the long stick to lift the large rock. "A fulcrum!"

A burst of adrenaline combined with mechanical advantage. Got it!

Grace dragged her injured body clear of the rocks. "Marcus! Tommy Boy!"

No answer.

Grace attempted to walk, but her ankle was badly strained and now rapidly swelling with the increased blood flow.

She attempted to move more rocks using mechanical advantage to find Marcus and Thomas. Dozens of rocks weighed hundreds of pounds.

Grace collapsed.

Grace helplessly lay on the ground, looked at the three canteens, and faced Peaksville to the east. "Dad, I need you."

L uke looked outside during study hall. "That's a toxic cleanup, right?"

Ruby watched. "Dangerous chemicals?"

Emma whispered. "Like what Mr. Light dropped on us?"

Amy scrutinized the ten strange individuals hired by the TSC sweeping the schoolyard. "It's a cover story. Street theater."

Emma laughed. "Nice white creeper van. Wonder if there's candy in there for the kids."

Amy smiled. "Candy?"

Emma elbowed her twin.

"How many hours are they going to sweep that same area?" Ruby asked.

Brianna nodded. "Same place. Over. And over. And over."

"You're right," Emma said.

Amy studied their HAZMAT suits. "White suits and respirators. What did they forget?"

"Gloves," Ruby said.

"Goggles," Luke said.

Aaron shook his head. "What a bunch of dipshits."

Amy pointed. "Look at their faces."

"They're ugly. But lots of people are ugly." Luke subtly put his arm around Ryan.

Ryan realized Luke's punchline and quickly wrestled Luke's arm away.

Amy pointed. "Check it out. Teardrop tattoos on their faces."

Ruby gasped. "Prison tattoos?"

Luke was shocked. "On school grounds?"

Aaron laughed. "The TSC *really* cares for adolescent health and safety."

G race cautiously approached the Rock Tower after an arduous three-hour, painful hike across the Rope Bridge and Trestle utilizing make-shift crutches.

"Is this one of those horrible dreams, Dad?"

Three half-full canteens and one leather Cabela's hiking boot were slung over her shoulder. Her swollen right foot, unable to fit in her boot, was wrapped in cloth torn from the lower half of her favorite Schweitzer Mountain Skiing shirt.

"One of those horrible dreams that lasts forever, Dad?"

Grace walked by the looming Rock Tower in the noon sun.

"I don't know if I can make it. I'm eighteen, but I'm still afraid of monsters, Dad."

Grace ignored movement in the rocky forest underbrush as she hobbled forward on crutches.

"They're the same monsters as the ones under my bed. Remember, Dad?"

Grace stopped and turned around. The fully-grown, injured male mountain lion now walked thirty feet behind her and matched her speed. Kiche's jaws and teeth had obviously wounded his normally-stealth, feline respiratory system. The North Idaho predator, although severely incapacitated, had death in its eyes.

Grace avoided eye contact with the large cat, faced forward, and continued homeward on her crutches.

The cougar menacingly followed her.

"The monsters with big eyes and big teeth, Dad."

. . .

I yelled in the darkness. "Grace!"

Thomas dejectedly sat in the magnetic mine. "Sorry, Marcus. This was all my fault."

"Tommy Boy, the mine entrance collapsed. You didn't do it."

"I got you into this mess. I shouldn't have doubted you."

I ineffectively attempted to move giant rocks blocking our escape. "Do you think Grace is alive?"

Thomas sensed my apprehension and illuminated his Casio G-Shock wristwatch. "By now, Grace is mustering a search party for us in Peaksville."

"You think?"

"Of course. The Safety Corps has search planes that can help."

Thomas and I didn't share the same heroes.

G race's forward speed on her homemade tamarack crutches was matched by the hungry mountain lion.

"Black bear? Fight back, Dad."

Fatigue and fear slurred Grace's speech.

"Grizzly bear? Play dead, face down, and protect, Dad."

The cougar reduced separation behind her to fifteen feet.

"Dad, what's mountain lion strategy? Fight or play dead?"

The hungry, marauding predator whistled during inhalation and sprayed a bloody mist during exhalation.

"Dad, I can't remember for big cats."

Grace suddenly remembered Jack's yell, stopped, and faced the two-hundred-pound animal. "Aaaaahhhhh!"

The cat stopped and unleashed its first wild, menacing snarl.

Roar!

Grace sighed. "Bad strategy."

Grace spoke nicely to the animal. "Please go away, Kitty Cat."

Roar!

Second terrifying snarl.

Grace turned away, faced the south and hobbled on one leg and two crutches towards Rainbow Bridge.

The hungry cat followed.

Grace was too afraid to look back again.

Grace exhaustedly addressed her pursuer. "Let's play a game, Kitty Cat."

"I'm going to close my eyes and count to ten. When I reach ten, Kitty Cat, you'll disappear."

Grace marched south into the noon North Idaho sun and closed her eyes. "One. Two. Three. Four. Five —"

The Cessna 182 and Bell 407 alternated school building overflights every two minutes.

Aaron maneuvered his lunch tray along the tracks. "I don't know how you guys could stand this. My head and heart are killing me."

Charlotte saw Aaron begin to wobble. "Ryan, help!"

Ryan grabbed Aaron's right arm and pulled him up. "I got you Aaron."

Ruby assisted. "Ryan, help him to the student lounge, I'll carry his food tray."

Emma bought Aaron his lunch and sat next to him on the couch. "You're burning up, Aaron."

Ruby noticed Luke's red face and felt his forehead. "Luke's burning up, too."

Gloria stood up. "I'll get Nurse Light."

Aaron coughed blood into a napkin. "Not the TSC, Gloria. They'll put us on drugs."

"Nurse Light is good." Gloria gently put her hand on Aaron's shoulder. "Trust me."

Gloria ran from the student lounge.

Amy agreed. "Nurse Light's our guardian angel. That's our little secret."

Nurse Light smiled when Gloria arrived. "Are you feeling better?"

Gloria whispered. "The pain is already gone after only four pills."

"Praise the Lord."

"We need your help. Aaron and Luke are ill. They're in the student lounge."

Nurse Light began to cry.

"What's wrong?"

"I love you guys so much. But I'm in danger."

"How can we help?"

"You can't stop inevitability, Gloria."

"What do you mean?"

Tears flowed down Nurse Light's face. "Gloria, did you know Ben was not my oldest child? Ben had an older brother."

Gloria hugged Nurse Light.

"I may be visiting him soon, Gloria."

Nurse Light wiped her eyes, grabbed her medical kit, and hurried to help Aaron and Luke.

· · ·

195

"You better be gone by ten, Kitty Cat."

Grace struggled southward on crutches through The Forbidden Zone with her eyes closed.

"Six. Seven. Eight. Nine. Be gone soon! Almost there, Kitty Cat!"

Grace opened her eyes. "And, Ten!"

Roar!

The male mountain lion leapt on Grace's back and knocked her to the ground. Grace instinctively remained prone, protected her neck with her hands, and clenched her elbows inward to protect her torso.

Slash!

The cougar tore at her exposed back and rib cage with its sharp teeth and claws.

Chomp!

Grace felt and heard her young life helplessly slipping away with each rip, slash and bite. The predator was actively ending her precious life.

"Dad, you always taught me to be the sheepdog!"

Rip!

Grace cried in agony, listening to the horrifying sounds of her demise.

"Where's *my* sheepdog, Dad?"

Her vision went blurry.

"Who protects *me*? It's not fair!"

Bang!

Grace heard a loud noise, faded away and lost consciousness.

CHAPTER FORTY-TWO

"Good afternoon, Peaksville High School students. Today is Thursday."
Dean Michaels commenced pre-dismissal announcements.

"Be advised that today's Air Quality in Peaksville remains 'Red.' Respiratory problems may result for non-compliant students not following TSC advisories. PsytoSCOPE Nanotech Corporation, a major local stakeholder in the kid-friendly 2013 CABESA Initiative, is accepting applications for summer internships. Peaksville State University Experimental Child Psychology Department is seeking high school participants in an ongoing study about stress and anxiety. Students can earn three hundred dollars weekly. Participants under nine years old require parent permission. Parents are invited to a Peaksville Foster Care workshop tonight at 7pm discussing absenteeism, mental health, adolescent chronic psychosomatic pain and parenting skills. School is cancelled tomorrow. Be safe out there. See you Monday."

Ryan and Gloria waited on the Elephant Rocks for Marcus, Grace and Thomas.

Brianna arrived from Peaksville. "I thought I'd find you both here. Any sign of the TFZ hikers?"

Ryan checked his watch. "Still waiting."

Gloria smiled. "Hi Bree!"

"How's Antoine?" Ryan asked.

Brianna sighed. "Nine days in a coma. I had to take a break early from today's hospital visit. It's getting more hopeless every day."

Gloria comforted her. "Antoine will wake up soon."

Ryan agreed. "He'll be fine. AJ's a strong kid."

"Who's in the raft?"

"What raft?"

Brianna pointed upstream as their raft slowly drew nearer. "That raft."

Gloria watched it approach. "Looks empty."

Ryan stood up, waded into Coldwater Creek, and intercepted the raft. "Someone's inside!"

"Gloria!" Brianna exclaimed. "It's your older sister! All bandaged up!"

Gloria cried. "Oh God, Gracie! You're all bloody! What happened?"

Brianna cried. "She's unconscious."

Ryan looked upstream. "Where are Marcus and Thomas?"

"What time is it, Tommy Boy?"

His G-Shock wristwatch illuminated the West Peaksville Neodymium Mine walls due to our hyper-adjusted rods.

"One hour later than the last time you asked, Marcus."

"Five o'clock?"

"Yep."

Thomas had repeatedly answered my next question many times. I needed to hear his answer again.

"Tommy Boy?"

"Yeah, Marcus?"

"Do you think Grace is alive?"

"I told you. Grace is already home. Trust me. Stop worrying, Marcus."

"Grace, Miss Lockwood called. She said you beat up a fifth grader," Mr. Becker said.

Grace politely ate her dinner. "Yes, Sir."

"Was she picking on you?"

Gloria and Gigi giggled.

"He's a boy, Dad."

"Why was he picking on you? You're only a fourth grader."

"He was picking on Gloria and Gigi."

Mr. Becker calmly drank his iced tea.

"Did you finish it?"

Grace looked at her dad and nodded. "Yes, Sir."

Mr. Becker, proudly wearing his USMC uniform, scooped mashed potatoes onto Grace's plate. "Wake up, Grace."

"Dad?"

"Wake up. Marcus and Thomas need you."

"I don't understand."

"You need to wake up." Mr. Becker gave a stern look. "Now, Grace!"

Grace Becker woke up in her bedroom and found Gloria and Gigi treating her wounds.

Gloria smiled. "You woke up. Feeling okay?"

Grace painfully shook her head. "What time is it?"

"Six o'clock."

Grace looked at the window. "Morning?"

"Evening."

Gigi yelled into the living room. "Grace woke up!"

Ruby entered the bedroom. "What happened?"

Grace looked around. "This doesn't make sense. The mountain lion. It killed me."

Charlotte entered and kissed her forehead. "You're alive, Sweetie."

Brianna cried tears of joy. "Grace, you floated down Coldwater Creek to us."

Grace looked around. "But I lost the fight, Bree."

Ryan, Luke, Aaron walked into her bedroom. "Where are Marcus and Tommy Boy?"

Grace unsuccessfully tried to sit up. "Oh no! The mine collapsed! The boys are trapped!"

Ryan stood in the doorway. "Luke, Aaron, let's go."

Grace disagreed. "Too heavy."

Ryan insisted. "We can do it, Grace. We have to go. Now!"

Grace cried. "Too heavy. Big rocks. Trust me."

Ryan wept and lost his temper. "Then what, Grace? I need to save my brother! He's all I got left!"

Charlotte looked at Chloe, Gigi and Jack. "Butters and Fiona!"

"What?" Ryan cried.

Gigi nodded. "Scottish highland cattle. Butters is a bull. Fiona is a cow."

Chloe nodded affirmatively. "I ride Butters around the farm. Butters can save them."

Charlotte looked at the boys. "Butters pulls carts. Butters pulls anything. Fiona goes everywhere Butters goes. We'll rig them with yokes."

Brianna held Grace's hand. "I'll stay with Grace!"

"Charlie, hurry." Grace gasped. "They're out of water!"

Charlotte looked around. "Everyone meet at the farm in ten minutes."

C harlotte and Chloe Epley haltered Butters and Fiona as the boys followed her instructions.

Ryan returned to the barn. "Charlie, two-hundred feet of rope is on the cart. What's next?"

Charlotte instructed Gigi and Jack. "Kiddos, take Ryan to the hay. Load up six seventy-five-pound hay bales."

Ryan, Luke and Aaron returned in sixty seconds covered in hay. "What about the darker green bales, Charlie?"

"That's alfalfa. Scotties enjoy the plain hay."

"Ok, then what's next, Charlie?"

"One fifty-five-pound bag of Sweet COB, one fifty-pound bag of range cubes, and one twenty-pound bag of apple-flavored horse treats. The brown bags will say *North40 Outfitters* on them."

Emma watched the boys pack for the TFZ. "What's Sweet COB?"

"Corn, Oats and Barley. Sweet means *with* Molasses, their favorite. It's a rare treat."

Ryan yelled from the barn. "What next?"

Charlotte shouted over the incessantly annoying Bell 407 rotor noise over the Epley farm. "Two twenty-gallon muck buckets!" She secured Butters to the yoke and cart.

Chloe haltered Fiona with no cart.

Ruby kept Kiche clear during the rigging. "They're so quiet."

Charlotte spoke and worked. "Scottish Highlands are a thousand-year-old heritage breed. They can go weeks without mooing."

Mrs. Epley brought a chocolate cake to the cart. "You may need this."

Luke smiled. "Thank you, Mrs. Epley!"

Butters looked back at the cart. "Moooo!"

Chloe fed slices to Butters and Fiona. "Sorry Luke, the cake is not for you."

Aaron laughed. "Luke can eat humble pie instead."

Madison scratched under Fiona's chin. "Are they dangerous?"

Charlotte looked around. "Safety brief! Cattle kick with back legs. Front legs are heavy but don't kick. But they step so don't get your toes squished. Our Highlands have never kicked a human. Stay clear just in case. The horns are weapons. They don't want to hurt you, but be careful. If a wolf, cougar or grizzly approaches, stay clear. They are a fold, not a herd. Butters and Fiona will pivot around shoulder to shoulder and fight the predator like Scotsmen. Like in *Braveheart*."

Ryan felt the sharp, thirty-six-inch horns. "Giant sheepdogs?"

Charlotte exposed Fiona's eyes by parting her brown hair. "Same hair style, too."

CHAPTER FORTY-THREE

The Peaksville students trekked west of Peaksville and enjoyed the final one hour of warm sunlight.

Gigi led D'Andre down into the TFZ intercepting White River. "Charlie, why aren't your Highlands afraid of Wolfie?"

"Butters likes dogs. Besides, Kiche keeps licking their noses."

Amy joked. "I noticed that Kiche enjoys licking cattle snot, Ruby. Is that instinct or learned LGD behavior?"

Ruby threw a rare spear into Amy's camp. "Learned from you, Amy."

Laughter from the evening TFZ rescue squad. "Roasted!"

"Careful, Ruby." Amy sighed and extended her index and pinky fingers and rotated her fist. "Mess with the bull, you'll get the horns."

Chloe smiled and scratched Fiona's chin from her left side. "You like dog licks, Fiona?"

Aaron scratched Butters as he walked. "Where did you get the cart, Charlie?"

"My dad built it for firewood retrieval in our woods. Notice how it is only forty inches wide, the same width as highland horns. Butters can pull it through trees as dad cuts. I mean he *used to* cut."

"It was perfect for Lover's Cave," Gloria said.

Emma Kernan carried Jack on her back in the setting TFZ sun. "Mr. Epley would be proud of you, Charlie."

Charlotte tried to smile. "I miss him."

Ruby saw Luke looking at Charlotte. "How much longer to Rainbow Bridge?"

Ryan pointed. "Starting to see it now."

. . .

C hloe handed Fiona's halter to Ryan after Rainbow Bridge and hitched a ride on the cart.

Charlotte maintained control of her two-thousand-pound bull in the darkness. "You got her, Ryan?"

"Good to go."

Charlotte coached Ryan. "Fiona likes it if you whisper things in her ear."

Ryan walked Fiona. "Almost there, Fifi. Can I call her Fifi?"

"Only if we can call you Fifi, Ryan." Amy joked in the TFZ moonlight. "By the way, Luke, hold those forearms up. Be ready to protect us if we see the mountain lion."

Luke cautiously scanned for movement approaching the Rock Tower.

Ruby's hand found Luke's hand.

Aaron stopped, pointed and whispered. "Look at Kiche."

Kiche smelled danger and positioned her body sideways between the threat and the children.

Madison whispered. "There."

Emma illuminated an object with her flashlight. "It's not moving."

Charlotte and Ryan stopped the Highlands and fed them apple-flavored range cubes.

D'Andre squeezed Amy's arm. "What is it?"

"It's the cougar. D-E-D. Dead."

Aaron utilized his flashlight beam. "Entry wound."

Ryan rotated the cougar's neck. "Exit wound."

Luke was confused. "Knife?"

Ryan examined the wounds. "Hunting rifle. High velocity. Possibly a .308 caliber or similar."

"Is that the cat that attacked me on Sunday?"

Aaron inspected closely and pointed his beam under its neck. "Bite wounds. Kiche throttled him there, remember?"

Ruby allowed Kiche to sniff the cat. "Someone saved Grace earlier?"

Madison Goodwell looked around. "A mysterious person makes a timely rifle shot six hours ago. Saves Grace. Bandages Grace. Carries Grace for three hours to Coldwater Creek through the mountain and loads her on the raft. This person is probably here. Tracking us. Right now."

The children vigilantly scanned the Rock Tower area for movement.

"It's okay." Ruby could sense Luke's fear and squeezed his hand. "The person is obviously good."

Madison illuminated the North Idaho forest and yelled loudly into the TFZ.

"Thank you, Guardian Angel!"

Ryan slipped Fiona a few range cubes with his left hand holding her halter in his right. "Marcus and Thomas are waiting. Let's roll."

"The Trestle crossing was easier than expected," Emma said as the young rescue squad walked the highlands down to the river.

Aaron examined The Rope Bridge. "What now, Charlie?"

Luke illuminated the cold river to reveal its speed.

"Let me check something." Charlotte found a long stick, leaned over the river holding the Rope Bridge, and measured the depth.

Ruby checked the stick. "Thirty-six inches deep average. Deeper in some places"

Charlotte held the stick up to Butters and Fiona. "They can cross with the boys' help. Butters first. Fiona will follow her protector. The cart stays here."

Luke got scared. "What do you mean 'help'?"

Charlotte laughed. "Luke, we need you to ride them across."

No response.

Amy smiled. "Will you require a cowboy hat for your crossing, Luke."

Luke looked at Charlotte.

"Just kidding. Ryan carries Kiche. Luke, Aaron, D'Andre, Ryan and Jack will then pull the highlands from the west side."

Chloe connected long ropes to Butters and Fiona's halters.

Charlotte slipped Butters some apple cubes, crossed, and yelled. "Butters! Come on, baby! Come on, baby!"

Butters snorted, ran towards Charlotte, and repeatedly leapt out of the river during his five-second passage. Fiona forded next in similar fashion.

Ryan gasped. "We didn't even need to pull."

Luke was shocked. "Holy cow! Bulls jump?"

Charlotte laughed. "Yes. Bulls jump."

Ryan looked uphill. "Lead the way, Charlotte."

For thirty minutes, Butters and Fiona pulled at least fifty rocks. Each rock averaged two hundred pounds.

Ryan anxiously examined the progress. "Charlie, can we send Gigi up top to check our progress?"

Charlotte handed Chloe and Jack the muck buckets and pointed to the river. "Can you guys water the Scotties?"

Gloria handed Gigi a flashlight and two water bottles. "Watch your step, Gigi. Tell us what you see."

Gigi climbed to a possible opening and examined with her flashlight. "Marcus! Tommy Boy!"

Ryan held Gloria's hand and whispered. "Oh, God. Please."

"Marcus! Tommy Boy!" Gigi yelled inside then turned to the rescue team. "I hear them! I'm going to bring these waters!"

Gloria yelled. "Gigi, no!"

Gigi disappeared into the West Peaksville Neodymium Mine. She climbed on top of the jagged rocks into the large cavern.

I saw the sixth-grader crawling our way holding a flashlight. "Gigi!"

Gigi handed us waters. "Drink these!"

Thomas and I had never had such a great tasting twelve-ounce bottle of water. "How's Grace?"

"She's with Bree at home. Let me go tell them you're okay."

Gigi crawled back outside. "They need more water. Keep pulling rocks. I'll wait inside with them."

She returned with six more bottles and kept us company for another thirty minutes.

Gigi told us about her big sister Grace's mountain lion encounter, the mysterious helper who shot the lion, the airborne gas attack, and the fake toxic cleanup crew in the schoolyard.

Butters and Fiona finished the job just after midnight.

Ryan ran inside, hugged me and cried. "Marcus, thank God you're okay, brother. Don't ever scare me like that again."

I had been worried about Grace.

Ryan was worried about me.

I *definitely* needed to be a better brother.

CHAPTER FORTY-FOUR

The morning TFZ sunlight beamed with precision onto my face into the West Peaksville Neodymium Mine from the east.

Chloe and Gigi giggled outside and brushed the Scottish highland cattle.

Luke and Jack prepared their fishing tackle.

I joined Aaron and sat on a boulder.

"Good morning, Marcus. Glad you and Tommy Boy are okay."

I nodded. "Thanks for the rescue."

Aaron smiled.

"Beautiful day."

"It's okay. Marcus, do you believe in forgiveness?"

"I guess so. Why?"

Aaron changed the subject. "Did you hear I got hit with that gas attack?"

"I heard. Headache?"

"First headache ever in my whole life."

"In your life?"

Aaron nodded affirmatively. "Marcus, you're my friend. I'm sorry about the last five years. And sorry about Derrick and Mr. Flynn. I'm sorry about everything."

I appreciated Aaron's kindness. "Thanks."

Aaron looked at me. "I'm not much of a forgiveness person. I'm more of a reciprocity person."

I didn't understand. "Reciprocity for what?"

Aaron looked at me and shrugged.

. . .

G race Becker woke up after the Bell 407's fifth pass over her home.
Brianna Lopez smiled. "Good morning, Sunshine."

Grace gently grasped Brianna's wrist. "Bree, there was a man in the TFZ!"

"Where?"

"Near the Rock Tower. I remember, now. The lion was mauling my back. I turned to look. I saw a mountain man. Then I blacked out."

"Is he the one who carried you to Coldwater Creek?"

"I don't know."

"Did he talk to you?"

Grace paused. "I heard my name. I remember. He yelled 'Grace' when the mountain lion was on me."

"Are you sure?"

"He yelled my name, Bree. I'm sure of it."

"You have a Guardian Angel, Grace."

Grace smiled.

Brianna patted the wound on Grace's forehead. "Why are you smiling?"

"My own personal Sheepdog protecting me."

D r. Hertz phoned General Voigt. "I'm sure you heard, Sir. The CABESA
Projects are in the TFZ again."

"Bud told me *some* of the Projects are in the TFZ."

"Twelve of sixteen. The four in Peaksville are midnight, dead, or in a coma."

"Damn. Bud failed to include those details."

"General Voigt, I'd like permission to cut 200 of my 250 Peaksville CABESA Command Center scientists and analysts loose for the weekend. They haven't had a 3-day weekend in four years. It's youth baseball and softball playoff season. My PIH scientists haven't attended one game this Spring."

"Will we still be able to reintroduce trauma and pain on the Projects in case they return before Sunday?"

"Doubtful, the PDS Electronic Warfare targeting experts warned. We'll require reintroduction of PstyoSCOPE imaging probes on Monday morning. Our Projects will potentially scramble the new aerosol ScatterSMART Lung Targeting Probes."

"Appreciate your candor, Doctor."

Dr. Hertz patiently awaited General Voigt's decision.

"I served thirty years active duty in the Air Force, so I understand all about missing youth sports and playoffs. Story of my life. Children grow up too fast. Cut your scientists loose. Tell them to take care of their families, courtesy of Peaksville Defense and Space."

"Thank you, Sir."

General Voigt looked at the large, embroidered American flag in his plush, mahogany-furnished Chief Executive office overlooking the PDS production lines. "Dr. Hertz, be sure to thank your PIH scientists for their patriotic service. I'll pass the news to the Queen Bee."

"God Bless You, Sir."

W e gathered around the Friday evening TFZ campfire after a long day of exploring, relaxing and talking.

I stoked the fire with a slightly charred cedar branch. "Thanks for saving Tommy Boy and me. Especially you, Charlie. I'll never forget it."

Charlotte humbly smiled as her Scotties lay on their bellies down by the river on a small, one acre patch of wild Rye and Timothy grass.

Thomas roasted a marshmallow at the end of a stick. "Hey Marcus."

"Yeah?"

Thomas displayed his flaming marshmallow. "I thought we were toast in the mine."

I was floored. "You lied?"

Thomas extinguished his marshmallow and winked. "Come on, Marcus. I'm a pessimist. I was just being nice. Keeping your hopes up."

"Thanks, Tommy Boy."

Gloria noticed Madison Goodwell silently crying. "Maddie, what's wrong?"

"Derrick is gone, and I haven't seen my dad in a year. I feel so alone."

Gloria hugged her best friend. "You aren't alone."

Emma rested on Aaron in the moonlight. "We're here with you, Maddie."

Kiche leaned onto Maddie's feet and emitted a low-pitched rumble.

Madison laughed and scratched Kiche's belly. "Ruby, your Livestock Guardian Dog would make a great therapy wolf."

Amy hastily avoided a group cry. "Luke, the fish is fantastic."

"Glad you like it. Jack helped."

Charlotte built a fish sandwich. "Yummy trout, Luke!"

"We did alright."

I looked in the small cooler. "How many fish did you catch?"

Jack held up ten fingers.

Luke mumbled. "We caught ten."

Amy attentively smiled. "Who caught the most?"

Jack shrugged.

Luke sidetracked. "Who's ready for another fillet?"

Aaron laughed. "You're changing the subject, *Mrs. Paul*. Who caught more?"

Amy smiled. "The graduating Senior or my twelve-year-old twerp brother?"

"What is this, *Survivor Island*? Do you like the fish or not?"

Aaron joked. We are simply trying to determine who the *real* man is, Luke."

Amy looked at her brother. "Jack, how many did you catch?"

Jack held up ten fingers.

"How many did Luke catch?"

Jack smiled and made a giant zero with his arms.

Amy joked. "Luke Bartholomew. *Not* a real man."

Ruby moved closer to Luke in the cool, mountain breeze for a hug.

Luke placed his arm around Ruby then looked at Amy. "Ha! Caught a fish."

"Come on!" Emma laced up her leather hiking boots in the afternoon sun. "Aaron and I found this awesome place! We're hiking there to eat lunch! Join us everyone!"

Thomas saw Charlotte lacing up her boots and stood up. "Sounds fun!"

Emma looked around. "Join us, Ruby?"

Ruby and Luke were studiously assembled with Chloe, Gigi and Jack on a sunny boulder outside West Peaksville Neodymium Mine. "You guys enjoy. We promised to play hide and seek with the kiddos after finishing math."

Emma and Aaron led us downstream to an amazing waterfall hidden in a lush valley surrounded by tall cedars.

Madison spun around below the quiet TFZ sky. "Great find."

Charlotte agreed. "It's beautiful."

I cautiously stood at the rocky edge of the waterfall and looked downward. "Eighty-foot drop?"

Thomas slowly leaned forward. "More like a hundred."

Ryan sat down next to Gloria on a sunny flat rock in the noon TFZ sunlight and opened his lunch box. "Remind me to never fall in the river at the Rope Bridge."

"Hold on a second, Ryan." Amy studied Ryan's lunch. "Everyone stop eating. What's that?"

Aaron, Amy's fellow velociraptor, triangulated on my brother. "I didn't know they still sold Spiderman lunchboxes in North Idaho."

Amy continued. "Did it come with a Spidey Thermos?"

"It's old. My mom packed it."

"Spiderman lunchbox." Amy smiled. "Old like grade school? Or old like Freshman year?"

We relaxed headache-free in the sun as Ryan remained downrange of Aaron and Amy's targeted scorn for the next couple hours.

Then we heard a distant scream.

"*Aaah!*"

Gloria sat up and exclaimed. "That's Gigi's voice!"

Ryan

Bang!

We momentarily chuckled at the metallic sound of Ryan's Spiderman lunchbox slamming shut, stood up and sprinted upstream to the mine.

I ran up the hill from the river bank. "What happened?"

Luke was pale and hyperventilating. "Marcus, there are five bodies! We found them playing deep in the mine!"

Ruby stood with the three terrified middle-schoolers. "Skeletons! Four of them were children!"

D uring the somber Saturday evening campfire, we were far less jovial.
Emma rested her head on Aaron's shoulder. "Class of 2020. I'm going to miss all of you this fall."

Charlotte wiped her eyes and scolded the Kernan twin. "No goodbyes yet, Emma. You'll make us all cry. High school isn't over yet."

Luke sighed. "The last few weeks have been a nightmare. I'm worried."

D'Andre teared up. "Antoine needs to wake up soon."

Emma hid her tears behind Aaron's shoulder.

Thomas taught me something in the mine on Thursday.

Energy can neither be created nor destroyed.
Hope, on the other hand,
can be created out of thin air,
multiplied and distributed freely.

I practiced what I learned from Thomas. "Antoine will wake up soon, DJ. He'll be accepting his diploma with us in two weeks."

Thomas immediately made eye contact with me. He knew I didn't believe it. Thomas harnessed his pessimism. "Yeah. Antoine will wake up any day now."

I reflected on my statement and determined that there was no such thing as 'spreading false hope' regarding an eighteen-year-old friend in a coma. Any hope was good hope.

Aaron gently transitioned topics to the five dead bodies in the mine. "Marcus, let me see that ring."

I handed Aaron the gold ring from the adult-sized skeleton.

Emma leaned over his shoulder to look. "Peaksville High School. Class of 2017."

Aaron examined closer. "Initials inside are BPL."

Peaksville High School
Class of 2017
BPL

C harlotte examined the ring in the bright moonlight. "Any identification on the four small children, Marcus?"

"Two were wearing Peaksville Middle School sweatshirts."

Aaron looked at me. "Peaksville isn't safe."

My father chose North Idaho because it was a safe place to raise children. But my father and little brother were dead.

Aaron was unfortunately correct.

CHAPTER FORTY-FIVE

D'Andre was the last to wake up on Sunday morning. "Wow, I feel great."
Chloe was curious. "Marcus, how does this mine help us?"
I packed my backpack and tied my boots for the trek home. "The magnetism."
Gigi was confused. "But how?"
I didn't pretend to have the answer. "Not sure, Sport."
Aaron reminded Gigi about the note. "It makes you invisible, kiddos."
I was confused. "Invisible to whom?"
Aaron shrugged.

I performed a headcount before the Sunday afternoon crossing. "Fifteen humans. Two wooly mammoths. One she-wolf. Ready to cross!"
Amy raised her hand and stared at Ryan. "I'm counting fourteen humans and three wooly mammoths."
Ryan flicked Amy's earlobe.
"Ow!"
Ryan smiled.
"Keep your bovine hooves off me!"
Ryan stopped smiling.
Amy smiled.
Splash! Splash!
Charlotte orchestrated two successful Scottish highland crossings and laughed. "They're getting good at this!"

Ryan completed another careful she-wolf Rope Bridge crossing.

Ryan pointed at his wet hiking boots from the east side. "Marcus, the lower rope is losing tensile strength!"

I waited on the west side, planning to cross last.

Chloe and Luke were midway.

"Careful, Luke. The rope has some play in it," I said.

Charlotte looked at Ryan's wet boots. "Chloe, strong hands."

Chloe's response was interrupted.

The lower rope broke.

Splash!

Chloe plunged, sunk and accelerated downstream.

Jack yelled utilizing perfect diction. "*Chloe!*"

Luke struggled, tucked inward, and suspended himself on the remaining two ropes.

I wasted one second. "Get her, Luke!"

Luke hesitated and fearfully shook his head 'no' and held onto the ropes. "The waterfall!"

I jumped into the river.

Splash!

Charlotte, Ryan, Amy and Emma ran downstream with rope.

Chloe struggled in the accelerating rapids. "Ah!"

I swam frantically in the cold, fast moving water to the middle-schooler.

Charlotte and Ryan positioned themselves on an overhanging tree trunk.

Amy and Emma sprinted past the hanging tree towards the waterfall.

"Catch Chloe!" I yelled, grabbed Chloe's jacket and steered her to Ryan and Charlotte.

Charlotte grabbed Chloe's arm. "Got her!"

Chloe was rescued.

Ryan pulled both Epley girls to safety.

The Venturi Effect accelerated me towards the waterfall. The river became narrower, deeper and faster. Ryan couldn't catch me.

I fought violently to swim laterally to shore. I remembered our peaceful lunch, yesterday. Today, the looming North Idaho rock formation terrified me.

"Marcus! Grab the rope!" Amy and Emma yelled with angelic voices.

Amy and Emma stood on different boulders holding a rope.

Dad used to hit me fly balls when I was younger. "*Marcus, you have to catch it. If you don't, you'll get hurt.*"

I caught the rope!

But Amy and Emma couldn't stop my momentum. They dug their heels into the ground and emitted terrifying screams. They didn't have the strength to interrupt my demise. I prepared for the inevitable. Unavoidable fate pulled me to the precipice. I contemplated water entry after my inevitable fall.

The twins were pulled into knee-deep water.

I let go of the rope to save them.

Ryan passed the twins, anchored himself on the final rock, and grabbed my drenched arm. "I got you brother!"

I flipped over the edge and hung over the one-hundred-foot drop onto the rocks below. The water was pulling me down. Our clenched arms were submerged.

Ryan's feet were sliding towards me on the wet, slick boulder.

I looked my brother in the eyes and struggled to speak with the water rushing over my face. "Sorry, Ryan." I unclenched my grip.

"Don't, Marcus!"

I broke loose.

CHAPTER FORTY-SIX

My name is Grace Becker. I'm eighteen years old. I'll graduate from Peaksville High School in two weeks.

Marcus told you the Flynn family story. Here is the Becker family story. Dad was Marine Corps infantry. Mom was an Army combat medic. Dad wanted three boys. Dad got three girls.

I don't know how this story ends. I'm scared.

CHAPTER FORTY-SEVEN

A my and Gloria sat in the Peaksville High School nurse's office awaiting the Monday morning TSC shots.

"How is Ryan?" Amy asked.

Gloria shook her head negatively.

"What about Grace?"

Gloria's eyes welled up with tears.

A rather rough-looking woman suddenly walked into the nurse's office in a white uniform.

Gloria quickly wiped her eyes and sat up straight.

The angry-looking fifty-year-old logged into the desktop computer, opened up a webpage and sloppily Googled medical equipment.

"Are you subbing for Nurse Light?" Amy asked.

No response.

Amy signaled Gloria by pointing at her own sternum.

Gloria silently looked at the woman's PDS neck lanyard.

Peaksville Defense and Space Corporation
CABESA Targeting Manager
Ms. Charity Ferguson

G loria tried to communicate with the odd stranger. "Are you a Nurse?"
"Nurse Light transferred. I'm her replacement."

The woman sat down at the computer monitor.

Gloria was sad. "Transferred?"

No response.

The woman leaned over and attempted to shield her webpage navigation.

Gloria nervously whispered to Amy. *"How to administer shot into arm?"*

Amy asked the woman. "Where is Nurse Light?"

"She got a new job somewhere else. Who's first?"

Gloria flinched.

The woman clumsily administered a painful shot into Gloria's arm.

"You're next, Amy."

"How did you know my name?"

"Gloria said your name."

Amy and Gloria made eye contact.

The woman immediately seemed angry.

Amy suffered through her awkward shot.

Gloria cried. "Nurse Light is coming back?"

No response.

Amy and Gloria walked to homeroom as the TSC Bell 407 initiated a slow, noisy hover over the Peaksville High School roof.

A m I dead?
I'm ready to wake up from my horrible dream.

What kind of God cures me of headaches for two weeks, only to make them return worse than ever?

What kind of God takes a boy who was dedicated to clearing all of the parasitic ivy from Peaksville Forest?

What kind of God takes five good, protective fathers in their sleep?

What kind of God puts a boy in a coma for two weeks?

What kind of God lets a boy accidentally drop his two brothers to their death?

What kind of God takes the only boy I ever loved?

The only boy who ever loved me.

It hurts too much.

"Grace?"

The Cessna 182 buzzed the roof of the student lounge.

Gloria repeated herself. "Grace?"

I regained situational awareness on the school couch and wiped the tears from my eyes.

Gloria's beautiful visage came into focus. "Gracie, you shouldn't have come to school today."

"I didn't want to be lonely."

Emma cried with me on the couch.

I looked at Gloria. "Is Ryan okay?"

"He stayed home."

Emma nodded. "Two brothers and a dad. Life isn't going very easy on Ryan."

The Bell 407 overflew our school roof.

Luke wiped his eyes and rubbed his temples. "I'm worried about Ryan."

I gently leaned on Emma's shoulder. "I can't do this anymore."

Max Burns, who had been absent for nearly two weeks, walked past the student lounge and stopped. Max looked Emma and me, burst into tears and whispered. "Sorry." He then quickly walked away.

Dean Michaels actuated the PA system. "Peaksville students, a quick midday announcement. We received sad news. Nurse Light, a member of our Peaksville High School family, died of injuries sustained in a car accident. Please join us for a moment of silence."

The Cessna 182 performed a low pass over Peaksville High School, interrupting the silence.

"Dean Michaels signing off."

Gloria cried. "Car accident? Nurse Ferguson said she was transferred."

Amy looked at me. "She's not a real nurse. Her lanyard ID said Peaksville Defense and Space Corporation CABESA Targeting Manager. She's a fraud."

I rubbed my arm. "That's why it hurt so bad."

Gloria pulled out a pill case and helplessly sobbed.

I looked at my sister. "What are those for?"

Gloria wiped her eyes. "Nurse Light told me on Friday she was in danger and she may have to visit her oldest son."

I was confused. "Ben's an only child."

"That's what she told me. She clearly said she would soon be visiting him."

I looked at Gloria's pill case. "Gloria?"

Gloria whispered. "Nurse Light gave me these pills two weeks ago. They seem to be working. Peaksville Hospital doctors lied to me a few months ago."

I waited. "Gloria?"

Gloria paused. "Grace, they wanted me to advance to stage four."

"What are you saying?"

My sister had cancer? My horrible dream continued. I fainted.

God was testing me.

. . .

C harlotte collected her homework and approached Luke near the water fountain. "How do you feel?"

Luke struggled to operate the water fountain. "I think I have a fever."

Charlotte gently held Luke's forehead. "Meet me at my farm in fifteen minutes."

Dean Michaels commenced pre-dismissal announcements. "Good afternoon. Today is Monday. Nine days of school remain. The Safety Corps Air Patrol continues to search for suspects responsible for the poisonous HAZMAT schoolyard substance that burned the lungs and throats of many students. All areas west of The Meadow remain off limits. Rule violators risk not graduating. Many flu-like symptoms persist today. Water fountains are secured. PSU Department of Experimental Child Psychology released a study detailing academic success. Students who respected authority were thirty-five percent more likely to receive good grades and fifty-five percent less likely to dropout. Peaksville Institutes of Health is inviting twenty high school students to participate in an ongoing study about heart arrhythmias. Students over ten years old can earn three hundred dollars per week. School is dismissed. Be safe out there."

Ruby caught up with Luke as the Bell 407 orbited overhead the schoolyard. "Hey, Luke!"

"Hi, Ruby. I'm in a hurry. Charlie told me to meet at the Epley farm."

Ruby sighed. "Everyone?"

Luke kept walking. "I think just me."

Ruby stopped. "Oh."

B rianna walked into Antoine's hospital room.

Emma wiped her eyes and sat in the courtesy leather chair. "Hey, Bree."

"Emma and D'Andre, how long have you guys been here?"

D'Andre shrugged. "Only two minutes."

"Did you tell Antoine about Marcus?" Brianna asked.

Emma nodded. "Can AJ hear us?"

Brianna nodded. "Definitely."

Emma looked at Antoine and whispered. "Please wake up, AJ. I'm sorry that I was mean to you."

Nurse Ferguson entered and walked to the notification board.

Brianna politely greeted her. "Hello."

No response.

She violently erased 'Nurse Light' and scribbled 'Ferguson' utilizing a dry erase marker. She walked towards Antoine's bed, observed the vital signs, and left.

D'Andre heard Nurse Ferguson leave. "What was that?"

Brianna Lopez sadly explained. "Ferguson erased Nurse Light and wrote her name."

C harlotte rigged the cart behind Butters in the red barn. "Luke! You're here!"

Luke smiled and stared at Charlotte's newly-braided hairstyle.

"Luke, help me with this yoke."

Luke dropped his homework and helped. "Where are you going?"

Charlotte smiled and scratched Butters under his chin. "Same place you're going. Back to the mine to collect dozens of neodymium magnet rocks."

"It's Monday."

Charlotte yelled over the TSC Bell 407 orbiting overhead her barn. "Just overnight!"

The rotor wash blew dust around as Luke spoke. "I didn't pack!"

Charlotte threw canteens, her 1970's red metal Coleman cooler and lighter fluid onto the cart near the hay and Sweet COB. "Got you covered."

"But the Rope Bridge is broken."

Charlotte threw several mountaineering carabiners onto the cart and smiled. "Got us covered. Saddle up, partner."

M rs. Becker answered the door. "Ryan, give me a hug. I'm so sorry. Your father, Derrick, and now Marcus."

Ryan cried in her arms on the porch as Mr. Burns passed overhead in the Bell 407.

"We're here for you. How's Mrs. Flynn?"

Ryan's sadness rendered him speechless.

"Here to see Gloria?"

"Actually, Grace."

"Come on in, Sweetie."

Mom entered my bedroom. "Someone's here to see you, Gracie."

Trying not to aggravate my mountain lion bite wounds, I slowly stood and walked to the living room. Ryan was sobbing uncontrollably.

"I tried, Grace."

I hugged him. "Oh, Ryan. I know you did."

Ryan wiped his eyes. "Please forgive me."

I hugged him again. "You didn't do anything wrong."

Ryan cried harder. "I better go, Grace."

I didn't make things better for Ryan.

Ryan left as the Cessna 182 buzzed down my street.

Peaksville *was* statistically the safest place in America. Our last murder was thirty years ago. But in two weeks, seven Peaksville sheepdogs were taken from us by wolves.

Why would anybody kill a sheepdog?

N urse Ferguson looked at Dr. Moriarty. "General Voigt said Queen Bee threatened to defund $250 billion from PDS, PIH, and PsytoSCOPE in the 2021 fiscal year."

"Why should innocent CABESA stakeholders suffer from TSC's inability to deliver simple 24/7 trauma?" Dr. Moriarty grumbled.

Nurse Ferguson stirred her Whiskey Sour in the smoke-filled tavern. "The Kernan boy talks."

"Since when?"

"Since this weekend. Project Jack accidentally said *ouch* after a Monday shot."

"What else?"

"TSC SIGINT recorded the twins coaching Jack not to speak to school personnel."

"At school?"

"Tucking him into bed. Amy and Emma actually had him reading Dr. Suess books aloud before bed."

Dr. Moriarty drank his beer. "What should we do, Charity?"

Nurse Ferguson sloppily grabbed a handful of free pretzels. "I'm just a PDS Targeting Engineer wearing a nurse's uniform. You're the PSU Experimental Child Psychologist, *Doctor* Moriarty."

"Actually, I'm not really a medical doctor. I just run the department."

Nurse Ferguson drank some Whiskey Sour and scooted closer. "That's not what you said last night."

L uke pensively stoked the campfire outside the old West Peaksville Neodymium Mine. "I should have jumped in to save Chloe. Marcus would still be alive."

Charlotte lay on her back and gazed at the peaceful TFZ sky. "It was an accident."

Luke grabbed Charlotte's hand. "I was scared, Charlie."

"It's okay to be scared."

Luke and Charlotte gazed at the stars.

Charlotte scooted closer as the cold evening air mass rolled down the mountainside like clockwork. "Luke?"

"Yeah, Charlie."

"How did you like the hot cocoa?"

"Great."

Charlotte whispered. "Are you chilly?"

"Little bit."

Charlotte nestled even closer, rested her head on Luke's chest and smiled in the moonlight. "I'll miss you this fall, Luke."

CHAPTER FORTY-EIGHT

Aaron and I snuck into the Peaksville High School Alumni Lounge on Tuesday morning. We flipped through the senior photos organized by year.

"Here it is. Class of 2017," Aaron whispered.

I held the gold ring up so Aaron could read it. "Initials BPL."

Aaron searched alphabetically using his index finger. "I'll be damned."

"What?"

"Brian P. Light. 2017."

My jaw dropped. "Nurse Light recently told Gloria that Ben had a brother. Ben calls himself an only child."

Aaron was angry. "They murdered Brian."

"*Who* murdered Brian?" I asked.

"The same people who murdered your dad."

I needed to know. "Tell me."

"This will be our secret." Aaron quickly paged back to the Class of 1987. "Ready?"

I whispered angrily and nodded. "I want revenge. I want justice."

Aaron suddenly slammed the PHS graduation photo boards shut as the Cessna 182 buzzed the school roof. "Not yet."

"Now."

Aaron whispered. "Too dangerous."

I was confused. "Too dangerous for you?"

"Too dangerous for *you*. Let's get out of here, Grace."

Once clear of the PHS Alumni Lounge, Aaron slipped a book into my hands.

I whispered. "*The Count of Monte Cristo?*"

"Read it."

"Then tell me who killed my dad."

The third bell rang.

"As you wish."

R uby looked at her watch in the student lounge. Her pensive countenance was an easy read. "Amy, what time to you have?"

The Cessna 182 orbited overhead Peaksville High School.

Amy iced her forehead. "Noon."

Thomas snored and slobbered on the couch.

"Tommy Boy," Aaron whispered.

I placed my hand on Aaron's knee. "He vomited twice. Let him sleep."

Our morning headaches intensified. "You okay, Emma?"

Emma signaled she may throw up again.

Aaron pointed to the cafeteria. "Charlie and Luke. They're back."

Ruby displayed a measured smile. "Hi, Luke!"

Charlotte handed me duct tape. "Plenty of three-pound magnetic rocks in this bag. You know what to do."

Ben Light curiously ogled our interaction from the north side of the cafeteria.

I covered my mouth and whispered. "Charlie, what about Chloe, Gigi, and Jack?"

"Middle School is done. Kiddos are wearing them."

The Bell 407 pulled into a slow hover over the roof.

Charlotte looked at her watch. "Butters is grazing on the soccer field. Luke and I need to stable him before Dean Michaels literally has a cow. See you in fifth period."

Ruby disconsolately watched Luke leave with Charlotte.

Being a teenager was difficult.

Especially in Peaksville.

A fter lunch, Mr. Burns angrily thumped overhead Peaksville High School roof at ninety knots and two hundred feet. "Drop Lock. I lost the Projects."

Mr. Light made one last attempt in his Cessna 182. "Confirm proper frequencies?"

"Affirmative," Mr. Burns transmitted on TSC Base Frequency. "They worked all morning."

Mr. Light entered a lazy orbit troubleshooting his MEDWEAP. "Didn't Charity introduce new PstyoSCOPE Lot-22 imaging probes yesterday?"

"Affirmative. Projects received double shots."

Mr. Light fumbled for his vibrating iPhone, climbed to five hundred feet, and transmitted on VHF. "Rug, standby five mikes. Swamp is calling on my cellphone."

Colonel Marsh initiated the phone call from the Pentagon to Peaksville, Idaho. "You there, Bud?"

Mr. Light entered an eighty-knot left orbit over the school, lowered his boom microphone and yelled into his iPhone. "Swamp, good to hear your voice!"

"I hear an engine."

"Warn me if the noise stops." Mr. Light joked.

Colonel Marsh laughed. "Ha!"

"Second thought, don't warn me. Queen Bee can't fire me if I buy the farm."

"That bad?"

Mr. Light sighed. "Our Projects learned to defeat the weapon targeting."

"Queen Bee should replace those derelict urchins with the retired PIH Spider Monkeys."

"She's more likely to replace me with a Spider Monkey."

"Spider Monkeys can't fly, Bud."

"Swamp, I taught you how to fly T-37 Tweets at Vance AFB."

Colonel Marsh laughed. "Good point. Anything's possible, I guess."

Mr. Light abruptly corrected his inadvertent altitude drop by yanking the controls backward. "Why did you call me, Swamp?"

"The USAF Chief of Staff recently did a presentation while seeking additional MEDWEAP funding. He said the Peaksville TSC is illuminating the Beacon of Freedom on the Shining City on a Hill."

"Thanks, Swamp. I needed that. Freedom isn't free."

"Amen, Brother."

"Rug is burning holes in the sky waiting for me."

"Fly safe, Bud."

"Famous last words."

Mr. Light stowed his iPhone and transmitted on VHF. "Rug, you up?"

"I'm up."

"Go cheap suit."

Mr. Burns dialed in VHF audio frequency 119.95 MHz. "Checking-in on cheap suit."

"Gas check."

"1+40 remaining," Mr. Burns replied.

"Rendevoux over Peaksville Hospital. Ready to cook Veggie Boy?"

"Born ready. Picking up his FREQ already."

Mr. Light instructed his TSC deputy. "Doc Hertz requested focused-beams to the head for thirty minutes. Veggie Boy almost woke up yesterday."

"I'll take brainstem at two-hundred feet. You take frontal lobe at three-hundred."

Mr. Light pointed his nose at the hospital. "Always hated his Squid dad."

"Seriously? You didn't like Navy Doc *'Whistleblower'* Jordan?"

"Serious as a heart attack."

Mr. Burns stabilized over the hospital. "Locked on?"

"Affirmative.

"Light him up."

O ur headaches, Ben Light's smile, and TSC overflights dissipated from a ten to a zero before the beginning of the sixth period.

Luke and Charlotte were hailed as Tuesday afternoon heroes.

Life was good.

Dean Michaels keyed the microphone at 2:55pm to initiate his ritual broadcast. "Good afternoon Peaksville students. Eight days of school remain. Internships opportunities exist at kid-friendly PsytoSCOPE Nanotech Corporation, Peaksville Defense and Space Corporation, and the Peaksville Institutes of Health. The PSU Department of Experimental Child Psychology study reveals a high correlation between juvenile delinquency and headaches. A thirty percent increase in juvenile delinquency increases headache severity by sixty percent. TSC Air Patrol search patterns will continue due to recent terror activity. Kid-friendly TSC keeps innocent citizens safe. School's out. Be safe out there."

The PA system transmission was punctuated by a one hundred and fifty knot flyby at two hundred feet by the Cessna 182.

Ben Light made eye contact with Ryan in the schoolyard, smiled and rubbed his eyes as if he were crying.

Aaron grabbed the back of Ryan's shirt. "Don't take the bait, Ryan."

Ryan flipped Ben the bird.

B rianna covertly taped a neodymium magnet rock to Antoine's calf in his hospital room.

"Hi Miss Lopez, visiting Antoine again?" Nurse Ferguson asked.

Brianna acted like she was adjusting his bed sheet. "Yes, Ma'am."

"Two weeks until Graduation. Excited?"

"Yes, Ma'am."

Nurse Ferguson picked up Antoine's chart. "I've been meaning to ask you. How are your headaches?"

Brianna was rattled. "Who, me?"

"I thought you told me you get headaches."

"No, Ma'am."

"Never?"

Brianna lied. "Never."

"Good for you! Must have been someone else who told me that. Would you like to work this summer at PSU Department of Experimental Child Psychology? Dr. Moriarty specifically requested you, Miss Lopez."

"Who's he?"

"The Department Director."

Brianna uncomfortably declined. "No, thanks."

"Your quality of life would dramatically improve, Miss Lopez."

Brianna internally reflected. "*This strange woman yields power over my life?*"

"I'm fine. Thanks, Ma'am."

"Okay. But think about your future." Nurse Ferguson exited Antoine's hospital room.

M r. Light transmitted to Mr. Burns on VHF 119.95, "Drop Lock on Veggie Boy."

"Concur."

Mr. Light climbed to five hundred feet to troubleshoot his PDS weapons. "You think they wheeled him into the lead-walled X-Ray room?"

"Not sure."

Mr. Light fumbled for his iPhone. "Standby, Rug."

Mr. Webster answered his phone. "Hey, Bud."

"Is that your G-Wagen outside Peaksville Hospital?"

"Affirmative. I see you both circling. What's up flyboy?"

"Did you just Drop Lock on Veggie Boy?"

"Affirmative. Cooked him for an hour. He went midnight two minutes ago."

"Copy, Web. Please call Charity to investigate."

"Wilco, Bud."

Mr. Light stowed the iPhone.

"Rug, you there?"

"Affirmative."

Mr. Light keyed the microphone. "Dr. Hertz has probably already called General Voigt to blame the TSC on the Drop Locks."

"The same Dr. Hertz that blamed us for blinding Veggie Boy's brother four years ago?"

"Same guy." Mr. Light rolled his Cessna 182 into a steep bank and pulled backstick towards Peaksville Municipal Airport.

Mr. Burns lowered his nose and accelerated. "I'll race you to the fuel pits."

CHAPTER FORTY-NINE

"Hello, Mr. Flynn."

Ryan entered the office and sat down in front of Dean Michaels. "Hello, Sir."

"I assume you realize why you're sitting in my office on a Wednesday morning."

Ryan was genuinely confused. "No, Sir."

"Yesterday, you made a terroristic threat towards a TSC Cadet."

Ryan was speechless.

"Aren't you going to defend yourself?"

"Sir, perhaps you have the wrong student?"

Dean Michaels read the TSC Report. "Mr. Ryan Flynn. Terroristic threat directed at Benjamin Light during Tuesday dismissal."

Ryan raised his right hand. "This is what I did, Sir. I gave him the bird."

"I know the bird. Lower your right hand, Mr. Flynn."

Ryan slowly retracted his middle finger.

"Peaksville High School does not tolerate terroristic threats. Especially threats aimed at authority."

Ryan replied. "Authority?"

Dean Michaels sighed. "Your brothers Marcus and Derrick were trouble makers. Don't follow in their footsteps, Ryan."

Blood uncontrollably rushed to Ryan Flynn's Irish face.

"Do you have anything to say to me, Ryan?"

Ryan quickly stood and walked out.

Dean Michaels spoke before Ryan exited. "You're dismissed, Ryan."

T he PIH CABESA Project Manager delivered harsh criticism via cellphone. "Bud, do we have to bring back to the PIH Spider Monkeys?"

"No, Dr. Hertz."

"Queen Bee is worried. They may scrub the 2021 Peaksville Project. We have families. I have five children. Ivy league schools are expensive. For your information, CABESA leadership may drop the TSC and switch to a Non-Governmental Organization to enforce law in North Idaho."

"That's unconstitutional, the TSC Officers have inalienable rights. This is a free country! This isn't the Soviet Union!"

"You have two weeks, Bud."

Mr. Light paused. "Dr. Hertz, soon your troubles will disappear."

"They better!"

"You have my word on it."

Click!

Mr. Light disconnected with Dr. Hertz and phoned Mr. Burns. "Rug, got something going on."

"The PsytoSCOPE aerosol ScatterSMART Lung Targeting Probes? I thought that was already a go."

"Parallel operation."

Mr. Burns paused and evaluated the tone of Mr. Light. "Sanctioned?"

"Not exactly."

"Potential flashback?"

"I'll keep you clear of the frag pattern."

"Where are you?"

"Filing my flight plan."

"Meet me in the pilot's lounge."

" G racie, we're all going swimming!"

I slammed my locker and stuffed my backpack. "Count me in, Ruby Kyle!"

Ruby smiled.

I caught Luke near the drinking fountain. "Luke, the rocks worked!"

Dean Michaels initiated his dismissal announcement. "Today is Wednesday. Ten days until the graduation ceremony. TSC Air Patrols operate 24/7 for the well-being of the citizens, especially the children. Peaksville State University released a study detailing a disorder called Perceived Pain Syndrome or PPS. The young mind routinely manufactures pain, discomfort, and psychosomatic symptoms. Twenty-seven percent of all children struggle with PPS. Perceived Pain Syndrome is normally associated with school truancy. To learn more about Perceived Pain Syndrome, please see Nurse Ferguson or confidentially self-report using a SMIR station."

Aaron looked at me, pointed up at the speaker, and whispered. "Horsecrap."

Dean Michaels continued. "Kid-friendly PstyoSCOPE Nanotech Corporation has summer internship opportunities. PNC is strategic partner of the TSC and major local funding recipient of the 2013 CABESA and Nanotechnology Initiatives. PNC helps the PIH eradicate cancer from our community. Accepting applications immediately. Air quality remains RED. School's out. Be safe out there."

I wondered how many of the 1000 Peaksville High School students believed the Dean Michaels broadcasts.

Hopefully zero.

But probably most.

E mma entered The Boxcar and towel dried her hair. "The rocks worked."

Charlotte winked and lounged inside The Boxcar after her swim. "I feel young again."

Luke laughed. "You're eighteen."

"You know what I mean."

I sat on the couch and cherished my friendships. "Seven more school days. I'll always remember you guys."

Ruby and Emma leaned on me as the kiddos entered The Boxcar.

I whispered to Jack. "Hey buddy, how's the talking?"

Jack smiled and whispered in my ear. "My sisters don't want me to speak at school until August."

Amy explained. "Nurse Ferguson keeps trying to get Jack to speak."

Emma agreed. "She knows."

Perhaps the Kernan twins were being overly cautious.

Slam!

The Boxcar wooden door slammed shut and a metal canister bounced into the retired train car.

Ryan yelled in the darkness. "Who's there?"

No response.

Click!

The door was mechanically latched from the outside before we heard footsteps running away.

Aaron quickly attempted to open the door. "Ryan! Luke! Give me a hand!"

Cough!

Ryan and Luke coughed!

Cough! Cough! Cough!

We instantly were all stricken with a fit of violent coughing and lung pain.

My first instinct was to yell for help. I couldn't yell. I whispered. "Hurts."

Bang! Bang! Bang!

The boys unsuccessfully pulled, kicked and body-slammed the sliding door. We were trapped and inhaling something insidious. Gas attacks were not supposed to happen to rural North Idaho children.

Our lungs and throats burned and ached.

I whispered. "Are we dying?"

Cough! Cough! Cough!

Nobody could hear my faint speech.

Click! Slam!

A person outside of The Boxcar unlatched and opened the door as the TSC Bell 407 hovered at one hundred feet overhead.

Madison looked outside and whispered. "It's Bree!"

Brianna emergently evacuated us from the noxious fumes.

Aaron and Ryan coughed and helped.

Tears streamed down our faces.

I looked at Brianna, pointed at my lungs and whispered. "Hurts —"

She helped me drink. It didn't help.

I cried so hard.

Brianna checked inside to make sure we all escaped. "What happened?"

Cough! Cough! Cough!

Emma wiped her eyes. "Someone locked —"

Gigi cried. "Oh, Bree —"

Aaron stood up, walked fifteen feet into the trees while coughing, and picked up a red lanyard and ID card from the forest floor.

Brianna read it aloud. "Charity Ferguson. Peaksville Defense and Space."

My horrible dream just got worse.

M y mom brought us iced teas as we recovered in my television room. "Pizza is in the oven."

Charlotte politely smiled in lieu of speaking.

Aaron looked around, sat up and painfully grumbled. "Tommy Boy."

I checked the living room. "He mentioned Peaksville Hospital. I warned him not to go."

Aaron nodded. "Same."

Luke remembered and whispered. "On the way here, Tommy Boy said he was going home."

Ruby lamented. "I hope he listens."

"Kid is stubborn." Aaron rubbed his forehead. "He still trusts the TSC."

"Still?" D'Andre questioned. "How?"

"Want the classic technical term?" Aaron sighed. "Stockholm Syndrome."

I looked at my watch. "Bree ran ahead to the hospital to check Antoine's magnet. If Tommy Boy goes there, she'll stop him."

Mom entered the TV room holding a paper. "Grace, a letter arrived from Congresswoman Abby Walker, Peaksville's U.S. Representative. This is in response to our letters two weeks ago requesting a Congressional Investigation. Want me to read it?"

I anxiously sat up. "Please."

Mom quickly scanned the letter embossed with official Congressional letterhead, sobbed and handed it to Gloria.

D*ear Mr. Becker, I want to take this opportunity to thank you for your letter regarding your family. Unfortunately, your situation appears to involve a legal dispute requiring resolution under the judicial system, and the Constitution mandates a separation of powers between the Judicial, Executive, and Legislative branches. Based on the information that you provided, it appears this is a matter outside the jurisdiction of the legislative branch, and I feel that my involvement in your present situation may be viewed as an interference in the judicial process. Mr. Becker, I am sorry that I cannot be of assistance at this time and your correspondence is being returned to you.*

S*incerely,*
   Abby Walker
Member of U.S. Congress

C hloe raised her hand. "Gloria, does that mean she's going to help?"

Charlotte hugged her sister. "No Chloe, she isn't going to help."

The Cessna 182 buzzed down our street as Brianna knocked on our door. "Tommy Boy is gone! They took him from Mrs. Stallworth at Peaksville Hospital."

"What happened, Bree?" Luke asked.

"I saw Thomas in the ER. He said his lungs and sinuses were burning. They repeatedly asked why. He initially didn't say. Nurse Ferguson threatened to charge Mrs. Stallworth with child abuse if he didn't say. Tommy Boy then described the gas attack to save his mother. They tied him to a wheelchair and drove him away in a white van."

I was terrified. "Where did they take him, Bree?"

Brianna cried and shrugged. "They wouldn't even tell Mrs. Stallworth."

CHAPTER FIFTY

Thursday morning. Seven more days of school.

The TSC Cessna 182 woke me up at four o'clock with monotonous subdivision overflights at five-minute intervals. They departed at six o'clock. Perhaps Mr. Light had to go home and cook breakfast for his wonderful son, Ben? Not sure.

Peace and quiet, finally.

Twenty minutes later, the TSC Bell 407 search helicopter began overflights at four-minute intervals.

So annoying! The noise aggravated my cardio-vascular system. I found my pulse and counted for ten seconds. Nineteen beats. Multiply by six. "114 beats per minute at rest? Can't be right."

Seemed too high. Morning math error? This time, I timed for thirty seconds. Fifty-nine beats. Multiply by two. "118 beats per minute. Oh, God. What's wrong with me?"

I showed Ruby. "Check this out."

Emma the Junior Olympian was sleeping next to me on the television room floor. I gently measured her pulse and showed Ruby. "124 beats per minute. Mine is about 115."

We measured Ruby's pulse.

Ruby gasped and whispered. "One-twenty?"

I leaned back and shrugged. "Maybe a high morning pulse was normal for an eighteen-year-old?"

Ruby shook her head.

Seven o'clock arrived too early.

Amy entered the room with Kiche at her side. "Rise and shine, losers! Pancakes everyone! Hot, buttery and steamy!"

I tried to smile. "Thanks, Amy."

During breakfast, my pulse seemed to drop below 100 BPM, but my headache and chest pain lasted all day.

R uby joined us in the student lounge for lunch. "I feel like I'm dying."

Charlotte agreed. "It's like a knife going through my chest."

I iced my forehead after the Cessna 182 noise subsided. "That Cessna woke me up at four. Where do they get all of their gas money?"

"Tax dollars funneled through industry." Aaron measured his own pulse. "I think I'm going to pass out. My heart is racing."

Emma made room on the couch and patted the seat. "Come here, Aaron."

Luke was pale. "Where do you think they took Tommy Boy?"

Aaron Webster replied. "I'll find out tonight."

I looked at my watch. "Fourth period starts in five minutes."

Ben returned his food tray, smiled at Ryan and walked towards his fourth period classroom.

Mr. Burns buzzed the cafeteria roof in the TSC Bell 407.

Ryan followed Ben.

Gloria sighed. "I hope Ryan doesn't hurt Ben."

Amy replied. "Why?"

"Can someone make sure Ryan isn't getting in trouble?" Gloria asked.

Amy laughed and stood up. "Come on, Bree."

Aaron looked at us and held his chest. "Operation RECIPROCITY begins this weekend. I have some things to show you all." He was definitely planning mischief.

I wanted in.

Aaron looked at me and whispered. "Read the prerequisite book, first."

Amy and Brianna returned their food trays, hustled towards their lockers, and heard banging in the hallway.

"Let me out!"

Amy stopped and placed her hands on her hips. "Bree, a locker is talking."

"I heard you, Kernan. Open the door," Ben Light said.

Amy touched the metal locker. "They finally did it! They invented talking A.I. lockers. Locker, what is your name?"

"Amy, this is Ben. Open the door."

Brianna Lopez laughed. "Fascinating technology."

"Locker, what gender is Ben?"

No response.

Brianna joked. "They have to iron some kinks out."

Amy continued. "Locker, has Ben ever kissed a girl?"

No response.

"Okay Ben. Don't tell on Ryan, and we won't tell on you. Deal?"

No response.

Brianna smiled at Amy.

Amy repeated herself. "Deal?"

"Deal."

Amy opened the locker and looked at her watch. "Better get to class, Mr. Only Child."

Y ou know you're in pain when you anxiously await your daily dose of truth from Dean Michaels.

Click!

I sighed and whispered. "Yes."

"Just a few Thursday afternoon announcements. Dr. Hands from KidCare Counseling Services will conduct an on-campus Stress Management Workshop Friday at 9 o'clock. A new Peaksville State University study reveals that second-hand smoke increases Childhood Lung Discomfort (CLD) by forty percent. Kid-friendly PsytoSCOPE Nanotech Corporation offers college scholarships for qualified Seniors. Please report classmates in need of counseling to any of the two dozen SMIR stations around campus. Confidentially provided and guaranteed to the reporting student. Some financial incentives may also apply. Six days of school remain. School is dismissed. Be safe out there."

Ryan slammed his locker. "Gloria and I are travelling to repair the rope. Come with us, Luke."

Luke sipped a bottle of cold water. "You read my mind, Ryan."

Ruby bumped shoulders with Luke. "Count me in. I'll bring Kiche."

D'Andre gathered his books in the hallway. "Ryan, can I go?"

Ryan prepared a gently-worded response. "You should travel with the Friday gaggle, DJ. It might be safer."

"My head hurts. My chest hurts. I can't wait. Please, Ryan."

Ryan paused. "Okay, buddy." Ryan placed his arm around D'Andre's shoulders. "We leave in one hour."

D'Andre smiled.

. . .

A aron and I visited Antoine in Peaksville Hospital.

Mrs. Jordan smiled. "Charlie and Bree beat you here. Join us!"

I hugged Mrs. Jordan. "Antoine's going to wake up soon. I really have a good feeling about it."

Mrs. Jordan held my hand. "Thanks, Gracie."

Aaron examined Antoine's I.V. connections. "Grace?"

Aaron's gears were turning. "Yes, Aaron?"

"Does Mrs. Becker know how to administer I.V.'s and feeding tubes?"

"Of course."

"Charlie?"

"Yes, Aaron?"

"Is Butters available tomorrow night?"

"Friday?" Charlotte asked.

Aaron nodded affirmatively.

"Butters is going out tomorrow night. He's getting his hooves done, then he has tap dancing lessons."

"Kidding?"

Charlotte put her hands on her hips.

Aaron sighed. "You're kidding."

Mrs. Jordan knew she was next.

"Mrs. Jordan?"

Nurse Ferguson lumbered into the hospital room, clumsily checked the vital signs, and exited without saying a word.

"One second." Aaron walked to the door, scanned the hallway, returned to Antoine's bedside and looked at Mrs. Jordan. "Are you —"

Mrs. Jordan interrupted, sobbed and hugged Aaron. "Yes, Aaron! Tomorrow night. The answer is yes!"

R yan unwound after his Thursday night Rope Bridge repair in the TFZ moonlight. D'Andre kept him company next to their fading campfire as Luke, Ruby and Gloria slept soundly in the West Peaksville Neodymium Mine.

"DJ?"

D'Andre continued Kiche's belly-scratch. "Yeah?"

"I miss my dad and brothers. I feel so alone."

"You're not alone, Ryan."

Ryan placed a dried cedar branch on the fire. "Why didn't God take me instead?"

"God chose you to stay and fight."

"Fight what?"

D'Andre paused. "The eternal fight. Against Evil."

Ryan stoked and rekindled the remaining embers. "I opt out."

"Ha!" D'Andre laughed. "It's not that simple. You can't opt out, Ryan."

"Why?"

"Because Evil opted you *in*."

CHAPTER FIFTY-ONE

"Good morning, Bud. Did I catch you at a bad time?"

"Getting weather in Base Ops. What's up, Boss?"

General Voigt sat in his executive leather chair. "When was the last time you spoke to Dr. Hertz?"

Mr. Light printed the latest METAR's and TAF's depicting significant weather in the area. "Last week sometime."

"Our PIH CABESA Director was found dead this morning. Had a heart attack in his sleep."

"Huh." Mr. Light stacked his flight planning documents. "He wasn't even that old."

"No, he wasn't that old, was he, Bud?"

Mr. Light collected his flight publications and typed Project frequencies into his PDS MEDWEAP. "Well at least he died doing God's work, developing medical weapons for America. He was a good man."

General Voigt overlooked the high-tech Peaksville Defense and Space production line from his office. "Bud, I'm going to be really blunt. No Extra-Judicial Killing unless sanctioned by Queen Bee or myself."

"Sir, I would never —"

"Colonel Raymond Gunnison will replace Dr. Hertz on Monday at PIH. Queen Bee wants a brief regarding the transition. Dr. Gunnison is a retired USAF Doctor, so he'll understand the CABESA Initiative, MEDWEAP testing and human experimentation."

"Perfect! Raygun was my Flight Surgeon during Operation ENDURING FREEDOM for two years in the sandbox."

General Voigt paused. "No more monkey business."

No response.

"Fly safe, Bud."

B en Light smiled at us during a Cessna 182 overflight before Friday homeroom. I whispered. "Maddie, it's a good thing Ryan's already in the TFZ."

Madison nodded. "Ryan wants revenge."

Amy rubbed her temples. "Me too."

Emma shrugged. "There's not much we can do."

I agreed. "Yeah, we're only eighteen."

Aaron Webster disagreed. "There's a lot we can do."

Brianna removed the ice from her forehead. "Like what, vote?"

"We can do a lot more than vote." Aaron whispered. "Operation RECIPROCITY starts tonight."

The first bell rang.

Aaron stood up. "Five o'clock at the Epley farm."

T he Rope Bridge repair team quintet slept well in the mine with Kiche after their Thursday evening journey and river passage project.

D'Andre gradually woke up to the sensation of a large wolf licking his face. "Kiche, stop."

Kiche continued licking his eyes.

He giggled in the darkness. "Stop."

The tall she-wolf nudged him.

D'Andre tried unsuccessfully to wrestle her down after covering his face didn't work. "Go to sleep, Girl."

She nuzzled her nose under D'Andre and playfully rolled him over.

"Okay, I'll let you out." D'Andre rubbed his eyes and faced the cave entrance. "But it's a cave. You could let *yourself* out."

Kiche wagged her tail.

Things were different. Yesterday, there was light or darkness. This morning, D'Andre distinguished a rectangular entrance framing the light.

"That's strange." D'Andre stood, closed his eyes, slowly walked to the light with his eyes closed and whispered. "Lord, I'm afraid to open my eyes."

Standing between the wooden stanchions of the West Peaksville Neodimium

Mine, D'Andre stretched his arms outwards, spread his ten fingers wide-open, faced the North Idaho sunrise and opened his eyes.

"Oh, sweet Jesus." D'Andre cried tears of joy. A cold, blue mountain stream flowed below. A bald eagle soared majestically above an adjacent rocky ridge. Several small birds darted between the trees. The tall cedars and tamaracks were green, brown, and full of life. "Thank you, Lord!"

Kiche playfully curled around him and panted.

D'Andre could see again! He wiped his tears, turned around, entered the dark mine and knelt next to Ruby and Gloria. "Girls, wake up!"

Ruby and Gloria awakened slowly. "DJ?"

"You're each so beautiful. Even more beautiful than I remembered."

"DJ?"

D'Andre held Ruby's face. "I can see you, Ruby!"

Ruby cried.

D'Andre held Gloria's face. "And I can see you, Gloria!"

Gloria screamed. "Oh DJ! You can see! DJ can see!"

"Ryan! Luke!" Ruby and Gloria hugged and kissed D'Andre. "Wake up! DJ can see!"

"I knew this day would come, buddy!" Luke stood and wept.

D'Andre smiled.

"Incredible." Luke wiped his eyes and laughed.

Ryan woke and sat up. "For real?"

D'Andre shined in the darkness. "For real!"

The five Peaksville children joyfully exited the mine.

Ruby petted Kiche. "Let's all take a nature walk!"

Gloria grabbed D'Andre's shoulders and gazed deeply in his eyes.

D'Andre smiled. "What are you looking at, Gloria?"

Gloria wept. "A miracle."

F riday dismissal arrived! One more week of school!

The PA system activated! "Good afternoon, Peaksville high school students."

Music to my ears! I looked at Aaron, smiled and stowed my *Count of Monte Cristo* book. Aaron read my mind. I wished I could read *his* mind. What did Aaron have in store for us this weekend?

Dean Michaels continued. "Final exams begin Monday. Graduation next Saturday for eligible seniors. Kid-friendly INLINE Pharmaceuticals is offering $100 per week to children suffering from daily headaches who would like to try their newest line of medication. School's out. Be safe out there."

. . .

The Cessna 182 orbited in a left-hand, twenty-five-degree angle of bank turn over the schoolyard.

"Jack!" Emma called her brother as he walked.

Jack collided into Nurse Ferguson.

Wham!

"Excuse me, Ma'am."

Nurse Ferguson watched Jack run to Emma. "You're excused, Jack!"

Emma whispered. "Jack, she's the one to avoid."

Jack whispered. "Sorry, she bumped me. I accidentally spoke."

Nurse Ferguson gave Emma a creepy look and lifted her iPhone.

"PSU Department of Experimental Child Psychology. How may I help you?"

"Dr. Moriarty, please. This is Nurse Ferguson."

"Stand by."

Dr. Moriarty picked up his phone. "Charity?"

Nurse Ferguson turned away from the Kernans.

"Confirmed. CABESA Project Jack speaks."

"I was afraid of that." Dr. Moriarty paused. "He *must* get his shot next Monday."

"I'll give him a double shot."

"I have to go drop off my kids at baseball practice. Meet me at Peaksville Tavern in thirty minutes for a *double shot* of whiskey."

Nurse Ferguson smiled. "Just what the doctor ordered."

The Epley family hosted campfire cheeseburgers and French fries while Aaron briefed the first element of Operation RECIPROCITY.

After dinner, we manned our stations at Peaksville Hospital.

Chloe, Gigi, and Jack excitedly rehearsed their roles in the hospital television lounge.

Gigi saw Aaron pass in the hallway. "Now?"

Aaron whispered. "Not yet."

The kiddos anxiously anticipated their cue as they listened to an INLINE Pharmaceuticals television commercial advertising their new psychotropic drug treating adolescent anxiety.

Chloe watched as Dr. Klein's 90-second INLINE ANXIETY commercial looped. Over. And over. And over. And over. "What's anxiety, Jack?"

"I don't know." Jack shrugged. "But I hope we start soon."

Chloe whispered. "I can't *wait* to start."

Aaron passed again.

Gigi pointed at her watch. "Now?"

Aaron leaned into the hospital television lounge and whispered. "Commence Operation ANTOINE in thirty seconds."

The middle schoolers excitedly counted down on their fingers.

"Three, two, one." Chloe smirked. "Now."

Jack giggled loudly and ran down the hospital hallway. "Tag you're it!"

Chloe ran and joked. "You're it!"

Gigi screamed and ran past the nurse station. "Tag you're it! Double-stamped it!"

"Children, this is a hospital!"

Chloe screamed. "Yes, ma'am!"

Gigi sprinted away. "Tag you're it, Jack! Triple-stamped it!"

The kiddos shrewdly escaped to the west wing before being scolded again.

"Can't triple-stamp a double-stamp!" Jack yelled as he ran away. "Can't triple-stamp a double-stamp!"

Aaron checked the hallway outside Antoine's hospital room. "Clear."

I smiled at Aaron then looked at my mom.

"Antoine, it's Friday night." Brianna whispered. "Time to rock and roll, buddy."

My mom quickly disconnected a few leads, left a few connected, and double-checked Antoine's vital signs.

Madison whispered. "You really are combat medic, Mrs. Becker."

"Gracie and Bree, lift AJ to the wheelchair. Count of three. One, two, *three*."

Outside, Gigi sprinted past the nurse station giggling. "You cheated!"

Chloe laughed. "*You* cheated!"

Jack serpentined down the hallway with his arms widely extended, imitating the Cessna 182's engine noise. "WAAAaaahhh!"

Hospital personnel reprimanded the twelve-year-olds as they rounded the corner. "Children!"

Nearby, Aaron raided the Supply Room with a medical grocery list in one hand and crowbar in the other. He quickly stuffed items into a black Samsonite suitcase on rollers then covered his tracks.

Amy looked at her watch and approached the nurse station.

"You probably can lift a lot."

"A little bit."

"A big strong male nurse like you?"

No response.

The young man attempted to perform his tasks behind the counter.

"You're so humble and wise. What's your name?"

"Chuck."

"Chuck. I like the name 'Chuck.' I bet you're strong like Chuck Norris."

Nurse Chuck blushed and continued his data entry.

Amy twirled her long blonde hair, hummed a Kesha song and leaned over the counter.

"Nurse Chuck? Do you want to type my phone number?"

No response.

"Are you ignoring me?"

The kiddos sprinted past Amy. "Five, four, three, two, one! Ready or not, here I come!"

Nurse Chuck yelled down the hallway. "Children, keep it down."

"Wow, Nurse Chuck. You are a man. A *real* man. I *like* the way you handled that. There are times when I like my men to be bossy. That was one of them."

Aaron wheeled the suitcase into Antoine's room and quickly unzipped it. "Mrs. Becker, what else?"

Mrs. Becker inventoried. "Perfect."

Aaron walked to the window and looked outside. "Transportation is ready."

Aaron and Mrs. Becker exited Antoine's room with the suitcase and asked a nearby nurse about cafeteria hours, prices, and preferred entrees.

Brianna and Madison pushed Antoine in a wheel chair towards the elevator.

I interrupted Amy's male nurse campaign. "Have you seen three children playing on this floor?"

The male nurse pointed to his right.

"Thanks!" I sighed. "What's the matter with kids these days!"

I intercepted a nearby Tech heading for Antoine's room. "Hello, what time does visiting hours end?"

"Nine o'clock tonight."

"And tomorrow?"

"Seven to nine, every day."

"What about Sundays?"

"Seven to nine."

"And Holidays?"

"Same."

The elevator door closed. "Okay, thanks!"

I walked by the nurse station, coughed and pinched Amy's rear.

"Ooh!" Amy leaned forward, halfway over the counter. "Goodbye, Nurse Chuck."

We all rendezvoused outside near our primitive getaway vehicle. I popped open a bale of hay with my Gerber knife and concealed Antoine. My mom utilized the red twine to tie and suspend Antoine's I.V.

Charlotte fed Butters an apple cube and held his halter. "Good boy."

Aaron stuffed the suitcase under the hay, smiled at the three kiddos and completed a headcount. "Let's roll."

We slowly walked alongside the Scottish highland pulling the covert farm cart partially illuminated by the low-flying Bell 407's navigation, strobe and search lights.

I giggled. "I can't believe we're doing this."

Aaron looked at me in the Friday evening civil twilight. "Grace, there's more tonight."

I didn't understand. "AJ's in the cart."

"Second phase of Operation RECIPROCITY starts in five minutes."

Brianna laughed. "Oh, no!"

Aaron unveiled his mischievous plan. "Operation TOMMY BOY."

I sighed. "Aaron, he's gone."

"Not quite. My parents are apparently the sloppiest TSC officers in town. Mommy Webster issued a TSC check to Mommy Michaels this morning for $3000. Guess what she scribbled in the memo?"

"What?"

Aaron paused. "Project Thomas temp housing Week #1."

Brianna exclaimed. "Those creeps!"

Aaron looked around. "Who's in?"

Emma smiled. "I'm in."

Amy raised her hand. "I'm in, Webbie. Dean Michaels loves to report child abductions. Let's give him one to report."

Aaron looked at me. "Grace, Mrs. Jordan is waiting at The Boxcar. Get AJ to the mine. The twins and I will catch up." Aaron looked at the Kernans. "With Tommy Boy."

I nodded. "Careful."

Amy locked knuckles with Emma. "Wonder Twin Powers: Activate!"

Aaron, Amy and Emma ran off in the moonlight into the wealthy district of Peaksville.

E mma whispered. "Nice house."

Aaron hid behind three cords of neatly stacked firewood between the twins and pointed. "That's Tommy Boy's bedroom."

Amy examined the impressive Michaels mansion. "How do you know?"

"Metal bars."

"Great." Emma whispered. "Dean Michaels is running a prison."

"More like a dungeon." Amy joked. "We warned him."

Aaron studied the branches of the White Birch tree. "Time to rescue Princess Thomas."

The twins smiled.

Aaron maneuvered through the shadows, holstered his Cabela's LED flashlight, and started up the White Birch.

Aaron felt the window, contemplated his escape and took the risk.

Tap! Tap! Tap!

The Buzz Lightyear drapery opened.

Aaron whispered. "Tommy Boy."

Thomas attempted to smile. "I like pizza." Thomas Stallworth slid the double-paned window upward and was separated from Aaron by seven cast iron bars.

"Can you get to another window or door?"

"French fries," Thomas replied.

"What?"

"I like pizza." Thomas stuffed his face with French fries.

"Are you drugged?"

Thomas extended his hand, spilled fourteen three-inch bolts into Aaron's hands and smiled. "I did this. Before pill time. Before the evening pills."

The Michaels family's Bernese Mountain Dog barked downstairs.

"Woof! Woof!"

The front porch light illuminated.

Aaron froze perched fifteen feet over the well-manicured, professionally landscaped lawn.

Mrs. Michaels walked outside with her dog. "Mommy loves good puppies. Are you a good puppy?"

The furry pooch dutifully smelled Aaron's footprints, went potty, and ran back inside.

"Good girl!" Mrs. Michaels closed the door and secured the porch light.

Aaron easily removed the unfastened iron bars and extended his hand. "Careful."

Thomas initially appeared to have the White Birch descent under control. He stepped outside, held a branch with his left hand and squeezed Aaron's hand with his right. "I think I'm good —"

Thomas wasn't good. Thomas fell immediately.

Aaron squeezed his hand.

The Wonder Twins ran to the rescue. "Drop him."

Aaron complied as he lost his grip.

"Gotcha."

Thomas smiled, stammered and tipped an imaginary hat. "Hello, ladies."

Amy planted a ridiculous kiss on his cheek. "You've been doing drugs, haven't you?"

Thomas smiled.

Emma helped Thomas stand. "Tommy Boy. Let's walk."

Amy looked back. "Where's Aaron?"

Aaron exited the bedroom window, climbed down the Birch, and jogged to his friends.

Emma laughed. "You climbed inside?"

"I did."

"Why?"

"Let's just say I left a calling card."

Amy smiled enthusiastically. "You peed on their carpet."

"Nope, better."

Amy guessed again. "You peed on their Buzz Lightyear drapery?"

"Let's catch up with Charlotte." Aaron hurled Thomas over his right shoulder. "Tommy Boy needs to ride with Antoine."

Thomas incoherently mumbled. "Mom."

Emma laughed. "I'm not your mom."

"Quiet." Amy corrected his sister. "He's imprinting on you."

Thomas repeated. "Mom."

Emma's eyes lit up. "You want us to tell your mom that you're okay?"

Thomas nodded affirmatively.

"I got this! I'll catch up." Emma sprinted into the darkness.

CHAPTER FIFTY-TWO

General Voigt slid his Ping 4-iron into his custom-made leather Nike golf bag and answered his iPhone. "Bud, I'm enjoying myself at Wolf Haven Country Club & Lodge on a Friday evening. This better be important."

"Projects are entering the TFZ."

"I figured. Most of them?"

"All of them, Sir."

"You mean *except* Veggie Boy and The Prisoner?"

"Project Antoine was stolen from Peaksville Hospital."

"That's horrible news. He could recover from his coma."

"Project Thomas was stolen from the Michaels mansion."

General Voigt disconnected the call.

Click!

Mr. Light anxiously leaned on his Cessna 182 in the Peaksville Municipal Airport fuel pits and watched his iPhone.

Ring!

General Voigt called back.

"Have Rug intercept them in The Forbidden Zone."

"Sir, weather is dogcrap."

"If I can hit range balls, Rug can fly."

"Sir, Bell 407 heading and attitude gyros tumble in the TFZ due to the rare earth metals."

General Voigt paused. "Then have Rug meet me on the flightline in twenty minutes to teach me how to fly the Bell 407."

"Not necessary. Rug will lift off in fifteen mikes."

"No more excuses."

General Voigt disconnected.

Click!

Mr. Light called Mr. Burns.

"Rug, when was the last time you flew into the TFZ?"

"Summer of 2017." Mr. Burns observed the low, inclement weather roll in from the northwest obscuring the mountain tops. "Remember?"

"Meet me in Base Ops."

G loria stroked Kiche's fur in the TFZ moonlight. "What a beautiful dog."

D'Andre leaned back and smiled. "What a beautiful day."

D'Andre watched Ruby cheerfully spill a bundle of sticks onto the campfire.

Ruby caught D'Andre looking.

"Mind if I look at you, Ruby?"

Ruby blushed and smiled. "It's okay, DJ."

D'Andre studied Ruby's face. "I closed my eyes for four years. And you grew up. You too, Gloria. You two are pretty as a picture."

Gloria got closer and stared deeply into D'Andre's eyes. "Truly a miracle."

"Hey DJ." Luke stoked the embers with a dry stick. "When my dad was alive, he prayed for your sight to return every night."

"Ah, yes. Coach Bartholomew." D'Andre leaned back and faced the stars. "Your dad taught me how to make a free throw."

"He loved coaching you."

"God, those were good times."

O rbiting Peaksville in his Cessna 182, Mr. Light utilized his weather radar to avoid fast-moving isolated evening thunderstorms and re-attempted radio comms with Mr. Burns. "Rug, this is Bud, how copy?"

No response.

Mr. Burns dialed up 119.95 MHz on his VHF and transmitted from The Forbidden Zone. "Bud, this is Rug, transmitting on cheap suit. Radio check." Mr. Burns struggled to keep his helicopter in VFR flight conditions.

Mr. Light circled Liberty Lake and nervously toggled UHF and set 303.0 MHz. "Rug, transmitting on Winchester. Request status."

Charlotte haltered Butters from Lover's Cave downhill into the TFZ. Her lumbering Scottish highland slowly pulled Antoine and Thomas in the homemade cart.

The TSC Bell 407 helicopter uncharacteristically arrived overhead in the TFZ, hidden in the low, dark overcast clouds. "Sounds like we have company."

My mom double-checked Antoine's vital signs in the light rain.

Emma caught us and whispered to Thomas. "Tommy Boy, your mom is happy."

Thomas whispered. "Piz-zaaaaah!"

Amy laughed.

Mrs. Jordan looked up as the red and green navigation lights appeared one hundred feet above our group, partially-obscured by the deteriorating weather. "Is this normal?"

"No," Aaron said.

Chloe whispered into my ear while piggy-backing down the hill. "Grace, who is the helicopter searching for?"

"Antoine and Thomas."

Chloe rubbed her temples. "To help?"

I hoisted Chloe higher on my back. "Try to sleep, Scout."

Mrs. Jordan looked at me. "Will it follow us to the mine?"

Aaron answered before I could reply. "Unlikely."

The red and green NAV lights and white blinking strobe seemed less than fifty feet from many of the taller, violently shaken cedars.

Emma hoisted Jack onto her back. "Mr. Burns is awfully low."

"Seems dangerous." Brianna wiped the light rain from her face. "Does Mr. Burns have windshield wipers?"

Mr. Burns transmitted on UHF while scud-running in and out of the low TFZ overcast. "Bud, checking in on UHF. How copy?"

Mr. Light orbited over Liberty Lake and climbed to improve radio reception.

Mr. Burns toggled VHF. "Bud, transmitting in the blind. No joy Project MEDWEAP frequencies. TFZ weather ceiling and visibility zero-zero. Developing vertigo. How copy?"

Mr. Light adjusted his VOX and SQUELCH and continued cycling between briefed frequencies. "Rug, this is Bud. Radio check."

"Bud, weather is absolute dogshit. Request permission to abort. Request permission to abort. Double-click if approved."

We anxiously continued downhill towards White River. The Bell 407 rotor blades made chaotic oscillating sounds.

Amy hurried forward. "Sounds like a washing machine out of balance."

I looked up. The red and green helicopter navigation lights developed a clockwise, circular rotation. The helicopter was suddenly yawing like a top. I hoisted Chloe higher and sped up.

I saw Aaron stopped fifty feet behind us. "Aaron! Run!"

"Keep walking. Be right there!"

I stopped and switched Chloe onto Amy's back. "Charlotte, keep walking! I'll wait for Aaron."

Amy hoisted Chloe and ran as the helicopter oscillations increased in magnitude.

Charlotte hustled Butters westward into the darkness as Brianna illuminated her path.

Crack!

The rotors impacted the trees one-hundred feet back.

I jumped behind a tree trunk and yelled. "Aaron!"

Aaron ran to me, stowed something into his backpack and led me away by my hand. "Let's go!"

Crack! Bang! Wham!

A violent chain reaction of thuds, booms and bangs erupted as the Bell 407 fell to the forest floor nearby. The helicopter burned after falling.

Crash!

"What was that?"

The TSC aircraft suddenly exploded and shook the entire TFZ valley.

Boom!

"That *was* a helicopter, Gracie."

"No! In your hands. You were pointing something at the helicopter."

Aaron flashed two empty palms illuminated by the burning helicopter. "You didn't see anything."

I didn't understand. "Should we try to save Mr. Burns?"

Aaron grabbed my hand and hustled me downhill, away from the fireball. "Let's go."

I whispered. "Tell me what you know, Aaron."

"Tomorrow."

G loria greeted us after midnight at the newly-repaired Rope Bridge. "Gracie! You got the package?"

I looked in the cart. "Two packages, Gloria!"

Ruby paused. "You found Tommy Boy?"

"You abducted him?" Luke joked.

Aaron smiled. "We *emancipated* him."

D'Andre yelled from the west side. "Hi, Mama!"

Mrs. Jordan saw her son in the moonlight. "Hi, Baby DJ!"

Luke giggled. "Your mom is going to freak."

Ruby nudged Luke. "Shhh!"

Ryan crossed to the east side and handed out safety devices. "Everyone connects to the carabiner *and* wears a float coat to cross."

Jack stepped forward, donned a vest, and hooked up to the carabiners. "I'm first."

Gigi and Chloe followed Jack.

We disconnected Butters from his yoke and cart and bribed him with range cubes.

No help required.

Splash! Splash! Splash! And crossed.

Ryan carried Antoine after my mom temporarily secured his I.V.

Ruby and Luke held Antoine. "We got him."

Ryan returned and slung Thomas over his shoulder during passage.

Thomas broke into song halfway across the rope bridge.

Skyrockets in Flight, Afternoon Delight
Skyrockets in Flight, Afternoon Delight
Skyrockets in Flight, Afternoon Delight

I was too tired to laugh. "Poor Ryan."

Amy giggled. "Tommy Boy knows one verse."

Lastly, Ryan returned and rigged Mrs. Jordan with the vest and carabiner connections. "DJ has a surprise."

Mrs. Jordan commenced her passage. "I love surprises."

D'Andre waited on the west side. "Careful, Mama."

Mrs. Jordan cautiously crossed the Rope Bridge.

Ruby and Gloria whispered the news to us.

I cried tears of joy.

Ruby pinched me. "Shhh! Crying will give it away."

I couldn't help it.

"Momma, it's a beautiful night, isn't it?"

"Yes, DJ."

"Momma, I haven't seen this many stars in five years."

Mrs. Jordan passed the midpoint. "Lots of stars, Baby DJ."

Amy laughed and whispered. "Baby DJ?"

Whack! Ruby slapped Amy's rear.

Mrs. Jordan stepped on terra firma below the West Peaksville Neodymium Mine.

"Momma, you look so beautiful in the moonlight. Just like I remember."

She slowly approached D'Andre, placed her hands on his cheeks and looked into his eyes. "Baby DJ? Is this real?"

"I can see, Momma! I can see! I can *really* see!"

"I knew it! I prayed so hard! I knew you would see again! Praise the Lord!"

It was a miracle.

Thomas monotonously sang '*Skyrockets in Flight, Afternoon Delight*' as we walked uphill to the West Peaksville Neodymium Mine.

Charlotte and I poured Sweet COB into a muck bucket for Butters and tied him to the largest tamarack tree we could find.

Gloria and my mom prepared Antoine's I.V. in the mine.

Ruby helped Jack, Gigi, and Chloe slide into their sleeping bags.

Thomas continued singing.

"It's one o'clock." I whispered from my sleeping bag. "Tommy Boy's not slowing down."

Amy agreed. "He slept on the cart for four hours."

Aaron sighed. "We should have made him walk."

"Skyrockets in Flight, Afternoon Delight!"

Emma whispered. "When will the drugs wear off?"

"Tomorrow," Aaron replied.

Thomas switched songs to our dismay. "*I can't feel my face when I'm with you.*"

I covered my head with a pillow and whispered. "Do something, Amy."

Amy plotted in the dark mine. "*Psst.* Tommy Boy."

Thomas stopped singing. "Buzz Lightyear, is that you?"

We giggled.

"It's Amy."

"Amy who?"

"Amy Kernan."

"Hello, Amy Kermit."

Laughter.

"Tommy Boy, *jones-ing* for a party-sized bag of Wavy Lay's potato chips?"

"Yeah, Man."

"You get the whole bag if you agree to my terms and conditions: No more singing."

Thomas didn't immediately reply.

Amy shook the bag of chips. "Deal?"

"Yeah, Man."

"Don't double cross me. Nobody double crosses Amy Kermit."

Thomas paused. "Okay, Kermit."

I shut my eyes, pulled my sleeping bag over my head, and tried to sleep through open-mouthed potato chip crunching. "Amy, why a party-sized bag?"

Ruby agreed. "Yeah, why not yogurt or *Jello*?"

The crunching stopped after five minutes.

And we slept.

CHAPTER FIFTY-THREE

I lounged on a heated rock with Kiche on the Saturday afternoon.

"Hey, big sister."

"Hi, Gloria. Where's mom?"

"Tending to Antoine in the mine."

Gloria joined me on the granite boulder and petted Kiche. "How'd you sleep?"

"Bad dream."

"Want to share?"

"In my dream, Marcus didn't jump in the river. Marcus survived."

Gloria smiled. "Sounds like a good dream."

I looked at Gloria as the cool mountain breeze gently blew the cedar trees. "Then I woke up. Alone. Which makes it a bad dream."

Gloria pointed down by the river. "See that little girl wearing overalls playing with Gigi and Jack?"

I watched Chloe giggling loudly and riding Butters. She had five squirrels slung over one shoulder and five speckled trout slung over the other.

"Marcus died saving that precious little girl, Gracie."

I rested my head on Gloria's shoulder.

Life was too complicated.

R yan sportily added lighter fluid to our ignited cedar campfire. "Now that's a fire!"

Brianna walked from the mine. "Hey Gracie."

"Hey Bree. How's AJ?"

Brianna shrugged. "Vitals good. Your mom and Mrs. Jordan are with him."

Gigi unpacked her marshmallow, Hershey bar and graham cracker supplies. "I hope Antoine wakes up soon."

Gloria leaned on Ryan. "He will, Sweetie."

Amy saw Jack and Chloe filleting fish and skinning squirrels. "Jack, what's for dinner, little buddy?"

Jack sheathed his Navy SEAL Pup survival knife. "Thirteen squirrels!"

Chloe smiled. "And fifteen trout!"

Amy found Luke hiding in the civil twilight. "Luke?"

Luke slouched.

Amy clapped three times. "Luke! Hot chick is talking to you. Pay attention."

"Hi, Amy."

"You fished with DJ."

Luke smiled. "Yes, Ma'am."

Amy looked at D'Andre. "DJ!"

"Amy!"

"How long has your vision been restored?"

D'Andre checked his watch. "Thirty-six hours."

"How many fish did Luke catch?"

"Exactly?"

"*Exactly.*"

D'Andre paused. "My vision's still fuzzy."

Luke gave D'Andre a victorious high five.

Charlotte opened a Diet Coke. "Tommy Boy. No singing? It's Saturday."

Thomas winked. "Sorry, Charlie."

I didn't want Thomas to escape well-deserved scorn. "Tommy Boy, how was your trip?"

Thomas drank river water from his canteen and shrugged. "I slept."

Madison laughed. "Tommy Boy even slept through a helicopter crash."

Aaron threw a stick in the fire. "That wasn't the 'trip' Grace was referring to."

"Oh, *that* trip. Yeah, Dean Michaels had me flying higher than the TSC Air Patrol since Wednesday night. Shots and pills. Every four hours."

Amy joked. "Sounds really cool —"

Luke nudged Amy and pointed to the middle schoolers.

Amy corrected herself. "It sounded like a cool, night breeze. Really, really cool."

Brianna stood up. "I'm going inside to check on Antoine."

"Bree, sit down," Aaron said.

"Please." Aaron wept. "I have something to say."

CHAPTER FIFTY-FOUR

E mma wiped Aaron's tears. "You okay?"

Aaron stalled a minute until he could stop crying. "Jack, let me hear that voice."

Jack Kernan sat in the campfire light. "What should I say?"

"That's perfect." Aaron pointed. "Jack, get my two backpacks."

Jack returned carrying two SwissGear backpacks. "These?"

Aaron nodded in the TFZ moonlight. "Two weeks ago, I snuck into my dad's secret TSC room."

Emma scratched his back.

Aaron paused. "Before I continue, everyone must promise three things."

I leaned forward, towards the campfire. Forbidden knowledge loomed. "Of course."

"First promise." Aaron sobbed again and quickly regained composure. "Everyone must forgive me."

"Why?" Luke asked.

Emma cried. "Okay, Aaron."

Charlotte looked around. "We promise."

"Sure." Gloria scratched Kiche's belly. "What else, Aaron?"

"Second promise." Aaron looked into our eyes. "Secrecy."

"Because you're in danger?" I asked.

Aaron shook his head. "Because *you* will all be in danger."

"We won't tell a soul," Charlotte nervously said.

"We all promise," Ruby said.

"Two weeks ago, I lost my temper. I wanted revenge," Aaron said.

He looked at me. "Grace, did you complete our reading assignment this week?"

Uh-oh.

Emma looked at me. "Reading assignment, Grace?"

"*The Count of Monte Cristo.*"

Aaron asked again. "Did you?"

I nodded. "I devoured that book in six hours on Thursday evening."

"Good. Then explain moral wounds."

I was being quizzed. "Moral wounds have this peculiarity. They may be hidden, but they never close."

"What else?"

I made eye contact with everyone in the campfire light. "They are always painful, always ready to bleed when touched, they remain fresh and open in the heart."

Aaron looked around the campfire. "What you will learn will inflict deep *moral* wounds. They will last forever. This knowledge may destroy you."

We all froze.

Emma grabbed Aaron's hand. "Please continue, Aaron."

"Grace, tell us about the dinner toast by Edmond Dantes to his teenage son."

"I'll try." I looked to the stars. "Life is a storm, my young friend. You will bask in the sunlight one moment, be shattered on the rocks the next."

I shook my head and cried. "Oh, Marcus."

"Gracie." Aaron encouraged me. "You're doing well."

Charlotte comforted me.

I continued. "What makes you a man is what you do when that storm comes. You must look into that storm and shout '*Do your worst, for I will do mine!*'"

Aaron smiled. "Bravo, Grace."

Charlotte hugged me and wiped my tears.

Aaron continued. "And so, my Peaksville friends, the third promise. You shall not harbor anger in your hearts. Promise me."

"No anger." D'Andre said. "We promise."

Aaron stood up. "Stand up if you can control your emotions. Stay seated if you will allow your emotions to control you."

Jack stood first, followed by Gigi and Chloe.

Charlotte, Ruby and I stood up.

Others followed.

Ryan and Amy remained seated.

Aaron waited. "Everyone or no deal."

"Come on, Amy." Emma whispered. "Stand up."

Amy looked around. "You are about to tell me who killed my Dad. I want revenge."

Aaron stood his ground. "No revenge, Amy. No anger. Will you settle for reciprocity?"

Amy jumped up and smiled. "I'm in!"

Heaven help those downrange of Amy Kernan.

Gloria whispered. "Ryan, stand up."

"I'm fine." Ryan sat with his arms crossed. "I'll hide my anger."

Aaron explained. "Ryan, I'm offering freedom. Since 2013, you were a prisoner to the CABESA Initiative. If you elect to be a prisoner to revenge for the remainder of your life, then we're finished."

"Ryan," D'Andre said. "Stand and join your brothers and sisters."

Ryan stood up, cried and hugged Aaron. "Okay man. Count me in. I'm sorry."

We all stood around the campfire and joined hands.

Gloria rested her head on Ryan's shoulder.

"Aaron, forgiveness, secrecy and self-control. We all promise."

Aaron placed sticks on the campfire. "Let's sit."

"Here it goes." Aaron mustered his courage and dropped a bombshell on us. "Two weeks ago, I learned that my dad heart-attacked your dads in their sleep."

We all sobbed for several minutes.

Gigi stopped sobbing barely long enough to speak. "Why?"

I wiped my tears and looked at Aaron. "How?"

"Drugs?" Luke suggested.

Aaron shook his head. "Who thinks they know what my dad does for a living."

Amy dragged her long sleeve across her eyes. "He drives around town and parks in his Mercedes G-Wagen near playing children."

Aaron nodded. "Sad but true."

I guessed. "Medical Equipment Engineer."

"Close."

Luke guessed. "LASER Engineer."

"Closer."

Aaron pulled something out of his backpack.

Ruby examined the eighteen-inch, black electronic device. "It's a telescope?"

"It's a MEDWEAP."

"A medical weapon?" Brianna asked.

Thomas examined at it and held it. "No such thing."

Emma gasped. "The burn marks on Dad's chest!"

Amy nodded. "From a LASER."

Jack was fascinated. "Can I see it?"

Aaron looked at Emma.

"It's fine."

Aaron handed it to Jack. "Don't turn it on."

I looked at Aaron. "You stole it?"

"After breaking a few others."

"Is your dad angry?"

"Yes."

"Does he want it back?"

"Yes."

"Did he ask for it?"

"No."

"Why?"

"He doesn't want the TSC to know it's gone. He also knows what my answer would be if he asked for it."

"What's that?"

"Dad, MEDWEAP's don't exist." Aaron looked at Thomas. "Anyone ever asks you about these, you answer like Tommy Boy. Say it again, Tommy Boy."

"No such thing."

Aaron nodded. "That is everyone's lifelong response."

"Things are a little tense in the Webster home?" Emma asked.

"Understatement of 2020."

Ryan inspected the PDS MEDWEAP. "Tell us more."

"The CABESA Initiative was signed into law in 2013."

I raised my hand. "Stands for what?"

"Cooperative Adolescent Biotech Experimental Science Act."

"Legal?"

"Secret law. Yes."

"Constitutional?"

"No. But it's a secret law and doesn't get challenged."

I was terrified but fascinated. "Keep going."

"Peaksville Institutes of Health runs the local CABESA Command Center. CABESA monitors the Projects."

Emma interrupted Aaron. "Projects?"

"You are Project Emma."

Emma turned pale. "Oh."

I leaned forward. "Tell us more."

"My Dad engineers them with taxpayer dollars. PDS builds them with CABESA taxpayer dollars. PIH buys them with tax payer dollars. TSC operates them with taxpayer dollars and fires them at Projects."

Charlotte interrupted. "When?"

"In your sleep, in class, in restaurants, in cars, everywhere."

Luke held the device. "Fires through windows?"

"And drywall. And roofs. And metal."

"Thermal targeting?" Ryan asked.

Aaron explained. "Electromagnetic interrogation primarily. CABESA was created to develop nanotechnology. PsytoSCOPE makes tiny nanotech RFID's called Imaging Probes. You each get a discreet frequency."

Charlotte gasped. "The shots!"

Aaron nodded. "Imaging Probes."

Amy exclaimed. "I knew it!"

I raised my hand. "Nanotech Imaging Probes inflict pain?"

"Negative. Imaging probes are uniformly-distributed targets in your blood. Your blood supply pools mostly in your head and hearts. Therefore, the MEDWEAP interrogates your frequency, illuminates your imaging probes, and fires at your illuminated head or heart."

"How does the neodymium magnet help?" Brianna asked.

"Magnets disable RFID's. Just like Cryptonite disables Superman," Aaron said.

"I got it. The Walmart cashier disables the RFID by swiping it on a magnet." Luke explained. "A credit card strip gets scrambled accidentally by magnets, also."

Brianna nodded.

Aaron agreed. "Good analogy, Luke."

Madison looked at Aaron. "The Lover's Cave notes. Yours?"

"Negative."

Jack pointed the MEDWEAP into the sky with his squirrel-hunting pellet gun resting in his lap. "Aaron, how do I fire this thing?"

"Simple. Power ON. Enter target frequency of Project. Then select a setting before firing.

F*requency:*
    1 Nausea
2 Pain
3 Arrhythmia
4 Flatline

"Flatline frequency?" Emma ran into the woods and vomited.
    I quickly followed.

Aaron waited.

Emma finished. "Keep talking, Aaron. I'm still listening."

Ryan stoked the campfire. "The TSC helicopter hovered over the cedars when Derrick fainted and died in Peaksville Forest."

"The TSC Air Patrol killed Derrick."

"I didn't see a LASER painting him."

Aaron explained. "Google estimates that 0.00038% of all electromagnetic radiation is visible by the human eye. MEDWEAP's, military LASER's, crowd control microwaves: All invisible to your eyes."

Ryan turned beet-red in the moonlight.

Amy crushed her empty can of Arizona Sweet Tea. "I want justice!"

"I want revenge," Ryan said.

Aaron remained calm. "Grace, what was written on the prison cave wall in *The Count of Monte Cristo*?"

"God will give me justice."

"Dantes scratched it out after being imprisoned for seven years. Didn't he, Grace?"

"He replaced the word *justice* with *revenge*."

Aaron continued. "Amy, the TSC killed Mr. Kernan. Do you believe you will get *justice* in the court system?"

Amy shook her head negatively.

"Ryan, the TSC killed Mr. Flynn and Derrick, and then you lost Marcus. What happens if you get *revenge*?"

Ryan dejectedly looked into the campfire. "Jail."

Aaron reached into his backpack and handed D'Andre the *Project Antoine* logbook. "DJ, my dad was keeping AJ in a coma. I'm sorry."

D'Andre paged through the PIH logbook and cried.

Aaron handed him the *Project D'Andre* logbook. "And my dad targeted your RFID eye inserts since 2015."

Brianna gasped. "Eye inserts?"

Aaron distributed the other logbooks.

I quickly flipped through *Project Grace*. "Holidays and Birthdays! I always vomited and fainted."

Aaron nodded. "Induced trauma."

Gloria cried. "I remember, Gracie. It was like clockwork."

Ryan fumed. "Sick bastards. No justice. No revenge. What do we get?"

Aaron stoically replied. "Reciprocity."

"What do you get?" Ryan asked.

Aaron stuffed the MEDWEAP into his backpack. "I'll tell you what I *don't* get. My graduation present was going to be any car under $100,000. This limit was imposed hide our wealth. That's gone."

Thomas retracted a marshmallow from the campfire. "Spider monkeys!"

D'Andre laughed.

"Okay, Tommy Boy." Amy chided Thomas. "You wish you were a spider monkey. We get it."

"No, seriously. I snooped around the Michaels home. The PIH retired sixteen laboratory spider monkeys in 2013. We replaced them."

"That's about when the TSC started hurting us," Ryan said.

"Nice work, Sir Thomas. Catch!" Amy tossed him a second party-sized bag of Wavy Lay's potato chips.

I sighed and face-palmed. "Shame on you, Amy."

After silently reading our MEDWEAP logbooks twenty minutes documenting years of covert medical experimentation, I stuffed the *Project Grace, Project Gloria* and *Project Gigi* logbooks into Aaron's backpack and cried with my two sisters.

Ryan returned the *Project Marcus, Project Derrick,* and *Project Ryan* logbooks to Aaron. "What kind of God allows weapons testing on children?"

Thomas tossed the *Project Thomas* logbook to Aaron. "I don't believe in God."

Aaron winked at me. "Hit it, Gracie."

I quoted *The Count of Monte Cristo* once again for Aaron. "It doesn't matter what you believe, Thomas. God believes in you."

CHAPTER FIFTY-FIVE

Mercedes Walker emptied a sugar pack into her grapefruit juice in the Nineteenth Hole. "I hope our back nine is faster than our front nine."

Krissy Moriarty agreed. "Too many old golfers on Sunday mornings."

Skylar Ferguson scooped a cupful of free pretzels. "I can't wait to leave this backwards flyover state."

Krissy Moriarty laughed. "My dad literally tried to convince me to attend Peaksville State University."

The three Coeur d'Alene Broadmoor Academy seniors jumped into their electric golf carts and sped to the tenth hole without paying for their drinks.

"Why is that worker yelling?" Skylar asked.

"We didn't pay," Krissy replied.

Mercedes Walker held the steering wheel with her left hand and finished her drink with her right. "My family doesn't *pay* for anything at Wolf Haven Country Club & Lodge. My mom only *makes* people pay."

Skylar skidded her wheels adjacent to the tenth tee box. "Is 2020 an election year for Representative Walker?"

Mercedes nodded. "Every two years these North Idaho Republican hillbillies vote for Mom."

"Any competition this November?"

Mercedes laughed. "No."

Krissy donned her golf gloves selected her seven-iron. "Mercedes, I wish you were going to Harvard with Skylar and me in August."

Mercedes sighed. "Mom is making me attend the Naval Academy in Annapolis, Maryland. Only one hour from her office in the Capitol."

Krissy took a practice swing. "I thought Congresswoman Walker hates the military."

Mercedes whispered. "She does, but the military loves my mom."

Skylar Ferguson smiled. "Love is blind."

Krissy Moriarty lined up her shot. "Like the blind love affair between your mom and my dad?"

Skylar face-palmed. "Ugh! Don't remind me."

Crack!

Krissy struck the ball. "My instructor keeps changing my golf swing."

Skylar joked. "First World problems."

Mercedes selected her eight-iron and adjusted her visor. "They promised my mom the Presidency in either 2024 or 2028."

Skylar choked on her pretzels. "Huh?"

Krissy flopped into the golf cart. "Who promised?"

Crack!

Mercedes Walker struck her ball without a practice swing. "The Syndicate."

CHAPTER FIFTY-SIX

I entered the West Peaksville Neodymium Mine for the fifth time on Sunday afternoon.

Mrs. Jordan smiled. "Antoine needs more time, Gracie."

I looked at my watch. "A few hours?"

My mom shrugged. "Maybe days. Maybe weeks."

My dad taught me to be a sheepdog. "I'll stay with AJ."

D'Andre stepped forward. "Me too!"

Emma joined us. "I owe AJ an apology. I'm staying."

"It's finals week. Go graduate. Mrs. Jordan and I will stay."

Mom was right.

Thomas looked at Aaron. "What about me?"

Aaron paused to think. "You're probably safer here, Tommy Boy."

"Saturday is graduation," Thomas said.

"If they take you again, we'll never find you. Let me work it."

Amy smiled and devilishly rubbed her hands together. "Tommy Boy?"

"Yeah?"

"Tell me more about the PIH spider monkeys."

"Mrs. Michaels yelled and called me a stupid replacement monkey when I resisted the drugs. Twice!"

"What else?" Amy asked.

"Dean Michaels is angry with Mr. Light."

"Why?"

"Not sure. Dean Michaels taunted him about spider monkeys during an argument. Apparently, a spider monkey named Jerome attacked Mr. Light years ago."

Amy smiled. "Jerome?"

"One more thing. The retired spider monkeys live in Coeur D'Alene on the 1000-acre Walker Ranch."

"Congresswoman Walker?" Aaron asked.

Thomas shrugged.

Amy smiled. "Bravo, Sir Thomas."

"And so," Aaron winked at me, smiled and quoted *The Count of Monte Cristo*. "Neglect has become our ally."

Charlotte prepared Butter's yoke and cart for the journey home.

Ruby fed Kiche one last time before the trip.

Brianna exited the mine and yelled down the hill. "Gracie!"

"Yeah, Bree?"

"I'm staying!" Brianna Lopez declared.

I ran back up the hill. "What about graduation?"

"Antoine is more important to me."

I hugged Brianna. "We'll cover for you."

Mrs. Jordan smiled. "Thanks, Bree."

Mom kissed me goodbye. "Love you, Gracie."

T he three middle schoolers hitched a ride on the cart after crossing the trestle. I looked at D'Andre. "You look preoccupied."

"Just thinking."

"About what?"

"The *Project D'Andre* logbook mentioned the TSC targeting my ocular RFID inserts thousands of times."

I walked and listened as D'Andre deconstructed his memories.

"In 2016, I was fitted for contacts. My vision was 20/40. The doctor asked me to look straight down while he held my left eyelids open. He inserted something on top of my left eye. He instructed me to rapidly look straight up. Said he lost it. Same procedure on the right eye. *Lost it again*! Grace, he inserted RFID's into the back of my eyes. That's when severe headaches started."

"Oh, God."

"I went blind within six months."

Amy interrupted. "DJ?"

"Yeah?"

"Doctor's name, please."

"Schultz."

"Is Dr. Schultz a Peaksville eye doctor?"

"Yes."

Amy looked at Aaron and smiled. "I'll take care of it."

After turning south at the Rock Tower, Ryan stopped and pointed. "Coyotes."

The scavengers devoured the decaying mountain lion in the late afternoon TFZ sun.

Kiche charged them.

"Kiche!" Ruby yelled. "No!"

The coyotes scattered.

Kiche returned with a smile.

"Top of the canine food chain." Gigi slipped her a treat. "Good girl, Wolfie!"

I laughed. "Kiche was outnumbered ten to one. How did she do that?"

"Kiche possesses what I lack," Luke said.

"What's that?"

"Confidence."

We passed Rainbow Bridge and trekked home above the White River.

"Hey, Aaron." Ryan said.

Aaron "Yeah?"

"Tell me about Operation RECIPROCITY."

"Are you ready?"

"Born ready."

For the next ten minutes, Aaron and Ryan walked and quietly plotted.

Kiche ran ahead.

"Aaron!" I exclaimed. "The crash site!"

The twelve-year-olds jumped from the Scottish highland-powered cart and ran ahead.

"Stay back, kiddos!" Emma said.

Aaron and Ryan approached the Bell 407 wreckage.

"What do you see?" Luke asked from a distance.

No response.

I slowly approached the charred cockpit. "Is that Mr. Burns?"

"It *was* Mr. Burns," Aaron replied.

Jack wandered around the debris. "Check it out!"

"Jack, don't energize it!" Aaron exclaimed.

Too late.

Jack actuated the black, two-foot, cylindrical MEDWEAP. "Hey Web! Mr. Burns had it set to *Flatline Frequency*!"

Emma retrieved it from her little brother and carefully walked it to Aaron.

Aaron checked the MEDWEAP logbook function. "Project Antoine!"

"What about Antoine?" D'Andre asked.

"The Safety Corps was trying to *Flatline* your brother in the cart as we left town."

D'Andre silently wept and was immediately comforted by Ruby.

Aaron stowed the MEDWEAP in his backpack.

Ruby and Luke loaded the middle-schoolers onto the cart.

Emma glared at the remains of Max's dad. "There's nothing more to see here."

We solemnly continued up the eastern face of Lover's Mountain.

Halfway through Lover's Cave, someone whispered my name. "Gracie."

"Who's there?"

"It's Ryan."

"What's up, Ryan?"

"I need to borrow your little sisters."

"It's eight o'clock on Sunday night."

"I'll have Gloria and Gigi home by eleven o'clock."

I laughed nervously. "Is it legal?"

Ryan paused. "No."

Aaron gently nudged me in the dark. "Don't worry, Gracie!"

"Home by eleven."

Brianna grilled the jackrabbit on the open fire. "Tommy Boy, you're a regular Davy Crockett."

Thomas added tamarack branches to the fire. "Marcus taught me how to trap game. I still can't believe he's gone."

"I miss him, too."

Thomas delivered grilled fish dinners into the mine for Mrs. Becker and Mrs. Jordan.

Brianna looked at Thomas. "Any progress?"

"Not yet."

"I wish Antoine would wake up. He loves barbeque."

"Soon, Bree."

The cedar trees waved in the cool evening breeze.

Brianna smiled. "Are you turning into a True Believer, like me?"

"Oh, I've always been a True Believer. Everyone believes things. I simply believed the wrong people instead of believing in my friends."

Brianna smiled.

Thomas earned a kiss on the cheek in the TFZ moonlight.

. . .

270

R yan Flynn stood in the Peaksville moonlight outside his Chemistry classroom window. "Any questions?"

Gigi Becker smiled. "What if a teacher is inside?"

Ryan whispered. "It's ten o'clock. We're fine."

Gloria Becker solemnly handed Ryan and Gigi each a tablet. "Amy said put these under our tongues if we get caught."

Ryan examined it. "Cyanide?"

Gloria smiled. "Breath mint."

Ryan laughed and lifted Gigi. "Commence Operation BROKEN NEEDLE."

Gigi reached in the unlatched window and spun the handle counter-clockwise.

Ryan looked up. "How we doing?"

"Little higher," Gigi whispered.

Ryan complied.

"She's in!" Gloria whispered.

Gigi stuck her head outside and pointed left. "Meet me at the double doors."

Gloria and Ryan sprinted to the north entrance.

The middle-schooler opened the doors and smiled. "Welcome to Peaksville High School, I'll be your night tour guide."

Ryan laughed.

Gloria scanned the dark hallways. "Now what?"

"Follow me."

Gloria attempted to turn the Nurse's Office doorknob. "Locked."

"Ready Gigi?"

Gigi smiled. "Born ready."

Ryan lifted Gigi to the unlatched two-foot by three-foot transom above the door.

Gigi landed like a cat on Nurse Ferguson's floor.

Gloria listened. "You okay?"

Click!

The twelve-year-old unlatched the door. "Oh, ye of little faith."

Gloria checked the vaccine cabinets. "Locked."

Ryan calmly slid open a drawer and reached deep inside. "Nurse Light's backup keyring."

"Nurse Light." Gloria smiled. "Still our Guardian Angel."

Ryan extracted three large shot boxes. "Bingo!"

Gloria found attached inventory certificates on the ten-pound boxes. "PsytoSCOPE Lot-22 Project Imaging Probes."

Gigi read the warning label. "Keep away from magnets."

Ryan whispered. "Aaron was right!"

Gloria scanned the hallway. "Let's go!"

271

Ryan, Gloria and Gigi hustled the TSC shot boxes towards the north exit.

"One last thing," Ryan whispered passing the Office of the Dean. "Gigi!"

Gigi set down her box and was quickly lifted up and through the open transom. *Click!*

Gigi opened the door and joked. "Step into my office!"

Ryan rustled through the file cabinets.

Gloria checked the hallways and whispered. "What are you looking for?"

Ryan opened and closed drawers. "I don't know."

"We better go, Ryan."

Ryan pulled out a green file folder, paged through the documents, and slammed the cabinet door closed. "Let's roll."

Gloria exited Peaksville High School. "Where do we hide these shot boxes?"

Ryan looked at his watch. "Lover's Cave."

CHAPTER FIFTY-SEVEN

Finals week arrived!

I leaned back on the hallway floor outside my English Literature classroom cramming plots, settings, themes and characters of our assigned Bradbury, London, and Stevenson classics.

Smash!

Nurse Ferguson threw her coffee mug against the wall. "Damn projects!"

Emma quickly sat with me and whispered. "What did Gloria do last night?"

I tapped Emma's leg and whispered. "Hold on."

Nurse Ferguson angrily marched past us towards the front office.

I smiled. "What day is today?"

"Monday."

"What happens on Monday morning usually?"

Emma gasped. "They didn't."

Click!

Dean Michaels energized the PA system. "Good morning, students. Monday morning TSC shots have been cancelled today for administrative purposes. Good luck on exams."

I smiled. "They did."

"Rug crashed, Ma'am."

"Hard landing?"

"You could say that," General Voigt said.

"How hard?"

"Fatal."

"Did TSC recover the weapon?"

"Not exactly."

"Explain."

"It may have burned in the fire, but —"

"But what?"

"The Projects may have recovered the weapon."

Click!

General Voigt waited thirty seconds before calling her back.

"Are you there, Ma'am?"

No response.

"Ma'am, something else happened."

"Of course."

General Voigt paused. "Lot-22 imaging probes were stolen from Peaksville High School last night."

"Some of them?"

"All of them, Ma'am."

No reply for ten seconds.

"Aren't you the CEO of Peaksville Defense and Space?"

"Yes, Ma'am."

"Don't I funnel billions of dollars to you so you can interrogate, target, and fire weapons at imaging probes?"

"Yes, Ma'am."

"So where are the probes?"

"Bud has been poking holes in the sky since six o'clock this morning. He thinks the imaging probes are hidden underground."

"Underground?"

"Perhaps in a cave, Ma'am."

"Of course. Children instinctively know to hide RFID nanotech Imaging Probes in caves. What's the matter with kids these days."

"The Peaksville Projects seem to have evolved, Ma'am."

"Speaking of evolved —"

"Ma'am?"

"Bud initiated the switch from spider monkeys to children in 2013, correct?"

"Affirmative."

"Bud selected the Peaksville Projects for this trauma-based program, correct?"

"Affirmative," General Voigt repeated.

"Perhaps Bud should inflict less trauma on me and more trauma on the Projects."

. . .

I stuffed my textbooks in my backpack and slammed my locker. "Luke! Aaron! How did you guys do on the Global Governance essay?"

Luke shrugged. "I spewed just enough rubbish about overpopulation solutions to pass."

I sighed. "Ditto. What was your overpopulation solution, Aaron?"

Aaron laughed. "Fewer Global Governance teachers."

"You didn't."

"I did."

"Aaron, that's a guaranteed downgrade to 75!"

"My dad is TSC. Ten to one odds she still gives me a 95. Membership has its privileges."

"Speaking of membership," Luke whispered.

Ben Light sauntered down the hallway, stopped nearby, pivoted away, and eavesdropped.

"Hi, Ben!"

"Oh, Grace. I didn't see you there."

Ben quickly departed.

Luke watched Ben walk away. "Web, why didn't you end up like him?"

Aaron looked around. "I'm not sure. Maybe it's learned."

I was confused. "But you didn't learn it from your parents."

Gloria tapped me on the shoulder. "Hi, Gracie!"

I smiled and hugged my sister and whispered. "You beast! Nurse Ferguson literally had a cow this morning!"

"Apparently."

Aaron looked at me. "After we finish tonight's operation, Mr. Light will go bananas."

I intentionally looked away from Aaron.

The Cessna 182 droned over the school roof.

I glanced back at Aaron. "After *we* finish?"

Aaron smiled. "Operation RECIPROCITY continues."

D ean Michaels commenced post-dismissal announcements as we walked toward the exit, headache-free.

"Good afternoon. Today is Monday. Just a few items. Submitting a false hoax into a Suspected Mental Illness Report station referring a TSC Cadet is a major infraction."

Gloria looked at Ryan. "You didn't."

Ryan returned a cheesy smiled. "I did."

Announcements continued. "The Peaksville Defense and Space Corporation seeks to develop and test anti-personnel electronic weapons by 2040 to fight terrorism. These technologies currently do *not* exist and may *never* be developed without future breakthroughs. Qualified students may apply for PDS internships. Final exams continue tomorrow. Graduation is Saturday for students without excessive absences. The TSC reported an unsuccessful child abduction over the weekend. School's out. Be safe out there."

Amy caught up with us outside in the schoolyard. "Gracie!"

I smiled. "Hey, Amy!"

"Dean Michaels is lying!" Amy exclaimed over the propeller noise.

"Amy Kernan." Aaron joked. "Master of the Obvious."

Amy complained. "We *successfully* abducted Antoine and Thomas! No recognition from the Dean!"

"We'll give you recognition tonight at Charlie's."

"Can I bring our new little friend to the Epley Farm?"

Aaron smiled. "Not yet."

B rianna Lopez joined Thomas Stallworth on the riverbank. "Any luck?"

Thomas smiled in the late Monday afternoon TFZ sunlight and lifted ten attached trout from the river. "Luck is not involved."

"Then it's skill."

"Skill is *definitely* not involved."

Brianna watched Thomas reel in another speckled trout. "Neither luck nor skill?"

Thomas recovered his small hook from the trout's mouth. "Only faith and patience."

"That works?"

Thomas smiled. "How's Antoine?"

"Nothing yet."

"Can he hear us?"

"I hope so! Today, I read Jules Verne's *Journey to the Center of the Earth* to him for eight hours."

"Fitting." Thomas smiled. "Deciphering clues. Magnetic caves."

Brianna agreed. "Everything old is new again."

Thomas disassembled his rod and reel.

"We're probably not graduating on Saturday," Brianna said.

"Aaron's working it."

Brianna sat on a boulder. "How?"

"We're graduating, Bree."

Brianna cried and shook her head negatively.

Thomas joined her. "Being stuck in the cave with Marcus taught me *hope*."

"Marcus died."

"Marcus died *saving Chloe*."

Brianna paused. "Does God have a plan for us?"

Thomas laughed.

"What's so funny?"

"Bree, you just read 100,000 words to a friend in a coma. You're already executing God's plan."

Thomas earned the second kiss on his cheek in two days.

"We're here," Aaron said in the Peaksville moonlight.

I examined the eight-foot chain link perimeter fence. "There's no gate."

Jack quickly jumped the fence, landed in the Peaksville Municipal Airport grass, and smiled at Aaron and me. "Commence Operation DENY FLIGHT."

I smiled. "That's where my parents met during the Bosnian Conflict."

"I knew that. That's why I picked the name." Aaron winked. "Waiting on you, Gracie."

"How exactly is this legal?" I asked from the top of the fence.

Aaron looked up at me. "My dad killed your dads *legally*. Who cares about legality?"

I landed in the grass. "Good point."

Jack pointed to the Cessna 182 on the flightline. "Over there!"

Aaron led the way. "Jack, you like airplanes?"

Jack nodded affirmatively and smiled. "My dad flew Navy airplanes."

"Where?"

"In Japan."

"Tomcats?"

Jack shook his head. "Greyhounds."

"Did you dad ever open the engine cowling and show you parts?"

"Not really."

"That's what we're doing tonight, Jack."

We arrived at the TSC airplane.

Aaron opened the engine cowling and removed a crow bar, hammer and pliers from his belt.

I nervously scanned the area as Aaron propped open the metal hatch with an over-center beam.

Crack!

"Okay." Aaron removed an engine part. "Jack, what's this?"

"Oil pump?"

Aaron shook his head and threw it into his bag. "Almost. Fuel pump."

Crack!

"What's this? Hint: It has *red* fluid leaking."

Jack examined the part. "Hydraulic part?"

"Hydraulic *what*?"

Jack tried again. "Hydraulic *pump*."

Aaron stowed it in his bag. "Good!"

"What are these?"

Jack smiled. "Electrical wires!"

Yank!

"Good!" Aaron ripped them out.

"And These?"

Jack stood on his tippy toes. "Oil lines."

"Good guess. Fuel lines." Aaron tore them out.

Aaron lay on his back under the Cessna 182. "Final exam, Jack. What kind of drain is this?"

"Hydraulic drain."

Aaron smiled. "Try again. It leaks something yellow, usually once per flight after the pilot drinks too much coffee?"

Jack giggled.

I looked at the drain as Aaron crimped it with pliers. "Why is Jack giggling?"

Aaron stood up, and explained. "Jack is laughing because... Jack, *you* tell Gracie why you're laughing."

Jack responded like a twelve-year-old. "When Mr. Light tries to use the relief tube under the seat, it will quickly back up and get him wet."

I tried to be mature. "Aaron, you dirty rat!"

"It's called *learning*." Aaron winked and hurled the parts bag over his shoulder. "Let's roll."

CHAPTER FIFTY-EIGHT

E mma approached me in the lunch lounge adjacent to the cafeteria. "Have you been called?"

"By whom?"

Emma pensively checked for TSC Cadets. "Dean Michaels."

"Why?"

"Interrogation."

"For everyone?"

Emma nodded. "Your name is on the list."

"What do I say?"

"Nothing."

Ryan joined us with his lunch tray. "I just spent one hour up in the Mother Ship getting probed."

"Was Nurse Ferguson there?" Emma asked.

Ryan nodded. "She asked about the shots, headaches, my dad, my brothers, Antoine, Thomas, and *things that I believe in*."

"Things you believe in? What do you mean?" I asked.

"Nurse Ferguson kept asking if I believed in weapons. Dean Michaels kept asking if the TSC is good or bad."

I gasped. "What did you say?"

"Not much. Nurse Ferguson was taking notes as if she was doing a psychological examination. I just kept shrugging my shoulders."

Amy laughed. "Ferguson's not even a real nurse."

Ryan pointed at Amy. "Dean Michaels even asked me that! He asked if I believe Nurse Light is a real R.N."

I looked at my watch. "Ninety-six hours until graduation."

"We can't let these people get away with this," Ryan said.

"Ryan, what do you hear?" Aaron asked.

"Luke chewing with his mouth open?"

Aaron laughed. "Besides that?"

Ryan smiled. "I only hear Luke chewing with his mouth open."

"Okay, what do you *not* hear."

Gloria smiled. "TSC Air Patrol."

Aaron looked at me and overdramatically crushed his small, cardboard milk carton. "Operation RECIPROCITY continues this evening."

"With or without our new little friend?" Amy asked.

Aaron paused and smiled. "With."

G eneral Voigt answered his phone and reclined in his plush leather chair. "Good morning, Bud!"

"Good morning, Sir."

"You're calling to tell me that you recovered the Bell 407 MEDWEAP, you recovered the stolen PsytoSCOPE imaging probes, you returned the vegetable to Peaksville Hospital, and the prisoner is sedated and drooling in the Dean Michaels high security dungeon."

"No, Sir."

"You want to bring back the spider monkeys?"

"No, Sir."

"Why are you calling, Bud?"

"My Cessna 182 has been vandalized."

"Let me guess. The Projects did it."

"Apparently so, Sir."

"Hard down?"

"Tango Uniform until Thursday. Some parts arrive today. However, some fuel and hydraulic lines require special-order machining and retrofit."

"Get the bird fixed."

"Yes, Sir."

"I won't relay this to Queen Bee," General Voigt said. "Thank me."

"Thank you, Sir."

. . .

Charlotte, Ruby, and I lounged near the campfire overlooking the Epley pasture.

"How's my chunky puppy?" Ruby rubbed Kiche's belly much to the wolfdog's chagrine. "How's my favorite chunky puppy?"

Kiche emitted a steady rumble.

I took in the view of the long-haired Scotties and beautiful horses, leaned back and closed my eyes. "It's so peaceful."

Charlotte carefully added firewood. "Where is everyone?"

I momentarily opened my eyes. "Aaron mentioned something about a little friend."

"Little friend?" Charlotte asked.

"Amy is involved," Ruby said.

Charlotte laughed. "Brace for impact."

I lay back and dozed off. "Wake me for dinner, Charlie."

I heard my name.

"Gracie!"

If I didn't reply, I could sleep more.

"Grace Becker?"

I was dreaming.

Someone kissed my cheek.

I mumbled. "Marcus, is that you?"

Amy giggled. "Again."

Another kiss.

I opened my eyes and froze as a defense mechanism. "Am I face to face with a monkey?"

Emma smiled. "A spider monkey."

"Did the spider monkey just kiss me?"

"Yes."

Another kiss.

I smiled. "Hey little buddy, you're cute."

Aaron laughed. "Grace, meet Jerome. Jerome, meet Grace."

I sat up. "The same Jerome that tormented Mr. Light? The retired PIH experiment monkey?"

Amy explained. "While Ryan, Gloria and Gigi executed Operation BROKEN NEEDLE on Sunday night —"

Aaron smiled. "I commandeered the Webster Mercedes G-Wagen —"

"And we liberated Jerome from the Walker Ranch," Emma said.

Jerome mounted Kiche for a ride around the campfire.

I smiled. "He's a rodeo monkey!"

Jerome dismounted and jumped into my lap.

Emma handed me a banana. "Hand Jerome this."

Jerome walked to the cooler, grabbed an Arizona Sweet Tea, handed the drink to me, and accepted my banana.

"Jerome only barters. One item for one item," Emma said.

I laughed and enjoyed the cold drink as Jerome carefully peeled the banana.

"Grace, are you well rested?" Aaron asked.

I shrugged. "Why?"

Aaron reached into his pocket and produced a lanyard, CABESA Initiative ID Card, and keyring. "Look at the picture."

I held the ID. "Your mother?"

Aaron nodded.

Amy smiled. "One of us can pass for Mrs. Webster."

I looked at Ruby, Charlotte, Madison, Gloria, and the Kernan twins.

"Dang." Mrs. Webster unfortunately resembled me. "Okay, what are we doing."

Aaron placed the lanyard and ID around my neck. "We're breaking into PIH's CABESA facility to steal a Domestic MEDWEAP Operator Master List."

I sighed. "You and me?"

"Not exactly."

"Will I be alone?"

Aaron put his hand on my shoulder. "I'll make sure you have a teammate."

"Swamp? Are you awake?"

"I am now, Bud."

"Sorry to call so late on a Tuesday night."

"It's Wednesday morning already in Washington DC," Colonel Marsh replied.

"Got five minutes?"

"I have five hours before battling the beltway traffic."

"Sorry, Swamp."

"Rough couple of weeks, huh?"

"You're tellin' me!"

"Sorry about your wife."

"Thanks Swamp."

"I heard Rug bought the farm on Friday. I served with him on a joint staff in Seoul. Great guy. Great pilot. Great American. Horrible loss."

"Thanks."

"What's up, Bud?"

"Swamp, the Peaksville Projects are breaking my balls."

"Don't they graduate soon?"

"Saturday."

"Bud, don't you have a cabin in the woods in North Idaho? Or maybe a pup tent, a Coleman propane cooker and some bear spray? Get out of the frag' pattern for a week or two."

"General Voigt would find me."

"Hang in there, Bud."

Mr. Light paused. "I'm starting to miss the spider monkeys."

Colonel Marsh laughed. "I know you don't mean that."

"Good night, Swamp."

CHAPTER FIFTY-NINE

I approached the gate guard of the well-lit, ten-story Peaksville Institutes of Health building at ten o'clock wearing mom jeans, mom shoes, a mom sweatshirt that said *PINK* on back, and a Starbucks baseball cap.

The PIH gate guard exited his shack and smiled. "Burning the midnight oil on a Tuesday night?"

Aaron briefed me fairly well.

I handed my CABESA Initiative ID Card and lanyard to the gate guard. "Preparing for the big inspection next month. Peaksville Defense and Space warned us about PIH layoffs and firings in 2021 if we fail."

He examined my credentials. "We don't want that. Do we, Mrs. Webster?"

I smiled. "Job security is job #1."

"Who's your little friend?"

"Oh, him. Jerome is a PIH Project from 2013. The inspectors from Washington DC wanted to review the CABESA spider monkey records. Jerome knows all the passwords to the Monkey Archives."

The gate guard smiled. "Your card, Ma'am."

"Thanks." I draped the lanyard around my neck, held Jerome's hand, walked through the PIH front door, and whispered Aaron's instructions to myself. "Elevator to Room 803. Act like you belong here."

We arrived upstairs. "Room 803. CABESA Guest Lounge."

Jerome impatiently made monkey noises while I rapidly cycled through my keys.

"Ooh, ooh, ooh. Ah, ah, ah."

"Found it," I whispered to my *teammate*.

I unlatched the lock, walked inside and removed Aaron's hand-written map. "Room 802 is next door, Jerome."

I was talking to a monkey.

I struggled to read Aaron's scribble. "Doctor Raymond Gunnison, USAF. New CABESA Director. Room 802. Lower Jerome from ventilation. Get 2020 Domestic MWOP Master List. Large red book."

I looked at Jerome.

Jerome instantly smiled at me.

Simple enough, right? I climbed onto the refrigerator via the counter with a bag of bananas. Jerome accompanied me. Possibly because of the bananas.

I removed the large ventilation diffuser and set it on the counter. "Ready, Jerome?"

Jerome kissed me.

"I'll take that as a 'yes.'"

My teammate and I entered the ducting, crawled next door, and peeked inside at the PIH CABESA executive office. "Bingo!"

I removed the Room 802 vent cover, lowered Jerome into Dr. Gunnison's office, and gave him a banana. "Red book, Jerome. Red book."

Jerome looked around, deposited his banana, climbed up into the duct and gave me a red *Swingline* stapler.

I smiled, accepted his gift, and handed him a second banana. "Red *book*."

Jerome quickly returned to the ventilation ducting with a shiny red apple.

I handed him a third banana. "Red book, Jerome. Big red book."

Jerome climbed down again.

For the next five minutes, Jerome picked up and examined about twenty things in the office: lamps, coffee mugs, pens, pictures, and USAF memorabilia.

Jerome left the third banana, climbed up and handed me a book.

I whispered the label of the five-pound book. "2020 Domestic MEDWEAP Operator Master List. Good job, little buddy."

Another kiss from Jerome.

We secured the ventilation diffuser, returned to the CABESA Guest Lounge, and quickly exited the well-funded PIH facility.

"Have a good night, Mrs. Webster," the gate guard said.

I smiled as my teammate handed him a banana.

CHAPTER SIXTY

"Hello, Bud?"

"Speaking."

"Hey, stranger. Raymond Gunnison, here."

Mr. Light smiled. "Raygun! I'm still emotionally recovering from my last full flight physical with you."

Colonel Gunnison laughed. "My apologies, Bud. One of the joys of turning forty in the Air Force."

"At least I didn't have to face you during the procedure. A little birdie told me that you're the new PIH CABESA Director."

"Checked in on Monday."

"Great, Doc."

"Aren't you the local TSC President?"

"Yes, Sir."

"Hey listen, Bud. I have a law enforcement question. Do you ever have problems with theft in the PIH facility?"

"No, why?"

"Last night, I believe the night cleaning crew stole a few items."

"Items?"

"Nothing much. My red stapler, an apple, and perhaps a book or manual."

"I'll check it out."

"One more thing, Bud."

"Yeah?"

"The thief left a banana in place of each stolen item."

No response.

"Bud, you still there?"

Mr. Light paused. "Bananas were left in the place of the stolen items?"

"Bananas."

"I'll check it out."

A aron and I arrived outside Peaksville Bread Company first.

"Why are we here again?" I asked.

"Amy wants us here at four o'clock."

"Operation RECIPROCITY?"

Aaron winked.

"Am I a participant?"

"Only a spectator."

I sighed. "Whew!"

Ruby, Luke, Madison and Charlotte arrived with the middle schoolers. "Hey Gracie! Want to *hang around* with us?"

"Want to go play on the *monkey bars*?" Chloe asked.

"Grace is our *gorilla warfare* expert," Jack said.

I attempted to ignore them.

"Grace has bananas in her ears!" Gigi said.

"My little sister betrayed me."

Aaron pointed down the street. "Speaking of betrayers, here comes Amy."

Chloe, Gigi, and Jack smiled as Jerome gave me a kiss. "Jerome!"

Emma accompanied Amy. "My twin sister is journeying back in time."

D'Andre laughed. "Nice pigtails and Peaksville Middle School sweatshirt!"

"This is for you, DJ."

"Really?"

Amy held Jerome's hand and walked downtown. "Walk this way."

We followed Amy and Jerome, slouched sideways and acted like monkeys.

"Ooh, ooh, ooh. Ah, ah, ah."

Amy stopped to scold us. "I tell the jokes around here."

We continued to a brick medical building.

Amy opened the door and turned around to brief us. "Behold Operation OPTOMETRY. Watch and learn, losers."

We followed Amy into Dr. Schultz's Optometry waiting room filled among ten seated patients.

Amy approached the counter holding hands with Jerome. "Is Dr. Schultz here?"

The nurses snickered at Jerome. "He's busy, sweetie. Do you have an appointment?"

"Can you pass a message?"

"Sure."

Amy turned to wink at D'Andre before continuing. "Tell Schultzy that I'm breaking up. I don't love him anymore. And I don't care what he says, I'm having it."

The shocked nurses dropped their jaws.

"Also, Jerome figured out that Schultzy is cheating on me."

One brave nurse spoke. "Who's Jerome?"

"My monkey."

Jerome smiled.

We tried not to laugh.

Amy walked towards the door, looked back and broadcasted. "And I left my Pre-Algebra book in the backseat of Schultzy's car. I need it for exams."

We exited quickly and hustled towards the Epley Farm for a scheduled pig roast.

D'Andre laughed and high-fived Amy. "That felt good, Amy!"

Amy was magnificent. The pigtails. The ridiculous theater performance.

Dr. Schultz made D'Andre live in darkness for four years.

Amy made D'Andre smile for four hours.

D'Andre's smile lit up our night.

Brighter than the campfire.

Amy was an angel.

CHAPTER SIXTY-ONE

I lounged with Charlotte, Ruby and the Kernan twins on Thursday morning. "Why are we here today?"

Charlotte leaned on Ruby. "True. Seniors are already finished with exams."

Ruby looked at the Kernan twins. "Where's Jerome?"

"Home," Emma said.

"Eating bananas and making monkey noises," Amy said.

Aaron arrived. "Think Jerome's up for some monkey business?"

Amy shrugged. "He's a monkey."

Aaron displayed a modified service dog vest. "I just finished this in the Art room. Think it will fit him?"

I laughed. "*Service Monkey*?"

"There's a document I want from PsytoSCOPE. Dean Michaels organized a tour after lunch for prospective interns." Aaron looked around. "But we're going to need a point man."

I sunk in my seat.

"A *Service Monkey* vest?" Luke arrived. "Now *that's* funny."

"You like monkey stuff, huh Luke?" Amy asked.

Luke nodded. "Doesn't everyone?"

"Luke, how would you like a summer internship?" Aaron asked.

Luke shrugged.

Amy smiled.

. . .

M r. Light called from Peaksville Municipal Airport after lunch. "Great joke, Web."

Mr. Webster smiled and leaned back in his PDS weapon lab chair. "Say again, Bud?"

"You and Nuke replaced my MEDWEAP with a banana."

"We did?"

"My Cessna 182 will be ready in two hours, I'll need it soon."

"It wasn't us."

"Come on, Web. You both know about my monkey issues."

"Where did you have it?"

"At the Peaksville Bread Company. In my briefcase. Between my legs."

"Someone put banana between your legs?"

"Yes."

"Come on, Bud." Mr. Webster sighed. "You know that my jokes have boundaries."

Mr. Light paused. "Was it Nuke?"

"Murdstone is about as funny as a heart attack."

"Damn."

W e arrived at PsytoSCOPE Nanotechnology Corporation for a Thursday afternoon tour for prospective interns. The spectacular $50 million complex in downtown Peaksville was probably the fanciest building in Idaho. Maybe even in Wyoming and Montana also.

Aaron and Amy entered first.

Luke entered next holding Jerome's hand.

Charlotte and I followed.

I whispered. "This looks just like the PIH."

Charlotte pointed to several giant murals of faceless, fingerless children swimming, studying and running through beautiful meadows. "Gracie, look."

"This place gives me the creeps."

An older executive with a German accent wearing a dark blue, pinstripe suit and well-polished leather shoes greeted us in the lobby. "Hello, young ladies and gentlemen! Welcome to kid-friendly PsytoSCOPE Nanotechnology Corporation. I'm Dr. Braun, the Chief Executive Officer. Before we begin the tour, can I offer you some drinks?"

Aaron responded for us. "No thank you, Sir."

"Very well. Please follow me."

Charlotte walked with Dr. Braun. "Is that a German accent?"

"Yes, dear."

Aaron continued small talk. "How long has PsytoSCOPE been in Peaksville?"

"We launched after the 2013 CABESA Initiative in support of young people like yourself. What's your name, son?"

"Aaron. Aaron Dorfman."

"Dorfman. Very interesting surname," Dr. Braun replied. "I had a young patient named Dorfman in Berlin in the 1980's."

Aaron nudged my arm. "West Berlin?"

Dr. Braun shook his head. "No, East Berlin. Well, then. Have a seat in our conference room."

We watched a twenty-minute movie called *PsytoSCOPE: I Sing the Body Electric.*

"We hope you enjoyed that presentation based on Walt Whitman's 1855 poem celebrating the human body."

Amy walked down the hall and whispered to me. "This creep better not try to celebrate my *glorious* human body."

I giggled. "Glorious?"

Dr. Braun addressed Luke as we entered the computer lab. "That is the first Service Monkey I've ever seen. Is he trained?"

"Yes, Sir." Luke sat at a computer with Jerome and accidentally laughed. "More or less."

Dr. Braun probed. "What medical discipline is your Service Monkey trained in? PTSD, Autism Spectrum, Diabetes?"

Amy stepped forward. "Luke has elephantitus."

"Elephantitus? Hmm, I've never —"

Amy quickly interrupted Dr. Braun. "It's really bad."

Charlotte helped. "I've seen it."

My turn. "I've unfortunately seen it twice."

Dr. Braun looked at Aaron.

"I've never seen it." Aaron slouched in his seat. "But I've heard stories."

Jerome smiled.

"Well, then." Dr. Braun paused then continued in his German accent. "On the computers, you will find an icon entitled *INTERN*. Click on it, fill out the questionnaire and complete the short aptitude test. I'll return in fifteen minutes."

Before I sat down, Aaron was already logged into his father's CABESA account.

"I'm in," Aaron whispered.

"We entered fictitious personal data while Aaron searched the company database.

"Found it."

Aaron plugged a thumb drive into the computer tower, dragged a file and whispered. "Twenty minutes, we'll need to stall."

"What is it?" Charlotte whispered.

Aaron turned his screen towards us.

I gasped. "The *North American Scheduled Depopulation Agenda* (NASDA)."

Aaron explained. "Personal details of over 300,000,000 American citizens. Their names, birthdate, nanotech Imaging Probe frequencies from flu shots and vaccinations, scheduled date of death, and medical cause of death."

Dr. Braun returned after fifteen minutes. "Does anyone need more time?"

Amy raised her hand. "Luke's elephantitus had a flare-up. His monkey went into action. I had to help. Can we have ten more minutes?"

"Certainly."

Aaron turned his screen again and whispered. "Gloria Becker. Scheduled death: 2022. Breast cancer. Nurse Light intervened and got caught."

I thought about my precious sister and whispered. "Oh, Gloria."

Charlotte gently placed her hand on my shoulder.

Aaron completed the download, logged out, pocketed his thumb drive, and stood up. "Got it."

We found Dr. Braun in the luxurious PsytoSCOPE lobby.

Amy shook his hand. "Kind Sir. On behalf of the students of Peaksville High School, we thank you for your magnanimous generosity. We certainly downloaded a great deal of information. Luke's Service Monkey now presents this token of our appreciation."

Wide smiles, firm handshakes, and one yellow banana was exchanged as we concluded our PsytoSCOPE tour.

T homas walked into the West Peaksville Neodymium Mine.

"Hey, Bree."

"Hey."

"How's Antoine?"

Brianna was gently weeping. "It's Thursday afternoon. We aren't graduating Saturday."

Thomas sat down in the candlelight. "It's okay, Bree."

"Mrs. Jordan and Mrs. Becker are estimating AJ may be in a coma for several more weeks."

"Several?"

Brianna nodded. "They're down by the river taking a break."

"They're trying to be realistic."

"Why is everything so heavy, Tommy Boy?"

Thomas scratched Brianna's back. "The Antoine Recovery Committee has two voting members, Bree."

"Who?"

Thomas placed his hand on Antoine's shoulder. "One is Antoine."

"Who is the other?"

"God."

W e heard a distant, indistinct voice.

I sat next to the Thursday evening campfire and looked around the barnyard. "Someone yell something?"

"Ruby!" Luke's mother stood on the farmhouse porch.

Emma pointed. "Charlie, that's your mom calling."

Charlotte yelled. "Mom?"

"Hurry! Bring Ruby!"

We all stood up and ran towards Mrs. Epley.

Ryan quickly pointed his flashlight beam into the barn and stables. "Where's Kiche?"

Charlotte sighed. "Maybe she ate the goats?"

Gigi ran with Chloe and Jack. "Wolfie!"

Ruby grabbed my hand as we ran. "I'm scared."

Mrs. Epley led the way. "I heard some unfamiliar yelping."

Ruby caught her breath. "Where's Kiche?"

Mrs. Epley pointed. "In the chicken coop. I'll get some water and towels. You all go in there and take a look."

Ryan approached the chicken coop. "Water and towels?"

Gigi ran. "Wolfie, were you bad?"

Chloe opened the door, peeked inside and closed the door. "Ruby?"

Luke tried to peek through the side windows. "How bad, Chloe?"

Chloe smiled. "Not bad."

Chloe blocked the door. "Is everyone ready?"

We solemnly nodded, expecting to see feathers everywhere.

Ruby ran to Kiche. "Good, girl!"

Kiche lay on her side with seven helpless puppies nursing on her belly while chickens lay on her back.

Jack gently petted some of the pups. "They look like little furry raccoons."

Ruby scratched Kiche's chin and whispered. "I'm sorry, I thought you were just getting a little chunky."

"How did she get pregnant?" Emma asked.

Amy laughed. "Oh, please."

"Yeah, who are you kidding, Emma," Aaron joked.

CHAPTER SIXTY-TWO

Colonel Marsh laughed. "Bud, I love Fridays. I love cherry blossom season here in Washington DC. But most of all, I love your phone calls. Let it rip!"

Mr. Light sighed. "Someone put a note on my BMW."

"Meter reader?"

"No."

"Secret admirer?"

"No."

"Jealous husband?"

"No."

"What did the note say?"

Dear Mr. Light, Payback's a banana. Signed, Jerome.

"Who's Jerome?"

"Jerome was a PIH spider monkey we retired in 2013. I tested MEDWEAP's on him. He hated my guts and tried to kill me, Swamp."

"Bud, you're going bananas. Buy a twelve pack of Rolling Rock, Cabela's hunting camouflage and some Spam. Go hide from Jerome in a cabin in the woods. Make sure you climb over six thousand feet to be safe. But don't fall asleep, that's when Jerome will come."

"Jerome escaped this week from the Walker Ranch."

"Jerome is real?"

No answer.

"You're being hunted down by a spider monkey in North Idaho?"

No answer.

Colonel Marsh paused. "How was his handwriting?"

"Worse than mine. Better than yours."

"Jerome sounds like a bad little dude."

"He is a *very* bad little dude."

"Does he do tricks?"

Mr. Light paused. "Yes."

"This. Is. *Awesome!*" Colonel Marsh laughed. "Hollywood could make a movie about this. You should get an agent."

"What should I do?"

"Watch out for flying poop and don't slip on any bananas."

Mr. Light tried not to laugh. "I'm serious, Swamp."

"Listen Bud, I know you're downrange of General Voigt's wrath. But with your Peaksville MEDWEAP testing, the USAF, PDS, PIH and PsytoSCOPE got trillions of Domestic MEDWEAP funding written into the budget since 2013. Chin up, buddy."

Mr. Light sighed. "Funding doesn't solve my primate problems."

"Humans are easy. Deny everything. Admit nothing. And make counter accusations."

"What about spider monkeys?"

Colonel Marsh laughed. "You're on your own."

"Thanks, Swamp."

"Could be worse. You could be flying a desk next to me here at the Pentagon."

"I wish. Don't be surprised if I become the new Fry Guy in the Pentagon cafeteria."

Colonel Marsh paused. "If everything goes south, just remember —"

"Remember what?"

"I take my fries with no salt."

"Mama, wake up."

Mrs. Jordan was sound asleep in West Peaksville Neodymium Mine.

"Mama, wake up, it's Friday morning."

Mrs. Jordan mumbled incoherently, half asleep.

"Mama, wake up."

"I'm tired."

"Mama, please!"

She sleepily responds, "Baby DJ, please let me sleep a little while longer."

"Baby DJ? Mama, it's me, Antoine."

Mrs. Jordan rapidly sat up, eyes wide open. "Antoine!"

Antoine smiled.

Her scream of joy woke Mrs. Becker, Brianna and Thomas. "Is it you? Am I dreaming?"

"It's me, Mama."

Brianna screamed in the darkness. "Is it real? Is it real? Oh God, I hope this isn't a dream!"

Mrs. Jordan grabbed Antoine and quickly ushered him outside into the morning TFZ sunlight. "Antoine?"

"It's me, Mama! I'm okay, Mama! I was just sleeping! But I could hear everything!"

The cedar trees sang loudly in the mountain breeze.

Mrs. Becker examined his vital signs. "Perfect."

Brianna hugged Antoine. "Could you hear me reading?"

Antoine nodded affirmatively.

"Tell me what I read."

Antoine quoted Jules Verne. "*While there is life, there is hope.*"

Antoine hugged Thomas. "What did I miss, Tommy Boy?"

"It doesn't matter right now." Thomas smiled. "We're just glad that you're okay."

Mrs. Jordan cried. "It's a miracle."

"Hello?"

"$70 million, Bud."

"Excuse me, Sir?"

General Voigt leaned forward in his leather chair and checked his calendar. "Our Peaksville Projects have been midnight for exactly seven days. The United States taxpayers spend $10 million per day to have CABESA test our MEDWEAP's."

"Copy, Sir."

"$70 million wasted, Bud. Money earmarked to benefit American children. The Queen Bee is threatening to pull $200 billion in 2021 CABESA funding."

Mr. Light preflighted his Cessna 182 at Peaksville Municipal Airport as General Voigt spoke. "Copy, Sir."

"Ten thousand CABESA-funded PIH Medical Professionals, PsytoSCOPE scientists, INLINE Pharmaceutical scientists, and PDS engineers in Peaksville have families to feed and children to raise. The Safety Corps is jeopardizing their futures through negligence."

"Copy, Sir."

"The Queen Bee said this is your final chance, Bud."

Mr. Light angrily pulled his wheel chocks and stowed his tie-down ropes. "Yes, Sir."

General Voigt paused. "No more screw-ups."

Click!

CHAPTER SIXTY-THREE

I whispered during the Friday afternoon, outdoor Peaksville School District 2020 Awards Ceremony. "Charlie, where's Aaron?"

"Aaron took Ryan, Luke, Ruby and Jack with him twenty minutes ago."

"Where?"

Charlotte shrugged and pointed to the cedar trees from the schoolyard. "They swung across Peaksville Creek into The Meadow."

The Cessna 182 approached the schoolyard student body.

Dean Michaels continued the outdoor presentation. "Now, we present the 2020 Support Staff Employee of the Year Award to: Dr. Hands of KidCare Counseling Services."

Amy stuck her finger in her mouth and simulated vomiting as Dr. Hands accepted his award. "Blah!"

Dean Michaels paused for ten seconds while Mr. Light abruptly performed a seventy-knot, two-hundred-foot pass over the Peaksville School District student body. "Please excuse the propeller noise. The Safety Corps operates to ensure the safety and security of Peaksville's children."

Emma whispered. "That was too low."

I nodded. "I saw his MEDWEAP."

Mr. Light peeled off to the left and set up for another low pass.

"Next, I would like to present the 2020 Employee of the Year award to: Nurse Charity Ferguson."

Nurse Ferguson accepted her award as the Cessna 182 thundered overhead.

"Three wing-spans above the ground," Emma whispered. "That's only one-hundred feet."

Mr. Light barely cleared the treeline.

"Were his wings rocking?" I asked.

"Unstable," Emma said.

"F.W.I.?" Amy asked.

"What's that?"

"Flying While Intoxicated."

I was suspicious. "Where is Aaron?"

Dean Michaels continued. "Before we announce the 2020 Student of the Year, D'Andre Jordan and Grace Becker, please join us."

D'Andre and I walked guardedly to the temporary schoolyard stage.

The Cessna 182 shook the ground during its third low pass.

D'Andre ducked and whispered. "What's wrong with Mr. Light?"

"Pardon the noise. The TSC is searching for child abduction suspects. Also, they continue to investigate the water contamination. Remember, freedom is not free."

D'Andre and I greeted Dean Michaels in front of one thousand students.

"Peaksville is a family. Recently, we lost family members. D'Andre and Grace, please accept these plaques in memory of students who passed away. Peaksville students, please offer a moment of silence for the deceased, Antoine Jordan and Thomas Stallworth."

"Bullsh —"

A loud, fake cough sounded from the back row of the audience.

What I saw next was a miracle.

I grabbed the microphone from Dean Michaels. "Sir, we can't accept. Two *other* Seniors want accept these gifts."

The crowd gasped as Thomas and Antoine stepped onto the stage.

D'Andre tearfully greeted his twin.

I handed Thomas the microphone. "We thank you for this thoughtful plaque. My name is Thomas Stallworth."

"And my name is Antoine Jordan. See you all tomorrow at graduation!"

Applause and cheers from the student body!

Dean Michaels grabbed the microphone. "Very well. Take your seats."

We mugged Antoine with hugs and kisses in the audience.

"The 2020 Student of the Year Award goes to —"

The Cessna 182 cleared the treeline in a slow, low flight profile.

"Benjamin Light!"

Whack!

Mr. Light clipped a seventy-five-foot cedar tree riddled with parasitic ivy. He overcompensated with maximum power and up elevator. He undercompensated with right rudder. The unfortunate result was a slow, sloppy, low-altitude left snap roll.

"Look out!" I yelled.

Crash!

The small airplane impacted the soccer field inverted at fifty knots and skidded to an upside-down stop, adjacent to Peaksville Creek, inside the soccer goal.

Amy yelled in her best Portuguese accent. "Goooooooooaaaaal!"

I slapped her knee and stood up to watch.

Ben dropped his plaque and ran towards the Cessna 182.

Luke emerged from Peaksville creek and ran to the scene.

Ryan, Aaron and Jack followed Luke wearing backpacks.

Dean Michaels advised Peaksville School District students. "Please be seated. The TSC has this under control."

"The TSC is hanging in his straps," Emma quipped.

I pointed at the airplane's engine compartment. "Fire!"

Luke beat Ben to the airplane, opened the cockpit door, unsecured Mr. Light, and dragged him free.

Flames rapidly filled the empty cockpit.

Ben pushed Luke aside and attempted to unfasten his father's MEDWEAP from his survival vest.

Boom!

Ryan blindsided Ben at full speed and knocked him down. "Back off!"

Mr. Light ran with the MEDWEAP.

Ruby screamed. "Go Kiche!"

Amy tapped my leg. "Are you seeing what I'm seeing?"

I smiled. "Pinch me."

Kiche ran from Peaksville Creek with Jerome riding bareback in his red vest.

Ryan began to chase Mr. Light.

"Stay back." Aaron grabbed Ryan. "Let's watch."

Mr. Light was a wounded gazelle being chased on the Serengeti by a circus act.

Jerome held Kiche's fur with his left hand. He waved his right high in the air for balance.

"Ooh, ooh, ooh! Ah, ah, ah!"

Mr. Light glanced back and screamed in terror. "No!"

The retired PIH spider monkey dismounted and tackled the TSC President.

"What do you want from me?"

Jerome unfastened Mr. Light's MEDWEAP and replaced it with a yellow banana from his red *Service Monkey* vest.

Mr. Light yelled. "It was for science!"

The emotional reunion between the *experimenter* and the *experiment* continued.

Jerome removed Mr. Light's Ray-Ban sunglasses, handed him a second banana, mounted Kiche, and galloped towards Ruby into the sunset with the MEDWEAP.

Amy nodded. "I've seen a lot of things in my life —"

I smiled. "Yeah?"

"But that. Was. *AWESOME*!"

CHAPTER SIXTY-FOUR

"W ho is Ben Gunn?"

Ruby Kyle smiled at the Saturday night Graduation Party at the Epley Farm. "What do you mean, Gracie?"

Antoine Jordan put his arm around Brianna. "I got this. He was Captain Flint's marooned ex-crewman who led Jim Hawkins to the treasure."

Brianna smiled.

"True." I nodded at Antoine. "But who is *our* Ben Gunn?"

"He saved your life, Gracie," Luke Bartholomew said.

Gloria agreed. "A true hero. Just like Nurse Light."

I looked at Aaron Webster. "Speaking of treasure, what ever happened to Brian Light's 2017 graduation ring?"

Aaron smiled. "Jerome trades bananas for MEDWEAP's. I trade high school rings for Tommy Boy."

Amy Kernan smiled. "Wait! Dean Michaels found it on Tommy Boy's pillow?"

Emma laughed. "Epic!"

Thomas Stallworth smiled. "Really?"

Amy joked. "You were too busy singing *Skyrockets in Flight, Afternoon Delight*."

A shooting star suddenly streaked across the North Idaho sky.

Gigi pointed and watched. "It's beautiful."

Cedar trees nearby in Peaksville Forest sang in the wind.

I closed my eyes. "Make a wish, everyone."

Ryan held Gloria in the Saturday evening moonlight. "I want Marcus back."

"Me too," I said.

"Me too." Chloe said. "Marcus saved my life."

`Madison cried. "I want Derrick back."

Charlotte cried. "I want our dads back."

Jerome walked over and handed bananas to everyone.

Jack smiled. "Thanks, little buddy."

Mrs. Epley arrived from the farmhouse. "2020 Graduates! Someone wants to meet you. Madison, close your eyes."

Madison smiled. "Why me? I'm only a Sophomore."

"You'll see."

A scruffy, bearded mountain man exited Charlotte's farmhouse wearing brown hiking boots, *Realtree* camouflage hunting overalls, a tattered and torn plaid shirt, and a Cabela's ballcap.

Gigi smiled. "Ben Gunn!"

"Maddie, it's me, baby," Mr. Goodwell said.

Madison opened her eyes and hugged her nanotechnology engineer father. "Dad! I had a dream about you! I knew it, I just didn't want to say!"

Charlotte smiled. "The jelly jars?"

Mr. Goodwell nodded.

"The gunshot?"

Mr. Goodwell nodded. "You fought the cougar too long. I had to wait for you to lay prone."

I hugged my guardian angel in the campfire light. "Thank you."

"There are others," Mr. Goodwell said.

Aaron leaned forward. "What do you mean?"

"Other CABESA Project towns. Shady Valley is the closest."

"Do the children know they're experiments?" Ruby asked.

Mr. Goodwell shook his head. "No."

"We have to help them," Aaron said.

"What if Shady Valley Projects don't want to be saved?" Thomas asked.

I looked at Thomas. "Say again?"

Thomas shrugged. "Derrick died. Five fathers died. Antoine was in a coma. I *still* went to the TSC for help. What if they go for to the TSC when we try to help?"

D'Andre agreed. "Tommy Boy has a point."

Antoine disagreed. "While there is life, there is hope. Correct, Bree?"

Brianna shrugged. "I'm not sure."

"There would be much danger involved," Mr. Goodwell warned.

"Everybody wants freedom," Ryan said.

"Not necessarily," D'Andre said.

"Everybody deserves freedom," Luke said.
Aaron looked around. "We have to *try*."
The twins nodded affirmatively.
Ruby agreed.
"And try we shall."

CHAPTER SIXTY-FIVE

Colonel Marsh summited the steps of the Lincoln Memorial in his USAF uniform. "Not in Peaksville anymore, Dorothy."

Mr. Light smiled. "That's for sure."

The two USAF veterans shook hands. "I heard about your Friday airshow."

"As did Queen Bee."

"Low altitude snap rolls, explosions. Even Jerome the spider monkey made an appearance."

No response.

Mr. Webster winked and smiled. "Sore subject."

Colonel Marsh greeted Ben Light. "Congratulations, 2020 Student of the Year."

The TSC Cadet beamed with pride. "Thanks, Swamp."

"Queen Bee defunded the 2021 Peaksville CABESA Project." Mr. Webster said.

"Thousands will lose jobs in Peaksville." Mr. Light said.

"*After* her November 2020 election," Mr. Murdstone said.

"This is my surprised face," Colonel Marsh joked.

"We live in interesting times," Mr. Light said.

"What now, Bud?"

"Tomorrow morning, we begin our Pentagon staff-weeny jobs courtesy of Queen Bee."

"What about General Voigt?"

"General Voigt is a triple-dipping cake-eater. Right now, he's probably giving the Queen Bee a pedicure at Wolf Haven Country Club & Lodge while drawing paychecks from PDS, TSC and the USAF."

Colonel Marsh laughed. "Voigt's callsign in Afghanistan was *Pigeon*. We had to throw rocks at him to make him fly."

Mr. Light proudly faced the Lincoln Memorial, shed a tear and read an inscription.

"The nation, under God, shall have a new birth of freedom. Government of the people, by the people, and for the people, shall not perish from the earth."

"Rug gave the last full measure of devotion to freedom," Colonel Marsh said. Mr. Light paused. "Washington DC. Land of the free. Home of the brave. Put's everything into perspective, doesn't it?"

"What about the Projects?" Colonel Marsh asked. "Justice?"

"Negative, Swamp." Mr. Light faced the western sky and crushed his empty soda can. "Revenge."

Colonel Marsh nodded. "Count me in, Bud."

"The Peaksville Projects will regret ever being selected for the CABESA Initiative."

EPILOGUE

EPIPHANY! *I hope you enjoyed Book #1 of FLATLINE FREQUENCY as much as I enjoyed writing it! Epiphany was written to entertain you AND make you laugh. This novel was designed to be very LOW-TECH and LOCAL. The young Idaho characters had no cars, no internet, no texting, no social media, and no cell phones. I combined a 1970 rural lifestyle, 2020 present day setting, and 2070 covert medical technology and advanced weaponry (hidden in plain sight).*

EXILE! *Don't miss Book #2 of FLATLINE FREQUENCY. The setting is 2027. The CABESA industry leadership and stakeholders have moved from Peaksville to Washington DC. Prepare yourself for cover-to-cover SUSPENSE, ACTION and ADVENTURE. Expect a HIGH-TECH and GLOBAL environment! Take a ride with the Peaksville CABESA Projects in the Airbus H225 Super Puma helicopter, F/A-18E Super Hornets, F-35 Lightning II, SOC Riverine boats, Gulfstream 650 ER jet, weaponized yacht, fishing charter boat, ski boat, SH-60 Seahawk, the USS Abraham Lincoln aircraft carrier, supertankers, Airbus 320 airliners, Freightliner tractor trailers pulling livestock and Air Force One. As a retired Navy Pilot who has landed on 10+ carriers and operated from 20+ countries, I wrote Exile to take YOU to exotic places such as Australia, Switzerland, Thailand, Singapore, Hong Kong, Dubai and Brunei. I PROMISE you'll enjoy Exile.*

    Expected release date: *February 2020.*
    Spoiler alert: *Expect a guest appearance by Jerome!*

. . .

EXOSPHERE! *Don't miss Book #3 of FLATLINE FREQUENCY. Exosphere will be out of this world!*
   Expected release date: *June 2020.*

Please leave a POSITIVE REVIEW for Epiphany on AMAZON!

Thank you,
      K.D. Buster

www.ingramcontent.com/pod-product-compliance
Lightning Source LLC
Chambersburg PA
CBHW031120210626
46816CB00016B/1739